Praise for
Keri Arthur

"Keri Arthur's imagination and energy infuse everything she writes with zest."
—Charlaine Harris

Praise for
Full Moon Rising

"Keri Arthur skillfully mixes her suspenseful plot with heady romance in her thoroughly enjoyable alternate reality Melbourne. Sexy vampires, randy werewolves, and unabashed, unapologetic, joyful sex—you've gotta love it. Smart, sexy, and well-conceived, *Full Moon Rising* left me wishing I was a dhampire."
—Kim Harrison

"A deliciously sexy adventure through a supernatural underworld that pulls you in and won't let go. Keri Arthur knows how to thrill! Buckle up and get ready for a wild, cool ride!"
—Shana Abé

"*Full Moon Rising* is unabashedly and joyfully sexual in its portrayal of werewolves in heat. Arthur spares no details, portraying werewolves, vampires, and supernatural beings with a sexuality and power that goes beyond the call of the full moon. Arthur never fails to deliver, keeping the fires stoked, the cliffs high, and the emotions dancing on a razor's edge in this edgy, hormone-filled mystery....*Full Moon Rising* is a shocking and sensual read, so keep the ice handy."
—TheCelebrityCafé.com

"Keri Arthur is one of the best supernatural romance writers in the world."   —Harriet Klausner

"Strong, smart and capable, Riley will remind many of Anita Blake, Laurell K. Hamilton's kick-ass vampire hunter....Fans of Anita Blake and Charlaine Harris' Sookie Stackhouse vampire series will be rewarded."
   —*Publishers Weekly*

"Fun and feisty...[An] effective crossbreeding of romance and urban fantasy that should please fans of either genre."   —*Kirkus Reviews*

"Well-done and entertaining."   —*Sunday Oklahoman*

"A sexy and fast-paced novel aimed at the mature reader...The author excels at showing not just characters, but how they interact as a society....The novel also rises above mere adult fantasy because the author carefully shows not just the juicy scenes, but their aftermath. This is not a novel where characters have sex and that's that; there are consequences and drawbacks to being a member of a race that simply can't deny sexual urges at certain times of the month. It may sound like great fun, but Arthur doesn't shy from the logical result of such behavior."

   —*Davis Enterprise*

"*Full Moon Rising* is the first book in a new paranormal series. It's sexy and exhilarating with characters that revel in their sexuality and take it anytime and any way they can get it....It's provocative and edgy with enough heat to scorch the paper it's written on. It's a pleasure to see that within a genre that is getting crowded with uninspired and repetitive stories, it is still possible for this author to create a unique and very strong heroine. For those who like Anita and Elena, the kick-ass and sensual Riley is worth a loud and satisfied howl. With books two and three already written and number four in the works, this will be a series to keep its readers hooked emotionally and sexually."

—ARomanceReview.com

"As the trend toward bolder and sexier heroines heats up, Australian author Keri Arthur tosses her hat into the burgeoning ring with the first book in her new supernatural series, *Full Moon Rising*. Arthur creates a shadowy and believable world where werewolves, vampires and other supernatural creatures co-exist with humans, and where Riley and her kind are held hostage by the monthly lunar cycles—like wolves, their mating practices are uninhibited and definitely not monogamous. Arthur also cooks up a nicely paced cloning plot that Riley has barely begun to unravel by story's end—leaving the door wide open for all kinds of possibilities. *Full Moon Rising* definitely grabs the attention and Keri Arthur is an author to watch."

—BookLoons.com

"Unbridled lust and kick-ass action are the hallmarks of this first novel in a brand-new paranormal series....'Sizzling' is the only word to describe this heated, action-filled, suspenseful romantic drama... keeps readers on their toes in constant suspense... breathtakingly scorching. *Full Moon Rising* sets a high bar for what is now a much-anticipated new series."

—CurledUp.com

ALSO BY KERI ARTHUR

THE RILEY JENSON GUARDIAN SERIES

Kissing Sin

Tempting Evil

Dangerous Games

Embraced by Darkness

The Darkest Kiss

Deadly Desire

Bound to Shadows

Moon Sworn

THE MYTH AND MAGIC SERIES

Destiny Kills

Full Moon Rising

A Riley Jenson Guardian Novel

KERI ARTHUR

A DELL BOOK | NEW YORK

Full Moon Rising is a work of fiction. Names, characters, places, and incidents either are the product of the author's imagination or are used fictitiously. Any resemblance to actual persons, living or dead, events, or locales is entirely coincidental.

2010 Dell Mass Market Edition

Published in the United States by Dell, an imprint of The Random House Publishing Group, a division of Random House, Inc., New York.

DELL is a registered trademark of Random House, Inc., and the colophon is a trademark of Random House, Inc.

Originally published in hardcover in the United States by Bantam Books, an imprint of The Random House Publishing Group, a division of Random House, Inc., in 2006.

ISBN 978-0-440-24638-1

Cover design: Jamie S. Warren Youll
Cover photo: © Photodisc Blue and Trinette Reed/Getty Images
Photo manipulation: Stephen Youll

Printed in the United States of America

www.bantamdell.com

2 4 6 8 9 7 5 3 1

THIS BOOK IS DEDICATED TO THE FOLLOWING PEOPLE:

Linda, for teaching me so much
Miriam, for taking me that final step
The Sock Monkeys and the Lulus—great writers
one and all

Full Moon Rising

Chapter 1

The night was quiet.

Almost too quiet.

Though it was after midnight, it was a Friday night, and Friday nights were usually party nights—at least for those of us who were single and not working night shift. This section of Melbourne wasn't exactly excitement city, but it did possess a nightclub that catered to both human and nonhumans. And while it wasn't a club I frequented often, I loved the music they played. Loved dancing along the street to it as I made my way home.

But tonight, there was no music. No laughter. Not even drunken revelry. The only sound on the whispering wind was the clatter of the train leaving the station and the rumble of traffic from the nearby freeway.

Of course, the club was a well-known haunt for pushers and their prey, and as such it was regularly raided—and closed—by the cops. Maybe it had been hit again.

So why was there no movement on the street? No disgruntled partygoers heading to other clubs in other areas?

And why did the wind hold the fragrance of blood?

I hitched my bag to a more comfortable position on my shoulder, then stepped from the station's half-lit platform and ran up the stairs leading to Sunshine Avenue. The lights close to the platform's exit were out and the shadows closed in the minute I stepped onto the street.

Normally, darkness didn't worry me. I am a creature of the moon and the night, after all, and well used to roaming the streets at ungodly hours. That night, though the moon rode toward fullness, its silvery light failed to pierce the thick cover of clouds. But the power of it shimmered through my veins—a heat that would only get worse in the coming nights.

Yet it wasn't the closeness of the full moon that had me jumpy. Nor was it the lack of life coming from the normally raucous club. It was something else, something I couldn't quite put a finger on. The night felt wrong, and I had no idea why.

But it was something I couldn't ignore.

I turned away from the street that led to the apartment I shared with my twin brother and headed for the nightclub. Maybe I was imagining the scent of blood, or the wrongness in the night. Maybe the club's silence had nothing to do with either sensation. But one thing was certain—I had to find out. It would keep me awake, otherwise.

Of course, curiosity not only killed cats, but it often took out inquisitive werewolves, too. Or, in my case, half weres. And my nose for trouble had caused me more grief over the years than I wanted to remember.

Generally, my brother had been right by my side, either fighting with me or pulling me out of harm's way. But Rhoan wasn't home, and he couldn't be contacted. He worked as a guardian for the Directorate of Other Races—which was a government body that sat somewhere between the cops and the military. Most humans thought the Directorate was little more than a police force specializing in capture of nonhuman criminals, and in some respects, they were right. But the Directorate, both in Australia and overseas, was also a researcher of all things nonhuman, and its guardians didn't only capture, they had the power to be judge, jury, and executioner.

I also worked for the Directorate, but not as a guardian. I was nowhere near ruthless enough to join their ranks as anything other than a general dogsbody—though, like most of the people who worked for the Directorate in *any* capacity, I had certainly been tested. I was pretty damn happy to have failed—especially given that eighty percent of a guardian's work involved assassination. I might be part wolf, but I wasn't a killer. Rhoan was the only one in our small family unit who'd inherited those particular instincts. If I had a talent I could claim, it would be as a finder of trouble.

Which is undoubtedly what I'd find by sticking my nose where it had no right to be. But would I let the thought of trouble stop me? Not a snowflake's chance in hell.

Grinning slightly, I shoved my hands into my coat pockets and quickened my pace. My four-inch heels clacked against the concrete, and the sound seemed to echo along the silent street. A dead giveaway if there *were* problems ahead. I stepped onto the strip of half-dead grass that separated the road from the pavement and tried not to get the heels stuck in the dirt as I continued on.

The street curved around to the left, and the rundown houses that lined either side of the road gave way to run-down factories and warehouses. Vinnie's nightclub sat about halfway along the street, and even from a distance, it was obvious the place was closed. The gaudy red-and-green flashing signs were off, and no patrons milled around the front of the building.

But the scent of blood and the sense of wrongness were stronger than ever.

I stopped near the trunk of a gum tree and raised my nose, tasting the slight breeze, searching for odors that might give a hint as to what was happening up ahead.

Beneath the richness of blood came three other scents—excrement, sweat, and fear. For those last two to be evident from that distance, something major had to be happening.

I bit my lip and half considered calling the Directorate. I wasn't a fool—not totally, anyway—and whatever was happening in that club *smelled* big. But what would I report? That the scent of blood and shit rode the wind? That a nightclub that was usually open on a Friday night was suddenly closed? They weren't likely to send out troops for that. I needed to get closer, see what was really happening.

But the nearer I got, the more unease turned my stomach—and the more certain I became that something was very wrong inside the club. I stopped in the shadowed doorway of a warehouse almost opposite Vinnie's and studied the building. No lights shone inside, and no windows were broken. The metal front doors were closed, and thick grates protected the black-painted windows. The side gate was padlocked. For all intents and purposes, the building looked secure. Empty.

Yet something *was* inside. Something that walked quieter than a cat. Something that smelled of death. Or rather, *un*death.

A vampire.

And if the thick smell of blood and sweaty humanity that accompanied his sickly scent was anything to go by, he wasn't alone. *That* I could report. I swung my handbag around so I could grab my cell phone, but at that moment, awareness surged, prickling like fire across my skin. I no longer stood alone on the street. And the noxious scent of unwashed flesh that followed the awareness told me exactly who it was.

I turned, my gaze pinpointing the darkness crowding the middle of the road. "I know you're out there, Gautier. Show yourself."

His chuckle ran across the night, a low sound that set my teeth on edge. He walked free of the shadows and strolled toward me. Gautier was a long, mean stick of vampire who hated werewolves almost as much as he hated the humans he was paid to protect. But he was one of the Directorate's most successful guardians, and the word I'd heard was that he was headed straight for the top job.

If he did get there, I would be leaving. The man was a bastard with a capital B.

"And just what are you doing here, Riley Jenson?" His voice, like his dark hair, was smooth and oily. He'd apparently been a salesman before he'd been turned. It showed, even in death.

"I live near here. What's your excuse?"

His sudden grin revealed bloodstained canines.

He'd fed, and very recently. My gaze went to the nightclub. Surely not even he could be *that* depraved. That out of control.

"I'm a guardian," he said, coming to a halt about half a dozen paces away. Which was about half a dozen paces *too* close for my liking. "We're paid to patrol the streets, to keep humanity safe."

I scrubbed a hand across my nose, and half wished—and not for the first time in my years of dealing with vampires—that my olfactory sense wasn't so keen. I'd long ago given up trying to get *them* to take regular showers. How Rhoan coped with being around them so much, I'll never know.

"You only walk the streets when you've been set loose to kill," I said, and motioned to the club. "Is that what you've been sent here to investigate?"

"No." His brown gaze bored into mine, and an odd tingling began to buzz around the edges of my thoughts. "How did you know I was there when I had shadows wrapped around my body?"

The buzzing got stronger, and I smiled. He was trying to get a mind-lock on me and force an answer—something vamps had a tendency to do when they had questions they knew wouldn't be answered willingly. Of course, mind-locks had been made illegal several years ago in the "human rights" bill that set out just what was, and wasn't, acceptable behavior from non-human races when dealing with humans. Or other nonhumans for that matter. Trouble is, legalities generally mean squat to the dead.

But he didn't have a hope in hell of succeeding with me, thanks to the fact I was something that should not be—the child of a werewolf *and* a vampire. Because of my mixed heritage, I was immune to the controlling touch of vampires. And that immunity was the only reason I was working in the guardian liaisons section of the Directorate. He should have realized that, even if he didn't know the reason for the immunity.

"Hate to say this, Gautier, but you haven't exactly got the sweetest scent."

"I was downwind."

Damn. So he was. "Some scents are stronger than the wind to a wolf." I hesitated, but couldn't help adding, "You know, you may be one of the undead, but you sure as hell don't have to smell like it."

His gaze narrowed, and there was a sudden stillness about him that reminded me of a snake about to strike.

"You would do well to remember what I am."

"And you would do well to remember that I'm trained to protect myself against the likes of you."

He snorted. "Like all liaisons, you overestimate your skills."

Maybe I did, but I sure as hell wasn't going to admit it, because that's precisely what he wanted. Gautier not only loved baiting the hand that fed him, he more often bit it. Badly. Those in charge let him get away with it because he was a damn fine guardian.

"As much as I love standing here trading insults, I really want to know what's going on in that club."

His gaze went to Vinnie's, and something inside me relaxed. But only a little. When it came to Gautier, it never paid to relax too much.

"There's a vampire inside that club," he said.

"I know *that* much."

His gaze came back to me, brown eyes flat and somehow deadly. "How do you know? A werewolf has no more awareness when it comes to vampires than a human."

Werewolves mightn't, but then, I wasn't totally wolf, and it was my vampire instincts that were picking up the vamp inside the building. "I'm beginning to think the vampire population should be renamed the great unwashed. He stinks almost as much as you do."

His gaze narrowed again, and again the sensation of danger swirled around me. "One day, you'll push too far."

Probably. But with any sort of luck, it would be *after* he'd gotten the arrogance knocked out of him. I waved a hand at Vinnie's. "Are there people alive inside?"

"Yes."

"So are you going to do something about the situation or not?"

His grin was decidedly nasty. "I'm not."

I blinked. I'd expected him to say a lot of things, but certainly not that. "Why the hell not?"

"Because I hunt bigger prey tonight." His gaze swept over me, and my skin crawled. Not because it was sexual—Gautier didn't want me any more than I wanted him—but because it was the look of a predator sizing up his next meal.

His expression, when his gaze rose to meet mine again, was challenging. "If you think you're so damn good, you go tend to it."

"I'm not a guardian. I can't—"

"You can," he cut in, "because you're a guardian liaison. By law, you can interfere when necessary."

"But—"

"There are five people alive in there," he said. "If you want to keep them that way, go rescue them. If not, call the Directorate and wait. Either way, I'm out of here."

With that, he wrapped the night around his body and disappeared from sight. My vampire and werewolf senses tracked his hidden form as he raced south. He really *was* leaving.

Fuck.

My gaze returned to Vinnie's. I couldn't hear the beating of hearts, and had no idea whether Gautier was telling the truth about people being alive inside. I might be part vampire, but I didn't drink blood, and my senses weren't tuned to the thud of life. But I could smell fear, and surely I wouldn't be smelling that if someone wasn't alive in the club.

Even if I called the Directorate, they wouldn't get there in time to rescue those people. I had to go in. I had no choice.

I took the cell phone from my bag and quickly pressed the Directorate's emergency number. When the operator answered, I gave them my details and told them what was happening. Help would be there in ten, they said.

Those people inside would probably be dead in ten.

I shoved the phone into my bag and strode across the road. Though I'd inherited a vampire's ability to shadow, I didn't bother using it. The vampire inside would know I was approaching. He'd hear the rapid beating of my heart.

Was it fear? Hell, yeah. What sane, normal person wouldn't feel afraid when about to walk into the nest of a vampire? But fear and I had been on many adventures together. It hadn't stopped me before, and it wouldn't stop me now.

When I reached the pavement, I stopped and studied the metal doors. Though the urge to hurry was beginning to beat through my brain, I knew that was the one thing I couldn't do. Not if I wanted to save lives.

The locks on the doors were simple padlocks. When the club was closed, they used a grate similar to the one over the windows to stop forcible entry. Which meant Vinnie, at least, was inside, and probably some of the wait staff.

I closed my eyes and breathed deep. Three different scents were coming from the left. The vampire and two others from the right.

I blew out a breath, then kicked off my shoes. Four-inch heels might be okay to party in, but they were shit when it came to fighting. At least, they were shit on the feet. The heels actually made damn fine weapons, especially when they were made of wood, like mine. Not only did they provide deadly little stakes when it came to dealing with vampires, but they were handy against everyone else, too. Few people ever thought that a shoe could become dangerous, but these *were* dangerous. Years of finding trouble in unexpected places had at least taught me one thing—always have a weapon handy. Sometimes a werewolf's teeth just weren't deterrent enough.

I rolled up my jeans so I didn't slip on the excess material, then tossed my bag into the right-hand corner of the doorway, out of the way and out of sight. After flexing my fingers, I stepped forward and kicked the door. It shook under the impact of the blow, but didn't open. Cursing softly, I kicked it again. This time it flew back with enough force to shatter the nearest window.

"Directorate of Other Races," I said, standing in the doorway and letting my gaze roam the darkness. I couldn't see the vampire hiding in the shadows, but I could certainly smell him. Why wouldn't most vampires wash? "Come out, or face the consequences."

Which wasn't exactly legal speak, but I'd been around guardians long enough to know they generally didn't bother with legalities.

"You ain't no guardian," a soft, almost childish voice said.

I rolled my shoulders, trying to ease the tension tightening my muscles. The voice came from the left, yet the unwashed scent was still coming from the right. Could there be two vampires? Surely Gautier would have told me . . . Then I remembered his nasty smile. The bastard had known, all right.

"I never said I was a guardian. I said I was Directorate. And the rest of my statement still applies."

The vampire snorted. "Make me."

Make me, not make us. The vamp was betting I didn't know there were two of them.

"Last chance, vampire."

"I can smell your fear, little wolf."

So could I. Could feel the tremor of it through my veins. But the smell of my fear was nothing compared to what was coming from the humans in the room.

I stepped inside the club.

The air to my right stirred, and the pungent aroma of death sharpened. I dropped. A shadow soared over my back, his stench so bad I almost gagged. The soft thump of his landing told me where he was, even if his scent was too close, too overwhelming, to pinpoint it exactly. I spun, and lashed out with a bare foot. The blow connected with solid darkness and the vampire grunted. Again air moved, giving me warning. I twisted, whipping the spiked heel across the darkness. Felt it scrape across flesh even as the vampire howled in pain. Again, it wasn't the voice of an adult—more that of a kid. Someone had turned youngsters. The thought sickened me.

Movement caught my eye. The first vampire had shaken free of the shadows and climbed to his feet. He swung around to face me, his eyes red with bloodlust, his thin features contorted with rage. Not only youngsters in human terms, but youngsters in vampire years, as well. But that didn't make them any less dangerous. Just a little less devious.

He ran at me. I dodged, then swung the shoe, hitting his jaw with an audible whack. He howled and lashed out with a clenched fist. I leaned back, felt the breeze of the blow brush past my chin. The reek of unwashed flesh swamped me again. Not the scent of the first vampire, but the second. And he was approaching fast. I grabbed a fistful of the first vamp's shaggy brown hair and yanked him around into the second vampire's path.

They hit with enough force to rattle *my* teeth, but it wasn't enough to knock either of them out. The first vamp somehow twisted around, his fist catching the side of my face with enough force to knock me off my feet. I hit the floorboards with a grunt, the shoes flying from my hands. For a moment, I even saw stars. Then the weight of one of the vamps hit, his body covering my length and pinning me to the ground. His stench flooded my senses, making it hard to breathe as his canines lengthened in the expectation of a feed.

Not on *my* neck, he wasn't.

I bucked, trying to get him off me, but he had his legs wrapped around mine to anchor himself. He laughed, and suddenly all I could see was bloodied teeth, slashing down.

"No way, you bastard." I forced an arm between us. His teeth slashed my wrist, slicing deep, and pain roiled white-hot through my body. Some vampires made the experience of taking blood pleasurable, but this one sure as hell didn't. Maybe he was too young. Whatever the reason, I screamed.

The other vampire laughed, which only served to fuel my anger. Strength surged though my limbs, momentarily obliterating the pain. As the vampire sucked greedily at my blood, I thrust my free hand through his hair, grabbed a fistful, then yanked his head back, dragging his teeth from my arm. As he squawked in surprise, I clenched a bloodied fist and hit him in the mouth as hard as I could. Blood and bone and teeth flew, and his squawk became a howl of agony. I bucked again and flipped him backward over my head. He landed with a crash on his back, hard up against the bar, and didn't get up.

One down, one to go.

And that one was flying through the air, diving straight for me. I scrambled upright and got the hell out of his way. The vamp twisted in midair, landing catlike, then swept with a booted foot, trying to knock me off my feet. I dodged the blow, then repeated it, battering *him* off his feet. He landed with a thump on his butt but quickly twisted around and dove forward. One fist smacked into my thigh and sent me staggering. The vamp was up almost instantly, teeth gleaming in the cold darkness.

I faked a blow to his head, then spun and dove for one of my shoes. It would kill the sucker if I hit the right spot, but the chances of his standing still long enough were next to nil.

Still, no matter where I hit, a wooden spike hanging

out of his chest would not only slow him down, but burn the shit out of him. No one was actually sure why, especially given that vamps could touch wood without problem. Current theories suggested it was some sort of chemical reaction between a vampire's blood and the wood—and *that* reaction was the reason a stake through the heart could kill a vampire. It set off a response that resulted in the cindering of all internal organs, in much the same way as sunlight crisped new vampires stupid enough to go out in it.

He snarled in rage and leapt for me. I grabbed the shoe, snapped off the heel, then rolled out from underneath him and jumped upright. As he spun around to face me, I drove the spike as hard as I could into his chest.

He moved, and I missed the right spot. It didn't matter. At that moment, anywhere was good. He stopped abruptly and stared down in surprise at the flickers of fire erupting from the wound. That's when I dropped him. He hit the ground and didn't move.

For a moment, I simply stood there, desperately battling to get some air back into my lungs. When I could breathe again, the pain hit—a tide that was almost all-consuming. I took a deep, shuddery breath and called to the wolf that prowled within.

Power swept through me, tingling through vein and muscle and bone, blurring my vision, blurring the pain. Limbs shortened, shifted, rearranged, until what was standing in the club was wolf not human. I remained in my alternate form for several seconds, panting softly and listening to the silence for any hint of movement, then began to shift back into human form.

The cells in a werewolf's body retained data on body makeup, which was why wolves were so long-lived. In changing, damaged cells were repaired. Wounds were healed. And while it generally took more than one shift to heal wounds as deep as the ones on my arm, one would at least stem the bleeding and begin the healing process.

Of course, changing shape while fully clothed is never a good thing for the clothes—especially when they were as fragile as the lace top I was wearing. At least my jeans were made of stretchy material, and usually managed to survive the change in reasonable shape.

Once back in human form, I knotted the remains of the shirt together, then swung around, my gaze searching the darkness for the humans who were here, somewhere. That's when the clapping began. It was a solitary tattoo that somehow managed to sound sarcastic.

I knew it was Gautier without even smelling him.

"You bastard," I said, as I turned back around to face him. "You just stood there and watched?"

There was nothing pleasant about his sudden grin. "You're right. You can handle yourself."

"Why didn't you help?"

He shoved his hands into his pockets and strolled into the club. "Only arrived back in time to see you shoving your shoe into the kid's chest. Interesting innovation, by the way."

I felt like raging at him, or, better yet, grabbing the other shoe and spiking it into his chest. But what would be the point? Gautier was twisted enough actually to enjoy the caress of fire across his flesh.

"I called the Directorate. Is that the reason you're here?"

He nodded and squatted beside the vamp I'd

spiked. "It isn't every day the Directorate gets an emergency call from a liaison. Jack put out an all-points to any guardians close to the area." He looked up. "Imagine the luck, me being so close."

Imagine, I thought sourly, and spun on my bare heel, walking to the corner where Vinnie, and a woman I presumed was one of the waitresses, lay. The big man had slashes across his arms, chest, and one cheek, but they weren't all that deep. His leg was twisted at an odd angle, and even in the dim light, I could see the white of shinbone. He'd somehow managed to wrap a tourniquet around his thigh, but even so, he'd lost a lot of blood. I wondered why the baby vamps hadn't sucked it up.

The woman hadn't escaped so lightly. Her shirt had been ripped open and her breasts deeply lanced. The vamps had suckled her like children would their mothers, and from the look of it, they'd bled her dry.

I squatted beside Vinnie. His gaze, when it met mine, was distant, shocked. "They followed me in when I opened. I didn't even see them."

I placed my hand over his. His skin was cold. Clammy. "I called an ambulance. They won't be long."

"Doreen? Is she okay? God, what they did to her—"

I glanced at the dead Doreen. Saw the echoes of terror in her lifeless blue eyes. What a goddamn awful way to spend your last moments.

My stomach stirred and rose. I swallowed back bile and squeezed Vinnie's hand. "I'm sure she'll be okay."

"What about the others?"

I hesitated. "If I go check, will you be okay?"

He nodded. "Me and Doreen, we'll just wait here."

"I won't be long." As I rose, there was an audible snap of bone. Gautier, finishing what I'd started.

Not that snapping vampires' necks actually killed them, but it certainly incapacitated them for a while. Long enough to drive a stake through their black hearts, anyway. Though Gautier didn't actually need to disable *any* vampire while he used the stake—he just enjoyed it. Enjoyed seeing the fear gather in their eyes as he raised the stake and drove it into their hearts. Which probably meant he was extremely pissed off at me just then, because I'd knocked both of the baby vamps unconscious, thereby robbing him of his pleasure. Why he was breaking their necks was anyone's guess. Maybe it was habit.

Maybe he just liked the sound.

I walked on past him like there was absolutely nothing wrong, like it was an everyday occurrence that rogue vampires were executed in my presence. Any other reaction could be deadly, because he was watching me like a cat does a mouse.

And I had no intention of ever being Gautier's mouse.

The distant wail of sirens bit through the silence as I squatted beside the three other women. All three of them were badly cut, and at least two of them raped. And as the soft squelch of wood being pressed into flesh, past bone and into heart whispered across the silence, part of me was fiercely glad. Those bastards didn't deserve a fair trial or justice. They didn't even deserve the quick staking they were being given.

The emergency crews finally arrived. As Vinnie and the women were tended to, I made a statement to the cops. Gautier flashed his credentials and walked out. But the look he gave me as he wrapped the shadows around his body suggested he and I were going to be at odds for a while yet. No real surprise there.

As soon as I was able, I picked up my handbag and got the hell out of there.

The night air was sweet compared to the nightclub, and I breathed deep, letting it fill my lungs and sweep away the foulness. Blood still rode the wind, but that was natural, especially since a lot of it was now on me.

What I needed was a nice hot shower. I slung my bag over my shoulder and headed home barefoot.

But I'd barely gone a dozen steps when the wrongness hit again, this time stronger than before.

I stopped and looked over my shoulder. What the hell was going on? Why was I feeling this when the situation inside the club had been sorted?

Then it hit me.

The wrongness wasn't coming from the club or the night. It was coming from a more distant place. A more personal place. A place that was forged from the bond of twins.

My brother was in trouble.

Chapter 2

Panic surged. Ten guardians had disappeared under suspicious circumstances in the last few months, and only two of them had been found. Or rather, only bits of two of them had been found. I swallowed heavily. My twin *couldn't* be the eleventh. He was the only family I had left since our pack had thrown us out. He was the only person who meant anything to me, the one person I couldn't live without. Losing him would kill me as surely as a silver bullet.

I took a deep breath and tried to calm my fears. Rhoan wasn't hurt, and he wasn't dying, because I'd have felt either of those.

He was just in some form of trouble, and, my fault or not, he'd been in trouble most of his life. He could handle it, whatever it was.

The last thing I needed to do was panic. But I *could* check. I retrieved my cell phone, pressed the vid button, then quickly dialed my boss, Jack Parnell. He was the current head of the guardian division, and one of the few vampires I actually liked. The other, Kelly, was a guardian and one of my few friends. Not only were they both nice, but they actually bathed like regular people.

Jack's bald features came online. He gave me a toothy grin, but there was an intentness in his green eyes that belied his jovial expression.

"Nice to see you're unhurt after your evening jaunt," he said, his tone cheerful and gravelly. "I'll expect your report in the morning."

"I'll write it up at home and e-mail it in. Tell me, have you heard from Rhoan?"

"About two hours ago. Why?"

I hesitated. I had to be careful what I said, because no one at the Directorate knew Rhoan and I were related, let alone twins. The fact that we shared the same last name was no clue, simply because every individual in a wolf pack shared the same surname. So everyone in our pack, related or not, had Jenson as a last name. And whenever someone new came into the pack, they legally changed their names to the pack name. It was the one way to differentiate origins between packs that shared the same coat color.

Most of those at the Directorate actually presumed we were lovers simply because we lived together—a theory neither of us corrected because it was far easier on us if they believed that. Of course, if they actually knew anything about Rhoan, they would have realized how unlikely our being lovers was.

I wasn't sure what Jack believed—he'd never said anything about the two of us, never asked anything about our situation. He gave the appearance of not caring either way, but after working for him for six years, I knew that was never the case.

"You're aware that werewolves often know when pack mates are in trouble?"

He simply nodded.

"Well, I've got that feeling now, with Rhoan."

"Life-or-death-type trouble?"

"No."

"Is he injured in any way?"

"No. Not yet."

He frowned. "So you simply feel he is in trouble?"

"Yes." Felt it through every fiber, and as strongly as I could feel the heat of the moon.

"I don't disbelieve you, Riley, but as he's not over-due, I prefer to wait. The mission he's on is a delicate one, and sending rescuers in could make the whole thing fall apart."

Like I cared about anything but my brother . . .

I took another deep breath and blew it out slowly. "But given the other disappearances, isn't it worth checking?"

"The others disappeared from a specific area. Rhoan's mission shouldn't take him anywhere near it."

"So you know where he is?"

"Yes." He hesitated. "Though you and I are both aware he doesn't always report changes of direction."

Wasn't that the truth. And if he *wasn't* where he was supposed to be, then finding him was going to be a whole lot of fun. "When will he become overdue?"

"He's due to report at nine tomorrow morning."

"And if he doesn't?"

"I shall decide then what to do."

"I want in."

"Riley, you're not a guardian."

Yet. I could almost hear the unspoken modifier. I could certainly see the amusement crinkling the corners of his eyes. Though I'd failed the tests, Jack, for some reason, held the firm belief that I had the makings of a great guardian. He'd told me so, lots of times. But because I'd already taken the test, he couldn't force me to take another. I was safe—at least until he found a way to make me do the damn thing again. Or until I played into his hands, as I suspected I might be doing.

"He's my pack mate. I don't intend to sit back and twiddle my thumbs if he's in trouble."

"Then report to work in the morning, and we'll see what happens."

Which was neither a yes nor a no, but about as much as I was going to get that night. "Thanks, Jack."

"Try not to scent anything else on the wind tonight," he said, voice dry. "It looks like an ant could knock you over right now."

"But only a very toned ant."

He laughed and hung up. I stared at the phone's blank screen for several seconds. If Jack wasn't going to be forthcoming with information, maybe I should try someone else. Like Kelly.

Guardians often discussed missions, so maybe she knew where Rhoan had been headed. I had no idea if she was actually home, but I knew for a fact she wasn't working. It was worth a try.

I dialed her number, but after three rings it clicked over to the answering machine. "Kel, it's Riley. Give me a call when you get home, no matter what the time." I hesitated, then added, so as not to panic her, "Nothing urgent. I just have a question."

I hung up, shoved the phone back in my bag, and walked home.

Only to find the night's weirdness had not finished with me yet. A vampire stood at my door.

A naked vampire, in fact.

I stopped and stared. I couldn't help it. He *was* naked, after all. And damn, he was *built*.

He had hair that might have been black, but just then looked brown with all the mud caked onto it, dark eyes that were anything but soulless, and a face angels would kill for.

His body was just as caked with mud as his hair, but underneath the dirt, it was lean and powerful—in an athletic sort of way. And to complete the perfect packaging, he was well endowed. Not the largest I'd ever seen, but mighty fine all the same.

The stairwell door slammed shut against my back, knocking me out of my admiring stupor.

"Hello," I said.

"Hello," he repeated.

A polite vampire. Amazing. "Is there any particular reason you're standing naked at my door?"

I was hoping there was. Hoping that maybe he was some kind of present. Granted, my birthday was quite a few months off, but a girl can always dream.

Though my dreams didn't usually contain naked vampires, especially mud-covered ones.

He answered my question with one of his own. "Is there any particular reason you're covered in blood?"

"I got into a fight. What's your excuse?"

He looked down, as if his state of undress was something he hadn't noticed until that moment. "I really have no idea how I ended up like this."

His voice was a low vibration that shivered through

my soul and made my toes want to curl. Damn if it wasn't the sexiest voice I'd ever heard on a man—dead or alive.

"But you do know why you're standing at my door?"

He nodded. "If you live here, then I am here to see you."

"Well, I can tell you, I don't get many bare-assed guys turning up on my doorstep." Which was partly what I'd been bitching about to my brother before he'd disappeared on his mission, and the main reason I'd half hoped this vamp might be a present. Rhoan tended to do things like that. Though admittedly, few vampires had a sense of humor, and most would not have gone along with such a stunt. "So, unless you can explain what's going on, you can march your pretty body down the stairs and out of our building."

"I need help."

Which more than likely meant he wanted Directorate help more than my personal help. Which was a damn shame. My gaze did another tour down his naked torso, and I couldn't help an almost wistful sigh. Okay, so I saw a lot of nice naked bodies at the werewolf nightclubs, but this vampire was definitely the best-put-together specimen of manhood I'd seen recently.

"Why do you need help? Did you flash your bits at the wrong man's wife?"

Annoyance flickered through his dark eyes. "I'm being serious. Someone is trying to kill me."

He might be serious, but it was hard to take him that way when he was standing there so calmly. Wouldn't the obvious action have been to report problems to the police, or even the Directorate? "There's always someone trying to kill vamps, and generally, you guys deserve it."

"Not all of us kill to survive."

Well, no, but the ones who did certainly gave the rest a bad rep. "Look, tell me what you want or go away and flash at someone else."

"You're a guardian for the Directorate of Other Races, are you not?"

"Nope. That's my flatmate."

"Is your flatmate here?"

I sighed. Why did all the pretty ones want to see Rhoan? "I don't expect him back until sometime tomorrow." Or later, if the feeling of wrongness in the pit of my stomach was anything to go by.

"Then I shall wait."

I raised an eyebrow. "Really? Where?"

"Here." He indicated the floor with an elegant gesture.

"You can't stay here." Mrs. Russel, the owner of this ramshackle ex-factory they now had the cheek to call an apartment block, would have a fit. The only reason she'd rented us a room in the first place was because it was against the law to discriminate against nonhumans— and because having werewolves in the building had the fortunate side effect of keeping vermin away. Rats, it seemed, didn't like us.

But finding a vampire sitting in her hall would tip the old cow over the edge and us out of the apartment. Mrs. Russel had a long-standing hatred of vamps— even though she celebrated every day the fact that her husband had become the meal of one.

"Especially when you're naked," I added. "It's against the law to loiter naked in public."

A fact I knew after having been arrested for doing

the same thing a couple of months ago—though I'd been in a park rather than a hallway. I'd escaped with only a small fine, but then, I had the full moon as an excuse. The silk dress I'd been wearing had fared no better against the change than my lacy shirt. Not that either event would stop me from wearing inappropriate clothing. The law might have problems with people running around naked, but werewolves didn't.

"The light is broken," he said, his voice so soft, so warm, that I again felt that shiver up my spine. "There are no windows, and the hall lies in shadows. No one will see me."

I'd seen him, but then, though he must have heard me coming up the stairs, he hadn't bothered shadowing. And that fact stirred uneasiness. As did the fact he was naked. It was no secret that I was a werewolf, and no secret that the full moon was only seven days away. And it was a very well-known fact that a werewolf's sexual urges rose dramatically in the seven days before the moon reached fullness. He might be bait.

Though why would someone want to bait me? Other than having a guardian brother, I was a nothing, a nobody. Maybe my apprehension for Rhoan was making me paranoid.

"If you're in trouble, why not go to the Directorate? There are plenty of guardians there to help."

"I cannot."

"Why not?"

Confusion flicked through the midnight depths of his eyes. "I can't remember."

Yeah, I was really believing that. "Would you mind stepping away from my door?"

He did so. I grabbed the keys from my bag and approached the door cautiously. He raised his hands, his expression a little amused as I unlocked the door and thrust it open. Once I'd stepped through, I relaxed. While many of the legends concerning vampires weren't true, the one about thresholds certainly was.

I tossed my handbag onto the nearby green sofa, then met his night-dark gaze. "Don't bite any of my neighbors, or I'll drag you down to the Directorate myself."

He gave me a smile that had my hormones doing excited little cartwheels. "I have perused the contents of this building. You are the only one here worth biting."

I couldn't help a grin. He might have been naked, he might have been covered in mud and up to no good, but he looked gorgeous and he smelled positively sweet compared to most of the vamps I worked with. Another time, another place, I might have been tempted to take his mud-covered bait, and to hell with the consequences. "Compliments won't get you through my door."

He shrugged, a small, somehow graceful gesture. "I speak only the truth."

"Ah huh." I half closed the door, then hesitated. "You really can't remember why you're naked?"

"At this moment, no."

Didn't remember, or was too embarrassed to say? I suspected the latter, though I didn't really know why, especially considering embarrassment was not an emotion any of the vamps I worked with ever felt.

"Fine. I'll see you later, then."

I closed the door, then headed into the bathroom for a shower. After that, I crawled into my rumpled bed and tried to catch some sleep. But the certainty that my brother was in some sort of trouble, combined with the fact that I had a hunky naked vampire sitting outside my door, up to God knew what, pretty much ensured that sleep was the one thing I couldn't find.

After an hour of tossing and turning, I gave up and got up. I pulled on my favorite Marvin the Martian T-shirt to ward off the slight chill in the night, then headed into the kitchen and grabbed a large glass of milk and the jar filled with chocolate chip cookies. Then, from the well-padded comfort of my favorite armchair, I ate, drank, and watched the night give way to a brilliant red dawn. When the sky show was over, I typed up my report on Rhoan's laptop, then e-mailed it to Jack. The phone rang a second later.

I leaned back in the chair and grabbed the receiver off the wall. "Hi, Kel."

Husky laughter drifted down the line. Kelly had one of those voices that would have made her an instant hit on the phone-sex lines. "And how did you know it was me?"

"Because I left a message on your phone, and because everyone else knows better than to ring me at this unholy hour of the morning."

"And yet you are up, which means you have a problem." She hesitated. "Is it just a desperate need for sane feminine conversation? Or is it something more serious, like needing that all-dick, no-brain of a mate taken off your hands?"

I grinned. Kelly didn't like Talon any more than Rhoan did, but at least she could see the benefits of keeping him around. Men as well hung as Talon weren't all that common. "Actually, I just had a question."

"Well, damn. I wouldn't have minded a bit of well-endowed werewolf action right now. But ask away."

"Did you talk to Rhoan before he left? Have you any idea where he was headed?"

"No, and no. Why?"

"I've just got a feeling he's in some sort of trouble."

"Not the sort that has taken ten of our number already, I hope?"

"No. Not yet, anyway."

"Good." She paused. In the background was the soft ticking of a clock, meaning she was in her quarters at the Directorate. The only clock in her own home was the mother of all grandfather clocks. It was so large—and so loud—that I was forced to leave the room when it chimed. "I'm due to go out again tomorrow night. I'll see what I can find if he's not back by then."

"Thanks. I owe you one."

"Get me into a club during the moon fever, and we'll call it quits."

I grinned. "Done deal. See you later."

"Arrivederci, bella."

I replaced the receiver, then rose and headed back to the kitchen.

I wasn't the world's greatest cook, and most days I tended to burn whatever it was I was cooking. But I could usually manage muffins, eggs, and bacon without too much damage. Luckily for my stomach, it was one of those days. As I dished it all up, I glanced toward the door and wondered if my naked vamp wanted anything to eat. Not that I intended offering myself. Rhoan always kept a good supply of synth blood in the fridge, simply because he needed it. We might be twins but I was more werewolf, my brother more vampire. He didn't have the extendable teeth, ate and drank normally, and could walk in sunlight as well as I, but when the full moon began to rise, so too did his need to consume blood.

I grabbed a synth pack from the fridge, then picked up my plate and walked across to the door.

My grubby but sexy vampire was sitting where I'd left him, in the shadows to the right of my door.

"Have you eaten?" I asked.

Surprise flickered through his eyes. "Are you offering?"

I grinned and tossed the plastic pack to him. "Hardly. But my flatmate always keeps a stock of synth blood. You're welcome to that."

He caught the pack deftly in one hand. "Thank you. It's most considerate."

"In other words," I said dryly, "the offer sucks, but you'll make do."

Humor touched his luscious lips. "You are very adept at reading people, aren't you?"

Only nonhuman races, and only because of what I was. I shrugged, and sat, cross-legged, on the safe side of the doorway. Even though he was a stranger, and probably up to no good, he was at least someone to talk to. While the lone wolf image wasn't one that fitted most wolves, it *did* apply to both Rhoan and me. We'd grown up in an environment that was hostile to our presence—to our very existence—and had become used to keeping to ourselves. Which meant, of course, that the art of making friends easily wasn't a skill either of us had. God, it had taken me forever to drop my guard and let Kelly in a little. We'd known each other for three years, and despite the fact that I called her a friend—a good friend—she still had no idea that Rhoan and I were related, let alone twins.

And while I had two mates I saw regularly, they

weren't exactly friends. Melbourne could be a cold city when you were basically alone.

His gaze slid down my barely covered bits—a touch that wasn't a touch, but left me burning. No surprise there. The moon heat, which was what we wolves called the weeklong phase in which the need to mate became almost all-consuming, had started. And while it didn't affect me anywhere near as strongly as full-blooded wolves, the burning need for sex was still hard to deny.

And if the moon-spun hunger was that strong already, I was in for a rough but exciting week.

"So," I said, trying to shake off images of mating with this vamp right there in the hall—and trying not to think of the delicious possibility of shocking Mrs. Russel's puritan sensibilities. "You obviously didn't come to your senses during the night."

"Well, that depends on how you define 'coming to your senses.'" Warmth sparkled in his dark eyes. "If you're referring to the fact that I'm still here, then obviously not. If you mean did I regain some memories, then yes."

"So you remember why you're here?"

"I told you that last night."

That he had. I was just curious as to whether he'd changed his story. "And as I said, if it's something urgent, just go to the Directorate. Any of the guardians will be able to help you."

"It's your flatmate I must see."

I speared some bacon, and dipped it into the yolk. "You another of his boyfriends?"

He jerked back so quickly anyone would have thought I'd hit him. "No, I am not."

I grinned. "No offense meant. It's just that many

vampires who are older than a century or two tend to swing between the sexes."

He studied me, face expressionless, eyes deep, dark pools the unwary could easily get lost in. "You are a werewolf, are you not?"

"Yeah." I tore off a chunk of muffin, covered it in egg, and ate it. Ladylike, that was me.

"Werewolves are no more intuitive when it comes to vampires than humans," he said softly. "So how is it you knew I was a vampire, let alone one who was more than two centuries old?"

I shrugged. "My flatmate is a guardian, and I work with guardians. You pick up on those things."

One look at his expression suggested he wasn't buying the lie.

"Can I ask another question?"

"You can ask. Won't guarantee I'll answer it."

His smile crinkled his eyes. Not only was he polite, but he had a sense of humor. Amazing.

"You are not the . . . shall we say, typical? . . . shape of a werewolf."

"Meaning I've actually got curves and boobs?" Boobs that had been my saving grace when it came to job-getting in the past. Despite the fact it was illegal to discriminate, few people wanted werewolves in their employ simply because the moon cycle meant wolves were away one week in four. But, thanks to said boobs, few people ever guessed what I was.

His gaze drifted upward. "Your hair is red, yet I thought there were only four packs—silver, black, golden, and brown."

I nodded. "Most people think that, simply because the number of red packs is extremely small and they're all somewhat isolated. They originated in Ireland, then migrated to the center of Australia. They mostly still live there today."

"Ireland and Central Australia are two vastly different locations."

Having visited Ireland eight years ago, I could certainly attest to that. I'd never seen so much rain in my life—at least until I'd gotten to Melbourne.

"They were chased out during the race riots of 1795. England was using Australia as a penal colony at the time, but there was plenty of land to be had so that's where they went." I shrugged. "I guess after the chill of Ireland, the heat of Central Australia was a dream."

"At that time, they could have had their pick of locations. Why go to a desert?"

"Who knows?" Not me, that was for sure. Pack history had never been my strong point. But then, they hadn't exactly gone overboard to teach us—after all, why would they bother when they had every intention of kicking us out once we hit adulthood?

Some wolf packs were tolerant of half-breeds. Ours wasn't. The main reason we'd been allowed to survive at all was the fact that our mother was the daughter of the pack's alpha—and had threatened to walk away from the pack if we were sentenced to death.

And yet when we had finally left, it had been as much of a relief for her as it had been for us. She loved us, we both knew that, but she'd made it very clear that she never wanted to see us again.

That decision had hurt—still hurt—and yet I could understand her need to regain a normal pack life. It couldn't have been easy raising pups who were unwanted by everyone but her.

"And the red pack are not lean, as other wolves are?" my grubby vampire asked.

"Mostly, no."

He nodded, his gaze rolling languidly down my body, somehow making me feel like I was drowning in sunshine. Which was a weird sensation to be getting from a creature of the night.

Though, to be honest, vamps generally weren't the ice blocks humans thought them to be. They only got cold if they weren't feeding enough.

I cleared my throat. "I wouldn't do that."

Amusement danced in his dark eyes. "Why not?"

"You know why not."

The amusement touched his lips, and my breath caught somewhere in my throat. Damn, when had dead men become so delicious?

"I wouldn't mind."

Well, actually, neither would I, but I had principles. At least until the moon fever *truly* hit. "You're here to see my flatmate, not me." I hesitated, and frowned. "You said last night someone was trying to kill you. If that's the case, why are you calmly sitting here in my hall?"

"Because they left me for dead. I doubt whether they'd bother going back to see if they succeeded."

"And you are naked and covered in mud because . . . ?"

"I was staked naked to the ground between a mound of mulch and a mound of topsoil."

I stared at him, not sure if he was being serious or not. "You were staked out in a garden center?"

"Apparently so. Luckily for me, they decided not to put a stake through my heart, but were simply content to watch the rising sun burn me."

"Which it obviously didn't."

He smiled again, but this time there was something ferocious about it. "The good thing about being over a few hundred years old is a certain amount of immunity to the sun. Something my attackers obviously didn't know. When dawn rose, I began screaming. They panicked and ran."

Suggesting, perhaps, that the men who'd attacked him were new to the vampire-hunting game. I leaned against the door frame and placed my half-empty plate on the dusty wooden floor. "Why didn't you just take over their minds and run them off that way?"

"I tried. They were blocked." He eyed me for a minute. "Much the same as you are."

I frowned. Rhoan had told me there was a gang of humans cruising the city in search of vamps to hunt down, but I was under the impression they were only teenagers. It was doubtful they'd be strong enough to overwhelm *this* vampire, let alone have developed tough enough mind-shields to keep him out. And while electronic shield technology did exist and did work, it was so expensive very few could afford it.

"Were they young?"

"No. Men, all of them, at least thirty."

That didn't sound good. "Perhaps you'd better go over to the Directorate. If there's a second gang active in the city, they'll need to know."

"I cannot."

"Why? My flatmate might not be back for days, and this really should be reported."

"Rhoan asked me to see him, and only him."

I raised an eyebrow. "I thought you didn't know my flatmate? And if you did, why didn't you ask for him by name last night?"

"Because last night I couldn't actually remember his

name, just his address. And I never did say whether I knew him or not."

Typical vampire. I'm sure the half that weren't salesmen were damn lawyers sometime in their lives. "Does that mean you've seen him recently?"

"Yes. Before those men caught and staked me out. That is how I knew this address."

Then maybe this vamp could help me find Rhoan if Jack and the Directorate wouldn't. "When was this?"

He frowned. "I'm not sure."

Damn. "So where did you see him?"

"I can't say."

"Then why did those men feel inclined to stake you out?"

"Something else I can't remember."

"There seems to be an awful lot you can't remember," I muttered, stuck between belief and disbelief.

"A regrettable side effect of being kicked several times in the head."

My gaze traveled to his forehead. There did seem to be shadowing under the mud, which might have meant bruising. "Have you got a name?"

"I have."

A smile twitched my lips. "Can you share it, or is it lost to the fog as well?"

"Quinn O'Conor."

"I'm Riley Jenson."

He leaned forward and held out his hand. I clasped it automatically, which was a stupid thing to do, really. He could have so easily hauled me out of the doorway had he intended me harm.

But the only thing he did was wrap his long, strong fingers around mine and squeeze lightly. And with the heat of his palm burning into mine, it was all too easy to imagine the gentle strength of those fingers sliding across my body, stirring the desire already building deep inside. I swallowed heavily.

"It's a pleasure to meet you, Riley Jenson," he added, his voice so soft it seemed to echo inside my head rather than through my ears.

I pulled my hand from his, but clenched my fingers to retain the warmth of his touch. That one reaction made me realize I had better be careful. Until I knew more about him, about what he was really up to, I'd better keep some distance. No matter how much my hormones were suggesting otherwise.

Yet curiosity was still stronger than caution.

"And can you remember what you do for a living?"

He nodded. "I own Evensong Air."

I almost choked. Evensong was the biggest of the three transpacific airlines, and had recently taken over the shuttle service to the space stations. Which made the naked vampire sitting opposite me a multibillionaire.

His face closed over. "Does that alter your opinion of me?"

"Like I've had time to form an opinion?" I grinned, and added, "But if it did, it would only be because I've never fucked a mega, *mega*rich guy before." Though I had certainly fucked your ordinary, everyday, garden-variety millionaire. Still was, in fact.

His laugh sent warm shivers down my spine. "One thing I love about werewolves—they're always forthright when it comes to sex."

"Had a werewolf or two in your time, have you?" Which wouldn't be entirely surprising. He was rich, he was gorgeous, and he was a vampire. They were one of the few races that could actually keep up with a werewolf in moon heat.

"One or two."

He didn't look as if he wanted to elaborate, and I wondered why. I watched him sip his meal for a second, then said, "I thought Evensong was owned by a Frank Harris?"

"He's the director and current face." Quinn shrugged. "Being a vampire has its restrictions. I will always need someone to run the business during the day."

I was betting Frank Harris was kept on a very tight leash, all the same. "So what is a successful business-man doing getting staked out by humans? I would have thought you'd be surrounded by the latest in security gadgets."

He frowned. "I wish I knew. It's most annoying, waking to find oneself staked out and having no idea why."

"I'm guessing it's even more annoying to discover you'd been overwhelmed by mere humans."

"Most definitely."

Amusement flirted with his mouth again, and my heart did the old flip-flop. Time to retreat, before I did something daft—like take this vampire's bait.

"Listen, I have to get ready for work. Would you like a coat or something? The weathermen reckon it's going to rain later."

A sensual smile flirted with his lips. "I appreciate the offer, but vampires do not feel the cold."

"Maybe not, but you're making *me* cold just looking at you." Which was actually the opposite of what was happening, but he didn't need to know that.

He shrugged. "If it makes you feel better, then I shall accept the coat."

I rose and grabbed one of Rhoan's coats from the

back of the door. At least Mrs. Russel's heart wouldn't go into overload if she did happen to see him. And as much as I liked pushing the old cow, I doubted whether we'd get another apartment this large or this cheap so close to the city.

After closing the door, I dug through the baskets of clean clothes until I found a suitable skirt and shirt to wear. Once I'd ironed them, I got ready for work. Quinn was still sitting in the hall when I left to walk down to the station.

The train was packed, and, as usual, I spent the entire journey with my nose pinned against the glass, trying to get some fresh air from the cracks between the panels to combat the almost overwhelming scents of humanity, sweat, and perfume.

I squeezed out at Spencer Street Station and walked the block to the green glass building that housed the Directorate. After going through the security scanners, then submitting my hand for print scanning, I took the elevator down to the basement levels, stopping at sublevel three. If the ten levels above ground were the public face of the Directorate—the areas that worked mainly by day, receiving the initial reports of crimes by nonhumans, processing the minor offenses, and doing other basic stuff like documenting reports of new vampire risings—then the five below were the heart. They were the area the public knew little about. There we tracked down, and took care of, the nastier stuff— the nonhumans who raped and killed and sucked dry. And we worked twenty-four hours a day, even if the majority of the guardians only hunted at night.

There were only one hundred of us down there, and seventy of those were guardians. The other thirty were officially known as guardian liaisons. We worked mostly on rotating eight-hour shifts, and our duties were basic but far from simple—nothing could ever be considered simple when dealing with vampires. We checked and processed information about the more serious crimes, gave the guardians their assignments once the sun had set, made their reports legible once the night was over, and kept the guardians who were in residence during the daylight hours supplied with food and drink.

Of course, most humans still thought vampires were forced to sleep during the sunlit hours, but that was a fallacy—and one most vampires were more than happy to perpetuate. Sure, most vamps couldn't go out into direct sunlight for fear of being fried, but that didn't mean they were comatose, either. Vamps didn't need to sleep any more than they needed to breathe. If vampires *did* sleep, then it was done either as a leftover habit from their human years, or out of boredom.

I was one of only three females doing the job, and the other two were vamps. Guardians weren't the easiest of folk to deal with, and only those capable of protecting themselves were assigned duty there.

Jack looked up from his computer screen as I walked into the room and gave me another of his toothy grins. "Morning, darlin'."

"Morning, Jack." I stripped off my jacket, plopped down on my seat, and looked into the security scanner. My iris was checked, identity confirmed, and the screen snapped into action. "You been here all night again?"

"What else would an ugly sod like me do?"

I grinned. "I don't know—get a life, maybe?"

"I have a life. It's called the Directorate."

"That's sad. You know that, don't you?"

"I prefer to call it committed."

"As in, should be committed."

He smiled. "Got your report. Nice job."

"Thanks. Any word from Rhoan yet?"

"Not yet." He glanced at his watch. "But it isn't nine, and your flatmate is never on time anyway."

I knew that well enough, and normally it didn't worry me. "Are you going to start a search if he doesn't report in?"

"Not immediately, no."

"Dammit, there's *something* wrong."

"We only have your gut instinct telling us that. And even then, you say it isn't serious. Forgive me, Riley, but if it isn't serious, it isn't enough to blow his mission."

Frustration surged through me. I blew out a breath, lifting the hair from my forehead. "Then I'll just have to do a little looking of my own."

Jack studied me for a minute, amusement touching the corners of his green eyes. "If you find something, you will let me know."

I raised an eyebrow. "That an order?"

"Yes."

"And will you share if you find anything?"

"Riley, Rhoan's a guardian, and the mission he's on is top secret. I can't share information." He paused. "Unless, of course, I was sharing it with someone who was willing to take a second guardian test."

"That's blackmail."

"Yes."

I shook my head. "And here I was thinking you were a nice vampire."

"There *is* no such thing as a nice vampire," he said.

"Just different shades of the same color. You'd be wise to remember that, especially here."

Wasn't *that* the truth. "I'm not going to take another test." I wasn't *that* concerned for Rhoan's safety. Not yet.

I tackled the pile of files in my inbox instead. The morning crawled by, and the sensation that Rhoan was in trouble neither waxed nor waned. Which was odd. If he *was* in trouble, and unable to get out of it, surely the danger should build? What the hell did it mean when it remained at the same level?

At lunch, I grabbed a sandwich and cola from the machine in the foyer, then headed back to do some info searching on the mysterious, but oh-so-delicious, Quinn.

There were lots and lots of yummy pictures— whoever started the myth that vampires couldn't be photographed was either a loony or had never actually tried it. And there were lots of articles, which swung between calling him a monster and hailing him as a savior of small companies. One article was all about a dead vamp found on one of Quinn's transport planes. Another mentioned expansions in his Sydney pharmaceutical company. And there was a small clipping about his engagement to one Eryn Jones—and a snapshot of the two of them together. She was a slender, brown-haired woman, and as pretty as hell. But then, I don't suppose someone like Quinn would end up with anyone dowdy. I glanced at the date on the top of the article—January 9. Six months ago.

He had to love her a *lot,* because vampires didn't often commit themselves to one person. Kelly had once told me it was simply too hard to watch someone you love wither and die while you stayed eternally young.

A vampire's only other choice was to turn their lovers into vamps, yet few relationships survived the turmoil of turning. Vampires tended to be territorial and two vamps couldn't often live in harmony.

A few articles later, I found an interesting one about Eryn herself—or rather, her mysterious disappearance. Quinn had apparently been questioned by police, but released, and the inquiries were "ongoing." Meaning the cops didn't have a goddamn clue.

Was this the reason behind the attack on Quinn? Did someone, somewhere, suspect that he was behind her disappearance? If so, why was he waiting at my place to see Rhoan? Was it something to do with the missing Eryn or something else entirely?

How did he even know Rhoan if he normally lived in Sydney?

Frowning, I did a search on his fiancée, but didn't come up with much more than the fact she worked for a well-known pharmaceutical company—one Quinn had apparently bought, then dismantled, several months after her disappearance.

Interesting, to say the least. Though God only knew how it connected to Rhoan's current troubles.

Jack came back in from his lunch break, and I got back to work. The afternoon crawled by, and though I kept glancing at the clock, no word came from Rhoan. Jack pretended to be totally oblivious to anything but whatever it was he was doing on his computer, yet I knew he was watching me. Knew he was waiting for me to say something. To ask about Rhoan and the possibility of a search and, of course, that pesky retesting.

Which I wasn't going to do until I'd exhausted my own avenues—and I intended to check them out as soon as I went home and changed. Unless, of course, the feeling of trouble sharpened dramatically.

At six, I signed off and got the hell out of there. Given it was Saturday, and late evening to boot, most of the usual pedestrian traffic had already gone home. There was even breathing room on the train.

Night was setting in by the time the train pulled into my station. I climbed out and walked up the platform to the exit. But the sensation that I was no longer alone crawled over my skin. I looked over my shoulder.

As usual, half the lights were out. Shadows lurked along the fence line and crept skeletal fingers across the platform itself. No one had gotten off the train but me, and no one or nothing hid in the shadows. Not that I could sense or see, anyway. I glanced across to the platform on the other side of the tracks. No one there, either.

So why did my skin prickle with awareness? An awareness I *knew* meant there was a vamp nearby, hiding in the shadows somewhere.

Why couldn't I pinpoint his location?

And why did the night feel suddenly hostile?

Frowning, I slung my bag over my shoulder and continued on up the platform. But as I neared the steps that led up to Sunshine Avenue, the sharp scent of musk, mint, and man teased my nostrils.

Not the vampire, but a wolf. The male of our species tended to have a slightly sharper basic aroma than males of other species. Or maybe it just seemed that way because we females were naturally more attuned to them.

I stopped abruptly. He stood to the left of the steps, hiding between the station's wall and the ramp for disabled folk. He was absolutely still, something that is extremely rare for us wolves. Unless asleep, we tend to fidget if we stay in one spot for too long. The energy of the beast, barely contained, was Rhoan's theory.

"I know you're there," I said softly. "What the hell do you want?"

The shadows parted, and the wolf stepped out into the light. He was rangy, mean-looking, and so much like Henri Gautier it could have been his brother. Only, as far as I knew, Gautier didn't have a brother.

"Riley Jenson?" His voice was guttural, thick, and so cold a shiver traveled down my spine.

"Who wants to know?"

"Got a message for you."

My heart leapt. While I didn't think scum like him would be a friend of my brother's, I wouldn't put it past Rhoan to use his like for a messenger.

"What?"

"Die, freak."

His hand blurred, and I saw the gun.

I moved, as fast as I could.

Heard the booming report.

Then there was pain.

Nothing but pain.

Chapter 3

"Riley?"

The voice was warm and familiar, but far away. Far, far, away.

"Riley, tell me what's wrong."

Despite the pain engulfing me, the soft question sent heat shimmering through every nerve cell. It had to be Quinn. No one else I knew caused that sort of reaction. But why the hell was he there, rather than haunting the halls of my apartment building?

And what did he mean by what was wrong? *I'd been shot, for Christ's sake.* That much had to be obvious, even to the simplest of minds.

God, it hurt. Burned.

"Is the bullet silver?"

Silver. The bullet was silver. *That's* why it hurt so much.

"Take . . . out." *Hurry.*

He swore. *Amen to that,* I thought weakly. My eyes

refused to open, my arm was numb, and the numbness was spreading all too quickly through the rest of my body. The wolf had missed my heart, but in many respects, it didn't matter. If Quinn didn't get that bullet out of my shoulder soon, I was one dead puppy.

I floated in a sea of molten agony, drifting in and out of consciousness, my body aflame and dripping with sweat.

Yet his voice reached me, dragged me back.

"I haven't got a knife. I'll have to use my teeth. It's going to hurt."

No shit, Sherlock. But the words stayed locked inside. The numbness had reached my neck and mouth, and breathing was becoming harder.

My shirt was torn away, then lips touched my flesh, a brief caress that made my skin tremble. Then his teeth were slashing down, slicing deep. A scream tore up my throat but seemed to lodge somewhere near my tonsils. His mind surged into mine and, like a cool and gentle hand, cocooned me, soothing the ache, easing the fire.

His teeth withdrew from my flesh, but were replaced by his fingers. There was no escape from the agony of his delving, no matter how much he tried to protect me. When he touched the bullet, moved it, I screamed again.

Then the bullet was gone, the fire was gone, and in its place normal, peaceful pain.

I reached to that magical place inside and called to the wolf. Power swept around me, through me, blurring the pain, healing the wound. But once I was back in human form, the world slid away.

It was dawn by the time it came back.

Several sensations struck me almost immediately.

My head was resting on what felt like flesh-covered steel, but the rest of my body lay on something hard and uncomfortable. There was a steady, aching throb in my shoulder, and a deeper burning down my arm. Even when silver didn't kill wolves, it could permanently maim. Fear touched my heart and I quickly twitched my fingers. They moved and I breathed a silent sigh of relief.

A cool breeze stirred around me, filled with the scents of humans and exhaust fumes, mixed with the tantalizing nearness of sandalwood, man, and mud. Somewhere to my right came the steady roar of passing traffic and, closer still, the rattle of a train drawing away from a station. Obviously, I wasn't in my apartment. Though I could usually hear the trains, my apartment didn't shake with the force of their passing like this place did.

I opened my eyes, and looked around. The room was small, shabby, and rubbish-filled. There were windows to my left, both barred and missing glass, and an open doorway to my right. Wooden seats lined the graffiti-strewn walls, and the floor was asphalt. Recognition stirred. We were in the goddamn waiting room at the train station.

I turned slightly to ease the ache in my shoulder and realized then my head was resting on Quinn's thigh. He was still wearing the coat I'd given him that morning, and, if the bare knee I could see was any indication, little else. Given his near nakedness, and the fact I had to be covered in blood, it was a wonder the police hadn't been called.

I lifted my gaze to Quinn's. Concern lingered in the dark depths, along with wariness. "How are you feeling?"

His voice flowed across my skin as sweetly as a caress, and deep inside, excitement stirred. If I was getting that sort of reaction in a situation like *this,* then the next moon fever really *would* be bad.

"I feel like shit." I gripped one edge of the seat and forced myself upright, away from him. "Why are we here? Matter of fact, why are you here?"

He hesitated. "I followed you home from the Directorate last night."

So he was the reason I'd been spooked on the platform. Though he obviously wasn't the only reason. "And why would you be following me when you're supposedly waiting for my flatmate?"

He stared at me for a moment, dark eyes now shuttered. "Because I wasn't sure you were who you said you were."

"And why would you think that?"

"I'm attacked, Rhoan has disappeared, and when I get to his flat, he suddenly has a roomie I know nothing about."

"Not surprising, considering you couldn't remember much of anything yesterday."

"True." He hesitated. "But even when my memory returned, I had no recollection of his mentioning he shared the apartment with anyone."

"And why should he have mentioned something like that?"

He shrugged. "We've been friends for a while. I think it odd he's never mentioned you were sharing."

"Well, he's hasn't mentioned you at all, buddy boy, so the distrust is completely mutual." I rolled my shoulder, then retied the remnants of my shirt to ensure my boobs didn't fall all the way out. Another fine for indecent exposure was not what I needed just then. "So tell me why we're here."

"I had nowhere else to take you. I'm a vampire, remember, and have limited options."

"A hospital is public."

He raised an eyebrow. "And here I was thinking wolves preferred to avoid hospitals where possible."

"We do, but there are a dozen other places you could have taken me." Like the café across the road that served hazelnut coffee and thick steak sandwiches. Right then, I needed both. Followed by a chaser of chocolate and maybe even a little sex.

My gaze slid down his body and came to rest on his lean, muscular legs. Okay, a whole lot of sex, preferably with those legs wrapped securely around mine . . .

I tried to get a leash around my rampaging hormones. It was *not* the time for such thoughts.

"A café is too public," he said, the amused glitter in his eyes suggesting he suspected the direction of my thoughts even if he couldn't actually read my mind. "Here, at least, I could ensure no one came near enough to disturb us, or see the state you were in. Anywhere else, I might have raised suspicions."

Meaning, of course, he was using the old mind-lock trick to keep people out of the room. "This place is usually pretty full, even on a Sunday. That's a fair amount of control you have happening there." More, in fact, than even Gautier had. It was an almost scary thought.

He considered me for a moment, then said, "And yet, despite that one moment when you were in pain, I am not able to touch your mind at all. That suggests a considerable amount of power on your part."

"I work with vampires. Believe me, I need to know

how to block you guys." I paused. "If you were following me, why the hell didn't you try and stop that madman?"

"Because I wasn't sure what he was up to until he pulled out the gun. Despite popular opinion, vampires are not faster than a speeding bullet."

I half grinned. "So you couldn't read him either?"

He raised a hand. A thin wire hung from a fingertip. "He was wearing a shield against psychic intrusion."

The nanowire was the latest development in nanotechnology for the protection against psychic intrusion. I didn't know how it actually worked, but I did know it only worked when the two ends were connected, and that it was somehow powered by the heat of the body. It wasn't yet available to the general public, and the Directorate was fighting to keep it that way. A lot of their information gathering came via psychic means.

And if that werewolf had a wire on, he obviously had either government or criminal connections, because they were the only ones who currently had them.

"Not being able to read him must have pissed you off."

"A little."

More than a little, if his expression was anything to go by. My grin became full-blown. "So what did you do when he shot me?"

"What do you think I did? I killed him."

Which was the vampire's answer to any problem— kill first, ask questions later. It was an okay solution if the problem happened to be someone who'd undertaken the ceremony to become a vampire, but pretty much useless with everyone else. The truly dead couldn't answer questions. "And the body?"

"Unfortunately, your attacker fell into the path of

an oncoming train. Services were delayed for some time while police investigated."

"And, of course, they will find no indication of murder."

"Of course." He studied me, and despite the amusement touching the corners of his eyes, his expression still held a lot of wariness.

He didn't entirely trust me, but hey, that was okay, because the distrust was completely mutual. He might be who he said he was, but as yet, I had no idea if he actually knew Rhoan.

"Have you any idea why that wolf tried to kill you?" he added.

I shrugged. "Shit like that happens all the time." Though admittedly, I'd never heard of a werewolf shooting a fellow wolf before. "We're shot at almost as much as you vamps."

In fact, most humans considered us one step *down* the ladder from vampires—thanks mostly to the many werewolf movies produced by Hollywood over the years. As a general rule, werewolves did not go crazy and hunt down humans with the full moon. Those who did were quickly dealt with within the pack. And it was extremely, *extremely* rare that victims of such attacks became wolves themselves—generally because few humans survived such attacks. But of the few who did, the change came only if there was wolf in their background anyway. But humans, it seemed, still preferred the Hollywood myth over reality. Or maybe vampires were just deemed sexier than someone who turned into an animal every full moon.

"Have you seen him before?" he asked. "Scented him?"

I shook my head.

"So how did he know you'd be coming home at that time? And why would he shoot you?"

"If you had bothered to question him before you killed him, we might actually have those answers."

He didn't react to my none-too-subtle dig. "Is it possible someone is trying to kill you?"

"That guy sure seemed intent on it."

He grimaced. "I meant, have you pissed off anyone lately?"

I grinned. "I'm a werewolf."

He nodded, his face solemn but a smile touching the corners of his eyes again. "In other words, yes."

"I'm quite capable of protecting myself, you know." Unless, of course, someone decided to shoot me at close quarters with a silver bullet again.

He rose, and the coat flapped open, revealing tantalizing glimpses of well-toned thighs. Heat slithered through me, a quick flick of longing that was only going to get worse as the days progressed toward the full moon.

"I'd better take you home."

I liked the sound of the "take" part, but wasn't so sure about the rest. It all just seemed a little too convenient at the moment. "Feel free to go elsewhere. I don't need an escort."

"Maybe not, but right now, until Rhoan returns, I intend to continue camping in your hallway."

Why? That was the question, and it was one he wasn't answering. "Why not go get a hotel room? There's one not far from here." Of course, it was frequented by hookers and druggies, but I didn't think he'd particularly care. He might be rich, but he was still a vampire, and at one time or another, most vampires had been down that path. Or so Kelly reckoned. "At least then, you could shower."

"If he is too much longer, I will."

He pressed a hand against my back as he escorted me out of the waiting room, his fingers seeming to burn against my spine. Combine that with the thick scent of sandalwood teasing my nostrils, and was it any wonder my pulse began to gallop?

Being a vampire, he was undoubtedly aware of my reaction. As if to confirm it, his gaze touched mine, dark depths rich with awareness and hunger. Not blood hunger. Sexual hunger.

Not only could I see it in his eyes, but I could smell it. On him. On me.

I blew out a breath and tore my gaze away from his. The force of a werewolf's aura, though usually well shielded, tended to go into overdrive and sometimes "leaked" during the moon phase, which was why most wolves didn't turn up for work during that week. There was nothing worse than being pawed or chased by humans when they wouldn't normally touch you with a ten-foot pole. Though I very much doubted Quinn was being affected by any leakage from my aura. I think it was more a case of plain old lust.

"Does the suggestion to get a motel room mean I'm not getting an invitation inside your apartment when you get home?" His hand slid down my spine and across my backside, a teasing touch that had desire flashing across my body.

"It certainly does."

"That's a shame."

My hormones thought so, too. But, luckily for me, my hormones weren't running the show.

Yet.

"And it'll remain a shame," I said. "At least until I know what you're truly up to."

We headed up the stairs and across the road to my street. Sunlight caressed him, warming his skin as we walked. He didn't flinch, meaning he was older than I'd thought. Generally, vamps didn't achieve any great degree of immunity to the sun until they were well over five hundred years old.

"If I wanted to kill you," he said, his dark eyes meeting mine, "I could do so now, and no one on this street would see, or hear, a thing. No matter how hard you screamed."

The fact that he made the threat so calmly, without the sense of menace that always cloaked Gautier's threats, made me believe him. And yet, perversely perhaps, my desire for him only increased. Like our animal kin, we wolves were genetically programmed to seek out the strongest mate. This vampire could certainly be classified as that.

But I couldn't dance with him, no matter how much I might want it, not until I knew the truth. And to discover that, I'd have to find Rhoan.

When we reached my home, I left him standing in the hall and headed for the shower. All the while fighting the urge to invite him in to share the water. Fighting the images of washing the mud from his wet golden skin and dark silky hair.

Even cold water didn't shake the fantasy or cool my reaction.

Once I'd stepped out of the shower, I padded over to the mirror and checked out the bullet wound. It was nasty—a puckered, red mess that more than likely would leave a scar. And I needed another scar like I needed to be shot again. I had more than enough scars littering my knees, hands, and back, all reminders of childhood scraps or less-than-bright explorations.

Not that there was a lot I could do about the new one. I dried myself, then headed into my bedroom to get dressed. If I was going to do the club circuit after work, I needed something suitable to wear. A knee-length skirt and sensible sweater, my current—and usual—work garb didn't cut it in any of the werewolf clubs Rhoan or I knew. Actually, most preferred skin, but if clothes had to be worn, then the fewer the better. I scanned my limited wardrobe and eventually chose a black microskirt and gauzy, dark green shirt. I threw extra undies and shirts into the bag, as Talon—the biggest of my two mates in more ways than one—tended to get a little rough on clothing during the moon phase, then I got down on all fours and looked under the bed for my green and glittery six-inch heels. Once they were retrieved from the dust bunnies, I shoved the shoes in with my change of clothes, put on my thick woolen coat, and left. Quinn was parked in what was becoming his usual spot, and it took every ounce of control I had to walk past him.

Jack was still at his computer when I arrived at work. "Any news?" I asked, as I threw my bag behind my chair and plunked down.

"Gautier took out the six suckers who were terrorizing the Footscray district."

Even for a vampire, the man was a freak. "I meant about Rhoan."

"I know."

"And?"

"There's no news."

"Have you sent anyone out to discover what's going on?"

"Yes, and he was seen where he was supposedly headed but apparently didn't stay there."

"And where was he supposedly headed?"

Jack gave me a crocodile-type smile. "Does that mean you've reconsidered taking the guardian test?"

"No."

"Then that is confidential information."

"Bastard."

He raised an eyebrow. "For someone who is so concerned, you're doing very little actually looking."

"I intended to look last night, but some moron decided I needed shooting."

The amusement fled his eyes. "What happened?"

"I'd just gotten off the train. He jumped out of the shadows and shot me." I shrugged. "These things happen to wolves."

I wasn't sure whether I was trying to reassure myself or him. After all, that wolf was the spitting image of Gautier, even if he did have a different smell.

"And your attacker?"

"Dead." I hesitated. "A train hit him."

"At least it saves on paperwork." He paused, then added, "So, are you going to look for Rhoan?"

"Straight after lunch."

"It'll be interesting to see who tracks him down first—you or Kelly."

I barely restrained my grin. Little did he know that Kelly intended to do that, anyway. Still, the fact that he'd taken that step meant he was taking Rhoan's disappearance more seriously than I'd presumed. "So you *are* sending her out tonight?"

He nodded, and I felt a little easier. With two of us out there, surely we'd find some clue as to what was happening to him. Because something definitely was, even if the sense of wrongness had yet to peak.

"Good," I said, and settled down to do some paperwork. But Jack's gaze was a weight I could almost feel. He was waiting for something, though what that something was, I had no idea.

"You planning to party this afternoon, are you?" he said after a while.

I glanced up at him, and he indicated the carryall. "Five days to the full moon," I said, by way of explanation.

He leaned back in his chair, expression bemused. "How come you wolves never get preggers? I mean, you fuck yourself silly for seven days, and nothing ever comes out of it. And you don't take contraceptives, from what I've heard."

"How can you call a whole lot of satisfaction nothing?" I replied with a grin.

He waved the comment away. "Really. I've always been curious about it."

"And you've never thought to ask a wolf? Or taken a wander through their thoughts to find out?"

"Never really cared enough to do either."

"So why ask now?"

"I hate silence."

"Yeah. Right." He hated silences as much as I hated the moon dance. Still, I couldn't see the harm in answering his question—and it wasn't like I hadn't been asked it before. "Werewolves don't take contraceptives, but we are electronically chipped to prevent conception. Don't ask me how it works, it just does. The chips are inserted under our skins at puberty and until they're taken out, we can't get pregnant."

It had been a pretty pointless exercise with me,

because apparently I had some weird hormonal imbalances that meant my eggs never made the journey down to my womb. The good thing about it was the fact I didn't menstruate. The bad thing, the fact I couldn't become pregnant without medical assistance. Even then, the doctors weren't sure if I would ever get pregnant or carry to term. Actually, most of them figured I was the werewolf equivalent of a mule—all the right bits but none of the functionality. But rules were rules, and there was no getting around them even if you couldn't conceive naturally.

"What happens if you do want to become pregnant?"

"You pay the government medicos five hundred bucks to take the chip out, and you can become pregnant within twenty-four hours."

"And the government forces this?"

"Yep."

He snorted softly. "Amazing. They have one rule for humans and another for everyone else."

"I'm figuring they don't want the world overrun with wolves."

"It's overrun with humans, and they cause more damn damage than the rest of us ever could."

"That's not a nice way to talk about your food source."

He shrugged and left it at that. Odd, to say the least. Midday eventually rolled around, and I climbed the stairs to the kitchen on sublevel two to check out the meals—which were mainly blood, and not the synth variety—for the guardians. Once it was all onboard, I escorted the trolley to the elevator then down to the fourth level.

The doors swished open and darkness greeted me.

I swore under my breath. The bastards were playing games again. And while darkness didn't worry me, the fact that there were over twenty vampires in that room, all of whom could become shadows in the night, made me wary. I couldn't watch them all, even with my vampire vision, and the security cams didn't work too well in darkness.

"If you fuckers don't turn on the lights, you can go hungry."

The lights came back on and Gautier's feral form strolled toward me. "Afraid of the dark, are we?"

I snorted and pressed the button on the trolley. With an electronic groan, it rolled forward and made its way toward the dining room. "Why don't you go have a shower, Gautier? You smell like shit."

He smiled, revealing bloodstained teeth. He'd fed before coming in, and I wondered who on. Was it an official source, or had he started hunting up his own meals?

"It's only blood, and the aroma is one I find intoxicating."

"Believe me, I know blood when I smell it, and what I'm smelling ain't blood."

I followed the trolley toward the dining room. Gautier followed me, a forbidding presence I could feel but not hear.

"Rhoan hasn't come back yet," he stated. "You heard from him?"

The small hairs on the back of my neck rose. He was so close I could feel the wind of his foul breath past my ear. But I didn't acknowledge him and didn't alter my pace, because that was what he was waiting for.

"He's on an assignment."

"The moon heat stirs for you wolves, doesn't it?"

"What's it to you?"

"Well, how are you going to cope without your lover?"

I snorted. "I'll find another. Werewolves generally aren't monogamous, you know." Not until they'd found their soul mate and sworn their love to the moon, anyway.

"Ever considered trying a vampire as a lover?"

His hand came down on my shoulder, his fingers pressing deep into my barely healed wound. Pain flashed white-hot through my body and I couldn't stop my knees buckling. Swallowing back bile, I kept going down until my knees hit the floor, then, before he could react, shot a hand to his crotch and grabbed a fistful of balls.

He made a gargling sound, and froze. Dead or not, vampires were still men and still very attached to their dangly bits.

"Touch me again, and you'll be finding these"—I squeezed his balls a little harder—"up in the vicinity of your throat."

His brown eyes were almost molten with fury and pain. I squeezed again and could swear I saw sweat break out across his brow. Impossible, surely, given Gautier's fierce reputation. Maybe it was just a trick of the lights.

"Do you understand me?"

His nod was barely perceptible. From behind us came the sound of clapping.

"Well done, Riley." Kelly's smooth and sultry voice came from close behind, and a little of my tension eased. If she was there, then my back was safe. "How about you give those sacks an extra squeeze for me?

The great Gautier in pain is such a rare but welcome sight."

Gautier's gaze went past me. "Watch your step tonight, bitch. You might just hit trouble."

"Oh, I'm so scared." Kelly's voice was dry.

I couldn't help smiling, but resisted the temptation to do as she asked and released him instead. I wasn't a fool—and if I inflicted too much damage, I'd catch hell not only from the Directorate, but Gautier himself. He wasn't above lying in wait for someone, and for all my bravado, I had no real desire to go head to head with the creep.

I rose and turned my back on him—which, in itself, was an insult of the highest form to a vampire like Gautier. His fury scorched my skin, but I didn't flinch and didn't turn around. Just kept on walking.

Kelly leaned against the doorway into the eating area, a wide smile softening her sharp features. "In a bit of a mood, are we?"

I grinned and tossed her a meal. "I'm just a little tired of being threatened."

"So I gathered. I'll have to pinch that move off you. It certainly immobilizes male quarry."

My gaze went to Gautier. Dark didn't even begin to explain his expression. Maybe I was crazy, but it cheered me up no end.

"You got any plans for Tuesday or Wednesday night?" I stopped the trolley and opened the sides so the other guardians had access.

Kelly shook her head, her black hair gleaming almost blue in the harsh lighting. "Nothing. Why?"

"The full moon is beginning to rise, so if you still want to catch a little werewolf action . . . " I trailed off and grinned.

"Oh, yes please." Anticipation flicked in her gray eyes. "The male of your species sure can show a girl a good time."

Ain't that the truth. "I'll ring Tuesday and we'll arrange a meet time."

She nodded and leaned forward a little. "I haven't heard any whispers here about Rhoan's mission, by the way. Jack's sending me out tonight, though, so if I find anything, I'll give you a call."

"Thanks. But be careful out there."

She smiled and touched my arm lightly. "The great Gautier doesn't worry me."

Well, he worried me. And I didn't like the way he was watching us. "I was thinking more about the disappearances than Gautier. I don't want you to join the ranks of the vanished."

"It's not something I want, believe me." Her tone was one of dry amusement. "But I will be careful."

"Good."

Once the trolley was empty of its packaged blood, the two of us dished out the coffee. But all the while, I was aware of Gautier's heated gaze. His expression reminded me of the man who'd shot me, and I decided to ask Jack about Gautier's background when I returned upstairs.

Once we'd finished serving, I walked the trolley back to the kitchen. Jack gave me a sweet smile when I got back to the office. "Like the way you handled Gautier."

I grimaced. "I just hope our bosses don't mind me roughing up their star guardian."

"You gotta show the guardians you're more than capable of protecting yourself down there, or there'll be trouble."

I nodded. Guardians seemed to have a whole different set of values than the rest of the population. Show the slightest weakness and they thought you were theirs to do with as they pleased. And while those in charge didn't condone the behavior, they weren't above turning a blind eye to it either, particularly if the guardians didn't kill their "toys."

I often wondered what would happen if the public or the press ever found out about some of the darker habits of those paid to protect them. Not to mention the true purpose of the guardian force—to kill without recourse to the courts or justice. Would there be outrage? Or would humanity simply accept it as a price that had to be paid for their safety?

Considering the unreasoned—almost instinctive— fear many communities had about the nonhumans in their midst, I pretty much figured it would be the latter.

Or that maybe they'd simply call for all of us to be shot. No nonhumans, no problems.

I propped on the end of Jack's desk and swung a leg. "Have you ever run a check on Gautier?"

"I ran complete checks on all personnel when I first came into this position." Jack leaned back in his chair. "Why do you ask?"

"Because I'm nosy."

"All wolves are, but that doesn't explain the sudden interest in Gautier or why you're now asking me about him."

I grinned. "I'm asking because you have a little more access to file information than I do."

A smile twitched his lips, but there was a coldness in his eyes that suggested he not only knew where I was going but had been waiting for it. And I knew in that moment that this was the reason he'd been trying to keep me talking before.

Though why he didn't just come out and ask his questions, I had no idea.

"What do you want to know?" he asked.

"Has Gautier got a brother?"

"None on record. His whole family is listed as dead, in fact."

"Well, the guy who shot me last night was the spitting image of him. Except that he was a werewolf rather than a vampire."

"Coincidence?"

"You don't believe in coincidence."

"No." He hesitated. "I've secured what's left of the body and have asked our scientists to do an autopsy and cell analysis. That way, we'll know if he is kin, or something else."

I raised my eyebrows. "So if you knew about the shooting, why not say something when I first mentioned it?"

"Because I wanted to see if you would mention it or want it followed through." He smiled. "Good guardians always finish what they start."

"So do good liaisons." I rose and brushed a kiss across Jack's leathery cheek. "And thanks for doing the check."

He actually blushed. "You're welcome. Now, hadn't you better get going? You've only a half day today, and you know how those upstairs feel about overtime."

"If it ain't approved beforehand, it ain't paid," I quoted, in my best Jack imitation.

He snorted. "Go find that flatmate you're so worried about before I *do* find a reason to make you stay."

With a grin, I bounced back to my desk. After

logging off, I grabbed my bag, waved him good-bye and headed out the door.

Though it was barely one, the sun had disappeared behind heavy clouds, and the day had become gray. I buttoned up my woolen coat, thankful I'd chosen it over the trendy, but short, leather one I usually wore when I did the club circuits.

I caught a tram to Lygon Street, but hesitated once I got out, sniffing the air and reveling in the mouthwatering aromas of meats, spices, and breads wafting down from the street's famed restaurant precinct. My stomach rumbled a reminder it hadn't eaten lunch, but I ignored it and walked on. Just then, I had deeper hungers to satisfy.

The Blue Moon was situated in a side street just off the corner of Lygon Street. Though it was my favorite club, the name always made me smile. It was such an obvious choice for a werewolf establishment that there were hundreds—if not thousands—of Blue Moons all over the world. Humanity at large probably thought we lacked imagination—but anyone who had ever stepped inside a club would know that definitely *wasn't* the case.

This Blue Moon was the smallest of the five werewolf clubs in Melbourne and the only one that allowed humans to enter—though it did have restrictions on which days, and no human was allowed to enter during the full-moon phase. The other clubs had a strict nonhumans-only policy, something the wankers in government were currently legislating to change. Which was amazing, really, when you consider that twenty years ago, the clubs weren't even legal and had regularly suffered raids from the police.

The doors swished open and Jimmy, the mountain-sized half-human, half-lion-shifter bouncer, gave me a grin in which half the teeth were missing. He'd lost them in a fight there a couple of weeks ago, and obviously still considered his toothless smile a badge of honor. And considering he'd come out on top of three wolves, the big man had a right to be proud.

"Hey, Riley," he rumbled. "Didn't think we'd be seeing you here until later in the week."

"I'm looking for Rhoan—do you know if he's come through?"

Jimmy shook his heavily maned head. "But I've only just come on shift. He could have come in earlier."

"What about Davern or Liander?" They were my brother's regular mates, men he'd been with for over two years. He had casuals as well, but if anyone might know where Rhoan was, it would be one of those two.

"Davern's been here since this morning, according to the security cams. Liander's usually over at the Rocker on a Sunday."

"Thanks." I paid my entrance fee and took a locker key. "What sort of mix we got this afternoon?"

He shrugged. "The usual."

Meaning there was a small smattering of vamps and shifters amongst all the werewolves. He opened the door. "Hope you're intending to change clothes. You know the house rules."

I patted his hand. "Heading to the change room first thing."

He nodded and closed the door behind me. I stopped at the top of the stairs and let my eyes adjust to the heavy darkness. Hologram stars blossomed across the midnight-colored ceiling, and the glow of the blue moon was only just beginning to dim their bright light. Tables and chairs, many of them occupied by wolves either mating or watching others mate, ringed the packed dance floor. Toward the back of the room, there were curtained booths for those who preferred to mate in some privacy, and they were also occupied. By the end of the week, when the force of the moon raged through our blood, those booths would have queues.

While most of those on the dance floor were naked, there were some who preferred something more exotic. A few wore leather outfits that clung to their bodies as closely as flesh, while others had donned more outlandish costumes that glittered and sparkled under the hologram moonlight.

The DJ was set up in the far corner, and the music he played filled the air with sensual and erotic melodies designed to seduce the senses. The room was heavy with the rich aroma of lust and sex, and desire rushed through my veins. All I had to hope was that I could control it long enough to find Rhoan.

But given the fierceness of that fever, I knew control would only be claimed by sating some of the need.

It was just too bad Quinn wasn't with me.

I frowned and thrust the thought away. Until I knew a whole lot more about the mysterious Quinn and his reasons for wanting to see my brother, I could not afford to do anything more than lust from a distance.

I walked down the steps and headed into the change rooms. After taking a quick shower to wash the smell of work and vampire from my skin, I put on my club clothes and did my makeup. Then I swept my long hair into a ponytail, shoved my bag into the locker, my credit card and locker key into the small pocket in my skirt, and headed out into the crowd.

Closer to the dance floor, the sensual beat of the music was accompanied by grunts of pleasure and the slap of flesh against flesh. The fever in my blood rose several notches and the deep-down ache that had started with Quinn that morning shifted into high gear.

But as much as I hungered to become part of the lusty, sweating crowd, I still had enough control to put business before pleasure. Davern was there somewhere, and I had to find him.

I skirted the edge of the dance floor, my gaze sweeping the tables lining the walls. Davern was near the rear of the room, close to the privacy booths. But he wasn't alone at the table, and I wasn't about to interrupt. Wolves, especially males, tended to get extremely violent if you did.

I grabbed a drink off a passing waiter—all of whom were mind-blind and nonhuman, which not only meant they could defend themselves if things got nasty, but the aura of a werewolf in heat had no effect on them. And while they were all normal men and women, and *did* get aroused, they were paid *extremely* well to ignore their hormones. Which was why jobs at all the werewolf clubs were most sought after.

I took a deep breath, inhaling the scents that swirled around me, allowing the atmosphere to soak through my pores, a richness that spoke of pleasure, indulgence, and carnal fantasies.

Was it any wonder humans were busting their balls to get into the wolf clubs? The sexual freedom of the clubs had to leave them feeling like kids in a candy store compared to the uptight, moralistic sensibilities currently being forced onto the human race as a whole.

Of course, having humans around during the full-moon phase would be a dangerous thing, especially considering there were some packs who liked their sex *extremely* rough. Humans just weren't designed to cope with a werewolf's idea of wild sex—which was why clubs Australia-wide were banding together for the first time in history to fight the government's plans. The last thing anyone wanted was a human casualty during the bloom of the moon—if only because the blame would be placed on werewolves and the clubs rather than the idiots who'd forced the change of rules.

As I looked back to the stairs, a man entered. He was tall and powerfully built, with chiseled features and dark golden hair. And the sheer sexual energy radiating off him was something I could feel even from where I stood. I'd met—and mated—with a lot of wolves over my twenty-nine years, but none of them had an aura as powerful, or as binding, as *this* wolf's.

Our gazes met. The heat so evident in the strange golden depths of his eyes echoed through the fibers of my being. Talon and I had been together for almost two years—which was something of a record for those who aren't soul mates. We knew each other extremely well sexually but were still basically strangers outside of the clubs.

He walked down the steps, stripping off his shirt as he did so and tossing it casually toward an empty table. His golden skin gleamed in the starry light and his leather pants showcased not only the strength of his legs but the size of his erection.

The force of his aura rolled before him, hitting the women nearest him like a tidal wave. Sighs and stares followed in his wake but he didn't stop, his gaze on mine as he strode toward me.

At six and a half feet, he was a big man. Even though I wore six-inch heels, he still dwarfed me by a good five inches. But when he moved, it was with the grace and lightness of a vampire. The selfish part of me hoped he didn't find his soul mate before I found mine, because we were good together. His brand of wild sex was something I wanted to keep enjoying for a while yet.

He stopped when there were still several feet between us, his gaze sliding casually down my body before rising to meet mine again. The lust that surged between us caressed my skin until it felt like I was glowing.

"I didn't expect to find you here this afternoon, little wolf."

His voice was a deep rumble, yet it flowed across my senses as sensually as a warm summer breeze. "I'm looking for Rhoan, and had hoped to ask Davern where he is."

His gaze momentarily went past me. "Davern won't be much longer, from the look of it."

"No, he won't." I was aware of the rising level of noise and pleasure coming from Davern's table, but part of me hoped he held off. I wanted to drink in the radiating force of *this* man awhile longer.

Talon took a step closer and my breath caught. The burning of the silver bullet in my flesh was nothing compared to the fire eating me at that moment.

His fingers brushed my cheek, then slipped down my neck and chest. It was a feather-light caress that felt as powerful as a sledgehammer. He flicked open the shirt's first button, then moved on to the next one. "The fever burns in you, little wolf. I can smell it."

So could I, and it was beginning to hurt. "It's a need that will have to wait until I talk to Davern."

"Really?" Another button gone. "And what is so urgent that you must speak to him during this time of celebration?"

"I got a call from Rhoan's mother." His mother was my mother, but Talon didn't know that. "As I said, I need to find him."

The last button came undone and he pushed my shirt open. His fingers skimmed up my stomach, sending quivers of anticipation scooting across my flesh. With deliberate slowness, his touch circled a breast, his gaze holding mine, drowning me in the flames of his desire as his caress gradually worked inward, reaching but not quite touching the aching, sensitive center.

Perspiration beaded my skin. His whisper-soft stroking moved to my other breast and by the time he'd finished circling to the center, I was close to screaming with frustration.

"Can I dance with you, little wolf?"

"After I talk to Davern, you can do whatever you want to me."

"A dangerous statement given the heat that sears us."

A smile teased my lips. I ran a finger down the hard planes of his chest and toyed with the top button of his pants. "And just what is it that you intend to do to me?"

He leaned closer. All I could smell, all I could breathe, was the musky, ardent odor of this wolf.

He brushed a kiss across my lips, then, with his voice little more than a gravelly growl, said, "I intend to fuck you senseless."

My heart slipped into overdrive. The intensity of

both his words and his aura suggested he was feeling
the moon as strongly as I, and, missing brother or no
missing brother, I was damn glad I'd come here today.
Misha, the second of my usual lovers, was gentle and
sweet, but Talon was fierceness and danger and excitement and power. When the moon rode me strongly, it
was Talon I wanted.

I raised an eyebrow. "Isn't that what you always do?"

His grin was wolfish. He wrapped an arm around
my waist and pressed me close, until it felt as if he was
trying to slip inside.

"This time I shall fuck you until you cry my name
to the moon." His breath caressed my mouth and his
gaze burned deep, until it felt like his desire singed the
very fibers of my soul. "Then I shall keep on going until you beg for me to stop."

"That could take a while," I teased, my breath little
more than a husky purr. "You sure you're up to it?"

"You will ache for no other lover tonight, little wolf,
be sure of that."

I wrapped a hand around the back of his neck and
pulled him down so I could kiss him.

"Davern's finished," Talon said after a while. "I
shall hire us a room."

I smiled. The Blue Moon was the only club that actually had privacy rooms available to rent. There
weren't many—four in all—but they were filled with
all the latest gadgets to cater to the more adventurous
types.

If Talon was getting a room, he was truly serious
about his hunger and his intentions, and expectation
coursed through me. Normally, we made out at the tables or on the dance floor, and that was pretty damn
fine. And while I couldn't give him the remainder of

the day, an hour or two of hard and heavy loving would certainly cure more than a couple of aches.

I flicked the top button of his pants undone and slid down the zipper. His erection leapt out at me, as if eager to be caressed. "Leave your pants hanging on the door so I know what room you have."

He claimed my mouth as fiercely as he undoubtedly intended to claim my body later, kissing me hard and long. Then he spun and walked away, leaving every inch of my body thrumming in expectation. I took a deep breath, but it did little to ease the ache.

After tying the ends of my shirt together, I made my way toward Davern. He was alone, nursing a drink, and looked up as I approached. He'd been drinking for some time because his eyes were more red than blue.

"Hey, Riley? How are you?"

I slid into the seat opposite him. He smelled of sex and sweat and alcohol, and I frowned. "I thought you were off the booze?"

"Got dumped this afternoon," he said gloomily.

It obviously wasn't too deep a relationship, because it hadn't stopped him taking other partners. "So?"

"So, he was a good fuck and I'll miss him."

I grinned and patted his hand in sympathy. "You drink too much more and you won't be up to finding more replacements tonight."

"It'll only take an hour or so to sober up, and besides, I feel like wallowing in self-pity right now." The hologram lights caught his black hair as he leaned back, lending it rich claret highlights. "What can I help you with?"

"I need to know where Rhoan is."

He raised an eyebrow. "Why?"

"Because I have a gut feeling he's in trouble."

The very lack of reaction in his bloodshot eyes told me just how little he cared for my brother—and for that alone, I wanted to smack his drunken ass.

"Serious trouble?"

I took a deep breath and blew it out. More to control that urge to hit him than anything else. "No, not serious trouble. I feel he needs help, that's all. He's gotten into a situation he can't extract himself from."

Davern snorted. "He's always doing that, and he always gets out eventually."

"Yeah, but this isn't a sexual situation." Yet even as I said it, I felt the slight lie. It *was* a sexual situation—sort of.

Which made about as much sense as Rhoan's staying in a relationship so long with an uncaring nitwit like Davern. He had to be a damn good fuck because he certainly didn't appear to have much else going for him.

"When did you last see Rhoan?"

"Last week. I believe he was with Liander until Sunday, though."

Then I'd definitely have to find Liander. "I don't suppose he said where he was going after Liander's?"

His bloodshot gaze went past me and I felt the hunger stir in him. Maybe he wasn't as drunk as I'd thought.

"He mentioned something about having to investigate Evensong Air."

Quinn's airline. Great. I grabbed Davern's hand, forcing his attention back to me. "It's very important I know exactly what he said about Evensong Air."

He blinked. "For God's sake, it was over a week ago."

"I know, but try to work your way past the sozzled brain cells and remember, all the same."

He frowned, and with his free hand reached for his drink. "He said there were some problems within Evensong and that he might have to go undercover. That's all. I swear."

I released him and flopped back in my chair. Rhoan was investigating Evensong and I had the vampire who owned the company camped out in my hallway.

Coincidence? Not likely.

And while I couldn't actually question Quinn himself without raising suspicions, I could certainly take the roundabout line of inquiry. Talon walked the same circles as Quinn, and if anyone could dig up dirt, it would be he.

But before I could ask him to do me a favor, I had to get past the sex.

Chapter 4

Talon's pants hung on the third door handle down the small hallway, and just the sight of them had anticipation gripping my lower body. The door opened as I approached, and there he was, golden, glorious, and hard with wanting.

His aura hit a heartbeat later, and it felt as if I was walking into an inferno of lust. If he'd taken me right there in the hall, I wouldn't have given a damn. But then, his aura had nothing to do with that. I was a wolf, after all, and exhibitionism was part of our nature.

He took my hand, kissing my fingers as he pulled me inside. Candles flickered in wall sconces near the bed, throwing yellow light across the red satin sheets and black walls. There was very little else in the room other than several benches of varying sizes and heights. Compared to the other rooms the club had available, this was pretty basic, and perhaps he'd chosen it for that reason. He wanted sex that was hard and fast and long, sex that was without distractions. Just him and me.

He closed the door, then pressed the panel to the left of the frame. "The psychic security screen is on," he said. "No one can hear us, no one can sense us. When I make you scream my name to the moon, no one but us will be the wiser."

He stepped closer. The light glittered off the twisted white gold chain around his neck, the only piece of jewelry I'd ever seen him wear and one that seemed to emphasize the corded power of his neck and shoulders. I pressed a hand against the hard planes of his chest, momentarily resisting the intensity of his aura. The heat of him flowed around me, through me, flaying my skin and stirring the hunger into a frenzied dance. That alone was warning enough to ask my questions right then, because who knew if I'd have the energy or clarity of mind after several hours of sex with him?

"You need to answer a question first."

"Sorry, don't like my sex with questions."

I grinned. "Well, that's the only way you're getting it today."

"Really?" He caught my hand, and though I could easily have resisted the force he applied to make me move backward, I didn't. I wanted him every bit as badly as he wanted me.

When my calves hit the smaller of the two benches, I stepped onto it and looked him dead in the eyes. It was a mistake, because the force of his aura crashed through me like a tidal wave, leaving me wet and so very ready for him. And just for an instant, I gave in to that wave and kissed him as fiercely as I wanted him.

It took a whole lot of will to break away, to ask the questions that had to be asked. Especially when he tugged at the knot holding my shirt together, his touch teasing me, arousing me, all the more.

I took a deep breath and tried to concentrate. "I need to know about Evensong Air."

"Why?" When the knot didn't come undone, he simply ripped the shirt apart and tossed it on the floor.

"That was a new shirt."

"Bill me," he growled, but treated the skirt and G-string a little less ruthlessly. "And answer the question."

My brain took a moment to click into gear and remember what question he was talking about. "Davern said Rhoan was investigating them, and I need to know why if I'm to have any hope of finding him."

"This call from his mother must be truly urgent if you're going to such extremes to find him."

My "yes" became lost in the sweet fever that flew through me as he began to trail kisses down my neck. When he caught a nipple in his mouth and sucked hard, I gasped and almost collapsed in pleasure. Somehow, through the haze of desire clouding my thoughts, I found the strength to add, "Death in the family."

"Ah." His fingers slid down past my belly, past my pubic hair, and deep into slickness.

For too many minutes, all I could do was groan in pleasure.

When I finally managed to gather enough brain cells together, I said, "You walk in the same circles as Quinn O'Conor. I need you to gather all the dirt you can on him."

His teeth were grazing me, teasing me, and all the while his aura washed me with heat and desire. Any other time I would have given in and gone with the flow, but I needed whatever help he could give.

He worked his way up to my mouth. "Promise to concentrate on the business at hand," he said, and nipped my lip hard enough to hurt. But it was a sweet pain, especially when his tongue immediately caressed the sting away. "And I'll promise to find out what I can about Evensong Air and its owner."

"This is urgent." But my fingers were straying down his back, my actions belying my words as I spread my legs and pulled him closer.

"So is this."

He pressed himself between my legs, sliding his cock back and forth, teasing, but not entering.

"If it was urgent, you wouldn't be teasing but doing."

He made a growling sound in the back of his throat, then, with one hard thrust, sheathed himself in me. I groaned in pleasure. Talon filled me, stretched me, in a way no other wolf did—and right then, I wanted to feel every single hard inch of him. I wrapped my arms around his neck, my legs around his hips, and pushed him deeper still. He cupped my butt, supporting me as he thrust and thrust and thrust, until it felt as if the rigid heat of him was trying to claim my entire body.

There was nothing gentle about this mating. Couldn't be, with the heat of the moon burning us both so fiercely. I rode him hard, needing it fast and furious, and Talon was more than happy to comply. Pleasure spiraled quickly and my climax hit, the convulsions stealing my breath and tearing a strangled sound from my throat. He came a heartbeat later, his body slamming into mine, the force of it echoing through every fiber of my being and shuddering through the wall behind me.

Once the tremors had subsided, I grinned. "That

was certainly a promising start, but it was way too fast to be seriously labeled fucking me 'senseless.'"

His grin was ferocious. "That was little more than taking the edge off our need. I made a promise, little wolf, and I intend to keep it."

If there was one thing I admired about Talon more than his physique, it was his ability to keep his promises.

But as good as it was between us, he didn't make me scream his name to the moon. That was the one pleasure I would keep reserved for the man who was my soul mate—wherever he might be.

After two hours of wild and sweaty sex, Talon took off to find another mate and I had a long, hot shower. Once dressed, I grabbed my bag out of the locker and made my way up the steps.

"Now, here's a wolf looking mighty pleased with herself," Jimmy commented as he opened the door.

I grinned. "That's because a good time was had by all."

He nodded. "There was a gent in here looking for you earlier."

"Really?" I said, surprised. "Who?"

"Vamp. He had a look around and came back out, asking if I'd seen you."

Shit. It had to be Quinn. He'd undoubtedly tried to read Jimmy, but I knew he'd have little success. Jimmy was mind-blind, just like the waiters.

Whatever Quinn was up to, he certainly was determined to keep an eye on me. "How long ago?"

"About an hour."

Relief swept me. The security system would still

have been in place then. He wouldn't have sensed me. "And you told him?"

"That you had been in earlier, but you'd moved on to the Harbor Bar."

The Harbor Bar was a good hour across town, giving me time yet to escape should he be on the way back. I rose up on tippy-toes and kissed Jimmy's leathery cheek. "You're a doll. Mind if I use the side entrance?"

"Go for it."

I swung on my coat and headed around the back. A blast of wintry air greeted me as I pushed open the back door and I shivered, half-wishing I had something warmer than a skirt to wear. Still, in the week of the moon heat, jeans generally weren't practical.

I slung my bag over my shoulder and loped toward the Rocker. I heard the club long before I saw it. There weren't many places in town still playing Presley's classic "Blue Suede Shoes," and absolutely none who'd follow it up with Chris Isaak's "Baby Did a Bad Bad Thing." I often wondered where the club managed to dig up some of the songs they played, as many of them had been released only on vinyl or CD, and those technologies had long since gone by the wayside.

Unlike the Blue Moon, the Rocker was bright, neon bright. Windows lined the main entrance, allowing curious passersby to peer inside. Nothing more than eating, drinking, and human-style dancing happened in the main room—those who wanted to mate did so in the privacy of the upstairs dance hall, far away from the public's prying eyes.

I went through the door and checked my bag and coat, then headed to the bar, ordering a cocktail and ending up with something pink and fluffy. With that in hand, I began my search for Liander. I found Misha first—he was coming down the stairs as I was about to go up them.

"Hey, pretty lady," he said, appearing out of the shadows as silently as a ghost. "Like that shirt you're almost wearing."

I smiled and kissed his pale cheeks. "Talon did another of his caveman tricks."

"I'm jealous." He grinned, his silver eyes sparkling as brightly as his hair in the glow of the neon lights. "He always gets to tear your shirts off."

"Play your cards right, and I might just let you tear off the skirt." Though after two hours of hard and furious sex, it wasn't going to be anytime in the immediate future. "You seen Liander about? I need to talk to him about Rhoan."

"Why? Is he in trouble?"

I gave him the same reason I'd given Talon, and he turned, offering me his arm. "Then I shall escort you to where he's currently demolishing a burger."

I smiled and hooked my arm through his. Talon might be a fantastic lover, but it was Misha I was comfortable with beyond the realms of sex. I *liked* Misha. I was never entirely sure that I could say the same about Talon.

Misha escorted me up the stairs and through the barnlike space that was the private dance room. Only half the benches and bean bags were occupied, which was odd, considering that the Blue Moon was packed and the full moon was drawing close. Liander was sitting on a sofa down at the far end, and he was alone—something else that was surprising.

I sat on the sofa opposite him and Misha slid in beside me. His thigh pressed against mine, and desire tingled across my flesh—a reaction that told me that no matter what I'd thought, the moon wasn't entirely finished with me yet.

"Nice drink," Liander said, by way of greeting.

I looked down at the fluffy thing. "I have no idea what it is. I asked for something sweet and got this."

"A warning never to ask for something sweet at an old rock and roll bar."

He leaned back, and sunlight danced across his sculptured cheekbones, making them shine a deep, rich gold. Which matched the highlights in his silver hair. I couldn't help smiling. Last week, he'd been blue. It was just as well he was one of the top special effects artists in the country, because he'd never be able to afford his ever-changing looks otherwise.

And it always made me wonder how the hell he'd survived the military's strict rules for ten years. It wasn't a place that appreciated individualism, and I just couldn't imagine Liander bowing to conformity. I'd asked him about it many times, but he'd merely shrugged and changed the subject. As far as I was aware, not even Rhoan knew the exact details about his years in the military.

Which was all very mysterious. And if he continued to be a prominent feature in my brother's life, I'd start digging. Not just because I was nosy—though I was—but because Rhoan was my twin and my pack. If there was something in Liander's background that could end up hurting Rhoan, I wanted to know about it.

"What can I do for you, Riley?"

"Have you seen Rhoan lately?"

He frowned. "Why? Is something wrong?"

I hesitated, mainly because I knew Liander actually loved my brother—even if my brother didn't feel the same way. Liander deserved the truth—or at least some semblance of it. But with Misha sitting beside me, I had to go with the same story. "I just need to get hold of him. You got any idea where he might be?"

"I thought he was on a mission."

"Davern told me he was investigating Evensong Air."

Liander grimaced. "That lush. He wouldn't know one end of a dog from the other these days."

I grinned. "Meaning?"

"Meaning Rhoan was investigating the owner, Quinn O'Conor, not Evensong Air itself."

My stomach sank. Just as well I'd listened to my instincts rather than my hormones. "I was under the impression the two of them were friends."

"They are, which was why Rhoan was so pissed at having to go undercover and investigate."

At least Quinn hadn't lied about that part of it. "Any idea what he was investigating?"

Liander shook his head. "You know he never gives away stuff like that."

I sighed and leaned back. "Then you haven't any idea where he might have gone?"

"I know he was checking out the street directory before he left."

I raised an eyebrow. "Don't suppose you know what address?"

"No. But I was sitting beside him and know the page number was sixty-nine."

I grinned. "No wonder you remembered it. Bit of wishful thinking there, huh?"

Amusement touched the corners of his silvery eyes. "In the end, there was nothing wishful about it."

"Lucky you."

"Indeed."

"There's a street directory at my place," Misha said. "If you want to check out what's on that page number."

I leaned over and kissed his cheek again. "Thank you."

He smiled into my eyes. "I can think of better ways to thank me."

The slow burn of passion ignited again. It wasn't the fierceness I'd felt earlier, but it was certainly a warning that this moon phase would be a bad one. And for the first time, I wondered if Talon and Misha were going to be enough to keep me satisfied.

I said good-bye to Liander and let Misha escort me downstairs to reclaim my bag and coat. Once outside the club, he pressed me back against the wall and kissed me. It was a slow, sweet possession that was so very different from the fierceness that Talon offered but just as arousing in its own way. Which was why I liked being with them both. In the two, I had my ideal man.

"I'll go get my car," he said, after a while.

"I'll wait."

He grinned, and walked off whistling. Five minutes later, we were roaring into the city at warp speed in his shiny red Ferrari—which he lovingly called his "bound to get a shag" wagon. Though why a werewolf, armed with an aura that could sweep all objections aside with little effort, needed a "shag wagon" was beyond any sort of reasoning.

Misha lived in the penthouse suite of a tower apartment building he'd recently purchased. It stood next to the Casino and the South Bank entertainment complex, and from what he'd recently said, the rent was making him huge gobs of money. His apartment, like him, was silver, but the coldness of it was offset by the brilliant views offered by the floor-to-ceiling windows and the splashes of vibrant colors tucked into odd corners. I never went too near the windows. Though I loved the view, I had a weird fear of heights that kicked in around twenty stories high. Fifteen was close enough to twenty to be cautious.

I dumped my bag and coat on the nearest chair and looked around. "Where's the street directory?"

"In the kitchen."

I raised my eyebrows as I headed that way. "Strange place to keep a street directory."

He gave me a grin as he walked around the bench and grabbed a couple of mugs from the cupboard. "Not when you have a business meeting to attend and are studying where the hell it is over breakfast."

I opened the directory and flicked to page sixty-nine. It didn't provide any immediate revelations.

"Do you know if there's anything of interest around here?" I slid the book across the bench toward him.

"The Moneisha Research Center is there." He indicated a spot surrounded by green.

I frowned. "Why does that name ring a bell?"

A smile tugged his lips. "It's only been in the news for the last week."

It wasn't that. I'd seen that name somewhere else, somewhere recently, but I'd be damned if I could remember where. I waved a hand. "You know I never read the headlines."

"Ah well, you've missed out on some interesting times." He pressed the button on the espresso machine, filling both mugs, then slid one across to me and sat down opposite. "Moneisha is apparently involved in gene research."

"So? Half the labs around the world are involved in gene research."

"Yeah, but Moneisha has *apparently* succeeded where others have failed."

I frowned. "Succeeded in what?"

"Pinpointing the cluster of genes that make a vampire a vampire. Word is they want to try and splice vampire DNA into the eggs of other races."

I stared at him. "You're kidding?"

He shook his head. "Hence the protests outside the labs for the last week and Moneisha's being in the news more than they would want."

"But . . . ?" Words failed me. I just shook my head and sipped at my coffee.

"Why would anyone want to do something like that?" he finished for me. "Imagine the supersoldier you could build if you could have all of a vamp's abilities and none of the restrictions, such as bloodlust and the inability to move around in daylight."

"I don't think I *want* to imagine something like that." It was simply too scary a thought. Vampires were bad enough—but soldiers with all of a vampire's skills and none of the restrictions? I shuddered. "Is the government behind Moneisha?"

"No. It's privately owned."

"Who by?"

He shrugged. "Last I heard it was owned by some company by the name of Konane."

Another name that sounded familiar. "And they are?"

"A research company. I can try and find out a bit more about it if you'd like."

"I would like."

I pulled the directory toward me and studied it for a few minutes. I had no idea if Moneisha was connected in any way to Rhoan, or if he was even headed that way. But there was nothing else on this map that seemed in any way a likely target, so I could only try. If I kept following his footsteps, sooner or later I was going to find some real information.

I checked the transport situation, noting there was a railway station within walking distance of the Moneisha labs, then closed the directory and pushed it toward Misha. "Thanks for that."

His smile touched his silver eyes as he reached across the table and took my hand in his. His fingers were warm against mine, his skin so pale. He caressed my wrist with his thumb, shooting slivers of desire up my arm. "How are you intending to get out to Moneisha?"

"Train. Why?"

"Would you like to borrow one of my cars?"

I raised my eyebrows. Misha was a collector of not only high-priced shag wagons, but vintage automobiles. At last count, he had about fifty antiques and five newer "classics" stored in the special parking lot underneath this tower. "You'd trust me to drive one of your cars?"

I couldn't help the surprise in my voice, and his smile grew. "Only one of the ones that I don't mind getting bashed up. I've seen you drive, remember."

"I know. Hence my surprise."

"There is an ulterior motive, of course."

His voice had dropped several octaves and slid through my system as smoothly as warmed chocolate. Talon might be excitement and raw power, but Misha was certainly passion. "And what might that be?"

"You have to return the car and the keys, and therefore might spend tonight with me rather than Talon."

I leaned across the table and kissed him. "A car would be far handier than public transport, so I just might be forced to accept that proposition." The hunger glittering in his eyes echoed through me, stirring the moon heat to life. "But why not get a down payment right now?"

"Why not indeed," he agreed, and pressed his hand against the back of my neck, holding me still as his mouth claimed mine.

As places to make love went, a kitchen bench wasn't that bad an alternative.

I checked the map for the umpteenth time, wanting to be sure I was headed in the right direction. On foot, I could find my way anywhere. Shove me behind the wheel of a car and I could get lost in a traffic circle.

Up ahead, the lights changed from green to red. The cell phone chose that moment to ring and I slipped the earpiece in as I stopped the car.

"Riley here."

"How are you feeling, little wolf?"

Talon's husky tones lost none of their impact electronically, and a warm shiver slipped down my spine. He didn't even have to touch me to turn me on.

"I've been with Misha, and I'm feeling fine."

Talon paused. Maybe he didn't like the thought that I could still need another after the pounding he'd given me.

"He can't do to you what I do to you."

His words held an edge that made me frown. Was Talon getting jealous? Surely not. "No. And sometimes that's a good thing."

The lights changed. I put on the turn signal and moved over to the side of the road. Given my driving record, talking to Talon while trying to steer the car probably wasn't a good idea.

His laugh skittered across my skin and made me hunger, yet there was also that rawness in it that stirred uneasiness through me. Sex with Talon was great, but if he was beginning to think there could be anything else between us, he needed his head examined. As a part-time lover he was fantastic, but I was *damn* sure I couldn't cope with him full-time. And not just sexually. Arrogance, and a complete belief in one's own superiority, was okay in the bedroom, but it would probably drive me crazy elsewhere.

"Can I see you again soon?" he said.

"I'm with Misha tonight."

"Then come now."

There was no hiding the annoyance in his voice this time, and I frowned. "Why do you suddenly have a problem with me being with Misha?" In the two years we'd been together, I'd had up to four other partners. It had only been recently that I'd settled on Misha and him.

"I don't. Well, I do when I want you and he has you, but it's not a jealousy thing, if that's what you mean." He paused. "How about I add a sweetener? I have that information you wanted."

"You ran a search on Evensong?"

"And the owner. Found a couple of interesting tidbits. You can come over to my place and collect them."

My heart accelerated. He'd never asked me to his place before—never told me much about himself at all, in fact, and curiosity stirred.

"When and where?"

He chuckled. "What are you doing right now?"

"Driving out to the Moneisha labs."

"You haven't got a car."

"Misha lent me one of his."

"No way. He's seen you drive and he adores his cars."

I grinned. "It's a Mercedes and he has several of them. He says he can afford to lose one."

Talon snorted. "I hope it's some bright color, so the other drivers can see you coming."

"It's red."

"Red *is* the color of danger."

"I'm not *that* bad."

"Oh yes, you are. I hope you're not driving while you're talking to me."

"I can multitask."

"Yeah, right. What street are you on now?"

I peered up at the nearby street sign. "On Burwood, near Oaklands Avenue. Why?"

"Because I'm going to send out an all-points warning to my people to get the hell out of the area."

"Bastard."

He chuckled. "Why are you going to Moneisha?"

"I'm probably chasing a wild goose, but that's where Rhoan might have been heading."

"Why would he be going there?"

"He's a guardian, so who knows? I'm just going to walk around the perimeter and see if I can feel anything."

"So how far off are you?"

"About ten minutes. Why?"

"Just trying to work out how long it'll be until you get here. I'm feeling hungry, little wolf."

My pulse slipped into third gear and the ache I'd thought Misha had sated became fierce again. Lord, what was I going to be like a day or so before the full moon? "So give me your address and I'll get there as fast as I can."

Not surprisingly, he lived in Toorak, a classy suburb filled with the superrich. I jotted the address down in my diary and hung up with the promise to be there within an hour and a half.

I continued on, and despite the aspersions on my driving skills, reached Moneisha without incident. After parking, I grabbed my coat and strolled toward the red-topped white buildings I could see through the guardhouse gateway. There were two sets of fences— a solid white concrete one that had to be at least eight feet high, and, farther in, a wire one. Even from across the road, I could feel the buzz of electricity running through the wire. I had no doubt there would be other security systems right through the lawns that surrounded the building.

The gray-suited guard shifted in his box, watching as I approached. I dropped my shields, and reached out to touch his mind telepathically. It felt like I was hitting a brick wall. Either he was wearing some sort of electronic mind-shield or was immune to telepathic touch. I gave him a cheerful smile and walked by, following the long, white wall. I wasn't sure what I hoped to find here, but I had to look.

I was about three-quarters of the way around when awareness shot through me. Joy leapt, and it was all I could do to stop myself from dancing. I'd found him. And while I had no idea why he was here, I had every intention of finding out. I stopped and heard the buzz of the security cam as it swung around to watch me.

Forcing myself to move, I crossed the road, then got out my phone, pretending to answer it as I leaned against the front fence of a house and studied the rooftops beyond the wall. There were two buildings, and they didn't appear connected to the main one.

They were also within six feet of the two fences. An easy enough jump if you could get past the security systems.

For the first time in my life, I wished I could communicate telepathically with my brother. But that was the one ability he didn't inherit from our mixed heritage. We both got the infrared vision and the ability to differentiate between nonhuman races and track them down, but he was totally mind-blind. Which was probably a good thing considering he worked with some of Melbourne's most dangerous vampires.

The camera was on me again. I couldn't stay there. But I had every intention of coming back later that night, when the darkness played into my hand and allowed me to use the vampire ability to fade into shadow.

I walked back to my car, but the vid phone beeped before I could get moving. "Riley speaking."

"Riley, it's Jack."

I grinned. "Hey, boss, there's no need to send Kelly out tonight. I've found our missing man."

"Really?" Amusement played around his mouth. "And where would that be?"

"Moneisha."

His amusement fled. "Why on earth would he be there?"

"Considering you won't tell me what mission he was on, that's not a question I can answer."

He laughed. "Would you like Kelly's help extracting him?"

"Does her help come with terms?"

"Most definitely."

"Then no."

"You won't get in there without some form of

Directorate help. Moneisha has more than just in-frared and electric fences guarding it."

"Why? What does it do?"

"Officially, it's a drug research center."

"And unofficially?"

"I have no idea."

"Is that why Rhoan was investigating it?"

"He wasn't supposed to be anywhere near it."

Because he was supposed to be investigating Quinn. The question was, why? My gaze went back to the white walls. If there was more than just infrared, how was I going to get past it? I didn't do this for a living. I could take care of myself, but I didn't have the training or the skills to get past major security. Which meant I had two choices—either I let Jack extract him or I strike some sort of deal.

The first option was obviously the sanest, but a nig-gle deep inside suggested that at this moment, it wasn't the right choice. Though I had no idea why it wasn't, I'd spent most of my life listening to my instincts. And though in the past that had often got me into trouble, I wasn't about to abandon the habit.

Still, I hedged. "Why would you even let me at-tempt to extract him?"

His smile never touched his eyes, and it was a strong reminder that no matter how much I liked this vam-pire, he was first and foremost a Directorate man. And in that moment, I knew the answer to my question, before he even said a word.

"I want you as a guardian, Riley. You have the po-tential to be as good as, if not better than, your pack mate."

"That doesn't exactly answer the question." But it did, all too clearly.

"It's a test, a taster, if you will. I've known lots of wolves over my lifetime, and if there's one thing I've learned, it's that you all have one serious flaw. Though for Directorate purposes, it's something of a plus."

"And that is?"

"You're all adrenaline junkies."

I snorted. "You aren't even in the right ballpark with that one." Yet even as I said it, Talon's image came to mind. Wasn't half the thrill of being with him the sensation of walking a knife's edge? That at any moment, his wildness could snap and become truly dangerous? "So this is the test you have when I won't take the test?"

"Exactly."

"You can't force me to be a guardian."

"I won't have to. It's inevitable, Riley. You and Rhoan are two peas in a pod—and you were both born for this type of work."

A chill ran through me at his choice of words. It wasn't chance. Nothing was ever said by chance when it came to Jack. He knew Rhoan and I were twins. "I'm not a killer."

"All wolves are killers. It's just that in today's society, the urge is well controlled."

"That's like saying all vamps are killers."

"All vamps are. Some just manage to channel it into other areas."

Like becoming guardians and killing with the approval of the state. I shivered. "So basically, you're saying that you intend reeling me in bit by bit."

"Yes."

"And the offer of help tonight—what strings come attached to it?"

"That you promise to take the test sometime in the future."

"Sometime? You're not setting a limit of when?"

He grinned. "There'll be no need to. You'll come to me eventually."

"You don't know me very well if you think that."

"I know you better than you know yourself," he said, his cold gaze burning with a certainty that chilled my soul.

He knows what we are. I licked my lips and hoped like hell the intuition was wrong. "Okay, you have a deal."

"Good. Drop by the office and I'll give you full details about Moneisha."

"I have some things to do first—could be a few hours."

"I'll be here."

"Surprise, surprise," I muttered.

He chuckled, and hung up. I slipped the Mercedes into gear and cruised back to the city, making it to Talon's as dusk began shifting toward true night.

His house—though calling it a house was a misnomer when it was so damn big I could see several levels clearly above the fifteen-foot fences—sat on a leafy acre right in the heart of Toorak. I drove up to the wrought-iron security gates and said my name into the speaker. The gates slid silently open.

The driveway snaked through stately elms, past manicured lawns, and finally presented the Old-English–style mansion in all its glory. It was a truly beautiful house, but it was a little hard to believe that only one man lived there. Obviously, Talon had more money than he knew what to do with.

I parked in front and climbed out, feeling more

than a little out of place in my old work skirt and sweater. The door swung silently open as I climbed the steps, and the red beam of a weapon scanner swept down me as I stepped through the door.

A security cam buzzed as it swung around, and I raised an eyebrow. "Why all the gadgets?" I said, sure there'd be microphones here somewhere.

"A millionaire can never be too careful these days." Talon's husky tones seemed to come out of thin air. "Take the stairs, first door on the left."

I did as ordered. The door slid open as I approached, and the room I entered was an office big enough to play football in. The walls were a cool, dusky blue, and the furniture chrome. Talon was sitting at a desk down the far end. He wasn't wearing a shirt, and I very much suspected he wasn't wearing any pants, either. A bottle of champagne and two glasses sat to his right.

"Stop," he ordered softly.

His aura hit me, snatching my breath, making my legs feel boneless. He was heat and longing and need, and I'd never felt anything so potent in my life. It had me ready for him in an instant, but the unease I'd felt in the car earlier increased. What he was projecting couldn't possibly be natural.

"Strip," he continued in that same, flat tone.

I kicked off my heels, then, with his gaze a fever that flamed my skin, did a little, teasing dance as I took off my sweater, skirt, and undies. By the time I'd finished, it wasn't just his aura making me ache, but my own desire.

He took a deep, shuddery breath, then reached for the champagne and poured two glasses. "Walk to the desk."

I strolled toward him, provocatively exaggerating the sway of my hips. The closer I got, the stronger his hunger burned, until it hit my senses like a blow and made my head spin.

He slid a glass across the chrome. "Down it."

"You don't have to get me drunk to have your wicked way with me."

"This is the best champagne you will ever taste, and it will fuel the evening I have planned for us."

There was nothing seductive in his words—they were said as a statement of fact, a choice in which I had none. And while in some ways it aroused me all the more, that deep-down sense of unease grew.

"I'm due at work by nine."

"Then you are mine until eight-thirty."

I couldn't help a smile. Given the heat he was projecting, the next hour and a half was going to be one wild ride. I picked up the champagne, raised the glass in toast, and downed it as he drank his. It might be the best champagne ever made, but it went down as badly as the cheap stuff and made my head buzz even more.

He offered me another and I shook my head, knowing I'd probably throw up if I had a second glass.

He pressed a small button on his desk. A slot opened close to me, and a folder appeared. "Your information on Evensong and its owner. But you can look at it later. Right now, I want you. Come here, little wolf."

At that moment, I felt like a lamb confronted by a very large and hungry wolf, and for the first time in my life, I wasn't sure I actually liked the sensation. Or that I wanted to be there, with him.

Or was it simply a matter of the champagne affecting my head more than I thought?

Swallowing to ease the burning in my throat, I walked unsteadily around the desk. His golden body gleamed under the caress of the lights, and hunger slipped through me, mingling uneasily with reluctance. There was no emotion in his face, nothing in his eyes beyond lust, and his erection seemed positively huge. Huge and blurry. I blinked but it didn't seem to ease the sudden fuzziness. He grabbed my hand and pushed me back against the desk. As my rump hit the cold metal, he nudged open my legs and thrust into me, deeper and harder than he ever had before. I groaned, trapped between pleasure and pain as he began to pound into me. The heat of him, smell of him, swirled around me, through me, and sweat broke out across my brow. The champagne sat uneasily in my stomach and I knew if he didn't ease up, I'd throw up.

"Talon, stop."

He grabbed my hips, his fingers digging into my flesh as he held me still and kept grinding into me. Even the wolf in me was beginning to dislike the sensation. I grabbed his hands, intending to push him back, but my grip felt weak and there was a strange buzzing in my head, making it hard to concentrate. Worse still, the light and the office seemed to be fading in and out of existence.

He came, and that was the last thing I remember clearly.

Chapter 5

Awareness drifted in and out, as if I were caught in a fragmented dream. Voices swam around me. Lights as bright as the sun burned into my eyes. Something cut my arm, and pain seared deep. Farther down, cold touched my stomach, sliding around like ice. The pain in my arm eased. Then, for a while, there was nothing but darkness.

When the fragments gradually returned, they formed a picture of rising pleasure. I drifted on silk, writhing and moaning, my skin on fire and every muscle screaming with pleasure. Hands stroked me. Heat filled me. Every inch of me quivered under the relentless assault, until I couldn't even breathe because the need for release was so strong.

I woke, to discover it was no dream. Talon was on me, in me, and I had the oddest sensation that I'd just been betrayed in some basic way. But the thought quickly fled as the convulsions began, curling through me like a tidal wave and pushing me into rapture. He came with me, but still he pounded into me, as if determined to ensure that every last drop of his seed spilled into me.

Eventually, he collapsed and rolled to one side. "You are amazing, little wolf."

I didn't feel amazing. I felt confused. Looking around revealed red walls instead of blue. Bedroom furniture rather than office. When had we moved there? I glanced at the clock on the bedside table, and saw it was close to eight-thirty. An hour and a half had passed and I couldn't remember any of it.

"We're in your bedroom?"

He turned on his side and rested his hand on my belly. "We've also been in the living room, the games room, and even tried the kitchen, because you said you were hungry."

There was an ache behind my eyes and a bitter taste in my mouth. I frowned and rubbed my forehead. "This is going to sound strange, but I can't remember any of it."

He grinned. "I think the champagne went straight to your head. You were pretty damn wild for a while there."

He was rubbing my stomach, his gesture possessive more than sexual, and for some reason, it disturbed me.

I grabbed his hand and threw it off me, and even that small movement had an ache rippling through my muscles. He obviously wasn't lying about the number of times we'd made love. But he was lying about something, I was sure of it.

I flipped the silk sheet aside. "I need a shower, then I have to go."

"En suite's to the right." He paused until I found the right door, then added, "Come back later tonight."

I turned on the taps, then, once the water was steamy, stepped into the shower. "As I told you before, I promised to be with Misha tonight."

"So come back afterward."

There was no way I was coming back to this house. It might contain the warmth of many colors, but it was cold. And I had the uneasy feeling something beyond sex had happened here, something I *should* remember.

"I promised Misha I'd stay with him."

"Then I pray something distracts him, because I want you to be mine, and only mine, this phase."

"Exclusive?" The thought made my body ache more than it already was. "I don't think so."

"Just one phase, not forever. I have a desire only you can fulfill."

I snorted softly as I washed off the soap. "Me and your seven other lovers."

He walked in as I turned off the taps. He tossed me a towel, then crossed his arms and leaned against the door frame. "The others haven't hair your magnificent color. Nor do they have your strength."

"Which is why I imagine you have seven of them."

He grinned. "And they certainly don't have your lushness. I want that lushness. I want—" He stopped, and his sudden smile was distant.

I had the strangest feeling that at that moment, he wasn't really with me, that he was lost somewhere in dreams that just might have dire consequences for my health. Which was daft. Talon was often ruthless, but I didn't think he'd hurt me.

"What I want, I get, little wolf."

He wasn't getting anything more from me. Not this

evening, anyway. I tossed the damp towel into the hamper, then said, "Are my clothes still in the office?"

"Yes."

"And that is?"

"Just down the hallway."

There was amusement in his expression, cold calculation in his eyes. I liked neither, and wasn't sure why. I'd seen both often enough in the last two years. Talon was an extremely successful businessman, and arrogance had always been a part of his makeup. Until very recently, it had never bothered me.

He followed me up the hall, a heat I could feel but not hear. I found my clothes, and the folder was with them, but before I could get dressed, he slipped behind me, his hands snaking around my waist to pull me back against him. He was hard again. He might be a wolf, but his hunger and his rate of recovery were definitely abnormal.

"Let me go, Talon."

"Tell me why you won't stay with me." His breath caressed my neck, and a second later, his teeth grazed my earlobe. This time, it wasn't pleasure that shuddered through me, but annoyance.

"Because I don't want to." I elbowed him hard enough to force a grunt. He backed away, and I got dressed. "And because occasionally it would be nice to have a bit of foreplay before sex."

He crossed brawny arms, his expression an odd mix of amused tolerance and steel. "I thought you liked it hard and fast."

"I do. Sometimes. But it would be just as nice to take some time."

"Then meet me for breakfast. We'll eat, flirt, fool around some, then do the hard, passionate sex."

I hesitated, but the truth was, the moon had me in its grip, and when that happened, it was simply easier to be with partners I knew than starting afresh with strangers. And as much as I enjoyed Misha, Talon was right. Misha couldn't do to me what Talon did to me. Couldn't satisfy me in the same way. It was an addiction all right, but his type of danger was far different from the one Jack was trying to force on me.

"I don't know."

"Then let's agree to just breakfast, and we'll see what happens from there."

I hesitated again, but only briefly. Addiction or not, I couldn't walk away from Talon. Not when the moon rode me like this. "Where?"

"The Kingfisher, in Collins Street."

The Kingfisher was one of Melbourne's boutique hotels, and from reports, spectacular. It also wasn't that tall, scraping in at nineteen floors. "Okay. But I also have to go to work and I'm not sure how long I'll be there. I can't give you a definite time." But not because of work, and not because of Rhoan. I needed time to recover from his demands.

"So call," he said, as he escorted me to the door.

But before I could escape, he pulled me close and kissed me. There was nothing gentle about it—it was a possession, an affirmation of right, and left me both shaken *and* stirred.

Yet relief was all I felt as I drove out the gates, and the sheer depth of it made me determined that I was never coming back to his house. And maybe, just maybe, it was a sign that after the current moon phase, Talon and I should part ways.

I glanced at the time, saw it was close to nine, and dug around in my bag to find the phone so I could call

Misha and tell him I had to stop by work. There were several voice messages waiting.

I hit the replay button, and Misha's rich tones filled the air. "Hate to do this, Riley, but it looks like I won't be able to keep our date tonight. My sister's had a car accident, and I've been called home. I could be gone for over a week. Keep the car until I get back. I'll call you."

The message had been recorded just after six—which wouldn't have been that long after I'd blanked out after drinking Talon's fine champagne. I hoped Misha was okay. Hoped his sister was okay. Wished he'd left me a number so I could get in touch with him.

I hit delete, then moved on to the next message.

"Riley, it's Quinn." The warm, sexy lilt in his voice caressed my skin as sensually as a touch. What was it about this vampire that affected me so? I didn't even know him, and yet I'd wanted him, even before the fever had hit. Which was strange, because I'd never felt an attraction that strong to anyone who wasn't a wolf.

"I'm not sure why you're running from me, but I *am* a friend of Rhoan's, and I seriously believe you're both in danger. We need to talk."

He paused, and I could hear music in the background. It sounded like Presley's "A Little Less Conversation," which probably meant he'd been at the Rocker when he called.

"Meet me on the Casino steps at eleven." He hesitated again, then added, "There's more going on than what you think. Meet with me. Please."

The call intrigued me, that was for sure. But until I'd talked to Jack, there was no way in hell I was about to risk going anywhere near Quinn.

I drove to work. Jack looked up from the computer screen as I entered, and his gaze widened.

"Darlin', you look like shit."

"Thanks, boss. That's always nice to hear."

He rose, grabbed my arm, and pushed me into the chair. "No, I mean it." He caught my face in his large hands, and stared at me. "Your irises are the size of footballs. Have you taken something?"

"Champagne that didn't agree with me."

"This is more than that." He grabbed the phone and ordered a medical team down to our floor, pronto. "I'll get them to take a blood sample, because I think you've been drugged."

Only one person really had the chance to drug me, and really, why would he bother? He was getting what he wanted. Yet I remembered the memory loss, and, as much as I didn't want to, I wondered.

"It's just a bad reaction to champagne." I wasn't sure who I was trying to convince—myself or Jack. "It's happened before."

In fact, this was the second time in as many months, though on the other occasion it hadn't happened so quickly. But I'd lost several hours, at least. I was going to have to stop drinking Talon's fine champagne, because it definitely didn't agree with me.

The medical team came in, took what looked like enough blood to supply the guardians downstairs for several days, said they'd analyze it straightaway, and left.

Jack sat on the edge of the desk. "You asked me earlier if I'd ever done a check on Gautier. Was it only to see if he had a brother or did you want more information?"

I leaned back in the chair and studied him for a moment. "This is another of your lures, isn't it?"

He grinned, confirming my fears. "A taste here, a taste there, and you'll be hooked before you know it."

I shook my head. "It's not going to happen. I'm not a killer."

He just raised an eyebrow. "Then you don't want to know any more about Gautier?"

I sighed and rubbed my aching head. "Of course I do."

"You knew he joined the Directorate about eight years ago?"

I nodded. He'd apparently arrived a year before Jack and two years before me. "And?"

"It appears that up until nine and a half years ago, Gautier didn't even exist."

I stared at him. "Impossible. I've seen his file. He has birth certificates, passports, citizenship cards, the lot, and everything was checked."

"Forgeries, one and all." His computer screen beeped. He rose and walked over to it.

"How can you be sure?" I asked.

"Because we have a very sophisticated system running here now, and there's nowhere you can't go if you have the access."

And Jack obviously had the access. Interesting. As the head of the guardian division, he'd naturally have access to more files than most, but his words suggested there was no place he *couldn't* go. Which, in turn, meant he either knew how to get around the system monitoring or that he had carte blanche when it came to access from the director herself.

Which begged the question—why Jack and not the other directors? Because the others didn't have it—

they always came to Jack when they wanted information about particular aspects in the guardian division.

I studied him a minute longer, then said, "But the same system would have checked his credentials when he first joined."

"Actually, no. His acceptance was handled higher up, then rubber-stamped down to us."

"How far up?"

He glanced at me. "Alan Brown."

Who was Director Hunter's second-in-command, and yet another vampire I didn't like. "You think he was pressured into accepting Gautier?"

Jack glanced at the screen again. "They've found no matches for recreational drugs," he said, then added, "Right now, I'm not sure what to think."

Somehow, I doubted that. I'm sure he had lots of thoughts about what was going on—he just had no intention of sharing them with me just yet. I tapped my fingers against his desk. "What would anyone have to gain by getting Gautier accepted here? He's an utter bastard, but he's also our best guardian, and has hardly set a foot wrong work-wise."

"Everyone knows Gautier wants my job, and eventually, the director's job. Maybe that's the plan." The computer screen beeped again. "No response to known prescription drugs."

Geez, the lab boys weren't kidding when they said they'd get on it straightaway. Either they'd cleared all the analysis machines just for this, or they'd had nothing else to do.

"I told you, it was just a reaction to the champagne."

"Maybe." He didn't sound convinced. "They're going to run through listed experimental drugs. Could take a while, though."

I shrugged, then added, "I doubt if Gautier would get the director's job. I think the old cow has plans of being in that seat for several centuries."

Amusement creased the corners of his eyes. "I know for a fact she has. Which leaves my job."

"But for all intents and purposes, you only oversee the guardian division. You're not the true power here, she is."

"True, but I have control over missions, and that alone might be all Gautier wants. The power to go after whom he pleases."

That thought sent a shiver down my spine. "Don't you dare leave, Jack."

"Believe me, I have no plans to do so."

"Good." I hesitated again, half-wondering if by even asking any more questions I was dragging myself further into Jack's world. "Did you ever discover if he has any kin?"

"No. He apparently came from Perth, but nobody there seems to remember him."

"And no one here thought that odd?"

"Apparently not."

But Jack had—and had done nothing except watch and wait. I wondered who else he was watching. "What about the shooter?"

"It appears he doesn't have a past beyond five years ago."

That raised my eyebrows. I mean, what were the chances of two almost identical people also sharing a lack of background? "What are the police saying? They automatically do DNA testing when the remains are unrecognizable, don't they?"

"They do, but they're not saying anything because I put a hush order on it."

"Why? Okay, he resembles Gautier and he shot me, but hell, werewolves are always getting shot by crazies."

"As I said before, I don't believe in coincidences. Especially when Gautier seemed to know about the bullet wound. Why else would he have touched your shoulder like that when, in all the time you've been here, he's barely done more than exchange insults from a distance?"

I blinked, remembering the watchfulness in Gautier's eyes. He *had* been looking for something. And though he was a vamp and could smell blood as easily as I breathed, the fact that I'd shifted shape to help the healing along then taken a shower meant there was no blood—fresh or otherwise—to smell. And barely healed wounds weren't visible in infrared. "It might have been dumb luck."

"Dumb luck has nothing to do with anything Gautier does. So the next questions are, why did the shooter resemble Gautier, how is he connected to Gautier, and why did he shoot you?"

I shrugged. "Maybe he just hates werewolves."

Yet that wolf had called me by name—and how had he known where I lived? With Rhoan and me both working for the Directorate, our apartment wasn't listed in the any of the phone directories. And it didn't make sense for Gautier to have given him the information. If Gautier wanted me dead, he'd do it himself—and with sadistic pleasure.

"That doesn't explain the likeness," Jack said.

No, it didn't. "So you think they could be related, despite the fact we can find nothing about either of them?"

"Not related by birth, but certainly connected."

"Connected how, then?"

"I think it very likely the shooter, at least, is a clone."

I stared at him. "They can't make clones—not ones that survive to adulthood, anyway."

"It's possible someone has, because your shooter is not the only dead person in recent weeks to resemble Gautier. And Gautier himself resembles a man who died some years ago. Plus, we discovered a lot of growth accelerant in the shooter's remains."

"What about DNA?"

"We haven't tested any against Gautier's yet."

"Why not?"

"Because we don't want him suspicious. We plan on taking some samples for testing during his regular physical."

Which was due in the next day or so, if I remembered correctly. "I guess you haven't talked to him, then?"

"No. At this stage, we're merely watching him. We're hoping he'll lead us to whoever is behind all this."

"That's a big risk, isn't it? What if he gets suspicious and runs?" The last thing we needed was Gautier off the leash. Just the thought sent a shiver down my spine.

"If he runs, he'll be killed."

Somehow, I didn't think it would be that simple. "So why does accelerant imply cloning?"

"Accelerant—at least in the tests currently being done on animals—is used to fast-track growth so the scientists can see what problems the clone might have when it reaches middle years."

"Where are the animal rights activists on that one?"

I muttered. "Is there any evidence of accelerant in Gautier's blood?"

"None at all—it would have been picked up in the six-month physicals."

So, he was either who he said he was, and the clones a mere coincidence, or he was somehow the source of the clones. Because if the dead man Gautier resembled was *truly* dead rather than vampire dead, then surely he couldn't be the source of Gautier and the others. "Do you think Moneisha is behind the clones?"

"We doubt it. It hasn't the facilities as far as we know."

"But Rhoan was investigating it?"

"No, he was checking a report that prostitutes were regularly disappearing from the St. Kilda district, and reappearing a week or so later, totally disoriented and having no idea where they had been."

"Human or nonhuman pros?"

"Nonhuman."

"If someone is trying to clone, maybe they need DNA samples to play with."

"Very likely."

His expression was that of a teacher pleased with the progress of a difficult student, and that irritated. Yet until I'd actually gotten Rhoan out, I'd have to put up with such expressions. And after all, time would tell which of us was going to win this particular battle.

Still, I felt an insane urge to irritate him back. "There's something about the attack I should tell you— I didn't actually kill the shooter. Quinn O'Conor did."

"I was wondering when you'd get around to telling me that."

I raised my eyebrows. "You knew about Quinn?"

He nodded. "I saw the security tapes."

"Vampires in shadows don't show up in normal security tapes."

He grinned. "No. But the rail system underwent a recent upgrade that included infrared systems being installed side by side with standard security. It's helped catch a number of criminals."

"That was kept rather secret, wasn't it?"

"Sometimes the public just doesn't need to know."

"Tell that to the civil libertarians." I pushed up from the chair and walked across to the machine to grab a coffee. "Why was Rhoan investigating Quinn O'Conor?"

Amusement touched his lips. "Oh, you are good."

"Was it the dead vamp found in his cargo plane?"

"Very good," he murmured, then nodded. "Turns out that vamp was a half-breed." He looked at me, and I knew, right then, that I'd been on the money before. He'd known all along what Rhoan and I were. "But one born in the lab, rather than naturally, like you and your twin."

I swallowed, but it did little to ease the dryness in my throat. "How long have you known?"

"Practically since you joined us."

And we thought we'd been so careful.

His smile was gentle. "Riley, I'm over eight hundred years old, and I've seen an awful lot in my time. I've met your kind before—you even have a name, do you realize that?"

The only name I knew was freak, and even then, until that man shot me, I'd only ever heard it in whispered tones from those in my pack who thought I was too young to understand.

"Dhampires," he continued. "The offspring of newly turned vamps, born to women who are usually attacked and raped in the vampire's first hour out of the grave, women who somehow survive. A one in a million chance."

"Our mother was a wolf."

"And I'm supposing she was in moon fever, because a werewolf would certainly best a newly risen vampire."

She had bested him—when it was over and his dying seed had somehow created life. "Why haven't you ever said anything?"

"Because I respect your right to privacy." He hesitated. "Though I have to admit, your birthright is part of the reason I want you on the team with Rhoan. I don't think either of you has tapped your full potential."

"And I want the whole picket fence and bundles of babies scenario, Jack, not long nights filled with bloodshed."

"Actually, I want you and Rhoan to form the start of a daytime guardian division. Right now, we are somewhat hampered by our ability to hunt only at night."

"Right now, your wants aren't even registering on my radar." I began to pace, taking care not to spill the lukewarm brown muck the Directorate had the cheek to call coffee. The moon was rising and I didn't have to see it to know it was happening. The power of it burned through my veins. "So why did a dead half vamp make you decide to investigate Quinn? There's nothing unusual in vamps occasionally dying on cargo planes, especially if they get their timing or packing wrong."

"This vamp suffocated."

I swung around to look at him. "Vamps don't really need air to survive, so how did he suffocate?"

"He was only half-vamp, remember."

"So he was too dumb to put airholes in the coffin?"

Jack grinned. "Actually, he had too much air."

That raised my eyebrows. "How can anyone have too much air?"

"He was half merman, that's how."

"A vampire merman?" I couldn't help the note of incredulity in my voice. "Why in hell would anyone want a cross like that?"

"I think hell had a lot to do with it. A hell run by fanatics determined to breed the perfect killing machine."

"I can't imagine a merman willingly being a part of research like that." They don't even like going to the doctors, for heaven's sake.

"I don't think willingness has anything to do with what is going on here."

"So why were you investigating Quinn?"

"It was just routine. He owns several pharmaceutical companies in Australia and the U.S. Of the ones here, the biggest is in Sydney. Sydney is where that vamp was headed."

"That doesn't mean he was headed to O'Conor's labs." I took a sip of coffee and screwed my nose up at the bitter taste. Still, with my head continuing to pound and my stomach beginning to growl over lack of food, bitter coffee was better than nothing.

"As it turns out, he wasn't, but we still had to check. Especially since Director Hunter wanted Quinn in on the investigation."

I swung around to look at him. *"What?"*

Jack smiled. "The older vampire community is not

a huge one. There are, perhaps, fifty vampires world-wide who have survived to reach their millennium years—and to do so means they are either extremely powerful or extremely canny. Quinn is both."

And for a vamp over one thousand years old, he was also very well preserved. "Why would she want him on the investigation, though?"

"Because he was already seeking the origins of the lab-made dhampire and the Gautier clones, and it is infinitely better if we pool resources and work together."

"Just how many clones are there?" That there might be more than two was a scary thought—and I could only hope they didn't all have a desire to shoot me with silver. "And why would he be investigating them? He's a businessman, not a cop or guardian."

Jack grinned again. "O'Conor's been many things over the years. A businessman is only the latest incarnation."

"That doesn't answer the question, Jack."

He nodded. "The truth is I can't actually stop him from investigating this, so it's better to have him working alongside us."

I frowned. "Throwing his ass into one of the cells upstairs would certainly stop him."

"The cells wouldn't hold me, let alone Quinn. Not with the sort of mind-power *he's* got."

A chill ran down my spine. "The Directorate is shielded. No one is supposed to be able to use mind-abilities within these walls."

"Most can't, and the cells will hold all but a very few."

But not him, and not Quinn, obviously. It was an almost scary thought that the two vamps I'd felt so comfortable with were far more dangerous than Gautier ever could be. "Why is Quinn investigating the clones?"

"He saw—and stopped—one in Sydney sometime ago. Apparently the clone was the image of a friend he'd thought dead."

Meaning the friend was the image of Gautier, if this "friend" was the dead man Jack had mentioned earlier. Part of me couldn't help wondering if the poor guy had been so depressed about his looks he'd killed himself. "A vampire friend, I take it?"

Jack nodded. "Quinn's also an old friend of Director Hunter. He recently contacted her about the matter— a professional courtesy, as he'd heard Moneisha mentioned while investigating and intended to come down to Melbourne and look into the matter further. Which is why she told me to bring him in on our investigations."

"Her okay doesn't make it legal to have a civilian involved in a Directorate case."

"In matters of civil safety, the Directorate can enlist whatever help it deems necessary. And it does give us the chance to intercede before he does anything illegal."

Somehow, I didn't think Quinn would be too bothered about legalities if push came to shove. "He left a message on my phone. He wants a meet tonight."

Jack nodded. "He contacted me once he'd regained his full memory. For the time being, I want you to work with him."

"Do you think that wise? I mean, if he's as powerful as you say, might he not be using his abilities to bend you to his will?"

"Director Hunter trusts him implicitly, so I must also."

"Director Hunter isn't infallible, as evidenced by

the fact she had no idea her vice president rubber-stamped Gautier's entry into the Directorate."

Jack grinned. He seemed to being doing a lot of that lately, and it was somewhat disturbing—if only because I suspected it meant he was extremely happy about how things were going when it came to his plans for me.

"Suspicion is an excellent habit for a guardian to have, you know."

So was knowing when to retreat—which was exactly what I intended doing just then. Besides, it was nearing eleven, which meant I'd have to get moving if I wanted to meet Quinn. "Tell me about Moneisha."

He glanced at the computer screen, said *"Moneisha, information portable,"* and a second later, a tiny chip sealed in plastic appeared. He picked it up and handed it to me. "All current information we have. Once you and Quinn have read it, destroy the chip."

I shoved it in my pocket. "Will do."

"Keep me updated."

I nodded and left. When I climbed into the car, I saw the file Talon had given me. A quick flick-through revealed nothing more than what I'd already seen. He hadn't even tried to do a thorough search on Quinn, and that was annoying. I didn't ask much of either of my mates, but when I did, I expected a little effort expended.

I shook my head, threw the folder down on the seat, and headed down to the Casino parking lot. It was close to eleven-thirty by the time I loped toward the Casino itself. Once I'd reached the main entrance of the big building, I swept my gaze across the people milling there. Humans, wolves, shapeshifters, and vampires, but none of them the man I was looking for. I turned, checking the surrounding area.

And found him not far away, sitting on the steps that led down to the quay. I walked over and sat down beside him, close enough that I could feel the warmth of him, but not quite close enough that we were touching.

"I didn't think you were coming," he said, voice conversational.

He'd actually showered and donned some clothes since I'd last seen him. His hair was indeed black, and so thick and silky my fingers itched to run through it. The coat I'd given him had disappeared, and he was wearing a burgundy sweater that hugged his lean form and framed his angelic features, and black jeans that seemed to emphasize the athletic strength of his thighs. He was sexy covered in mud, but the clothed version . . . wow.

"What happened to the coat?" An inane thing to say, but my brain was too busy battering down my hormones to think of anything more intelligent.

He glanced at me, eyes darker than the night itself, and totally unreadable. "I left it at my house to be washed. Blood from your wound had soaked into it."

I raised my eyebrows. "So you do have a house here?"

He nodded. "In Brighton."

It figured. Toorak was only for the would-be billionaires, like Talon. "I talked to Jack before I came here."

"Then you know I mean you no harm."

"Well, no. I know you're currently helping the Directorate's investigations, but I very much suspect you'll do your own thing if it happens to suit you better."

He smiled his seductive smile, and my hormones did an excited little shuffle. "You do read people well."

"Meaning, of course, that I'm right not to trust you fully."

"I didn't say that."

Didn't deny it, either. "Jack wants me to work with you tonight."

"Meaning you've found Rhoan?"

"He's at Moneisha."

"Moneisha? That's surprising."

I did up my coat. The chill coming off the river was seeping into my bones, and the warmth flowing from Quinn wasn't enough to combat it. The goose bumps prickling my skin were threatening to become mountains.

"Why? I thought you were investigating Moneisha yourself?"

His dark gaze met mine. "Jack told you?"

"Yes. And it annoys the hell out of me that you simply didn't come out and tell me you were working with the Directorate. Rhoan might be rescued by now if you had."

"I couldn't remember the truth—only various bits and pieces of it, originally—and by the time I *did* remember it all, you'd run."

"Well, naked vampires camping out on my doorstep or following me home do tend to raise suspicions."

"I had to be sure you were who you said you were. As I said before, Rhoan never mentioned you." His gaze came to mine, his expression briefly curious. "You cannot be lovers."

"No, we cannot." I didn't bother going any further. The fact that we were twins was something he didn't need to know. Though if Jack had guessed, surely

Quinn, who was apparently far older, would as well. "Tell me what you know about Moneisha."

I had the information chip Jack had given me, but was interested in seeing just how free with information Quinn was going to be. Jack might trust this vampire implicitly, but I wasn't so inclined.

"My investigations have led me to believe we have two branches of research happening—one doing cloning, one doing the crossbreeds. On the surface, neither seems to be connected to the other. While I doubt Moneisha is behind either, I think it *is* part of the chain. There's certainly a lot more going on behind those walls than what is being reported."

"I'm going in there tonight to get Rhoan out."

He raised an eyebrow. "Alone?"

"Jack suggested I take you."

"Someone covering your back is always a good idea."

Having *this* vampire covering my back *wasn't* such a good idea. Not when the moon was riding me so hard. I glanced at my watch and saw it was nearly twelve. "Look, do you mind if we continue this conversation inside?"

"You're cold?"

"Starved more than cold. I haven't eaten anything since breakfast."

He rose and offered me a hand up. His fingers were warm against mine, gentle yet strong. It was all too easy to imagine those hands on my body, caressing and teasing.

Though his expression remained flat, the surge of his desire washed over me like a summer storm. He might have his shields up on full to protect himself from my aura, but that didn't stop the awareness zinging between us.

"What would you like to eat?" he said softly.

You. I cleared my throat and stepped away a little. The night was much colder without his touch. "A burger would be good."

He nodded and, ignoring the slight space I'd put between us, pressed a hand to my back and guided me forward. Heat flared where his fingers rested, rolling through the rest of me in waves.

"There's a nice restaurant down near the Swanston Street end," he said, his voice a musical caress that made me want to sigh.

"Do nice restaurants sell burgers and fries?"

"This one does. Tell me what you discovered about Moneisha."

"Security is tight, and they apparently have infrared cameras."

"That's going to be a problem."

I took the microchip from my pocket. "Information and floor plans."

He smiled. "Then perhaps we should grab takeaway and make our way to my office."

"You have an office close by?"

He pointed to the white building that dominated the skyline a block away. "My office is on the top floor."

I looked up . . . and up. "And you don't get height sickness?"

I certainly did, but it didn't have anything to do with my dual heritage. It was an end result of being thrown off a mountain when I was a pup. Why the fear manifested in buildings, I have no idea, especially when I could still climb mountains and be fine as long as I didn't go near any cliffs.

He raised an eyebrow. "Do you?"

"Sometimes."

"Then perhaps we shall keep to one of the lower floors."

"Unless you want me puking over your undoubtedly nice carpets, that could be a good idea."

He nodded. We reached the restaurant and he bought me a burger, fries, and Coke, refusing to let me pay for it. I sipped the drink as we moved on to his building. Security let him in after an eye scan, and we took the elevator to the tenth floor. Another eye scan later, and we were in a section that consisted of endless rows of desks. He led me through them and into an office at the far end.

"Chip?"

I was tempted to hand him one of the French fries, but didn't think he'd see the humor in it right then. So I handed him the microchip and sat on the edge of the desk, one leg swinging as I munched my food. The screen popped into existence after security confirmed his identity yet again. He slipped the chip into a slot and it disappeared into the depths of the desk. A second later, floor plans appeared.

"Where did you feel Rhoan?"

I pointed a greasy finger at the appropriate wall and the screen shimmered slightly. "There's about six feet between the walls and the roof, but there's a camera close by and I would imagine it's infrared."

"There's another entrance here." He pointed to a spot just past where I'd found Rhoan. "And a small guardhouse."

"That might be a good point of entry, if we could distract the guards."

He nodded. "They have laser sensors here and

here." He indicated the two spots. "And it looks as if they also have sensor beams set one foot above the outer wall."

"Fuck."

"Crude, but appropriate." Amusement flirted with his lips again as he leaned back in the chair and studied the plans. "Though one foot leaves enough room to get under if you are aware of its presence. If Rhoan is still in there, it's going to take some planning to get him out."

"What do you mean, 'if'?"

"They've got cameras. They would have seen you walking around the perimeter."

"So? They wouldn't know me from a bar of soap."

"If Moneisha *is* involved in making either the cross-breeds or the clones, that may not be true." He studied me for a moment, dark eyes flat and somehow chilling. He reached into the pocket of his jeans. "I found this on that werewolf who shot you."

He dropped the small button into my palm. I looked at it, not sure what to make of it. My confusion must have shown, because he added, "It's a camera. A very powerful, very experimental, camera."

"They watched me being shot?" I couldn't believe anyone would be so...I stopped the thought. I worked with guardians, so yes, it was certainly possible to believe someone would be bloodthirsty enough to enjoy something like that.

"He never intended to shoot you in the heart. He wanted to maim, not kill."

I took a quick swig of my Coke and regretted it the minute it hit my already churning stomach. "They couldn't have known you were there, and if you hadn't have been, I would have died."

"True. But he also had a small medical kit on him,

meaning he could have been intending to retrieve the bullet himself."

"So why shoot me, then patch me up? What was the point?"

"Maybe they wanted to watch your reactions."

I went cold. "But that would mean—"

"If they're holding Rhoan for what he is," he said gently, "then they undoubtedly suspect what you are, too."

"But no one—" I broke the words off. If Jack had guessed, maybe others had too. "There's nothing on our birth certificates, and we've told no one." I fixed my gaze on him. "I can't believe Rhoan told you."

"He didn't. I guessed. Werewolves generally do not make good guardians because they cannot sense the dead. Yet he has senses as keen as my own." He paused. "And you blurred in an effort to avoid that bullet. Something else werewolves cannot do."

I slipped off the desk and began to pace. "What I don't get is the why? They're creating their own freaks. Why would they need me or Rhoan?"

He caught my hand as I passed him, stopping me in my tracks. "You are not a freak."

There was anger in his voice, in his eyes, as if the mere idea I could think such a thing offended him greatly. I found myself smiling. "Easy for you to say. You're just a common old vampire."

"And you are a miracle of existence. Never think otherwise."

My smile grew. "You know, I could really get to like you."

His sudden grin was devilish. "Does that mean I get to dance with you sometime soon?"

"It just might." Once I'd gotten Rhoan out. Once I knew for sure Quinn was playing it straight.

"Good." His gaze went back to the floor plans. "I can think of two reasons why they might want you and Rhoan. First because you both appear to have integrated your dual heritage very well."

I went back to pacing. It was better than sitting still. Or sitting close to a treat I wasn't able to sample just yet. "And the second?"

He looked at me. "Your almost identical looks."

That stopped me. "What?"

"All the clones so far have been the image of the guardian known as Henri Gautier."

"Apparently so."

"Meaning they come from the one source."

"The friend you thought was dead."

He nodded. "Well, the dhampire found in my plane looked nothing like Gautier, meaning he came from a totally different source material altogether."

"Yeah, so?"

"So what if they don't know, or believe, that dhampires can be born naturally? What if they think you and Rhoan are lab creations? *Successful* lab creations that they *didn't* create?"

I stared at him as the implications sank in.

If that were true, my brother and I were in deep shit.

Chapter 6

hat really makes as much sense as them choosing to clone the same butt-ugly image over and over again." I paused, remembering as soon as I'd opened my big mouth that the butt-ugly image had apparently originally belonged to his friend. Presuming, that is, his dead friend was the source of the clones and not another clone himself. To cover my gaffe, I quickly added, "And surely if the people who attacked me already had Rhoan, I'd feel a greater sense of danger where he was concerned."

"Not necessarily. Not if Moneisha is merely a collecting point. Maybe the people behind that lab are merely getting samples and don't know yet what they really have."

I eyed him for a moment. "So you knew Rhoan was in St. Kilda investigating the disappearances of the pros?"

He nodded. "I was with him most of the night."

"Why did you leave? It's not as if dawn would have threatened you."

He grimaced. "No, but hunger could."

I raised my eyebrows. "And you couldn't have taken blood from the pros?"

"I could have, but I prefer not to." His smile touched his eyes again and damned if it didn't make my knees go weak. "I only bite someone while making love, and I do have a preference for women who are not in the game."

The thought of him biting my neck while thrusting slow and deep made me all goose pimply and hot. Man, I was really going to have to take this vampire for a test run before he disappeared out of my life.

"So Rhoan disappeared after you'd left?"

He nodded. "Rhoan was dressed like a hooker so he didn't stand out on the streets while hunting information. I was in the shadows watching, and reading thoughts."

Meaning they might have suspected that Rhoan had a guard, because they'd only snatched him once Quinn had left. Either that, or they'd thought Quinn was a watchful pimp. I walked to the windows and stared out. We were only ten floors up, so there wasn't all that much to see but more buildings. I let my gaze drift to the southeast. The reason for Rhoan's capture wasn't really important. Getting him out of there before they realized he wasn't *just* a wolf was.

I swung around. "We have to go."

Quinn didn't try to stop me, which was good, because right then I probably would have tried to flatten him. I say tried, because I very much suspected he was one vampire I *wasn't* equal to. There was something about him, something under that calm, sexy exterior, that suggested greater depths than any of the vampires I worked with. Even Jack.

And if Jack was wary of this vampire, then I sure as hell should be.

All Quinn said was, "We have to prepare first."

"I can shadow. They won't see me."

"They have infrared. You said that yourself."

I stopped at the door and took a deep breath. He was right. But it did little to ease the anxiety suddenly knotting my insides.

I glanced over my shoulder. "What do you suggest?"

He retrieved the chip from the desk, then rose and walked toward me, all grace and beauty in a lean and powerful package. "A little game of dress-up."

I could think of a lot of games I could play with this vampire, and dressing up was certainly up there on the list. But I very much doubted he meant the type of dressing up *I* was imagining—more's the pity. "Meaning?"

"Meaning, if Moneisha is looking for prostitutes, why don't we give them an easy one to snatch?"

"Wouldn't they be a little suspicious of a pro suddenly appearing on a quiet suburban street?"

He gave me the chip, then pressed a hand into my back again, guiding me toward the elevators. "Not necessarily. There's a working brothel one street down from Moneisha. Hopefully they'll think you're just walking to work."

I slanted him a sideways glance. "And how would you know there's a working brothel one street away?"

"A good investigator discovers what he can about a target area."

"Yet you said only moments before that you preferred to avoid prostitutes."

"I do." He gave me another of those grins. "I'm a billionaire. Women throw themselves at me all the time. I have no need to pay for it."

Which didn't exactly answer my question. "And do you not-pay-for-it often?"

"Quite often. I have needs, like any other man."

I was hoping he'd assuage some of those needs with me. And as soon as I got my brother out.

The doors closed behind us and the elevator dropped. My stomach flirted with the idea of puking, then decided to settle again. "So where are we going?"

"To buy camouflage." His gaze slid down my body. "The skirt is nice, but it doesn't quite stretch into pro territory."

Well, no, but all I had to do was take off the coat and sweater, reveal the torn shirt, and you had come-get-me material right there. "It's nearly midnight. There are not going to be any shops open."

"When you have the money, the shops are always open."

The glass front doors slid open as we approached and the cool evening air swirled in. It was thick with the aromas of smog and humans, but underneath it lay something else. Musk and mint and man. The same combination that had been on the wolf who'd shot me.

I stopped and heard something else. A scream of air, as if something fast and deadly was tearing through the night toward us.

I threw myself sideways and knocked Quinn out of the way. He cursed, his arms going around me, instinctively cushioning my body with his as we fell to the ground. He grunted as we hit, and his eyes widened. Air hissed, and I twisted around to look. Something cut through the night just above us, something that was wood rather than metal, with a deadly pointed end.

An arrow.

The fact that it was all wood suggested it had been aimed at Quinn, but the reality was, an arrow in the heart wasn't going to do *either* of us any good.

It hit the glass behind us and ricocheted harmlessly away. Footsteps whispered across the sounds of the night. Our attacker, on the run. I broke away from Quinn's embrace, flung off my bag, coat, and sweater, then shifted shape. In wolf form, I bounded after the bastard.

"Riley, wait!"

It was a command, one I ignored. The would-be assassin was running toward South Bank, perhaps hoping to shake any pursuit in the crowd gathered near the Casino. Meaning he either didn't realize I was a wolf, or he had no idea just how keen a wolf's hunting sense was.

He kept running, looking over his shoulder as he did so, barreling into people and thrusting them out of the way. I loped after him, lithely avoiding the idiot humans who screamed or stepped into my path rather than out of it. The man ahead was another Gautier, right down to the long, greasy ponytail. He was obviously aware that he was being pursued, but he was looking over the wrong shoulder and I was drawing closer and closer. His scent was cloying, the minty smell barely covering the growing odor of death and decay. I wrinkled my nose and resisted the temptation to sneeze.

He didn't head over the bridge, as I'd expected, running instead into the Clocks poker machine venue. I shifted shape, retied the shirt, then strode in after him.

He weaved through the machines, not quite running. I kept back, out of sight. His scent lingered in the air, a trail I could follow anywhere, even in a venue layered with so many conflicting odors.

Another aroma joined the throng—sandalwood. I smiled and glanced over my shoulder. Quinn was three feet behind me, my bag slung casually over his shoulder.

His dark gaze was filled with anger as it met mine. "You could have gotten yourself into trouble running off like that." He handed me my sweater, and I put it on as he added, "It might have been a trap."

It still could be. Who knew where Gautier's double might lead us? "That arrow was aimed at you, not me."

"It would have got me, too." He reached out, catching my hand and raising it to his mouth as we walked. The brief caress of his lips across my fingers was unlike anything I'd ever felt before. Sweet, and yet at the same time, erotic. "Thank you," he added softly.

I took a deep breath, trying to control my suddenly erratic pulse.

Ahead, our would-be murderer ducked through a door and disappeared. I looked up at the sign above the door and smiled. He'd gone to the toilet. Perfect.

"You mind the door." Quinn handed me back my bag and coat. "I'll have a little talk with our friend."

"Anyone else in there?"

His gaze narrowed slightly, and I knew he was using his infrared vision to check. "No."

"Good."

I followed him in, but stopped just inside, leaning back against the door as it closed. I have to say, the smell of men's toilets was never pleasant, no matter how much air freshener they used. Not that I'd been in all that many, but hey, it was one way of avoiding the queues in the women's during intermission at the theatre or concerts.

The urinals weren't occupied, but one stall was. It had to be our man. Why he thought he'd be safe behind the closed door of a toilet was anyone's guess. Maybe he didn't get out amongst vamps or werewolves much.

Quinn raised a foot and kicked the door open, then blurred so fast one second he was there, and the next he wasn't. There a brief flurry of sound, flesh smacking against flesh, then a squeak that was more a note of pain than fear. It wasn't Quinn's squeak.

Silence fell. No conversation, no nothing. But I knew what was happening. Quinn was raiding the other man's mind.

The door behind me bumped slightly, then someone knocked. "Sorry," I called. "Closed for cleaning. Someone vomited."

The gent on the other side cursed and walked away. "You'd better hurry, Quinn. Security will have seen us come in here. We probably haven't much longer before they investigate."

He came out five seconds later and closed the stall door before walking over to the basin to wash his hands. I watched him for a moment, then my gaze drifted back to that closed door and I felt a sudden chill. "He's dead, isn't he?"

"Yes." He didn't look at me, just finished washing his hands, then tore off some paper towel to dry them.

"How?" I hadn't heard the snap of bones, so he certainly hadn't broken the other man's neck.

"Heart attack." His dark gaze met mine and the coldness there chilled me. "An easy thing to do when you can read their minds and know their worst fears—and have the empathic capabilities to enforce the belief those fears are currently happening."

So he was empathic as well as telepathic. That certainly explained why he was catching my aura so strongly, despite my shields and his. "He died of fright?"

"I'm afraid so."

He dumped the paper in the bin and walked toward me. I would have backed away had I had anywhere to go. And while I recognized it was a ridiculous reaction, I just couldn't help it. As much as I was certain I could protect myself, I had the strangest feeling that, against this vampire, there was no defense.

"We'd better get out of here," he continued, in that same soft, flat tone. "Security is coming."

I opened the door and walked out. Sure enough, two men in black security outfits were walking toward us. They didn't look at us, didn't even appear to notice us, and I knew Quinn had touched their minds, diverting their attention away from us.

His fingers pressed into my back, but this time I stepped away from his warm touch, walking quickly through the room and out into the night. I stopped at the curb, crossing my arms and drawing the cool, flavorsome air deep.

He stopped behind me, a heat I could feel more than hear. "I scared you."

"Yes."

"Why? You work with guardians. They do far worse than what I did in there."

"I know. But I expect it from them. I didn't expect it from you."

"I'm a vampire. That's what we are."

"Yeah, but for some reason I'd been hoping you were different." That the exterior gloss was fact, not merely a show. But that was my problem, not his. Hell, it wasn't as if he hadn't warned me that he could kill as easily as he drank blood. And, truth be told, the demonstration hadn't really killed my desire for him. "Did you uncover anything useful?"

He was silent for a moment, then said, "He was partially blocked. I caught images. Moneisha's not where these things are coming from."

I glanced over my shoulder. He wasn't even looking at me, but staring up at the cloudy sky, his expression thoughtful.

"What images?"

"It's underground. Lots of concrete, bright lights, white walls, that sort of stuff."

"Nothing recognizable in the way of scenery?"

He shook his head and finally looked at me. His eyes were shuttered. "It could have been anywhere. Any country."

Great. "Then let's go get Rhoan out."

"Disguises first."

"Where? It's midnight and there's not a lot open." Not a lot beyond restaurants, clubs, and the Casino, that is.

"As I said before, that doesn't mean a lot when you have money."

A point he proceeded to prove by having the largest retailer in the city open its doors so we could shop. "Can you do tarty?" he said, as we headed up in the elevator to the women's floor.

I grinned. "I'm a wolf. We do tart better than the tarts."

A smile warmed his dark eyes. "I've noticed that about wolves. I shall leave you to your own devices, then, and go get the supplies I need." He glanced at the assistant. "Anything she wants. Charge it to my account." His gaze came back to me. "I'll meet you downstairs in half an hour."

Half an hour wasn't long when you'd just been given full use of unlimited credit, but hey, I wasn't about to bitch. I wasted ten minutes simply walking around looking, and eventually went for the thigh-length silver snakeskin boots, simply because I'd always wanted a pair. But I settled for the four-inch heels rather than the six-inch, just in case I had to run. I combined those with a barely decent blue net skirt that was way too short to be described as micro, and a silver crop top that had peekaboo holes for my nipples. To complete the effect, I went for a bright blue wig and blue-toned skin makeup. Then I headed into the change room to make the transformation.

As I studied my reflection in the mirror, I decided I did slut superbly well. The blue wig and skin toning made my smoke-colored eyes glow a bright blue, and the skirt and shirt flirted with indecency but left enough covered to stop the cops hauling me off to charge me. I shoved my jacket on, put my other clothes in my bag, and walked downstairs to meet Quinn.

He was waiting, several bags at his feet. His gaze went to my hair, then slid down to my face, and a mix of surprise and hunger flitted through his eyes. The surge of his desire nearly scorched my skin.

"Rather keen on the blue, are we?" I teased.

He didn't deny it. Couldn't, when I could so easily smell it. "I don't get a preview of the rest of it?"

I grinned. "And spoil the surprise?"

His gaze slid down, lingering on my leather-clad ankles. "I've got a feeling the surprise could be heart attack material."

"Isn't that the effect you want?"

"Yes." He bent to pick up the two bags, affording me a glimpse of laser guns and some sort of electronic sensor. I didn't even know they sold that sort of stuff here, and I shopped here frequently. But maybe they had a special section set aside for billionaires.

He gave the manager a huge tip, then escorted me outside. "Did you come in a car?"

I nodded. "It's in the Casino parking lot."

"Then we'll leave it there and go in mine. They might have taken note of your car earlier."

We walked down the street, heading back to his building. My heels clicked against the pavement, a tattoo of sound as rhythmic as the beat of desire burning through my blood. I felt good in the blue clothes, sexy rather than slutty. Not that I minded slutty if the occasion was right. And if it hadn't been for the fact that I needed to get my brother free that night, I would have offered to take Quinn's neat packaging for a quick test drive.

His car turned out to be a black Ferrari—sleek, sporty, and hot. Much like the man himself. He opened the door for me and I climbed in.

"So, what's the plan?" I said, once we were under way.

"If you look as good beneath as I think you do, all you'll have to do is walk up the street and every camera in the vicinity will be on you."

I grinned. "And then?"

"You find a way to keep those cameras on you while I either get over the wall or get through that second entrance and try to find a way to get Rhoan out."

I raised an eyebrow. "It'll take two of us to get Rhoan out, won't it?"

He shrugged. "It might. But first off, we'll have to find out if he's in there, then we have to discover just how well guarded he is. It may not happen tonight."

So he thought. I, on the other hand, was damn sure that, one way or another, Rhoan was coming out of the place that night. "If you do a drive past first, I might be able to tell you if he's still in there."

Quinn nodded. We cruised through the streets, the streetlights blurring past at a speed that suggested he wasn't keeping to the legal limit. I suppose when you were a multibillionaire, a ticket or two didn't really make that much of a dent in the bank balance.

We reached Moneisha in record time, and he slowed to cruising speed. I studied the white walls but didn't feel anything. I said as much to Quinn.

"It might be because you're in the car. Maybe you have to be closer to feel him."

Maybe. And maybe he was simply gone. I tried to ignore the unease sitting like a weight in my stomach, and said, "I'll have to do a walk past."

Quinn turned into a side street and stopped well out of camera range. "I'll drive past in five minutes and stop. You can pretend I'm a potential client and come talk to me. That way, if he's not there, we can simply drive away."

I raised an eyebrow. "Why don't we simply lower our shields a little and use telepathy?"

He gave me a glance that could have meant anything. "I don't think so."

"Why not?"

"Because you're a wolf in moon heat, and your aura is so strong that I can feel it even with my shields up."

"And this is a bad thing because . . . ?"

"Because when I make love to someone, I prefer it to be in comfort, not in the confines of a cramped sports car."

I grinned. "I've never done it in the front seat of a Ferrari. It could be fun."

"It could be dangerous."

I laughed. I couldn't help it. "You know, for a man who's seen a thousand years pass by, you have some pretty staid ideas."

"And you're a pup who hasn't yet had the time to appreciate the finer things in life—like making love in luxurious surroundings."

"Hey, I fuck millionaires, so I already know all about luxury. Danger and discomfort can be just as thrilling, believe me."

He shook his head. "I'm going to have to teach you better."

I grinned. "Or maybe you just need some of that stuffiness shaken out of you."

"In the twelve hundred years I've been around, I've tried it all. Believe me, I know which is better."

"But in all that time, I bet you ain't met someone like me." I gave him a saucy grin. "I'm going to rock your world, vampire."

His smile just about smoked my insides. "You're welcome to try."

My hormones were all for trying right there and then, but I had a brother to rescue first. I opened the door and started to climb out. Quinn reached across the car, his fingers wrapping around my knee, a heat that burned past the snakeskin leather and slithered deep into my bones.

"There is one thing I must make clear, though," he said, his low tones holding a hint of warning.

I glanced at him. "What?"

"There can never be more than a casual dance between us. I have no intentions of getting seriously involved with another werewolf."

I raised my eyebrows. "What makes you think I want anything more than casual? I'm a wolf—and like all wolves, I want the soul mate and kids ideal. You can never offer me that."

"I'm just warning you."

"So I consider myself warned." I slipped out of the car and took off my coat, throwing it back inside. His sharp intake of breath made my grin widen. "Consider this outfit *your* warning, my dear vampire."

I blew him a kiss and slammed the door before he could make any sensible reply. Grin still wide, I strolled down to Acacia Street, crossed the road, and began an exaggerated, saucy walk far enough away from the walls for the cameras to see me. A soft buzz filled the silence as they began tracking me.

I sensed Rhoan within minutes. He was still there, still in those same rooms I'd sensed him in earlier. I sighed in relief. All we had to do was try to get him out.

Lights cut across the darkness behind me. I kept walking, listening to the throaty purr of the engine, knowing it was Quinn simply because I could sense him with the same ease I was currently sensing Rhoan.

He stopped beside me and the window slid down. I

strolled over and leaned down, flashing the cameras an eyeful of butt.

"He's there."

"Right now, with you looking the way you're looking, I'm not particularly worried if he's there or not."

"So the front seat of the Ferrari is suddenly looking good?" I teased.

My phone rang before he could answer. He reached into my bag, clicked the flashing vid button, then held it up so I could talk without blowing our cover.

Jack came online, and he didn't look happy. "Riley, where are you?"

"Outside Moneisha," I said. "Why?"

"Well, when you grab Rhoan, don't bring him to the office. There's been some trouble."

"What kind of trouble?"

"Someone's just tried to kill me."

"A pretty stupid someone, I'd say."

Jack gave me a crooked grin. "Well, yeah, seeing he missed his target and was caught. Unfortunately for us, he killed himself before we could question him too much."

I frowned. "Where did this all happen?" I couldn't imagine a shooter getting through the Directorate's street-level doors, let alone down to the guardian levels.

"I was on my way home."

"I thought the Directorate was your home?"

"Only most of the time."

"So whoever sanctioned the shooting knew your movements pretty well."

"Exactly. And combined with Rhoan's disappearance and the attempt on your life, I think we'd better start playing extra safe. Once you snatch Rhoan, don't go home or come here. They'll expect those, so go somewhere else and ring me once everyone is safe."

"Will do."

He hung up. Quinn put the phone back in my bag, then said, "So where do you intend taking him?"

"I'll worry about that once I get him out."

He considered me for a moment, the heat that had been so evident in his eyes moments before totally gone. "I could fly him up to Sydney and have him checked there. They certainly wouldn't expect that."

No, they wouldn't. But I wasn't about to let Quinn loose with my brother—not when I didn't know if I could trust him. Not when I'd been attacked, and now Jack. Okay, so he'd been attacked too, but it all still seemed just a little too convenient. Just because Jack trusted him didn't mean *I* had to. Hell, how could I even be sure if Quinn had pulled that camera off my shooter? What if it was just an attempt to gain my trust?

Though what would the point of that be, when, as he'd already said, if he intended me harm, he could well and truly have done it already?

I worried my bottom lip for a moment, then said, "I don't know if that's wise. After all, whoever is behind this made an attempt on your life, as well."

"We don't know if that's connected."

I snorted. "So it's just a coincidence that my shooter and your attackers happened to be genetically engineered clones? Give me some credit for intelligence."

He grimaced. "I'm sorry. But Rhoan needs to be checked. We can't take him to a hospital here because we can't be certain how far this thing extends. You can't take him to the Directorate for the same reason. So our next best option would be to take one of my private planes to my labs in Sydney and have him checked there. Besides, Melbourne is not a safe place for you to be if they're trying to get rid of everyone involved in this investigation."

"I'm not involved. I'm just rescuing Rhoan."

"That shooter makes you involved, whether you want to be or not."

A gate to the right of us creaked open. I looked sideways. A brown-skinned man appeared, the hunger in him thick and sharp. A werecreature of some kind, though he didn't feel like a wolf.

"He's wearing a guard's uniform," I noted softly, looking back at Quinn. "Could be the opportunity we want."

"Could be." He reached into the glove box and withdrew some thick tape. He tore off two pieces and handed them to me. "You think you can get him through those gates and keep him distracted long enough for me to get in there?"

I stuck the tape to my palm. "I'll try. Make sure you drive off like a rejected customer."

He nodded. "Once we get Rhoan, we'll take him straight to Essendon airport. I have a plane there that could be ready in the hour."

He seemed pretty damn determined to get Rhoan to Sydney, and that only made me more convinced it was better to do the exact opposite. I didn't answer and pushed away from the car. Quinn planted his foot and the car took off with a squeal of rubber.

I strolled leisurely toward the guard. He was tall, broadly built, and muscular—very desirable, until you looked into his eyes. They were brown, and held no humanity at all. Just hunger and death.

The heat of his aura hit me a heartbeat later. The

moon heat surged in response, leaving me breathless, hot, yet very uneasy. There was an undercurrent of brutality in what he was projecting, and I very much suspected that sex with this man would not be pleasant . . . maybe not even survivable.

"Are you werecreature?" The guard's voice was gruff with the urgency I could feel vibrating through him.

"My mother was wolf."

His gaze slithered downward, coming to an abrupt halt where my nipples poked through the shirt. "That explains the heat I feel from you."

I shrugged. "If you hunger, there's a cost."

He smirked. "How about we do a deal?"

I raised an eyebrow. "What sort of deal?"

"I won't report your activities here to the cops and, in return, you mate with me and my buddy."

Christ, there were two of them. Just what I needed with the moon burning in the night sky.

I pursed my lips, pretending to consider the proposal. After a moment, I said, "Not here. Is there somewhere more . . . intimate we could go?"

He grinned, gave the camera a thumbs-up, then motioned me to follow him. As I walked through the first gate, I slid a piece of the tape across the magnetic lock. A second later, the guard caught my hand and pulled me roughly toward him. My heart started hammering and I barely resisted the instinct to deck him. But only because the surge of his desire suggested his actions were born of hunger rather than suspicion.

He pressed me close. His body felt on fire, and, like the Gautier clones, he smelled faintly of mint and musk and freshly turned earth. Did that mean he, too, was a clone? Or was he something else completely different? Perhaps another of those lab-bred crosses?

The waves of his aura were blasting me with hot desire, hardening my nipples to the point of pain and making my pulse race—all physical signs of a response I didn't feel inside. But I couldn't let that reluctance show. I had to make him believe I was as eager as he or there'd be trouble.

He pressed a hand into my back, his fingers sliding down my spine, his touch hot yet sending chills skating across my skin. His breathing was rapid, fanning my cheek with foulness.

"You feel good, wolf."

I forced a smile and pressed my groin against the thickness of his erection. "As do you," I purred. It wasn't a lie. I was a wolf, the moon was in bloom, and the need to mate was rising. The heat of him pressed against me did feel good—even if the rest of his packaging made me want to throw up.

His mouth came down to mine and it felt like I was kissing death itself. His hand slid under the skirt and began fondling my rear. I shuddered, partly in pleasure, partly in pain. His touch made me eager, yet it also bruised.

When his fat fingers tried to slide farther, I pulled away and placed a hand on his chest. "Not here. Inside, out of the cold."

His grin was full of hungry anticipation. He caught my arm, pulling me roughly forward. I managed to slide the tape across the second gate and hoped like hell it worked. I could handle one man with no problems, but I very much suspected I might not be able to handle the blast of two hungry auras—not for long, anyway.

We approached the guardhouse, and the aura of the second werecreature hit. It felt like I was drowning in a sea of lust, one that had my blood surging even though the sane part of me quailed at the thought of mating with those two sickos.

Not that I intended letting the charade go that far. Unlike my brother, I was telepathic, and I could use that power to protect myself just as well as I could use my fists. And in cases like this, telepathy was the far better weapon.

The first guard opened the door and ushered me inside. The room was small, containing little more than monitors, chairs, and a phone. The second guard was the exact duplicate of the first—brown on evil brown. And like the first guard, there was something base, something corrupt, in the energy he was projecting.

He rose, expectation shining in his eyes as he hitched the waist of his pants and gave me the once-over. I obviously met with his approval, because his eagerness burned the air.

The first guard reached for me, something I felt rather than saw. I spun out of the way, covering the movement by catching his hand and pressing it against one breast. His fingers caught my nipple, squeezing hard.

I ignored the pain and forced a smile. "Hadn't you better ensure we're not disturbed first?"

The second guard reached for the phone. I pushed the first man backward. "Strip."

He grinned and quickly obeyed. I looked down, and felt the blood rush from my face. His cock wasn't only thick, it was barbed, in the same way that a cat's is barbed. He'd tear me apart if he got inside.

He stepped toward me and I pressed my hand against his chest again. "Wait for your friend." I kept my voice to a low purr. "It's more fun when there are two."

The second man made a strange sound in the back of his throat and hurriedly completed the call, telling whoever it was on the other end they were going on patrol and wouldn't be back for half an hour.

I ordered the second man to strip when he'd finished his call and lowered my shields a little.

Their hunger hit like a club, and I found myself fighting a lust stronger than I'd ever felt before. But behind the hunger came the excited buzz of their thoughts. These two weren't shielded, weren't psychic, and were very easy prey. I took a deep breath, then lowered my shields completely, and surged into their minds. Made each one look at the other and believe he saw me.

They fell into each other's arms and began to mate. I closed my eyes, not wanting to see it, hating what I was doing even though it was a far better option than letting either of them touch me.

The door crashed open. I spun, fists clenched, ready to confront whoever it was. Only it was Quinn. His gaze met mine, and the relief so evident there stirred me in ways I'd never thought possible. Then his gaze swiveled toward the two on the floor.

"Interesting way of dealing with the problem." His voice was flat, yet I saw the muscle in his jaw jump, as if he was battling not to laugh.

"Better than letting them touch me. Their penises were barbed."

"That would suggest werecats."

I nodded. "If their smell is anything to go by, these two came from labs, not nature." I crossed my arms and tried to ignore the sounds of their mating. The tremors of desire running through me were growing sharper. I wasn't sure how much longer I could hold out against need.

"Go find Rhoan," I said, voice sharp. As much as I wanted to find him myself, the truth was, Quinn had far more experience than I in skulking around. He was a thousand-year-old vampire, after all. "I'll stay here with these two."

He hesitated. "Will you be okay?"

I ignored the concern in his voice. "Just go."

He did. I leaned back against the wall as the slap of flesh on flesh and the grunts of pleasure echoed around me, rising to a crescendo that sawed at my nerves. When the two on the floor were finally still, I made them both get up and get dressed, then sat them down in the chairs.

By that time, sweat was beginning to run down my cheek and my head was beginning to hurt. I'd never really used my abilities to this extent before, and had never realized just how much energy it sucked. It was worse than being with Talon for eight hours.

I glanced at my watch. Quinn had been gone for fifteen minutes. We had maybe another fifteen before someone thought to check these two.

Or would have had, had luck been on our side.

Alarms bit through the air, the noise piercing. A second later, the door was flung open and Quinn appeared, Rhoan limp over one shoulder and a laser gun in his free hand.

"Hurry" was all he said, all he needed to say.

I glanced at the two men, wiped their minds of everything that had just happened, and ran out the door. I pulled the tape off the gates, locking them behind me, then blurred into the night and ran after Quinn.

It was three blocks before we came to the car. Quinn

exchanged the gun for his car keys and opened the doors. "We'll head straight for the airport," he said, as he bent to place Rhoan in the car. "I'll call ahead so that the plane is ready by the time we get there."

Like hell he would. There were times when I was more than a little careless about my own safety, but I sure as hell wasn't going to risk my brother's any more than I had to. He wasn't just my twin, he was my pack. The two of us had to look out for each other, simply because we were all the other had since our mother's pack had thrown us out. And until I'd actually talked to Rhoan, heard his side of the story, then Quinn was still on my may-not-be-trusted list.

Which meant I was going to have to lose the delicious man yet again. I could only hope that if he *was* innocent, he'd forgive me.

As he was straightening, I thrust a hand against the back of his head, forcing him forward, bashing his head against the roof of the car as hard as I could. Which was *damn* hard.

He never really stood a chance—and it just went to prove that even a thousand-year-old vampire could be taken unawares. I caught him as he fell, grunting a little at the force of his weight, then dragged him across the pavement, and over the fence of the nearest house. He fell into the shadows of several thick bushes and, for all intents and purposes, was hidden from sight.

I ran back to the car, slipped into the driver's seat, and drove away as fast as I dared.

Chapter 7

It took ten minutes to stop looking in the rearview mirror for any sign of pursuit and begin to relax. I glanced at my brother, still slumped in the passenger seat, and touched a hand to his neck. His pulse was steady, his breathing even. Yet I didn't feel any easier. Until he woke, until I knew for sure he was okay, I couldn't.

Which left the problem of where to go while that happened. If I couldn't go home and couldn't go to the Directorate, then really, I only had one other choice.

Liander.

He'd protect Rhoan every bit as fiercely as I would, simply because he loved him. I reached for my phone and quickly dialed his cell phone number. He wouldn't be home, not with the moon in bloom.

He answered on the third ring. "Riley," he said, surprise in his voice. "What's up?"

"I found Rhoan."

"He okay?" The edge was back in Liander's voice and I relaxed a little more.

"He's unconscious, so I'm not sure. We need somewhere safe to retreat."

"My office," he said instantly. "It has plenty of security, and there's a loft where he can sleep it off."

I glanced at the time and saw it was almost three. "I'll be there in twenty minutes."

"I'll meet you out front."

I got there in fifteen, but it didn't matter because Liander was waiting, anyway.

"Jesus," he said, as he dragged Rhoan from the car and hauled him over his shoulder. "He looks like he's been through a marathon."

"In some ways, he has." A marathon of milking, I suspected. "Let's get off the street, then I'll try to explain what has happened."

He nodded. Once he'd checked himself through the eye scan and fingerprint scanner, the huge red metal door that dominated the front of the cheerless brown brick building opened, revealing the soft golden glow that was Liander's workshop. I stepped through, my gaze scanning the many half-finished bits of latex humanity and monsters. "You've got another movie contract?" I asked, scanning the line of ogres, trolls, and wart-nosed witches.

He nodded as he closed and relocked the doors. "A fantasy project. I've actually had to take on two apprentices."

"Excellent."

"Indeed it is." He walked toward the stairs, taking them two at a time, as if Rhoan's weight was nothing more than that of a babe. "What happened to him?"

I hesitated, but only briefly. Liander was ex-military,

and knew how to keep a secret. And while Jack might have a problem with me telling Directorate secrets to non-Directorate personnel, I doubted Rhoan would. Not in this case, anyway. And he was the only one whose opinion I really worried about.

"He was in St. Kilda trying to find out why hookers were being snatched off the street, and got snatched himself."

Liander carefully placed Rhoan on the bed, then touched his neck, checking for a pulse before he began taking off my brother's clothes. "So where did he end up?"

"The Moneisha Research Center. We think they're a collection point for nonhuman sperm and eggs."

He shot me a surprised look. "Really?"

"Really." I walked across to the small washbasin area and grabbed a soft cloth and a small bowl, then flicked on the tap and waited for the warm water to arrive.

"Well, that certainly explains the bruised and swollen state of his genitals." He shook his head. "No moon dancing for this young wolf this month, that's for sure."

"And won't that piss him off."

Liander gave me a grin. "Truly," he said, as his gaze skated down my body. "Can I just say you're looking wonderfully tarty for a change?"

"Thanks." I added some soap to the warm water, then carried the bowl and cloth over to Liander. "He doesn't seem to be hurt."

I was looking for reassurance more than anything, and Liander wrapped an arm around my shoulder, giving me a light squeeze. "I'd say he's just dehydrated and tired. There don't seem to be any injuries other than bruising, but I'll get a friend over to check, anyway. She's a doctor."

"Good idea."

Liander took the bowl and cloth from me and carefully began to wash Rhoan down. I fidgeted for a moment, then walked across to the small window, staring out at the moonlit sky. The force of the heat that shivered through my body was a warning that I better get to one of the clubs sooner rather than later.

"Go," Liander said, reading the surge of desire, not my thoughts. "He'll be fine with me."

I swung around. "You'll ring the minute he wakes?"

"You know I will."

I walked across the room and kissed his cheek. "Thanks."

He smiled. "I'll buzzer you out when you near the door."

I headed out. Once down on street level again, I grabbed the cell phone and called Jack.

He answered on the first ring. "You safe?"

"As houses. Rhoan's unconscious, though, so I haven't been able to question him."

"Then perhaps you'd care to tell me why you decided to knock Quinn unconscious."

"Well, he was insisting on taking Rhoan to Sydney. And I'm sorry, but I'm not going to fully trust the man, no matter what you say, until I talk to my brother."

Jack laughed. "Darlin', you are going to make such a wonderful guardian."

"Not in this lifetime, I'm not." I hesitated. "How is Quinn?"

"He's got a sore head—and he deserves no less for

being so foolish as to turn his back on someone he barely knows."

"So he's there with you?" I paused. "Actually, where are you?"

"I'm back at the Directorate for the time being. Quinn's booked himself into one of the vamp hotels to sleep off his headache."

At least he'd be safe there, as most of the vamp hotels guaranteed the safety of their patrons. "Which one? I need to return his car." I didn't want to leave it at Liander's, simply because whoever was behind Moneisha might have recognized the car and be looking for it. For the same reason, I didn't particularly want to drive around in it. Besides, given my less-than-spotless driving record, it wasn't a particularly good idea to be driving a car I could never afford to fix.

"He's at the Gatehouse," Jack said.

Which was in Little Collins Street, and not all that far from the Kingfisher. I wondered if Talon would be there yet. "I'll get Rhoan to ring you once he's awake."

"Do that. And Riley? Be careful out there. Rhoan may be safe, but I doubt the danger is over for any of us yet."

"Will do."

I hung up, then stared at the car for a few seconds, debating the option of ringing Talon as opposed to simply going to the club. Talon might be up to something, but I doubt he'd actually hurt me. Whereas, if I went to the clubs and mated with strangers, I had no such assurance.

In the end, that was what swayed me. Talon was the only man I could class as safe just then. I dug my phone out, and called him.

"Little wolf," he said, voice a throaty growl. "This is a pleasant surprise."

"Can you meet me at the Kingfisher in twenty minutes?"

He chuckled. "By the sound of your voice, the moon rides you hard."

"You have no idea," I muttered. "Let's forget breakfast."

"Good. Niceties were never my style anyway."

Which is why I would have called him rather than Misha, even had Misha been available. At that moment, I didn't need niceties. I just needed the ache eased as quickly as possible—and if Talon could be depended on for anything, it was quickness.

"I've already booked the penthouse suite. I'll be waiting in front of the hotel."

I hung up, jumped into the car, and zoomed into the city. After giving the car and keys to the Gatehouse's parking attendant and leaving instructions for Quinn to be informed of its return, I loped across to the Kingfisher. Talon was already there, waiting at the top of the steps.

I undid my coat as I climbed the steps toward him, and his desire swirled around me, hot and strong and demanding. I welcomed that heat, breathed it deep, letting it mingle with the urgency already pounding through my veins. Sweat broke out across my brow, and it was all I could do to restrain the desire to rip off his clothes and taste his readiness right there on the steps of the hotel.

"Like the boots," he growled. "Those I think you can keep on for a while."

He caught my hand and we hurried into the hotel,

all but running past the lobby elevators into a second, more secluded area.

"Private elevators," he said, swiping a keycard through the slot. "It'll take us direct to the penthouse."

I couldn't wait for the penthouse. My blood burned, my heart hammered like a steam train, and the ache was all-consuming. I wanted sex, and I wanted it *now*.

The doors slid open. Not waiting for him to take control, I pushed him inside, pressed him against the wall, then, with one hand, pulled him down to claim his mouth. With my free hand, I undid his pants.

He growled deep in his throat, and lifted me. I wrapped my legs around him and pushed him deep inside, a groan escaping at the sheer glory of it.

"You feel wonderfully tight, little wolf. It tells me you didn't have any lovers last night. Tells me I'm your first this morning."

"Shut up," I said, my voice breathy, "and just fuck me."

He chuckled softly, then got down to business. The elevator began its ascent, and the whine of machinery mingled with the rasp of our breathing, the slap of flesh against flesh, and the grunt of need. The moon's heat was fierce, and so was I. I rode him hard, desperate to claim every inch of his rigid heat, to feel him fill me. A pressure began to build low in my stomach, fanning through the rest of me in slow waves. The air was so thick and hot and needy I could barely breathe. Then he found that spot deep within, his flesh hitting it again and again and again. The slow waves became a molten force that flowed across my skin, making me tremble, twitch, drawing unintelligible words from my mouth.

And still I drove his flesh into me, deeper and deeper as his breathing became harsh, his tempo more urgent. His urgency pushed me into a place where only sensation existed, then he pushed me beyond it.

He came with me, his warmth spilling into me as his body went rigid against mine.

The elevator came to a stop. For a second, neither of us moved. His breath fanned my cheek, ragged gasps I echoed. Yet he was still hard inside me, and I knew the fiery, urgent need burning through his blood wasn't satisfied. Knew, because I felt the same.

The door opened. He put me down, zipped up his pants, then pulled me into the corridor. We were barely inside the room when he took me again.

It set the scene for the rest of the day. Sex that was hard and fast. Anywhere and everywhere.

It was early afternoon before the fever faded and either of us was able to rest. By then, we were in one of those swim spas that seemed bigger than my whole bedroom. Walls of glass surrounded us on two sides and would have allowed us the view of the city and the bay had the rain not come in and turned the world gray.

I floated in the bubbly heat, the faint scents of lemon and lime teasing my nostrils as I flicked water up with my toes, watching the droplets glitter in the cold afternoon light.

"You seem pensive, little wolf."

I looked at him. He sat on the molded bench seat down the far end, golden arms stretched out along the edge of the spa, muscular body touched with the warmth of the water.

"Just worried about Rhoan." Liander hadn't yet phoned, and that couldn't be a good sign. If he didn't ring in the next half hour, I was calling him.

"You found him."

It wasn't a question, more a statement, which was odd. I nodded. "He wasn't well, so I've a friend at home watching him." I might trust Talon with my body, but I wasn't about to trust him with my twin's safety.

"He's a wolf. We're strong by nature. He'll be okay."

I nodded again. I knew that, but the worry was, what had Moneisha been doing to him? Just because there'd been no visible cuts or bruising didn't mean there weren't any. Didn't mean deeper damage hadn't been done.

"Champagne?" Talon asked, reaching for the half-empty bottle near the steps.

I shook my head. "No. It doesn't seem to agree with me."

He poured himself a glass and drank it down in one gulp. It seemed he liked the bubbly stuff the way he preferred his sex. And as much as it was physically satisfying, part of me was beginning to hunger for more. Though what that more was, I couldn't really say.

My gaze drifted back to the gray-clad sky. What would it be like to make love with Quinn? It would surely be good—after all, with a thousand years behind him, he'd have had the time to sharpen and refine his technique. Something I doubted Talon would ever do.

"Have you ever thought about the future, little wolf?" Talon poured himself another glass of champagne, then leaned against the wall again.

I slanted him a curious glance and wondered where he was headed with a question like that. "No, not really. Why?"

"So you have no idea where you want to be in ten, or twenty years' time?"

"No." Mainly because no one seemed to know how much time I *actually* had. Werewolves generally lived somewhere between one hundred fifty and two hundred years. But vampires were eternal, unless killed. No one knew which side of the fence I would fall on. So far, my development was slower than a wolf's normally would be; but, by the same token, I wasn't years behind the norm.

I tended to treat the longevity problem the same way I treated the whole fertility problem—by not really thinking about it. When it became a problem, *then* I'd worry.

"So you've had no yearning for children or marriage or anything like that?" he asked.

"Of course I have—but the time isn't right yet for such things."

He reached out as I drifted near to him, snagging my hand and tugging me closer. As I settled on his lap, he said, "And if it was?"

"Then yeah, kids and marriage would definitely be on the agenda." I could feel the rising force of his erection, but for the moment, he made no attempt to enter. "What about you? Do all these questions mean the lone wolf is actually thinking about settling down sometime in the near future?"

He laughed. "No. But I do want a son. I want my name carried on in the next generation."

I grinned. "All males want a son, but sometimes they get daughters."

"There are ways to ensure gender."

"I prefer to rely on nature." Although if I relied on nature, I'd never get pregnant.

"So you do want to have kids sometime in the future?"

I frowned. Hadn't I just answered that question? "As I said, yes. If I meet the right man."

"And if you don't?"

"I don't know. I'll worry about it when the time comes."

His hands slid down to my hips, shifting me, then holding me still as he slid his cock deep inside. And while the lingering moon heat had me half-ready to take him, his continuing avoidance of *any* form of foreplay was beginning to annoy.

And I said as much.

He merely grinned. "When the moon rises high, sex is what matters, not foreplay."

"It may not matter to you, but it does to me." I pried his hands off my hips and pushed away from him, kicking water in his face as I floated back to the center of the spa.

Surprise flitted through his golden eyes. He hadn't expected me to be so strong. "You weren't so concerned about the foreplay this morning, little wolf."

"That was this morning. This is now."

"There's no satisfying you females, is there? No matter what we do, we're wrong." Though it was said with a smile, the spark of anger lit his eyes. He didn't like being denied, even for something as simple as sex.

"What is foreplay going to cost you? Ten? Fifteen minutes? Not much, in the scheme of things."

"Do I satisfy you, little wolf?"

"Mostly."

"Then what is the problem?"

I shook my head. I'd beaten my head against this particular wall before and knew from past experiences that nothing would ever change. Talon was what he was—I either put up with it or left.

Still . . .

"The problem is you just presume. You never even bother to ask."

He studied me for a moment, expression one of thoughtful consideration. I had a bad feeling that our relationship was about to change in some unfathomable way.

"Then I have a question for you, little wolf."

Though that bad feeling was growing, I grinned faintly. "The answer is no, you can't have sex with me just yet. I'm enjoying floating in the bubbles right now."

"That wasn't the question."

Like I didn't know that? "Then what is?"

"Will you have my child?"

Surprise hit like a club but I somehow managed to say, *"What?"*

"I want you to carry my child."

"But . . . " My voice faded. Was he absolutely crazy? Maybe the heat of the spa had fried a brain cell or two. Surely he had to realize I wasn't about to take the risk of having kids with a man I didn't love. "We're not soul mates."

"So? I don't want to swear eternity to the moon, little wolf. I just want a son."

"So wait for your soul mate."

"I don't want a soul mate. I want to take my pleasure when and where I choose. But I also want a son to carry my name and take over my empire when I die."

Empire? Lord, his businesses weren't *that* big . . . were they? I shook my head, unable to believe he was actually serious. "So why me?"

"Because you are unlike any female I have met, and a son of ours would be strong."

"This is madness, Talon. I don't want a child with you—or anyone else—at this moment. And just in case I've never mentioned it, there's a history of conception problems in my family. That's why the red packs are so few."

Which wasn't a lie. The red packs were small in number for *precisely* that reason. Which is why none of my earlier doctors had picked up the real reason behind my fertility problem. They'd all been working on the premise that I'd inherited the barrenness that ran riot in our pack, and hadn't tested any further.

"We have read your medical files—"

"We?" I interrupted, annoyance in my tone. "What do you mean by 'we'? And how the hell did you get my medical files?"

"There is nothing that can't be bought if you have the money. And I am, of course, talking about the specialists I have consulted. It is their belief that all you need is a series of injections to help ovulation."

If he and his experts believed that, then they'd obviously gotten hold of my earlier medical records and not the more recent ones from my Directorate-approved, and therefore carefully screened, doctor. No one could get into *those* files without an alarm being raised back at the Directorate. It wasn't common procedure, and while the precaution had made me feel a little easier about using a Directorate doctor, I'd always wondered why Jack had implemented the procedure for me. Of course, his reason was now pretty clear. He'd known all along what I was and was keeping my secrets even as he kept an eye on what was going on within my system.

Those protected files were the only ones that mentioned my being a half-breed as the major factor in my fertility problems. And from what I'd been told, there *wasn't* a drug currently on the market that would help me ovulate.

Even so, Talon's smug smile had my fist clenching, but I somehow resisted the temptation to smack him one. "Talon, if I have a kid with you, I'm locking myself to you for the next ten years or more. Few wolves are willing to take on the pup of another."

"No other wolf would be allowed to. What is mine is mine."

"I'm not spending the next ten years in an exclusive arrangement with you. I enjoy what we have, but I don't want it permanently."

"So I'll raise the kid myself."

I shook my head. "If you think I'm going to go through all the trouble of trying to conceive just to hand my baby over to someone else at the end of it, you're crazy."

"I'm not crazy, but I *am* serious. I want you to have my child."

How could he believe I'd actually agree to something like this? Surely, in all the time we'd spent together, he must have learned something about me. Yet as I stared at him now, I realized the answer was no. Talon didn't see me as a person—just a willing sexual partner he now wanted babies with. "The answer is no."

"At least take some time to consider it."

"No." I climbed out of the spa.

He watched me, golden eyes filled with cold determination. "I always get what I want, little wolf. In the end, you will do this."

"No, I won't."

He gave a lazy smile that had wariness skittering through me. I didn't like that smile. Didn't trust the gloating underneath it.

"You may not have a choice."

I grabbed a towel off the chair and began toweling myself down. "What do you mean?"

His lazy, confident smile made the wariness grow. He was up to something, something more than what he was admitting.

"I mean, I've put out word that you and I have reached an exclusive agreement for the next couple of months. You can turn to no one but me during the moon heat now, and I will not provide what you want until you agree to my terms."

Anger rose, and it was all I could do not to launch myself at him and punch that smug, cold smile from his lips. "Misha will be back soon. And he'll be told the truth."

He raised an eyebrow. "Misha will not fight me over you."

The certainty in his voice sent chills down my spine, if only because it sounded like he knew Misha far better than I did. Which was stupid. As far as I knew, they'd met less than half a dozen times. Hardly time enough to form any depth of friendship.

I chucked the towel on the chair. "What we have is good, but I *can* live without it. If you don't give this crap up, I'll walk away for good."

"I have put a lot of thought into this, little wolf. A lot of time. I don't intend to give it up until I get what I want."

"The answer is, and will remain, no." I swung around and walked through the door to get my clothes.

His chuckles followed, brushing ice across my skin. "We'll see, little wolf. We'll see."

I didn't bother answering, just put on my super short skirt and top, and got the hell out of there. But I had a feeling Talon's surprises weren't over yet.

$\mathcal{M}$y phone rang as I was walking out of the hotel. I dug around in my bag until I found it and was relieved to see it was Liander.

I flicked the receive button, and said, "Is he okay?"

"I'm fine, sis."

Relief swept through me and tears welled. I blinked them away fiercely, and said, "Really?"

"Well, I'm not going to be doing much dancing for the next couple of days, but other than that, yes."

"So they were milking you? Nothing more?"

"As far as I know. They had me chained with silver, which was why I couldn't escape."

"Have you been checked over by Liander's doctor friend?"

"Yeah. I'm fine, as I said, just as sore as hell and walking like a man who's been in the saddle too long."

I grinned. "Nothing new in that, brother."

He snorted softly. "I wouldn't mind if it was self-inflicted."

"So now all we have to do is find out why Moneisha are in the market for sperm."

"To do that, we may have to break in there again, and that's not going to be easy." A bell dinged, and I looked up to see the sleek silver tram approaching the stop outside the hotel. I hurried across the road. "Have you talked to Jack yet?"

"Yes. He told me to stay here—he's coming to us."

"Did he tell you someone tried to kill him?"

"Yes." He hesitated. "He also told me Kelly has gone missing."

Something inside froze. "But . . . but she wasn't supposed to be looking for you. She was supposed to be on another mission entirely."

"She was. Jack's sent out searchers. They'll find her."

Rhoan's tone was meant to be reassuring, but all I could think of was the other guardians who'd disappeared of late. I didn't want that happening to Kelly. Didn't want it happening to anyone I knew, or even to anyone one I hated.

With one exception. "Gautier threatened her last night. Has Jack questioned him about it?"

"Yes. Gautier's many things, sis, but he isn't a fool. I doubt he'd attack another guardian."

"Gautier would kill anyone who got in his way." Especially if he thought he could get away with it.

"Kel's a survivor. She'll be okay."

She might be a survivor, but if Gautier had gone after her, then she was dead meat. Though I guess she *did* have more of a chance against him than whoever was behind the mutilations of the other guardians.

"If he's hurt her—" I just couldn't say killed her. I didn't even want to think about it. "I'm going to kill him." Blow his brains out, then stake his rotten heart.

"If he *has* hurt her, you won't have to. Jack will."

Maybe. Maybe not. Gautier was our best, after all. I blew out a breath and changed the subject. "Jack knows about us."

"He's known for a long time. You can trust him, sis."

I'd thought I could trust Talon, too, but after the discussion we just had, I wasn't so sure.

"Where are you now?" he added. "Or rather, how long will it take you to get back here?"

"I've been with Talon at the Kingfisher." I glanced at my watch. "It'll take me about half an hour to get there, because I have to go to the Casino parking garage and collect Misha's car—"

"Misha lent you one of his cars?" The surprise in Rhoan's voice came through loud and clear.

"I'm not that bad a driver—"

"This from the woman who has wiped out how many cars in the last ten years?"

"Eight," I mumbled. "But only two of those accidents were my fault."

"The jury is still out on the other six, though."

"I just got your ass out of jail, brother, so you could play nice for a little while."

He chuckled softly. "If you insist."

"I do." I hesitated, then added, "Jack's going to try to drag me into this investigation. I don't want to be involved any more than I am, Rhoan. I don't want to be a guardian."

"I know." The amusement fled from his voice. "And I'll do what I can to keep you free, but when it comes to this particular case, I don't think there's any escape."

Which is not what I wanted to hear.

He paused, then added, "You might want to ring Talon and Misha, and just warn them that work is creating problems that may spill into your private life. Tell them to be careful."

"Misha's gone back to his pack, and I have no intention of speaking to Talon for the next couple of days. He's being a bastard."

"Always has been. You just couldn't see past the sex."

"True. But then, the sex was damn good." Or it had been, until recently. What had changed, I wasn't sure. Certainly Talon hadn't.

"Just be careful, Riley."

Like I needed to be told that. "See you soon, bro."

I hung up and caught the tram down to the Casino. If I didn't get Misha's car out of the garage soon, the fees would cost me more than the old Mercedes was actually worth. I took the elevator down to sublevel three and headed out across the concrete expanse. Water dripped in the distance, and up ahead, lights blinked, sending shadows scurrying through the concrete paddock.

Sound whispered around me—the soft scuff of a heel, followed by the faint caress of mint in the air. I stopped abruptly, muscles tense as I looked around. There was no one else there . . . and yet there was. My gaze swept across the shadows filling the distant corners. A vampire lurked there—but he wasn't what I sensed. It was something else . . . something stranger.

I sniffed. The air was a mix of dampness and exhaust fumes, but underneath it lay something old. Something rotten.

Something almost dead.

My stomach stirred. I clenched my fist and forced my feet to walk on. The car was only two rows away—closer than the elevator. Not that I could retreat that way even if I'd wanted to because whatever that smell belonged to stood between me and the elevator.

Air caressed my cheek with foulness. The vampire was on the move. I dug the keys out of my bag and clicked open the car. The taillights flashed in response, briefly illuminating my surroundings with cheerful yellow.

I opened the car door and threw in my bag. My neck prickled a warning and I spun. Something glittered in the air—a thread of silver arrowing toward me.

I swore and ducked out of the way, but it was too close, too fast, to avoid. It sliced through my coat into my arm, biting deep into my flesh. Pain slithered through me, and with it came a cold sensation. Icy fingers began spreading from the wound, reaching up toward my shoulder and down toward my hand. I wrenched the thing free, but it felt like half my arm came with it, and I couldn't help screaming.

When I held the thread up, I saw what remained of the barbs on the arrowhead. Saw the flesh hanging off them.

Warmth pulsed down my arm, and from the shadows came a surge of blood hunger, a force so strong it almost knocked me over. Sweat broke out across my brow, yet the coldness was spreading, making me tremble.

Air screamed. I blinked, switching to the infrared of my vampire vision, and saw the blur of heat rushing at me. I swung, kicking the vamp as hard as I could. But my movements seemed to be in slow motion, and the vampire easily avoided the blow.

His fist swung. I ducked, felt hair stir as his hand skimmed the top of my head, then rose, fist clenched as I cut upward. The blow hit him under the jaw and knocked him off his feet. The force of it numbed my fingers. I shook my hand, trying to get some feeling back.

Sweat stung my eyes and obscured my vision. I blinked, but it didn't seem to help any. The vampire was little more than a smudge of red as he scrambled back to his feet and rushed at me.

He lashed out again. I blurred, but it felt like my feet were stuck in glue. The vampire's blow smashed into my chin and sent me sprawling backward. I hit the car door with a grunt and fell sideways to the floor, my breath leaving in a whoosh of air. Pinpoints of lights were dancing before my eyes, and I wasn't sure if it was lack of breath or something else.

Then the vamp hit me, his body covering mine, hot and heavy. Though gasping for breath and fighting the blackness threatening to consume me, I heard the vampire's snarl. The shadows were unraveling around him, revealing gaunt features and dead brown eyes that were identical to Gautier's. His teeth were extending, saliva dripping from the points in expectation of the feed.

I thrust my hands between us, and tried to push him away. I might as well have been trying to move a mountain. My strength was slithering away, the darkness coming in, and close by the dead thing.

Watching, waiting.

I didn't know what it was. Didn't care. Just knew I couldn't let it get me.

The vamp's teeth sank into my flesh, and heat flashed white-hot through every cell in my body. The sounds of his greedy sucking filled the air, the last thing I'd ever hear if I didn't do something soon.

I took a deep breath and gathered the last of my fast-fading reserves. Energy surged through my limbs. I grabbed the vamp's head, ripped him away from my flesh, and twisted his neck hard.

Bone snapped. Breaking his neck mightn't kill him,

but it sure as hell would immobilize him and allow me to get away.

I rolled him off me, then grabbed the car door and pulled myself upright. The parking garage whirled around me and, for several seconds, I simply stood there, battling for breath as sweat dripped down my face and blood ran from my neck and arm. There was a bitter taste in my mouth, my throat was drier than the Sahara, and my heart pounding so erratically it felt like it was going to leap out of my chest.

Something had been on the arrowhead. Something meant to knock me out.

Ahead, a creature that was cool and blue moved toward me. It seemed to flow rather than walk, shimmering brightly one moment, fading out of existence the next.

I blinked, not sure what I was seeing. Or if I was actually seeing.

Then the smell hit me. This was the dead thing. The thing I couldn't let get me.

I tried to climb into the car, but my legs had become lumps of unfeeling ice and suddenly I was toppling sideways again. I hit the ground with a grunt, gasping for breath as the blackness rushed in.

The last thing I remember seeing were the hands that reached for me.

Hands that were blue and suckered like a gecko's.

Chapter 8

Awareness returned slowly. It came as an ache—a throbbing heat that radiated from hot spots in my arm and my neck, with smaller flares of warmth coming from my wrists and my ankles.

Noise surrounded me. My heart, beating nine to the dozen in time with the pain. Above that, the throbbing beat of a bass, a rhythmic tune that seemed to pound through the metal underneath me, mingling with the deeper, throatier roar of an engine.

Laughter drifted past—deep, powerful and male. With it came scents—musk, mint, and decay, entwined within the metallic odor of blood. Blood that was stiff and heavy on the sleeve of my coat.

I cracked open my eyes. There was nothing to see but blackness. I blinked, and realized the blackness was a cover of some sort. Pinpricks of light spotted the material, indicating it was daylight. I wondered if it were the same day, or another.

Laughter edged across the noise again, and through the musky foulness of the blanket covering me I caught a whiff of alcohol. I hoped that meant my captors were drinking, that it wasn't just another odor coming from the blanket covering me. The chances of escape escalated if the men were boozing.

I shifted slightly, trying to ease the ache in my arm. Chains rattled, scraping harshly across the metal flooring underneath me. The surrounding noise stopped, and I froze.

"She awake?" The voice was deep, guttural.

There was several beats of silence, then, "Nah. I told you, they pumped her with enough juice to drop an elephant. She won't wake for at least another twenty-four hours." The second voice was a mirror image of the first.

Silence fell again. I listened to the hum of the tires against the road and, after a while, drifted off to sleep. The slamming of a car door woke me sometime later.

The road noise had stopped. So too had the throaty roar of the engine. The sharp odor of the two men had faded somewhat, and I could hear only one intake of breath.

It might be the only chance I had to escape. I lowered my shields a little, feeling out the thoughts of the man still in the van. Unlike the guards at Moneisha, this man was shielded from psychic intrusion.

I swore under my breath. That one fact would make escape more difficult. The only chance I really had now was if I could somehow get the man's attention and get him in the back of the car with me.

And the best way to get a man's attention? Flash some breast, of course.

I shifted a hand. Metal clinked against the metal

again. Obviously, I'd been chained, and if the burning
on my wrists and ankles was anything to go by, those
chains were silver. I couldn't claim my wolf form until
they were off.

In the front of the van, the man stirred. I held still,
waiting, until the squeaking of the seat indicated he
had gone back to whatever he was doing. Slowly, carefully, I undid the buttons on my coat, then pulled up
my sweater. Once my breasts were free, I flicked off
the foul-smelling blanket and rolled onto my back. I
kept my eyes closed, my breathing slow and even, as if
I were still out of it.

The seat squeaked again, then came a sharp intake
of breath. Desire surged around me, a hunger as sharp
as any wolf's.

For several seconds, nothing happened. Then the
van lurched as the man moved into the back with me.
The scent of mint and death became so strong my nose
twitched. Only with those scents came a feeling of
wrongness. This man wasn't human, wasn't wolf,
wasn't even a shapeshifter or vampire. He was something else, something I'd never come across before.

And whatever he was, he was dying.

The heat of him caressed my skin. His breathing
was short, sharp, the smell of his desire so strong it
stirred the moon fever in me.

He stopped. I cracked open an eye, watching as he
reached for me. His eyes were a muddy brown and
filled with hungry intentness. Around his neck was a
thin piece of wire—the psychic shield. Get that off,
and his mind was mine.

His fingers ran across my breasts, his touch hot and
somehow foul. Bile rose in my throat, but I resisted the

urge to move. He smiled, revealing teeth that were as pointed as any vampire's but stained black and rotten.

It took me a moment longer to realize those teeth were actually extending. He was going to feed . . . on my breasts.

I lurched up, chopping a hand across the windpipe with as much force as I could muster. He made a gargling sound, his eyes wide as he struggled to breathe.

I gave him no time to think, no time to react, just ripped the wire from his throat, almost garroting him in the process. With the wire gone, I lowered my shields and surged into his mind, swiftly taking control.

I thrust him back against the wall of the van. Pain burned up my wounded arm, and sweat broke out across my brow. There wasn't a lot of strength in my grip, and I was forced to switch hands. The chains chimed, jarring against the sound of the stranger's harsh breathing.

Using my free hand, ignoring the increasing pain, I gripped his face and forced him to look at me. "Where has the other man gone?"

His voice was as flat and as lifeless as his eyes when he answered. "For a crap."

So I had maybe five minutes more, at best. "Where is the key for the chains?"

"He has them."

I swore softly. "Where are we?"

"In a rest stop near Seymour."

Which was only about forty-five miles out of Melbourne. Obviously, not enough of the elephant juice had gotten into my system, because I'd slept little under an hour. "Where are the keys for the van?"

"In the ignition."

"Move into the passenger seat."

He obeyed. I wiped the sweat from my eyes and knew from the pounding ache beginning behind my eyes that I couldn't hold that depth of control for much longer.

I threw off the blanket and looked down at the chains. They were definitely silver, not metal, but luckily, they weren't tethered to anything in the van. They'd wanted to restrict my movements, but hadn't expected me to wake before they'd reached their destination. I pulled down my sweater, climbed into the front of the van, and started the engine.

"Where were you taking me?"

"Genoveve, then Libraska."

The first name rang a distant bell. I'd heard it somewhere before. But at present, I didn't have the time to worry about it or to question him any further. I had to escape before the second man came out because I very much doubted if I'd have the strength to battle two of them.

"If you've got a phone, give it to me."

He did.

"Has the man in the toilet got one?"

He nodded. I swore softly. The minute I took off in this van, they'd be ringing their superiors to report the fact—and there wasn't one thing I could do to prevent it. There were limits to my mind control and I wasn't about to hang around just to destroy that second phone. It wasn't worth the risk.

"Climb out and go to the toilet."

Again he obeyed. I leaned across the seat, locked the door, and threw the van into reverse. The tires squealed against the bitumen, and out of the corner of my eye I saw someone running out of the men's toilet, pants flapping around his knees.

Smiling grimly, I shoved the van into gear and sped off. The control I had on the second man snapped, and the pain of it rebounded through me, as sharp as glass. I glanced in the rearview mirror and, through the blur of tears, saw the second man running after me. He was fast. Vampire fast.

I flattened my foot. The old van shuddered and began to pick up speed, blowing smoke as I sped out of the rest stop and headed for the free-flowing traffic on the Hume Highway.

A quick glance in the mirror told me the second guard was almost close enough to open the back doors. I didn't think I could eke any more speed out of the van, so I did the next best thing—cut from the merge lane into the left lane, right in front of a car. Tires squealed behind me. I looked up to see a Ford slither sideways, clipping the rear of the van and throwing me forward. As I battled to keep the van straight, the Ford spun into the path of the guard, throwing him up and over the hood. He landed on the strip between the merge lane and the left lane, and didn't move.

I sped on. I'd escaped. Now I just had to get back to my brother. One thing was certain—I couldn't do it in the van. It was too hot—because of the accident, and because my escape was undoubtedly being reported back to those behind the kidnapping attempt.

I took the off-ramp to Seymour and eased up on the accelerator. The last thing I needed was to be picked up by the cops. I cruised through town, turning into a side street near the outskirts. This I followed until I came to a crossroad. After looking both ways, I headed right, simply because it was a dirt track that disappeared into trees.

When I was deep within shadows, I pulled off the

road and stopped. It was then that reaction set in. For several seconds, I didn't move, simply sat there, sucking in breath and swallowing bile, my whole body trembling.

Eventually, I found the strength to move. I grabbed the phone, then opened my door. The chains on my legs weren't long, forcing me to jump down rather than climb.

Evening was coming on, painting the patches of sky visible through the gums with red. The air was cool, filled with the scents of eucalyptus and grass. In the distance, cows mooed, and, beyond that, water rustled.

I shoved the phone in my pocket and headed that way. I needed a drink more than I needed anything else. Besides, I had to put distance between me and the van.

But walking through scrub isn't easy, particularly when chained. By the time I had reached the river, my throat was parched, my head pounded, my muscles were protesting every step, and the trees were doing a mad dance around me.

I dropped to my knees on the muddy riverbank, and greedily scooped up some water. It tasted of dirt, but it was wet and cold, and that was all that mattered. I splashed some over my face and neck, then washed the blood from my left hand.

Kookaburras laughed in the distance. I would have laughed with them, had I the energy. What a mess. So much for Jack's thinking I'd make a good guardian.

With a sigh, I stripped off my coat, then tore off the sleeve of my sweater to reveal the wound. It was another mess—swollen, red, with a hole as big as my fist. It had scabbed over, and was no longer bleeding, but it didn't look good. I needed to change to my wolf shape, needed to let my natural healing capabilities do their stuff. But with the chains on, I was trapped in human form.

I wet my sleeve, washed down my arm, then wrapped the cloth around the wound. As bandages went, it wasn't particularly hygienic, but I didn't have any other option. Besides, the cool wetness felt good against my feverish skin. I put my coat back on, then rose and studied the surroundings.

Where to now?

I rubbed my throbbing head and stared almost blindly at the trees on the other side of the small river. I couldn't go back to town with the chains on, couldn't risk going anywhere near the freeway. I needed help and I needed it fast, as I had a vague suspicion my arm was going to get a lot worse. I had the phone, but did I dare use it? Satellite tracking was so sophisticated these days, they could pinpoint to the millimeter anything that had a satellite chip in it—and most phones did.

That thought made me pull the phone out of my pocket. It wasn't on, but did it matter? I didn't know. Couldn't think. I stared at it for a moment longer, then threw it onto the ground and stomped on it, before kicking the broken remains into the river. Better safe than sorry.

For several seconds, I simply stared at the horizon and swayed, wondering what I should do. Then I made my decision and walked into the river, angling sharply across it. The chains snagged on every rock, and after what seemed the hundredth time, it occurred to me that I should lift them out of the way.

I finally reached the bank and pushed myself into a lope. Through the blur that was beginning to overtake my mind came one thought—I needed distance between me and the van.

The red flags of dusk faded into night. The chiming of the chains mingled with the chirruping of crickets, and in the long grass to the right and the left, small creatures rustled. Overhead, the moon was rising, a presence I could feel more than see. I ran on. Sweat bathed my body and my muscles shook. Every breath seared my lungs, yet it was nothing compared to the pain flowing from the wound on my arm. It felt like someone was holding a hot iron to my flesh, and just burning, burning.

I stumbled across the road before I even realized it was there. I staggered back, chest heaving as I battled to suck in the air my body desperately craved. The sign danced and blurred before my eyes, and I blinked. It didn't seem to help much. With a shaking hand, I wiped the sweat from my face, and tried to focus. Baker's Road, God knew where. I looked up and down the dusty expanse, seeing no hint of civilization either way. I sniffed the air. The faint smell of spring caressed the night—jasmine. Not something normally found in the wilds of the bush. There had to be a house somewhere close.

I headed back to the trees and walked parallel to the road. Cows mooed nearby and I moved back to the road. A building came into view—it didn't look to be a house, more a two-story tin shed that had power lines running to it. Maybe—hopefully—a weekend retreat. One that was unoccupied.

I stopped and switched to the infrared of my vampire vision. No red splotches indicated life anywhere close—nothing beyond the cows, anyway.

Relief surged, leaving me trembling and weaker than ever. I forced my feet to move on and listened intently. There was nothing to be heard beyond the crickets and the cows. The scent of jasmine got stronger, and

I sneezed. Half the shed was covered in the vine—obviously, the owners didn't get hay fever.

The door was locked. I stood back and kicked it, almost toppling in the process. The door flew open, and the cow nearest me snorted and leapt away.

The scents of vanilla, red gum, and mustiness flowed from the shed but were quickly overpowered by the jasmine. I stepped inside and closed the door. Though it was pitch-black, my vampire vision allowed me to see that the room was a combined kitchen, dining, and living area, all in one big expanse. What looked like stairs were near the back, presumably leading upstairs to the bedroom. And near them, a phone.

Relief surged through me and I staggered over. Plonking down on a step, I reached over and picked up the receiver. Dial tone. If I'd had the energy, I would have danced.

The numbers were a smudge I couldn't make out, forcing me to dial through touch more than sight. I called Jack rather than Rhoan, simply because my brother would have felt my distress and would no doubt be out looking for me—soreness or no soreness. And while Liander would be with him, my fuzzy brain couldn't recall his number. As the phone rang, I leaned against the banister and tried to ignore the pounding in my brain and my arm. Tried to ignore the fact the darkness seemed to be closing in on me.

"Parnell here."

I closed my eyes, never in my life more relieved to hear my boss's gruff tones. "Jack, it's Riley."

"Jesus, girl, where are you? We found your car—"

The world was spinning, burning, darkening, and time was something I didn't have much of. Not before that darkness claimed me, anyway. I cut him off. "I'm

somewhere in the wilds beyond Seymour. In a shed,
on a Baker's Road. There are cows . . . and jasmine."

"Riley? Keep the line open, and we'll do a trace."

"They're tracing me," I said. "Hurry . . . "

My voice faded, and the blackness sucked me away.

When awareness surfaced, it was once again to the
sensation of pain. In my arm, my wrists, and ankles.
Burning, agonizing pain.

I shifted, moaning softly, trying to escape the heat
and yet unable to. Cool cotton caressed my skin as I
moved, and it was then I realized I was no longer on
the stairs, but somewhere warm and soft. Water
touched my forehead, icy against my fevered skin.

"It's okay," a velvet rich voice assured. "You're okay."

How could I be okay when it felt like I was lying in
the middle of an oven? "Quinn?"

"Yes. You're safe, Riley."

I licked dry lips and forced my eyes open. His face
hovered above me, angelic face expressionless but dark
eyes lit with fury.

"I'm sorry," I croaked, "but I couldn't let you take
Rhoan to Sydney. Not until I'd talked to him."

"Don't worry about it."

"Where are we?"

"Still at the farmhouse."

I swore softly and tried to rise, but my muscles felt
like water. He held me down easily.

"They'll find us," I protested.

"If anyone finds us here, I'll deal with them."
Though his tone was flat, his expression left me in no
doubt as to *how* he'd deal with them. "For now, you
need to rest."

"I can't." I sounded like a petulant child, and that's exactly how I felt. "It feels like I'm on fire."

"I know." His voice was grim. "Rhoan will be back soon."

"From where? Why isn't he here?"

"Hush," he said softly. "Just rest and conserve your strength."

His words were an order my body seemed eager to obey. I closed my eyes, but the burning would not be ignored. I shifted my hand, trying to find a more comfortable place to rest it, and heard the clink of chains. "Why are they still on?"

"Because there's nothing here strong enough to cut them." His mind surged into my mind, a cool force that would not be denied. *Sleep, Riley.*

Against my instincts, against my will, I did.

When I next woke, the pain had finally eased. I lay in darkness, and no longer felt like I was under the grill setting in an oven. The ache in my arm had muted, on a par with the pain coming from my ankles and wrists. I shifted, and was relieved to hear only the whisper of the sheets. The chains had finally gone.

I opened my eyes. Saw shadows mingling with strings of cobwebs. I blinked, noted the corrugated iron roof beyond the cobwebs, and realized I was still in the shed. The air was dusty, rich with the scent of wood and smoke and vanilla. But overpowering that was the warm scent of spice and leather. A scent I'd recognize anywhere. I smiled and looked left.

Rhoan sat in a chair near the bed, his short red hair sticking out at all sorts of angles, his bare feet propped up on the dresser, legs slightly apart. He wasn't wearing jeans, simply black boxers, but he did have a sweater on. Again, it was black. Considering his love of bright colors, finding him in basic black was quite a surprise.

His smoke-colored gaze met mine, and I saw the relief there. "I was beginning to wonder if you'd ever wake."

His voice was etched with tiredness, and I raised an eyebrow. "The wound was obviously worse than I'd thought."

He took his feet off the dresser and walked carefully over. The bed creaked as he sat down. "Worse is an understatement."

He picked up my hand and held it to his chest, just over his heart. The steady beat reverberated through my fingers, and I knew, without his saying a word, just how close I'd come to leaving this life.

"Don't ever try and die on me again, you hear? It's not allowed. Ever."

Tears touched my eyes, and I blinked them away. "But it was just an arrow—"

"An arrow made of silver," he cut in. "With barbs that had been designed to break off in your flesh and travel through your system. You were being poisoned, inside and out."

Horror recoiled through me. No wonder I'd burned. I swallowed, but it didn't seem to ease the dryness in my throat. "But why would they do that if they were after the same thing from me as they were from you?"

He shrugged. "Jack's theory is that a woman is born with all the eggs she'll ever have, whereas a man keeps on producing sperm. Maybe those eggs were all they really wanted."

They were bastards. Whoever they were, they were bastards. And crazy ones at that. "So how did you get the barbs out?"

"With an experimental medical scanner Jack borrowed from the Directorate. One barb had reached your shoulder, the other two had headed down your arm." He hesitated. "You were delirious by that time. It wasn't easy."

His tone suggested something had happened, and it wasn't hard to guess what. Once the silver had been removed, my natural instincts would have taken control, whether or not I was delirious. I took a deep breath and released it slowly. "Whom did I attack?"

He grimaced. "Quinn. Savaged his arm pretty badly before we gained control again."

Attacking the man I wanted to seduce was not the brightest thing I'd ever done. "Has he wolf in his background?"

"No."

At least that was one good thing—we didn't have to keep an eye on him the night of the full moon. "So how long was I out?"

"Twenty-four hours. It's Tuesday, and four in the afternoon."

"I hope you let Jack know I'm not going to make it to work."

He smiled. "Jack knows. He's still downstairs."

I yawned, then asked, "Why?"

"Because another attempt was made on his life. Until we know what's going on, this shed is our temporary headquarters."

"I'm sure the owners will be pleased about that."

"The owners are currently overseas and not expected back for another two weeks. We're as safe here as we would be anywhere."

"Only problem with that is the fact we're out in the middle of nowhere."

"That means squat in this day and age." He grinned, kissed my fingers, and rose. "You feel ready for something to eat?"

"I suppose." I paused. "What about the moon? We can't avoid what it does to us, and out here, it's going to prove a problem."

His smile faded, and he scrubbed a hand through his short hair. "I know. Liander's here, but given what you said on the phone about Talon, I didn't think you'd want him close."

"I don't."

"Then Quinn is a possible solution for you. His behavior over the last twenty-four hours certainly suggests he's interested."

I grinned. "I know for a fact he's more than a little interested in some werewolf action."

A smile touched his lips, but his eyes sparkled with worry. "Be careful with him, sis."

My earlier wariness of Quinn came back in a rush. "Are you two actually friends?"

"Yes, and that's why I'm giving you the warning. I think he's the type you could fall for. Just . . . don't."

"He's not a wolf, so he hardly qualifies for the type I'd fall for." I paused, then added, "So why the warning?"

"Because a wolf almost destroyed him, and he's sworn never to get involved with another one."

"He's already given me that speech. What did that wolf do?"

"I don't know the details. I just know he will never again trust another wolf."

"He trusts you."

"Only up to a point." He shrugged, as if it didn't matter, and didn't hurt, when I knew it did. Like me, Rhoan didn't have all that many good friends. "Just take the sex if it's offered and walk away when it's over. Trust me, it's all you'll get anyway."

"It's all I want, so it should be no problem."

He studied me for a moment, then leaned forward and kissed my forehead. "I'll get you something to eat. You stay here and rest."

I caught his arm before he could move away. "Any word from Kelly?"

He hesitated, then shook his head. "They're still looking, though."

I closed my eyes, but no matter how much I tried to stop it, fear still rose. Though I guess no news was good news inasmuch as that it still allowed hope. I had to cling to that. Had to.

He placed his hand over mine and squeezed lightly. "She'll be okay, sis."

I nodded and released his arm. He walked away, still looking like a cowboy who'd spent too many days in the saddle. I took a breath and let it out slowly, then lifted the sheet and took stock. My left arm was bandaged from shoulder to fingers, and my right wrist and both ankles were also bandaged. I could move my bandaged fingers, even though it hurt, so once again I'd been lucky. But how much longer would my luck hold? Sooner or later, those bastards would get me—unless we got them first.

Of course, to get them, I had to become part of Jack's team. Had to take yet another step to giving him what he wanted—me, as a guardian.

"Everything is still there, if that's what you're checking."

Amusement played in the depths of Quinn's warm voice, and I looked up with a smile. "A girl likes to see these things for herself."

The smile teasing the corners of his luscious mouth warmed his dark eyes, and both did strange things to my pulse rate. The moon might not have risen yet, but the fever was beginning to burn through my veins, thanks to his presence.

He grabbed the chair Rhoan had vacated and pulled it close to the bed. "How are you feeling?"

"Fine," I replied politely. "How are you feeling?"

The smile grew. He brushed a finger down my cheek, his touch lingering near my mouth. "At least your skin no longer burns."

He wasn't feeling it from *my* side. "How's your arm?"

The bump under his sweater suggested I'd done a good job—his left arm appeared to be bandaged as much as mine.

He shrugged. "A vampire heals almost as fast as a wolf. I'll be fine in a day or so."

"I'm sorry I attacked you." I smiled slightly, and added, "Both times."

His fingers drifted down my neck, trailing heat across my skin. His expression was distracted—a look that had nothing to do with blood hunger, and everything to do with a man being confronted by a naked woman. "Both events were instinctive. There's nothing to forgive."

His touch reached my shoulder and skimmed the bandages. Goose bumps fled across my skin, a sensation that owed nothing to fear or pain.

"But there's something we need to talk about."

His gaze came back to me. Fires burned in the black depths, a heat I could feel through every fiber. "I want you."

It appears werewolves weren't the only ones up front when it comes to sex. "Good."

His fingers skimmed the rise of my breasts, and my nipples woke to painful life. My mind might be advising caution, but my body was screaming *yes, yes!*

"When?" He was speaking softly, the lilt of Ireland caressing his voice, sending my already erratic pulse into overdrive.

"Soon," I said, voice breathy. "Not now."

His fingers slipped under the sheet, taking an agonizingly circular route to my aching nipples. Slowly, teasingly, he rolled his thumb across one hard nub. "That's a shame."

My hormones thought so too. "Tell me about the wolf who hurt you."

He stopped, but his fingers were so warm against my skin it felt like he was branding me. Then his gaze met mine, and I saw the hardness there. Rhoan was right. This man would never give me anything more than sex. The wolf who had been here before me had totally destroyed this vampire's heart.

His touch left me, and while I regretted that, curiosity was still stronger than desire. One of these days, I was going to have to leash my curious instincts before they landed me in water too hot to get out of. Or, in this case, out of luck with one of the sexiest vampires I'd ever come across.

He leaned back in the chair, his face expressionless. "Why?"

"Because Rhoan warned against getting too involved with you, and since he rarely gives that sort of advice, I'm wondering why he chose to do so now."

Surprise touched his stern features. "Rhoan said that?"

"You've said that, too," I reminded him. "I'm gathering that we werewolves are good enough for a dance or two, but nothing more?"

His gaze met mine, the dark depths cold and hard. "Basically, yes."

"Meaning, you hold the all-too-human view that werewolves are little more than whores who have little or no control over their base instincts?"

"Yes."

I snorted, inexplicably disappointed. "And here I was thinking that a thousand years might have knocked a little knowledge into your brain."

His smile was grim. "A thousand years *has* knocked knowledge into my brain. And my experiences with wolves have confirmed my beliefs."

I thought back to the pictures I'd seen of his fiancée. Remembered the articles saying she'd disappeared. "Eryn was a wolf, wasn't she?"

His nod was short, sharp.

"What did she do?"

His hesitation was brief, but nevertheless there. His reluctance to talk about the subject was obvious, and yet he was. Did that suggest he wanted me more than he wanted to keep his secrets?

"We met during a moon phase," he said, voice low and devoid of the sexy lilt. "But the fever continued on after. I couldn't get enough of her. I thought it was love."

I raised an eyebrow. "And it wasn't?"

"No. It was a drug called *Everlasting*."

I frowned. *Everlasting* wasn't a drug I'd ever heard of—though there were certainly plenty of them to be found in the clubs. "What does it do?"

"Imitate the moon fever in races other than were-creatures."

My gaze widened. "That's dangerous."

"Very. Thankfully, it was only experimental. Eryn was working for the company developing it and decided to do a little field test. I was the subject she chose."

Then she didn't research well enough, because anyone with half a brain could see you didn't want to mess with this particular vampire. "So she never loved you?"

"Oh, I'm sure she loved my money."

I blinked at the sheer depths of anger so evident in his flat tones. "What happened?"

"I bought the company, then destroyed the whole project."

"So *Everlasting* is no more?"

"No."

"And what about Eryn?"

"Last I heard, she was working in a whorehouse in Sydney." His sudden smile was ferocious. "A suitable occupation for a wolf who was little more than a slut after money."

I stared at him, knowing he'd taken her mind, altered her self-image. Made her believe she *was* what she'd become. A shiver ran through me. As punishments went, it was as cold as you could get.

"And what do you think I'm after?"

"Nothing more than sex." He hesitated, then gave me a slow, sexy smile that had my hormones scrambling and toes curling. "Which brings me neatly back to my original question—when?"

"My brother insists I eat and regain some strength before I do anything too vigorous."

"And I intend for it to be *very* vigorous."

Oh, man . . . "How about we seal the deal with a kiss?" Because if I didn't at least taste him, I might just explode with frustration. Though it was very possible that I would explode even if he *did* kiss me.

He leaned forward, his hand cupping my cheek as his mouth captured mine. It was a kiss unlike any I'd ever experienced—a long, slow possession that left me gasping for breath and hotter than I'd ever been for a man.

I couldn't wait to see what he could do when he had the time to explore more fully.

"Your brother's climbing the stairs with your dinner," he whispered, brushing his lips across mine a final time before he sat back.

I took a deep breath, but it was filled with the scent of him, the richness of sandalwood combined with sheer masculinity. He smelled good enough to eat. Or at least nibble. And lick.

"My brother has always had bad timing," I muttered.

Quinn chuckled softly and rose. My gaze slipped downward, and I noted with pleasure he wanted me every bit as badly as I wanted him.

"Sorry to break in on your fun," Rhoan said as he appeared. "But you have to eat before you go expending too much energy."

"And so do I," Quinn commented, giving me a look guaranteed to make my insides combust. "Though synth blood is not my meal of choice right now."

He disappeared down the stairs, and I suddenly remembered how to breathe.

"Are you sure there's no wolf in his background?" I said, sitting up so Rhoan could place the tray on my knees.

Rhoan grinned. "The man is potent, I'll give him that. Damn shame he's straight."

I gave him a long look. "Don't tell me you hit on him."

"Hell, yeah. Wouldn't you if you walked into a bar and saw him?" He placed the tray on my knee and sat down. "He refused nicely, we got talking, and the rest, as they say, is history."

"This was how many years ago?" I picked up my knife and fork and studied the mess on my plate. I think it was bacon and eggs, but I couldn't be sure. A cook my brother wasn't.

"Only one."

"So why haven't you introduced us?"

It was his turn to give me a long look. "This from the wolf who rants about all vampires being arrogant pigs?"

"Well, all the ones I've met have been. Quinn isn't."

"He can be on his bad days, believe me." He rose again. "If you're feeling up to it after you finish that, come downstairs."

I nodded. "Why has Jack allowed Liander to stay?"

"Because this is looking bigger than the three of us can handle." He shrugged. "Liander's here because I need him, and because he's one of the best makeup artists in the country."

I raised an eyebrow. "That sounds like a plan."

"It is. When you come down, we'll enlighten you."

"And just what am I supposed to go downstairs in? My birthday suit?"

He grinned. "We retrieved your bag from Misha's car. It's on the chair near the stairs."

He headed back downstairs. Once I'd eaten the mess he'd laughingly called a meal, I shifted shape to help the burns along some more, then threw on some clothes and followed him down.

Everyone was sitting at the table, including Liander.

"How you feeling, darlin'?" Jack asked, his green eyes sweeping me in a concerned, fatherly way.

"A little achy, but otherwise fine."

He nodded. "You want to tell us what happened?"

I sat on the last remaining chair and proceeded to do that.

Rhoan frowned. "Genoveve and Libraska aren't research facilities I've ever heard of."

"Nor I," Jack agreed. "We may have to go through the records to find them. If they are on the record, that is."

"What do you mean?" I reached for one of the apples sitting in the middle of the table. "I thought all research facilities, whether government or private, had to be listed?"

"Only in the last fifty years. There were a lot of places, particularly military ones, that were built in the twentieth century that were never recorded—for security reasons. It was a volatile era."

"What about the thing that attacked her?" Quinn asked. "That doesn't sound like any creature I've heard of."

"No. But if they're playing around with the basic building blocks of life, who knows what they've come up with?" Jack glanced at me. "You up to a little more investigating?"

I raised an eyebrow. "Like I have a choice?"

"There's always a choice."

I snorted softly. "Between you trying to railroad me, and these nutters coming after me, I think choice has temporarily flown out the window."

He didn't bother to deny my allegations, merely smiled. "You are going to make such a wonderful guardian."

"You're better off chasing after Liander than me—you'd have more hope."

"He's already come after me," Liander commented, his silver eyes sparkling with a combination of amusement and annoyance. "And I have temporarily been seconded into this outfit, whether I like it or not."

"Well, you were military, and you do slide in rather well." Rhoan's smile was decidedly wicked. "And just think of the advantages—me, primarily."

Liander grinned. "Why do you think I'm here? At least I don't have to share with the lush."

"Bitchy." Rhoan's smile widened.

"The truth," Liander said, voice dry.

"Enough," Jack said, and glanced at me. "We're planning a two-prong attack. An accident has been planned that will wipe out the power in the Ferntree Gully area. Rhoan and I will break into Moneisha and do a little investigating."

Which left me with Quinn. The thought had my hormones doing an excited little dance. "Surely Moneisha will have backup generators?"

"And probably handheld scanners," Quinn added.

Jack nodded. "But the generators only handle essentials, and we can avoid any guards, whether or not they're holding scanners."

"And in the meantime, I'll be doing what?" I asked.

"Searching the paperwork in Alan Brown's office."

"How? All the offices upstairs have eye scan locks."

"They do. Except the scanners have mysteriously started acting up the last twenty-four hours, and all staff have been issued with special keycards and codes until the problem is resolved."

"Convenient," I said dryly.

He merely smiled. "Alan Brown has a long-known

habit of bringing prostitutes into his office. Unfortunately, Brown took some coffee that didn't agree with him earlier this afternoon and went home sick. He won't wake until tomorrow."

"And how was this managed? You and I both know Brown wouldn't touch anything you gave him with a ten-foot pole. And you couldn't exactly ask any of the guardians to tamper with his coffee, because you don't know whom to trust right now."

Jack nodded. "But I know I can trust the director."

I raised my eyebrow. "Alex Hunter? The woman is a bitch."

"And that bitch is my sister."

Trust me to put my foot in it. Or open my big mouth, as the case might be.

Rhoan laughed, and Jack reached across the table, patting my hand comfortingly. "It's okay. She *is* a bitch, most times. But she wants to know what is going on every bit as badly as us. The Directorate is her baby—she was one of those who pushed to get it set up—and she has no intention of letting it be used for nefarious purposes. As of this weekend, you, Rhoan, and I are on special assignment and reporting directly to her."

Meaning I was taking the first step down that guardian path. And there wasn't one damn thing I could do about it. If I said no, he'd lock me away somewhere safe, and that would be almost as bad, not only because I was a wolf who couldn't stand enclosed spaces for long but because some warped part of me *wanted* to be involved. I might not want to be a guardian, but these bastards had come after me twice now, and the wolf wanted revenge.

I glanced at Quinn. "But how are we going to get

into Brown's office when Quinn looks nothing like Brown?" He was far, far too handsome, for a start.

"He will by the time I've finished with him," Liander said.

"You think you can do something tarty for me as well?" I couldn't risk wearing the blue wig and makeup again, just in case it set off alarms somewhere.

Liander grinned. "You have no idea how long I've been wanting to redo your look. You have to keep up with the times, Riley."

It was a comment he'd made more than once. I stuck my tongue out at him before looking back at Jack. "When are we moving?"

"As soon as everyone is ready. Liander will be holding the fort here."

"And we meet back here afterward?"

Jack nodded. "Let's move it, people."

I grinned. He sounded like the old army sergeant he'd once been. I rose, munching on my apple as I headed back upstairs for a shower. Raiding Alan Brown's office wasn't exactly what I'd been hoping to do tonight, but at least I was with Quinn.

And come hell or high water, it was going to be the night I rocked his staid little world.

Chapter 9

*Y*ou could have hired a less conspicuous car," I said, accepting Quinn's offer of help as I climbed out of the Porsche.

He shrugged and slammed the door closed. The doors locked automatically, and the car beeped softly as the alarm was set. "It's fast, comfortable, and besides, I'm half-thinking about getting one. This is a good way of testing it."

The stiff breeze caught the thin gray strands of hair that had been combed over his newly bald cranium, standing them on end like flags. Match that with a goatee beard, puffy cheeks, and a small beer belly, and you had the picture of a man well past his prime. It was hard to believe that under all the makeup there was one incredibly handsome individual. I grinned.

"Liander should get a medal for the work he's done on you."

He took off his coat and put it around my shoulders,

then slid his hand down my arm and twined his fingers through mine. Heat trembled through me, and the fires of need leapt into focus. It was barely nine in the evening, and the moon had only just begun to rise. Yet the fever was a slow burn in my blood, a force ready and able to explode. I took a deep breath and tried to ignore it. Yet I couldn't ignore the caress of his body's heat as we strolled toward the Directorate building a block away. Couldn't ignore the tension emanating from him, a tension that spoke of a need as great as my own.

"He hasn't done such a bad job on you, either." The soft lilt in Quinn's voice had disappeared, thanks to the modulators inserted into his cheeks. What came out was Brown's harsh tones. "Though I think I prefer the blue toning to the white. It makes you look too ghostly."

Which was the effect Liander had been going for. Apparently, ghostly was going to be the next big fashion trend. Personally, I agreed with Quinn. White contacts, white hair, and powder white skin were just too spooky.

But at least I'd been able to keep my sexy boots, though he'd swapped the peekaboo shirt and microskirt for a thigh-length dress that was little more than gossamer, and very similar in design to the outfits Brown's tarts wore in the security vids we'd viewed. Brown liked his women naked and ready to go, it seemed.

Which is probably why Quinn had wrapped his coat around my shoulders—I was wearing zip underneath the gossamer, and in the gleam of street lighting all was revealed. I didn't particularly care, but Quinn had made a couple of comments about indecency and respectability that had made me smile.

It was going to be so much fun dragging his complacent sexual views out of the ordinary and into the extraordinary.

We climbed the steps and walked to the Directorate's main doors. Quinn pressed the code keys, then swiped the card. As the doors swished open, the red beam of the scanners ran down us. Neither of us was carrying weapons, so we didn't set off any alarms. And there was no problem with the handprint scanner, either. Liander had covered that—with a little help from Jack and the prints he'd taken from the files.

"Assistant Director Brown," the guard at the desk said, his eyes all but popping out of his head when he saw me. "We weren't expecting you in this evening."

"Got a little business to attend to," Quinn replied, his grin lecherous as he patted my behind awkwardly.

He had Brown's movements down pat, and I bit the inside of my cheek, trying not to laugh.

"I'll have to code an elevator for you," the guard said. "We locked them down for the night."

Quinn nodded, and the guard scooted ahead of us. He unlocked an elevator, but didn't step back, forcing me to press past him to get into the elevator. As I did, he slid his hand across my rear, taking a quick feel.

Quinn moved so swiftly it was only when I heard the crack of bones that I realized something had happened.

"No touching the merchandise on *my* money." His voice was flat and cold, and the guard paled.

"Sorry, Director," he stammered.

"Do it again, and I'll have you fired."

He let go of the guard's hand and stepped into the elevator with me. I waited until the door closed, and said, "That was a bit much. The tapes show that's a somewhat regular occurrence when Brown brings his women in."

"I don't care. That man has no right to touch you."

"We're here in disguise. We have to follow the pattern set."

He glanced at me, eyes unreadable thanks to the blue lenses he had in. "That may be your game plan, but it's not mine. Not when it comes to something like that."

"Brown's not a gentleman, and he certainly doesn't mind sharing. Remember that."

"I'm not Brown. You remember that."

The doors opened before I could reply. Quinn pressed his hand into my back, guiding me down the shadow-filled hall. Warmth pooled around his fingertips, lapping across the rest of my skin in waves. The fever flickered in response, surging through my veins. It was ignorable—but for how long?

Cameras tracked our progress up the hall. When we got to Brown's office, he pressed in the code, swiped the card, then motioned me inside.

The lights came on as he reset the lock. I stopped in the middle of the room and looked around. Though I knew the basic layout of the office, the sheer size of it still surprised me. It wasn't as huge as the office Talon had in his house, but it was still pretty amazing. Nor was the furniture the standard-issue cheap stuff we got downstairs. This was mahogany and leather right down the line.

I tossed the jacket on the nearest chair and moved down to the far end of the room.

"Lighting level dim," Quinn said behind me.

His voice had an edge and I looked at him. He

smiled grimly. With all his makeup, it wasn't a pretty sight.

"That dress you're almost wearing is dead see-through in bright lights."

I struck a pose and batted my eyelashes innocently. "And you don't like the view?"

"Oh, I love the view, but unfortunately, I need to concentrate on what we're here to do."

I grinned and motioned to the seemingly blank wall in front of me. "So do you want to open the cabinets so we can start?"

"Cabinets open," he said, tone still gruff.

There was a soft click, and the wall slid aside. I walked to the cabinets at the far end, my smile growing as I heard the soft groan behind. Obviously, the dress was see-through in dim lights too.

"I don't know what Jack hopes to find," I said, pulling out the first drawer. "Surely Brown is not stupid enough to keep anything incriminating in his office."

"It would certainly be a lot safer than keeping it at home," Quinn commented from the other end. "This place normally has more security than Fort Knox."

I raised an eyebrow. "And you know this because . . . ?"

A smile tugged his lips—lips that were still full and lush and oh so kissable. "Because I've had a somewhat less-than-respectable past."

So Jack had said. "You robbed Fort Knox?"

"Their security wasn't as sophisticated back then. Certainly not strong enough to keep a determined vampire out."

No wonder he was megarich. I shook my head and

he chuckled. "It wasn't the first bank to suffer unexplained losses."

"You made a habit of it?"

"I had several brief flurries into crime. Respectability gets boring after a few centuries."

I raised an eyebrow. "So how far into the current respectability phase are you?"

"Far enough for it to start feeling old." He pointed to the cabinet I had open. "If you don't start looking, we're never going to get out of here."

And I wanted to get out of there, because I wanted to make love to him. Whether or not he was still wrapped in an ugly outer layer.

I began flicking through the paperwork. In this age of electronic marvels, it was amazing just how much paper was still used. Of course, paper was no longer just paper, more a special form of recycled plastic, but it felt the same and was used in the same copious amounts that it ever was.

It was a half hour before we found something.

"Financial costings," Quinn said. "For an unspecified project." He flicked through the papers with a frown. "The project wasn't approved by the Directorate."

I opened another drawer. "Nothing unusual in that. From what Jack says, a good half of the projects presented to the board are turned down."

His gaze met mine. "This was for genome research. The proposal was presented fifteen years ago."

I frowned. "Why would he be keeping something like that?"

"Why indeed?" He tossed the folder on the nearby chair and continued searching.

The drawer I'd opened was filled with boxes and

boxes of fingertip-sized silvery disks. I plucked one free and grinned. "What's the betting Brown likes to record his exploits for posterity?"

"Is there anywhere here we could check them?"

"Yeah, but we can't go through all of them. It'll take years."

"Check a couple from each box. I'll continue searching the drawers."

I flipped the disk across to him. "You check. I don't need to be looking at other people making love right now."

"Neither do I, believe me."

"Yeah, but the consequences of your getting all hot and bothered are far different from a werewolf's getting all hot and bothered."

He smiled. "Ah, but getting a wolf hot and bothered definitely has its benefits."

"Not at this precise moment it doesn't."

"You have a point. Just select some and we'll examine them later."

I grinned. "In the privacy of a bedroom, perhaps?"

The words were barely out of my mouth when movement caught my attention. Soft steps in the hall outside, coming toward the office. I blinked, flicking my vision to infrared. The walls melted away, revealing two men. Though they were little more than red heat blurs, the metal at their sides suggested guards.

"Quinn," I warned softly. "Guards are headed our way."

He swung round, eyes narrowed slightly. "They've been told about the babe Brown has in his office, and intend to check her out under the guise of a regular security check."

The fact that he could read their intentions when

the building had psychic blocks situated right through it only confirmed Jack's earlier statement that the Directorate would never hold a vampire like Quinn. And the wolf in me reacted to the knowledge with fierce desire.

"Apparently," Quinn continued, "Brown lets them get away with it, as long as they keep quiet about what he does in here."

"If Jack knows, it's no state secret."

"I'd suggest Jack knows more about what goes on in this place than most of the directors." He paused again. "The guard downstairs is asking them to make sure the camera is on. Which cuts out attacking them."

I met his gaze. "We attack them and we warn Brown and whoever else might be behind all this that we're on to them. We can't risk that yet."

"So we give them what they want—a show." He walked over to one of the visitor's chairs and sat down. "You'd better get that beautiful butt of yours over here, because they're almost at the door."

I did as directed and sat on his lap, my thighs straddling his hips, legs stretched wide either side of the chair. It was a devastatingly intimate position that had the blood pounding through my veins and yet it wasn't anywhere near intimate enough for my liking. I slid back and, before he realized what I was up to, quickly undid his zipper, freeing his cock from all restrictions. Then I wriggled over him until he was right under me, hard flesh against wet.

He groaned. "Jesus, Riley, don't move or I'm gone."

I grinned. "We are supposed to be giving those men an eyeful."

"And that's all I intend to allow them." He touched a hand to my face, his fingers so warm against my skin.

"When I make love to you for the first time, it won't be with an audience at my back. And it will be somewhere decidedly more comfortable than an office."

"You are *so* old-fashioned. And an audience can definitely add to the spice." I wriggled a little, just to tease him some more. The tremor that ran through him was fierce, as was his intake of breath. "Besides, if you just sit there like a store dummy, they're going to suspect something is wrong."

The grin that touched his lips was decidedly wicked. "Oh, I have no intention of just sitting here."

His hands skimmed my sides and lifted the gossamer creation away. He dropped it beside the chair, then slid one hand around to my spine, pressing me forward until my nipples brushed his mouth.

His breath was hot and damp across my flesh, sending goose bumps rippling. Then his tongue replaced his breath, and slowly, languorously, he worked his way toward an engorged point. When his lips surrounded it, sucking it deep inside his mouth, I trembled, a helpless sound of pleasure escaping.

He chuckled softly, a throaty sound that was as seductive and as arousing as his touch, and moved his attention to my other breast.

The door clicked open. The breathing of the two men rasped against the silence, a sound that roughened, quickened. I couldn't have given a damn what the two men were seeing or feeling. Not when every fiber of my being thrummed with pleasure.

Quinn cupped my breasts, lightly pushing them together, his tongue sweeping from one hard nub to the other. I squirmed on his lap, enjoying the press of his erection, the way he pulsed and twitched.

When he finally pulled away, I groaned. His hands

slipped down to my hips, holding me still, then he leaned his head against the back of the chair, and said, "I believe you've seen enough for one night, gentlemen."

The door closed. Footsteps moved away.

"Oh God," I said, my voice ragged. "You can't stop now." I'd *die* if he stopped.

"I have no intention of stopping just yet." Though it was Brown's voice, the heat, the passion, so evident within it stirred my already aching senses.

His hand slid up the inside of my spread thighs, his fingers grazing me. I shuddered, thrusting into his touch, sure I was going to bust if he didn't get on with it. "Stop teasing," I moaned, when he did it a second time.

He chuckled again, then wrapped his free hand around my neck and pulled me down. His kiss was hot, lavish, branding and possessing my mouth in a way no other man ever had.

As his mouth claimed mine, his fingers slid between us, pressing into my slickness, caressing, delving. I shifted, giving him greater access, moaning when his fingers slipped inside. Then his thumb pressed into my clit, and he began to stroke, inside and out. I shuddered, writhed, as the sweet pressure built and built, until it felt as if every fiber of my being was going to tear apart from the sheer force of pleasure.

Then everything did, and I grabbed his shoulders, my fingers digging into his flesh as the tremors rolled through me.

After what seemed like ages I remembered how to breathe again. "Wow," was all I managed to say.

"Wow indeed." His voice was a mix of male satisfaction and simmering tension. "Feel a little better now?"

"I'm feeling a whole lot selfish now, actually. Which

is why"—I shifted, capturing him, driving him deep—"I think I should return the favor."

His hands came down on my hips and held me still. Then he smiled his dangerous smile and sent my pulse rate skittering again. "When I make love to you, Riley, it will be after a long, slow, seduction of your senses. I like to do things properly the first time."

Bedevilment ran through me. He really didn't know much about werewolves if he thought I'd let him get away with a statement like that. Or without taking some pleasure himself.

And there was more than one way to give pleasure, as he'd so amply shown. I raised an eyebrow. "Really?"

"Really. I told you, I'm an old-fashioned man."

"Then I guess I'd better rise and get back to the business at hand."

"I guess you'd better."

I placed a hand on his chest, holding him still and in place as I threw one leg over his. His erection, all veins and knots and hard, hard flesh, looked positively painful, his flesh red and glistening with my moisture. Keeping one hand on his chest, I leaned forward and kissed him, long and slow. Then, before he could react, I dropped to my knees beside him, claimed his erection with one hand, and ran my tongue around the tip. He jumped, then groaned. "Jesus, don't—"

"Don't what?" I murmured, running moistened lips up and down his shaft.

"This is dangerous. Any delay is dangerous."

There was a desperation to his voice that made me smile. This vampire wanted what I was offering, no matter what his words were saying.

"I love the taste of danger." I ran my tongue back up to the tip, and added, "And I love the taste of you."

I took him in my mouth. Drew him deep, sucking and tasting and teasing him, until his movements became desperate and the salty taste of him began seeping into my mouth. I sucked again, harder this time, and he came, fiercely and violently, his whole body jerking with the force of it.

When he was done, I licked the tip of him and looked up. "So how did the old-fashioned man enjoy that?"

"You're a witch." He shook his head, as if still unable to believe what I'd just done. "And as I said, any delay could prove costly. Even glorious ones."

I grinned. "Going out with a tent pole is dangerous. The guards would be wondering what you were actually doing in here."

"True." He gently pushed me upright, then handed me the dress. "Shall we continue investigating?"

I was half-inclined to continue what we'd started, but he was right about one thing—we were there to work, not play.

We continued searching the drawers. I was on my final one when I found a folder marked "White Phantom Project." It wasn't anything I'd ever heard of—though I was hardly in a position to hear or see anything top secret—but something about the name stirred my curiosity. Inside, there were old floor plans, building sketches, and the like, as well as the names of several people who no longer worked for the Directorate. I handed the folder across to Quinn. "Look at this."

He took it and had a quick glance. "It doesn't give us much." He glanced at the name on the spine, and his frown deepened. "You know, Genoveve is a form of Guinevere, which is both French and Welsh. I believe Guinevere means either white wave or white phantom."

"So?"

"So, white phantoms are a form of vampire."

I raised my eyebrows. "Really?"

He nodded. "It's a bit of a stretch, but at this stage, I think we can afford to grab at anything."

He tossed the folder on the chair with the other one. We finished searching our prospective drawers but didn't find anything else. I picked out a couple of the disks, then Quinn relocked the cabinets, grabbed the folders, and walked across to the phone.

"All calls from the offices are recorded," I said, as he picked up the phone.

"I'm not intending to use it." He held out a finger. On it was a pinhead-sized dot. "The latest in bug technology."

"The Directorate's a government department. It's regularly swept."

His smile made my hormones do their jig again. "My labs are developing this one, and so far, it's gone undetected in a number of government buildings."

I raised my eyebrows. "And why would you be bugging government offices?"

"Not all offices. Just those trying to place sanctions on my businesses."

"And, handily, you just happened to be carrying one of these little bugs around in your pocket?"

"No. The labs developing them are in Melbourne. I went there yesterday and picked one up." He smiled at me. "Of course, I've now warned your boss what I'm up to, so I daresay I'll have to develop new spying methods."

He placed the dot on the base unit, then walked around the table and held out a hand. "Shall we go?"

I glanced at the wall clock as I wove my fingers in his. "Jack didn't want us to meet back at the farmhouse until five. That gives us three hours to fill in before we have to leave for Seymour." I met his gaze and tried to restrain my grin. "What do you think we should do to fill in the time?"

"Feel like a coffee?"

"No."

He unlocked the door and wrapped a hand around the handle. "How about a midnight snack?"

"It's well after midnight and the only thing I'm interested in sampling right now"—I swept my gaze down the front of him—"is something I've already tasted."

"Do you always talk this dirty to mates?"

I laughed. "My dear vampire, I haven't even begun to get dirty yet."

Amusement and desire vied for prominence in his eyes. "That almost sounds like a threat."

"Take it any way you want. As long as you take me, I don't care."

"Oh, you can be sure that I intend to take you." His sexy grin teased my hormones as he opened the door. "Just not here. Out you go."

I went, and ran nose first into someone who was little more than shadow. I yelped, and jumped back, my pulse going a mile a minute. But even before the shadows found form, I knew it was Gautier. His smell wrapped around me, a noxious scent that made me want to scratch at my skin. Quinn's hands came down on my shoulders, his fingers pressing deep, as if warning me not to speak. Like I *needed* a warning.

"Director Brown," Gautier said, oily tones soft and somewhat respectful. "I thought you'd gone home sick."

"I had. Now I'm back. What do you want?"

"Nothing. Just doing my nightly check."

He was lying. I knew for a fact Radford was supposed to be doing the rounds that week, not Gautier. So why was he there, nosing around the executive floor? Did he suspect something was wrong, or was he up to business of his own? Business that meant ill for the Directorate?

"Then why were you standing at my door?" Quinn said, voice a perfect imitation of Brown's sharp bark.

"Thought I heard voices. And, as I said, I didn't know you were here, sir."

He was still lying. And was that a bead of sweat on his forehead? What on earth had Gautier been about to do?

"Well, now you know the source of the voices, I suggest you continue your rounds."

Gautier hesitated, took a glance at the cameras, then wrapped the shadows around himself and disappeared. I switched to infrared, watching him retreat until he disappeared into the stairwell.

"Let's go," Quinn said, locking the door before grabbing my arm and propelling me down the hall.

I waited until we were in the elevator, then pulled my arm free of his grip. "Gautier suspects us."

He raised an eyebrow. "How do you know that? You can't read his thoughts any more than he can read yours."

"No. But I could read his expression—"

"A vampire like Gautier doesn't have expressions."

"It was there—just a brief flicker. Something you said made him suspect us."

"Then we're getting out of here as fast as we can. We can't risk him getting help and maybe cornering us."

No, we couldn't, because I'd seen Gautier in action. And while I had no doubt that Quinn could handle the likes of Gautier, it would be a different story if Gautier called in help. And there were at least twenty vampires sitting in the vaults of the place, just itching for a good fight.

We exited the building and made our way down the street. Though I heard no sound, the hairs on the back of my neck rose.

"We're being followed," I said softly.

"I know. But the closest one is not a vampire—the heartbeat is too regular." His fingers tightened on mine. "Let's head for the car and see what happens."

We didn't alter our pace, just kept walking. The tall buildings around us blocked out most of the wind's fury, but though it was after midnight, the night was far from quiet. The moon was riding high and wolves were celebrating all over the city. Even the traffic was heavier than normal.

Yet through all the noise came a whisper of movement. It was more a sigh of air than anything else, and it was coming at us fast. I caught the sharp tang of musk and man, and anger surged through me. It wasn't Gautier.

I pulled free from Quinn and swung round, catching Talon's reaching hand before he could pull the wig from my head.

Surprise ran through his eyes. I squeezed his fingers

a little harder, and the surprise became pain. "And what do you think you're doing?"

"I gather you know this gentleman." Quinn's voice was flat and yet I sensed the amusement in it. Maybe he liked the sight of pain being inflicted on others.

"I'd use the term 'gentleman' loosely. But yeah, I know him." I released Talon's hand, throwing it back against his chest. "What the hell are you doing here? And how did you find me?"

He grinned, but it never touched his eyes, which were cold and hard as his gaze moved from me to Quinn and back again. "A wolf always knows where to find his mate."

"*This* is your mate?" Quinn's voice was scathing. "Good Lord, I thought you had more taste than that."

"Mate as in sex partner, not mate as in permanent relationship. This jerk has just decided he needs a kid from me and has laid claims without my consent."

"There are laws against that, you know," Quinn said conversationally. "Though I've always found a good beating works as a far better deterrent."

"Now, there's a thought." I pushed Talon hard in the chest, knocking him back several steps. Surprise flickered in his golden eyes.

"What the fuck do you think you're doing?" I continued sharply. "What right have you got to come here after me?"

The false smile slipped away, and what remained was cold and hard. God, what had I ever seen in this man? "You're mine, little wolf, and I don't intend to share. Even with a dead man."

"I belong to no one but myself. And how do you know he's a vampire?"

Talon snorted, his expression impatient as his gaze

briefly swept past me. "It's Alan Brown, isn't it? Seen him on the recruiting ads."

If it *had* been Alan Brown, Talon would have been dead meat. Brown was another of those vampires who didn't treat fools—or those who didn't respect his so called "superiority"—lightly. "So how did you find me?"

"Easy. I checked out what shifts you were supposed to be on this week and came here to wait for you."

He was lying. Why I was so certain, I didn't know. Certainly there was nothing in his eyes or his expression that gave him away.

"You broke into my apartment?" And how could he have found my schedule in all that mess when half the time I had trouble?

He shrugged, his gaze sliding down my body, becoming heated when he saw what I was wearing. Or almost wearing. "I like, little wolf."

For the first time, the fierce burn of his aura had little effect. It was as if some sort of veil had been raised between us. I felt the caress of his desire but it no longer stirred the fever. Maybe because I'd finally glimpsed the real Talon and hadn't liked what I'd seen.

He reached out to touch me, but I slapped his hand away. "Have you given up on that crazy idea of yours?"

"It's not crazy. And a child of ours would be perfect."

Maybe it would. If it lived. If I lived. "I have no intention of having a child with you, so get over it."

His expression was hard, determined, but I saw something else in his eyes that scared me—amusement. Gloating. "You will have no choice in the matter, little wolf. I intend to ensure you do not find relief with anyone else. Including dead men."

Anger surged, and I hit him. I'd never condoned women hitting men any more than I did men hitting women, but right then, with the smug smile teasing his lips and the I-know-something-you-don't look in his eyes, I just couldn't help it. He didn't see it coming, and it landed on his chin with every ounce of strength I could muster. Which was quite a lot. His head snapped back, and he was out before his back hit the concrete.

"Good punch," Quinn commented. "Remind me never to make you angry."

"All you have to do to avoid it is remember that *this* particular wolf doesn't take people trying to take over her life too lightly."

Which, in many ways, was what Jack was trying to do—but at least he was giving me maneuvering room. Talon wasn't—he was making his statements like it was already a fait accompli.

I knelt beside Talon and felt for a pulse, just to ensure the smack in the back of the head hadn't killed him. The pulse was there, nice and steady. He was just knocked out.

I scanned the street as I rose. Our other watcher was still out there, hidden in the shadows, watching the proceedings. If it was Gautier, we could be in serious trouble. Even if he didn't suspect Quinn, he'd probably be more than a little suspicious of my identity by then.

"Let's get back to the car."

Quinn nodded, placed his hand against my spine, and escorted me the remainder of the way. "So tell me," I said, once we were in the car and zooming out of the city, "why would you think I'd be willing to make love to you if I had a permanent mate?"

He gave me a look that suggested he wished I'd missed the intent behind that particular statement. "Because I've heard the promises wolves make, and I've never met one who actually keeps them." He slowed the car as the lights ahead changed to red.

"What happened between you and Eryn was about money, not promises. You said that yourself. Don't condemn a whole race because of the actions of one goddamn wolf."

"It was more than one." He looked at me, blue-lensed eyes flat and hard to read. "I seem to have a somewhat fatal attraction to your race."

Ire swam through me. I was sick and tired of other races judging werewolves and deeming us unworthy or lacking. Why? Because we saw sex as a celebration, something that should be enjoyed rather than something that must be hidden away behind doors and darkness? Vampires drank blood to survive, and many killed their food supply, and yet the world in general deemed them more worthy of respect than us.

It made no sense, especially given sex was used to sell everything from Band-Aids to cars. I mean, whom did we really hurt with our moon dances? Sure, the aura of a wolf could make the unwilling willing, but few wolves bothered using it. We didn't need to when we could get what we wanted within our own race.

"You know, most of the vampires I work with are little more than stinking killing machines. That doesn't mean I think the whole damn race is the same."

His shrug was nonchalant, and yet the fierceness of his grip on the steering wheel suggested he was taking this conversation anything but casually. This Eryn—and whoever else was behind his less-than-stellar opinion of werewolves—really *had* done a number on him. "What I personally think of werewolves has nothing to do with anything."

"It does when you think we're nothing but prostitutes—and remember, you're the one who said you'd prefer to avoid pros."

The lights turned green, and he drove off at warp speed. "I don't consider wolves prostitutes—you don't sell yourselves, for a start. But I do think you are all far too free and easy with your bodies."

"And yet you seem all too willing to jump in and enjoy the offerings."

He gave me a somewhat amused look. "Underneath the vampire is a man—and no man in his right mind would say no when the packaging is as delightful as yours."

"That is such a *human* attitude—hate the race, but won't pass up the opportunity for a freebie all the same."

"At least I'm being honest—more than what your so-called mate is being, I'd say."

I let the change of topic slide. We could argue forever on his all-too-human grievances against wolves and never get anywhere. "Talon has always been arrogant, but I never thought he'd go this far."

"How long have you been together?"

"Two years."

"Is that not a long time for a wolf? Maybe that's why he thinks you have an agreement?"

My smile felt tight. "We've never been exclusive. At this particular moment he has seven other lovers, while I have one." I glanced at him. "And one prospective. In years past, he's had up to ten, and I've had three or four others. And he has no intention of giving up his harem for anyone."

"A wolf with lots of stamina, obviously."

"Yeah." Talon was all stamina, no finesse.

"Then what's the problem?"

I crossed my arms. "The problem, as I said before, is the fact he's decided I'd make the perfect mother for his children."

Quinn seemed to contemplate this for a few seconds, then said softly, "There's nothing wrong with wanting children with the woman you love."

"No, there's not," I agreed sourly. "Only we're not soul mates and he doesn't love me. He just wants to implant me with his kid."

Quinn glanced at me. "You don't want this?"

"No. I told you, we're not soul mates. I enjoy the sex, but that's it. And I'm certainly not about to risk my life having a kid with someone I don't love."

"Why would you be risking your life?"

I sighed. "Because of what I am. I can't conceive naturally, and my specialist doesn't know if I'll ever be able to carry to term. He's even suggested that pregnancy could actually kill me."

His surprise rippled around me. "Why?"

"Because recent results suggest my system might consider the fetus a foreign body and attack it. And, in the process, perhaps kill me." I shrugged. "He is of the opinion that if I want children, it could only happen with the help of drugs and under strict medical supervision. Even then, there is no guarantee."

"Not something you'd risk for someone you didn't love."

"Exactly."

He paused for a beat, sweeping onto the Tullamarine Freeway, then asked, "Do you want children?"

"Yes. If I ever meet the right wolf."

"You're young yet. Plenty of time."

I'd heard the same thing from Rhoan many times, and I didn't believe it now any more than I did then. What wolf wanted a women who might never be able to give him children? The ideal of family, of passing one's genes on to the next generation, was as ingrained into the werewolf culture as the moon dances and sexual freedom. We could no more help the desire to breed when we found our soul mates than we could the urge to celebrate the rising moon. It was part of what we were.

Which is the other reason why Rhoan and I had been allowed to survive. Half-breeds or not, we were at least another generation in a pack that had fewer and fewer pups every year. Our genes were pack genes, even if watered down.

Quinn swept the Porsche into the middle lane and pressed the accelerator. The car shot forward to something resembling light speed.

"There is a speed limit on this freeway," I said dryly.

"It's after midnight. Can't think of a better time or place to test this baby out." He glanced at me, the blue lenses in his eyes gleaming brightly under the freeway lights. "So basically, the problem is the fact he won't accept no for an answer. Why don't you just use telepathy to force him to accept it?"

I frowned at him. "I can't."

"Because he's blocked?"

"Because I've known him for two years. I can't force my will on him like that."

"As I said, why not? Sounds to me he's trying to force *his* will on *you*."

Well, yeah, but that was Talon. His wants had always come above everyone else's. But using words and strength was far different than using psychic talents. Besides, if I did do that, I'd be no better than he was. "Telepathy is a defense. I refuse to use it for anything more."

"Yet you used it at Moneisha just fine."

"That's different."

"It's not, you know."

"Rescuing my brother is defense of pack, nothing more."

"If you say so." He glanced in the rearview mirror, then said, "That wolf doesn't seem the type to accept his wishes being denied."

"He'll get over it." Yet I remembered the look in his eyes, remembered his vow that he always got what he wanted, and wondered.

I shifted in the seat and studied Quinn for a moment. "So what about you?"

He didn't return my look. "What about me?"

"How long did it take for you to get over Eryn?"

His smile was both wry and bitter. "I think current evidence suggests I'm not."

It certainly did. "So how long were you with her?"

"Nine months."

"When did you discover what she was doing?"

His expression was grim. "Not nearly fast enough." He hesitated, then added, "Four months ago."

Only four months. No wonder he was still hurting. No wonder he was still so angry. "And how long has Eryn been assigned to the whorehouse?"

"Two months." He shrugged. "It took time to buy her company."

"And are you intending to leave her there?"

"Yes."

"The punishment doesn't fit the crime, you know."

His sudden grin was savage. "She created her bed. Let her lie in it for eternity. I don't care."

The harshness of his words was a sharp reminder that this was a vampire I sat beside. A rare vampire, granted, in that he apparently still had the capability to feel, but a vampire all the same. And he could obviously be as cold and as cruel as any of his race.

"If you didn't care, you wouldn't have reacted so harshly," I noted.

He didn't say anything, but we both knew I was right. He looked in the rearview mirror again, and a prickle of unease ran down my spine.

"What's wrong?" I twisted around, saw the distant flash of red-and-blue lights. "Cops or emergency services?"

"Cops, I think."

I grinned. "So much for the theory that this was a perfect night to test this beastie's speed."

"True. But unlike you, I'm not above using my psychic skills to get me out of trouble."

I raised an eyebrow. "You obviously haven't read the papers lately." Not that I actually had, either. Jack had told me the news over lunch one day.

He glanced at me as he slowed. "What do you mean?"

"All police and emergency services have been issued with psychic deadeners as part of their everyday kits."

He swore softly. I just kept on grinning. Behind us, the blue-and-red lights drew closer, revealing the candy colors of the police car. Quinn pulled over to the side of the freeway and two cops climbed out. One moved toward Quinn's side, the other to mine.

We both lowered our windows, and Quinn said, voice ultrapolite, "Is there a problem, Off—"

His words were cut off by an odd popping sound. He jerked wildly, then became still, and though my concern surged, I had no chance to see what was going on.

Not with the barrel of a gun appearing two centimeters from the end of my nose.

Chapter 10

"Don't move," the cop behind the gun warned. "Or you'll taste lead."

What happened to the right to remain silent and all that crap? That they didn't even bother to say the words meant they were after us specifically.

Obviously, it *had* been Gautier in the shadows. But why would he send state coppers after us rather than Directorate personnel?

Though we *had* stopped, maybe the reason was that simple. We would have been more suspicious of an un-marked car swooping down on us so quickly.

My fingers tightened around the door handle, but otherwise, I obeyed the cop's orders. The fact that Quinn hadn't reacted in any way had me worried. Until I knew what was going on, I intended to play along with the current scenario.

"We were only speeding," I said, forcing fear into

my voice. "Surely pointing guns at us is a bit of an overreaction?"

The cop ignored me, looking over the top of the car again. It suggested they considered me no threat. They'd learn soon enough just how wrong they were.

"The vamp out of action?" the cop with the gun asked.

"Yeah. The new tasers certainly do the work."

Tasers. Great. That was all we'd needed. Though the weapons had been around for a while, it had only been recently they'd developed one with the right electrical current to affect vampires every bit as efficiently as humans. Quinn would be out of action for hours.

A hand reached into the car and, out of the corner of my eye, I saw the wig being tugged off. "It's definitely not Brown."

So Gautier *had* been suspicious of Quinn rather than me. I wondered what Quinn had done or said to tip him off.

"You want to call the retrieval in to headquarters," the gunman continued, "and ask what they want us to do with them?"

The other cop made a grunt of agreement and walked away. I waited a few more seconds then grabbed the gun, wresting it from the cop's hand as I thrust open the door.

He staggered backward with a yelp of surprise. I threw the gun into the back and flowed out of the car, knocking the cop out before he knew what had hit him.

A booming retort bit through the silence. I dove for the shadows along the side of the road, heard the scream of air, and the sharp sting of pain as the bullet scraped my rump, then I hit the ground and rolled to my feet. Wrapping the shadows around myself, I ran toward the other car. The second cop was still standing near the car door, his gun aimed at the spot where I'd disappeared from sight.

I shook my head. When were the authorities going to learn and stop pairing two humans together? It made no sense, not with the introduction of recent incentives that included a fresh, free blood supply to vamps who joined the force. Of course, the Directorate skimmed the cream, while the psych and physical tests prevented a good percentage of the remainder from joining the cop ranks. But there was such an influx of applicants it could take years for the cops to work down the remaining list.

I picked up a small stone and padded quietly to the back of the car. The cop was starting to look around. I tossed the stone, waited until it clicked against the road up ahead, then let the shadows unravel and ran at him. He never stood a chance. I had the speed and power of both wolf and vampire, and he was only human. I tucked his unconscious body into the car, turned off the camcorder, then collected the second cop and shoved him into the car as well. Then I ran back to Quinn.

I didn't bother feeling for a pulse, mainly because the slow metabolic rate of vamps would make it extremely difficult to find one at the best of times. I unclipped his seat belt and dragged him around to the passenger side. Once he was safely belted back in, I ran around to the driver's side and started the car. Cop central would have called in reinforcements once they'd seen what was happening. We had to get off the freeway, and get rid of the Porsche, as quickly as possible.

But I didn't take the first off-ramp, continuing on instead to the Mickleham Road exit. The mob Quinn had hired the Porsche from had a depot at the airport, but I couldn't risk taking the car there with Quinn unconscious. Mickleham Road had an old hotel not far from the freeway, one with the parking tucked nicely around the back and stairs rather than elevators to the rooms. I'd get a room and dump Quinn there, then get rid of the car and return.

I pulled off the wig and took out the lenses as I waited for the lights to turn green. Looking a whole lot less ghostly, I pulled into the hotel and stopped at the side of reception rather than out the front under the bright lights. After grabbing my purse from the security box behind the passenger seat, I did up my coat and climbed out. No sense in giving the woman the wrong idea.

As it turned out, I shouldn't have bothered. The woman at the counter wouldn't have cared who rented the room as long as they paid up front. When I not only paid up front but asked for their best room—which turned out to be their one and only honeymoon suite—she practically danced on the spot. Obviously, times were a little tough with all the new hotels opening at the airport.

I drove around to the back and parked. After opening the room's door, I half carried, half dragged Quinn up the stairs, mighty glad the place was almost empty or that no one came out to investigate the source of all the noise. Explanations weren't something I could be bothered with just then. I made him comfortable on the bed and wrote him a note, leaving it on the table with the folders, the gun, and my wig so he'd see them all if he woke, then headed out.

Returning the car proved no problem, so I headed

over to the less exotic rental area and hired an every-day-type Ford.

By the time I got back to the hotel, an hour had passed and Quinn was still out of it. I grabbed the phone and dialed Jack's vid phone, which had been left with Liander. Only it wasn't Liander who answered, it was Jack.

"What are you doing back?" I asked, worried something had gone wrong.

"We got in and out faster than we'd expected. Listen, I can't talk long. Alex tells me a tracer has been placed on this number. You've got one minute, max."

"Gautier ran into us as we were coming out of Brown's room. He didn't recognize me, but something tipped him off that Quinn wasn't Brown. He set the cops after us. We were pulled over, and Quinn's been tasered unconscious. It could be a while before we get there."

"Alex mentioned that an alert had been placed on the car. She didn't countermand it because we want to see where this all leads. You obviously coped."

"Obviously," I said dryly. "And no, I'm not hooked on the adrenaline rush of it."

He laughed. "Did Quinn place the bug?"

"Yes. And we found a couple of interesting files that speak of a White Phantom Project."

"Good. Don't worry about hurrying back because the cops have set up security checks on the freeway, and they'll be there until peak hour. We can't do anything else now until we have the cover of darkness again, anyway."

A whole day to play with Quinn. How cool was that?

"What grid reference are you?" he continued.

I hesitated, trying to remember the codes, then converting the name of the hotel into something that resembled map references. I passed them on, and he grunted.

"Call if there's trouble or if you shift location."

"Will do." I replaced the receiver, then walked over to the old spa that dominated the corner of the room. Big enough for two to play in. My smile grew when I saw the line of essential oils against the wall. Paying for the honeymoon suite had its benefits.

I threw the coat and dress on the nearby chair and continued on to the bathroom to inspect my shot butt.

It wasn't bad, just a scrape that stretched from one cheek to the other. It hadn't even bled much. I took a quick shower to wash all of Liander's goop from my skin, then toweled off and padded naked to the bed. Quinn didn't stir when I climbed in beside him. I half wished I'd taken the time to strip him completely, because skin was far better than cloth to curl up against. But right then, I didn't have the energy to get up and complete the task. Besides, my imagination was up to pretending. With a smile teasing my lips, I closed my eyes and went to sleep.

When I woke hours later, it was to the reality of flesh pressing against flesh and the pounding of desire through my veins. Breath caressed my shoulder, punctuated by butterfly kisses that sent shivers of pleasure coursing through me.

When I stirred, his fingers brushed from my hip to my stomach and flowed upward. My breath caught in anticipation. Tension quivered through every muscle, so that when his thumb rubbed one aching nipple, it felt like I was going to explode. For several seconds, I couldn't even breathe, the need was so bad.

"Do you know how frustrating it is to wake beside a beautiful woman," he said, the seductive lilt back in his soft voice, "and find yourself fully clothed?"

Oh, I understood frustration, all right. I'd been experiencing it, in one form or another, since he'd walked naked into my life.

"Clothes have never stopped anyone with determination." I turned around to face him. His dark hair was damp and his face free of the muck that had made his handsome features ghastly. I ran a finger down his still-wet cheek and outlined his lips. "How are you feeling?"

"As horny as hell." His lips parted, drawing my fingertip into his mouth, sucking on it gently. Anticipation crashed through me. I couldn't wait for him to sample other parts in the same manner.

"How are you feeling?" he continued, after a few moments.

"Much better now that you're awake and aware."

His hand was resting on my hip again and the heat of his touch flared through me, spreading like a wave that had my whole body tingling. He might want our first "real" lovemaking session to be a long slow seduction of the senses, but I didn't think he had much hope. Not given the need that surged between us.

"Do you remember what happened last night?"

He frowned, but there was a distracted look to his eyes as his fingers began another agonizingly slow journey up my body. "Not much after that cop reached my door."

"He used a taser on you. Gautier did suspect us."

"Lucky, then, that the woman with me was capable enough to take over when things got tough."

I grinned. "Very lucky. Had to give the Porsche back though. You'll have to settle for a Ford."

"Right now, the car is the last thing on my mind."

I raised an eyebrow, a smile playing on my lips. "So what *is* on your mind?"

"This." His hand slipped behind my neck, his fingers tangling in my hair as he brought my lips to his. Suddenly we were kissing as if our lives depended on it. And maybe they did, because I'd sure as hell bust if he didn't fully consummate the tension that had been simmering between us since the beginning.

After what seemed like hours we came up for air. The rapid pounding of my heart was a cadence that filled the silence, accompanied by the heated rush of blood through my system.

I opened my eyes, stared into his. Saw the desire burning bright—desire that was both sexual and blood need. He was controlling both urges, but the first only just.

He kissed me again, and whatever slivers of control *I'd* had were totally and irreparably smashed by the force of it. By the passion behind it.

No one had ever kissed me like that before.

But right then it wasn't his kiss I wanted. I was ready for everything he could give.

I pushed him onto his back and climbed on top, claiming him in the most basic way possible. He groaned, his hands sliding to my hips, pressing me down harder. I arched upright, echoing his groan at the way he filled me, completed me, in a way not even Talon had. It was almost as if I'd found that one perfect piece of the puzzle, the one and only fragment designed to perfectly fit the space that was me.

He began to move, and thought became impossible.

All I could do was move with him, savoring and enjoying the sensations flowing through me.

Then he reared up and pulled my legs around his hips so that I was sitting in his lap, impaled by his body, my breasts crushed against his chest. His dark eyes burned into mine, stirring me in ways I'd never thought possible.

"I want to be kissing you when I come inside you," he all but growled.

The words were barely out of his mouth, and I was there, kissing him, tasting him, my arms wrapped around his neck, holding him close as he moved inside me. My body quivered with the sensations tumbling through me, my thighs clenched against his sides as the pressure built and built, until I felt so tightly strung that everything would surely break. Then everything did break, and I was unraveling, groaning, with the intensity of the orgasm flowing through me. His kiss became as fierce as his body, and as he poured himself into me, his mouth left mine, his teeth grazing my neck. I jerked reflexively when they pierced my skin, but the brief flare of pain quickly became something undeniably exquisite, and I came a second time.

When the tremors subsided, he took my face between his hands and gently kissed me. "Now that the edge has been taken off need, we can get a bit more serious."

"Can't get much more serious than what we just did." My lips were close to his, and as he breathed out, I breathed in. It felt as if the very essence of him was invading every pore.

The heat in his gaze lit fires deep in my soul, yet I had the strangest feeling that I hadn't even begun to plumb the depths of what this vampire could do to me.

He brushed another kiss across my lips, then said, "How much time do we have left to us?"

"All day. Jack doesn't want us back until dusk."

"Then I have time enough to seduce you as I'd originally intended." He paused, and his devilish grin made an appearance, causing my heart to stutter. "And time enough to make you scream."

I smiled. What a very male thing to say. "I don't scream for anyone."

He raised an eyebrow. "Then you haven't been loved right." He lightly slapped my hip. "Off, woman. I have a seduction to attend to."

I slipped to one side and stretched out on the bed. He twisted around, retrieving the gossamer dress from the chair. "Let me tie your hands together."

"Why?"

"Because this is about me pleasuring you. I don't want you touching me just yet."

Excitement surged, and I held out my hands. I'd tried restraints in the past and couldn't really say that I'd tripped on the experience, but the dress was flimsy and I could tear free if I needed to. He tied my hands together, then sat back and spent a minute simply looking at me. The hunger in his eyes made me grin.

"See something you like?" I teased, shifting my hips provocatively.

"I see lots of things I intend to taste. But for now, turn over."

I did as ordered, then watched him walk over to the spa. The man looked great from all angles, but he certainly had a fantastic butt. He leaned over the tub, giving me not only a view of great butt, but well-hung balls and lovely muscular thighs as he grabbed one of the essentials oils. "Cinnamon should do, I think."

He'd picked my favorite scent. I smiled, watching him walk back, amazed to see that he was more than ready to go again. A vamp's stamina was indeed every bit as good as a werewolf's. He knelt at the end of the bed, poured a large dollop of oil into his hands, and rubbed them together.

"Close your eyes," he ordered.

I did as he bid, and sighed in pleasure when his thumbs pressed into the arch of my foot. As he deftly began working the oil into my skin, the rich scent of warmed cinnamon curled through the air, arousing my senses almost as much as the gentle, erotic caress of his fingers. Gradually, he worked his way up my leg, his fingers weaving a spell that left me both aroused *and* relaxed.

When he finished one leg, he started the other. I was all but thrumming with pleasure, totally enjoying every nuance of this sensual pampering.

"What happened here?" he said, his finger lightly tracing the bullet burn.

"One of the cops tried to rearrange my rump."

"Obviously he doesn't know perfection when he sees it."

"I think he was more worried about the fact his partner had just been knocked out by a scrap of woman."

He was straddling me now, his fingers working their way up my back. If I'd been a cat, I would have been purring.

"I don't think anyone would call you a scrap of woman."

As if to emphasize his point, his fingers brushed the sides of my breasts, sending tingles of electricity through every nerve ending.

"Well, I'm certainly not an amazon."

His smile was a warmth I felt rather than saw. "On the outside, no. But inside, there's a warrior desperate to get out."

"No warrior, just a woman ready and willing to defend herself and her pack."

Quinn's fingers worked their magic on my neck and shoulders, and by the time he'd finished, I was all but boneless. And as horny as hell. When he climbed off, I sighed in disappointment. I'd more than half hoped he would have finished what he'd started and take me from behind.

"Roll over," he commanded again.

I did. He drew my arms over my head and tied the free end of the dress to the headboard. Then he moved down to my feet and began the whole massage process again, this time holding my gaze every inch of the way and taking extra care, and extra time, once he'd got to my breasts. It was an erotic and sensual experience, and by the time he'd finished, every inch of me was quivering with the need to have him deep inside.

But the carnal glint in his eyes, and his sexy, knowing smile, suggested he had no intentions of hurrying.

"Now it's challenge time." His low, rich tones vibrated across my skin, as intimate as any kiss. "I intend to make you scream for me, Riley."

"Not a hope in hell." Yet even as I said it, I had a vague suspicion that if any man could, it would be this vampire.

He reached across me, placing the capped oil on the bedside table, then leaned down and brushed a kiss across my mouth. "Then let the games begin," he said, his breath as hot as the glint in his dark eyes.

I grinned. "Go for it."

And he did. Using mouth and tongue alone, he left no part of my upper body untouched or unexplored. He discovered erogenous zones I had no idea existed, and exploited them to the full, bringing me to the crest of orgasm time and again, only to back away each time, until sweat sheened my body and every inch of me vibrated with the need for release.

Then he moved down.

When his tongue flicked over my clitoris, I jumped in sweet bliss, a whimper escaping my lips. He chuckled softly, his breath fiery against my moist skin. Then he suckled on me, and that was the end of any form of restraint on my part. I leapt over that edge with abandon, twisting and moaning and shaking as he continued to stroke and suckle me.

The trembling had barely subsided when he said softly, "Are you ready to scream for me, Riley?"

His breath caressed my thighs, a kiss of air that had me quivering. I closed my eyes, enjoying the sensation, wanting him inside and yet wanting to prolong this lovemaking session as long as I could.

"I told you, I don't scream for anyone."

It came out breathy, and he chuckled softly. "Then I shall continue as I am."

He did. And every bit as thoroughly as the first time, only this time he used his hands rather than his tongue and mouth. He brought me to the edge so very quickly, but this time offered no release, backing away, claiming my mouth, kissing me fiercely and thoroughly, until the threatening tremors had subsided. Then he started all over again.

I'd wanted foreplay, and now I was getting it—in spades. Only I wasn't sure if I was going to survive it much longer.

"Please," I panted. "Oh, God, please . . . I need you . . . inside."

He knelt over the top of me, his body as hot and as sweaty as mine, his grin wicked. "You know the price."

"Yes, yes, anything. Just do it."

He reached above me, undoing my hands, then shifted slightly so that the long hard length of his erection nuzzled me, seeking but not entering. "Shall we take it long and slow?"

I made a strangled sound and he chuckled. "Didn't think so."

With one swift, hard stroke, he was inside, and it was such a sweet, glorious relief I almost wept. Then he began to move, thrusting deep and strong, and there was no calm, no control, in any of his actions now. It was madness and passion and heat and intensity, and though I could barely even breathe let alone think, I knew this is what I had been seeking, what had been missing in my life. Because it was more than just sex, more than just a connection of bodies and desire. It was almost as if in this one, glorious moment in time, we'd become one, physically *and* spiritually.

Then his teeth entered my neck, and everything exploded into ecstasy. Together, we fell screaming over that edge, plunging into a sea of bliss more powerful than anything I'd ever experienced.

When I remembered how to breathe again, I took his face between my palms and kissed him long and slow. "That was amazing."

He rolled to one side and gathered me in his arms. "And I made you scream."

His warm, sexy tones held a hint of contented male

arrogance and I smiled. "Only because I needed you inside."

He chuckled softly and brushed a sweaty strand of hair from my forehead. "Sounds to me like I have to prove it was no fluke."

And I thought Talon had stamina. I smiled and dropped a kiss on his chin. "Sounds like."

Over the course of the day, he did indeed prove it was no fluke.

But late in the afternoon, as we lay hot and sweaty and entangled in each other's arms, I knew I was in deep, deep trouble. Because the intensity that burned between us suggested this vampire could be more than just a sex partner.

It didn't matter that I barely knew him. Didn't matter that he didn't want me in *any* way other than physically. I had no more control over my emotions than I did the moon urges.

I wanted him. Wanted to explore the full boundaries of what we had.

Only *that* was the last damn thing *he* wanted.

But as I'd warned him not so long ago, I was a wolf ready to fight for what she believed in.

And I was more than willing to fight for the possibilities that lay unexplored between me and this vampire.

Well, well," Rhoan said, his gaze jumping from me to Quinn and back again as we walked up the path toward him. "Looks to me like a good time has been had by all."

I grinned. "We didn't have a pack of cards handy, and had to do *something* to while away the time."

His gaze centered on the bite scar on my neck. Quinn had been careful to keep using the same entry point, so that I didn't have bite marks littering my neck. But we'd made love more than a few times, and the wounds were taking a little longer than normal to heal.

"Hope you didn't exhaust her too much. We have a lot planned for tonight."

What he was really saying was that he hoped Quinn hadn't taken too much blood, and we all knew it.

Quinn placed a hand on Rhoan's shoulder and squeezed lightly. "I took no more than necessary." He looked at me, a smile touching his lips. "And if you're worried about anyone getting exhausted, try worrying about me."

"I didn't hear any complaints at the time," I said dryly.

His smile grew, making my hormones do their mad dance. "Nor are you ever likely to. You can exhaust me anytime you like." His gaze switched to Rhoan. "Where's Liander? I need to return his modulators."

"Inside cooking dinner. Apparently he likes my attempts about as much as my sister does."

Quinn's gaze took in mine for a moment, then he headed inside. I followed, enjoying the view before heading upstairs to get some decent clothes on. Then I went back outside and plopped down on the bench beside my brother. "So, how did last night go?"

"A cinch, once the power was knocked out. The guards were out in force, but there weren't any vampires amongst them, and both Jack and I were careful to neutralize our scent beforehand."

"Did you find anything?"

He snorted softly. "Sperm and eggs, and lots of them."

"Did you find and destroy your lot?"

"I believe so. We found some interesting files, but other than that, nothing. As we suspected, Moneisha is little more than a collecting point. It's not where these duplicates are coming from."

"So they weren't set up for research of any kind?"

"Yeah. But basic stuff."

I frowned. "I thought it was Moneisha who had isolated the cluster of genes that make a vampire a vampire?"

He gave me a perplexed look. "Where did you hear that?"

"It was apparently reported in the newspapers."

"Not in any I've read."

Now *I* was confused. "Maybe we don't read the right papers."

"Who told you that they had?"

"Misha. He said there'd been protests outside Moneisha because of their genetic research."

"There have been protests all right, but mainly because they've been buying up residences in the area with the intention of expanding."

"Maybe Misha mixed up a couple of stories." Yet even as I said it, I doubted it was the case. Misha had the best memory I'd ever come across.

"Maybe." Rhoan didn't sound any more convinced than I was.

I chewed on my lip for a moment, then asked, "Have you found out any information about Konane?"

"Who?"

"Konane. They apparently own Moneisha."

"Where did you hear this? Because I know Director

Hunter is still working her way through the paper trail."

"Misha told me."

He frowned. "I wonder how he knew?"

"I can ask, when I next see him."

"Tell Jack and see what he says." He paused. "So how come Gautier suspected you?"

I shrugged. "I don't know. He was standing at the office door as we were coming out. Maybe he heard something."

"Those offices are soundproof."

"Then either he has a nose as sensitive as a wolf or something Quinn said tipped him off. Though what that could be, I have no idea."

Rhoan frowned. "You know, the few times I've worked with him, I've noticed he has extraordinarily keen senses for a vamp. If he *is* one of the lab-built creatures, then maybe he *has* got the nose of a wolf."

I leaned back against the sun-warmed wall of the old shed. "Has Jack checked all the military installations? Couldn't this be a government program?"

"The military is certainly working on implanting vampire genes into other nonhuman races, but from what Jack says, the longest any of them has lived is a couple of years."

I remembered the smell in the parking garage. Remembered the feeling I was facing dead—or at least dying—things. "Whoever is behind this, I don't think they're having much luck in the longevity stakes, either."

"They're living long enough to do some pretty nasty stuff."

I raised an eyebrow. "Like what?"

He hesitated. "You know we've had ten guardians

gone missing?" When I nodded, he continued, "From what we can glean from the remains of those we've found, it appears they might have been forced to fight for their lives in some kind of arena."

I closed my eyes and prayed that Kelly hadn't joined their number. Hadn't become just another means of testing some madman's grotesque creations.

She didn't deserve that sort of end. None of the guardians had.

But once again I shoved the thought away, not wanting to face the hurt of it until the moment hope was totally gone and I knew for sure she was dead. "Obviously, the bodies were dumped in areas out of the sunlight; otherwise, there wouldn't be any remains to study. Which in itself suggests someone wanted the Directorate to find the remains."

He nodded. "Jack says there was an enormous amount of growth accelerant in the body of the vamp they discovered in Quinn's plane. And the prelim results Quinn got back on Gautier's clones also show high dosages."

I frowned. "Sounds like they don't really care if their creations live all that long."

"Maybe just long enough to complete a task." His expression was grim when it met mine. "A vampire's body degenerates pretty quickly once he's dead. Can you think of a better killing machine than one designed to get in, do its job, then self-destruct before any evidence can be pulled from it?"

"It's not something I actually want to think about." I watched a willy wagtail flit across the backs of the nearby cows. "How come Gautier has been allowed to stay with the Directorate? Especially after his clones started appearing everywhere?"

"We think Gautier is working with someone in the Directorate—someone other than Alan Brown. Until we can ferret that person out, Gautier stays. It's better to have an enemy where you can watch him."

"You're not exactly watching him now."

"Director Hunter is."

"Ah." I closed my eyes, listening to the wind keening through the nearby gums. The storm that had hit Melbourne earlier that afternoon was on its way. "As a guardian, Gautier has to undergo regular health checks. I'm gathering nothing out of the ordinary has ever been found?"

"No. And Jack's told you about his history—or lack thereof."

"Yeah. Bit by little bit."

Rhoan grinned. "He wants you in the program, sis, and he's just trying to reel you in."

"So he's already said."

The man in question came out of the trees as I spoke.

"Riley," he said, a smile touching his lips but his eyes all seriousness. "We need to talk if you can give me a moment."

I glanced at Rhoan, who shrugged at my unasked question. I pushed to my feet, and said, "Sure."

Jack followed the path back into the trees and I trailed him. We walked down to the dam and stood on the edge, watching dragonflies buzz the water.

"What's up?" I said, after a moment.

"Something you may not like." He looked at me, green eyes hard with anger. "You remember the blood sample I took?"

My stomach dropped. "Yes."

"We got some interesting results back."

I briefly closed my eyes, not sure I really wanted to hear this. "So, I was drugged?"

"Yes. There was N529, a fast-knockout drug designed for use on nonhumans, and one which is not due to come onto the market until next month. The other was ARC1-23."

I raised an eyebrow. "Which is?"

"It's a drug that's still on the experimental list because of the serious side effects it appears to have on some nonhumans." He hesitated. "It seems someone is trying to get you pregnant."

Chapter 11

For several seconds I didn't react, simply stared at him. Then anger surged and I clenched my fists, wishing I had something—someone—to hit. "I'm going to kill the bastard."

Actually, killing him was too quick. Maybe I'd settle for ripping his fucking balls off.

"I gather you know who's behind it?"

I nodded and began to pace. "One of my regular mates was talking about me having his child recently."

"But you didn't consent to take this drug?"

I snorted. "Hardly. If I ever do take the risk of having kids, it'll be with someone I love, not with someone I just fuck."

"Have you still got the chip in your arm?"

"Shit." I ran my fingers up my arm, and found the small lump under my skin. Relief slithered. Thank *God*.

"We need to do more tests," Jack continued, obviously reading my relief correctly.

I frowned. "Why?"

"Because the quantities of ARC1-23 in the blood sample suggest you've been given this drug over a couple of months, and, as I said, it's known to have some serious side effects."

I pushed my hair away from my face and began to pace again. The anger surging through my body wouldn't allow me to remain still. "What kind of side effects are we talking about?"

"It seems the drug can mutate once in the body, altering not only its own chemistry but the chemistry of the host."

"That . . . that . . . "

Jack nodded, as if in understanding. "The drug had passed all lab trials, so they decided to run a series of tests on some volunteers who were having trouble conceiving, using a mix of humans, shifters, and werewolves. Of the fifty who were in the first trial, ten were unaffected. Thirty became pregnant, and had normal gestations and births, with neither the parent nor the child showing any adverse reactions to the drug. The remaining ten, however, began to transmute in one way or another."

With the way my luck had been running of late, I wouldn't be one of the lucky ones who was completely unaffected. I wouldn't even be one of the ones who got pregnant. I blew out a breath and changed my mind. I was going to rip the bastard's balls off, *then* kill him. "Why did it affect some and not others?"

"Studies undertaken suggest it might have something to do with the fact that the ten who changed rather than getting pregnant were all of mixed heritage."

His expression was grim and somewhat speculative.

I didn't have to read his thoughts to know he was thinking about *my* mixed heritage. I felt like screaming. Jesus, as if I didn't already have enough weirdness in my life.

"So where did they find so many crossbreeds?" Breeding between nonhuman races—especially other shifters and werewolves—was extremely rare. Though we were sexually compatible, something in our genetics made it next to impossible for one breed of shifter to impregnate another naturally.

"They advertised throughout Australia. Natural crossbreeding may be rare, but it does happen."

"How long was it before the side effects became apparent?"

"The trial was conducted over a year. It was six months before the side effects started to show. Up until then, everything had been proceeding exactly as expected."

So I had months to wait before I'd know one way or another. I kicked some stones out from under my foot, watching them splash into the water. Dragonflies buzzed the ripples, their wings jewel-like in evening light. "And how is the drug taken?"

"Via injection, once a month."

I closed my eyes. Talon had been giving me the injections for at least two months, then. Why else had I been blacking out after drinking his "fine" champagne? "I knew he was single-minded when it came to getting his own way, but I never thought he'd go this damn far."

"I gather we're talking about Talon Lasalle?"

I squinted up at Jack. "How did you know?"

"Had him investigated." His sudden smile was wry. "You may think of yourself as little more than a paper pusher, but the truth is, you work in a sensitive area and know more about the workings of the place than most of the directors. The Directorate has many enemies, and the information you and the other liaisons hold could be extremely useful to those intent on our destruction." He shrugged. "So I know exactly who all my people spend time with."

"You investigate everyone we come in contact with?"

He snorted softly. "Hardly. We haven't the manpower. Just those who feature prominently in your life. The only reason Liander is involved in this mission is because I know all there is to know about him—and his exemplary record in the military. He'd make a good addition to the new team I want to set up."

"You'd have as much hope conning Liander as you've had with me."

"He's not as stubborn as you."

I ignored the gibe. "So what did your reports say about Misha and Talon?"

"Talon is a very successful entrepreneur with fingers in all sorts of pies—and many of those companies have fingers in other pies, not all of which we've tracked down yet. He's ruthless when it comes to getting what he wants but has never stepped beyond the law—as far as we know."

"Until it came to wanting a kid," I muttered. "What about Misha?"

"Misha's even more difficult to pin down. He's very successful, but as yet we're not exactly sure how."

I frowned. "He owns Rollins Enterprises."

Jack nodded. "Which has suffered five years of substantial losses, yet Misha's personal fortune keeps getting larger."

"Undoubtedly thanks to good investments." Like the South Bank apartment complex.

"Damn good. Only, as yet, we can't locate all of them."

I stared at him for a moment, not sure what to think. "You think Misha's a crook?"

"I honestly don't know, because both the gold and silver packs are notoriously tight when it comes to giving out information about pack members and money. I do know he's covered his tracks very well, and my instincts suggest he's up to something. While I doubt *that* something involves the Directorate, I *am* sure it involves you in some way."

I rubbed a hand across my eyes. The day that had started out so well was becoming positively shitty. "Why haven't you mentioned this before now?"

"Because I haven't any evidence that he *is* up to something. My instincts could be wrong. It wouldn't be the first time."

I took a deep breath and released it slowly. Misha and I were going to have a heart-to-heart when he got back. If I didn't get answers that satisfied me—and Jack—he was struck off my list, right alongside Talon.

And to think only a couple of days ago I'd been blissfully happy with them both.

"So how did Talon get hold of ARC1-23 if it's not on the market?"

"It's his company doing the fertility research."

Fingers in every pie, as Jack had said. "He doesn't know I'm part vampire. He probably thought it was safe to give to me."

"That doesn't excuse what he's done."

"No." I paused, trying to calm another rush of anger. "So what happens now?"

He considered me for a moment. "He'll be charged, of course."

As long as I got to him first, I didn't care what they did to the bastard. "I hear a 'but' after that."

He nodded. "The military badly wants to explore the possibilities of this drug, and Talon is the key to their getting their hands on it."

Meaning, of course, they weren't about to let anything happen to him until they did. "I'm gathering it's no longer being marketed as a possible fertility drug?"

"It's undergoing a larger trial, and test applicants are being carefully screened. After all, it worked for a good percentage of the test group."

I took another deep breath, then asked the one question I'd avoided. "So what, exactly, does it do?"

"It appears to enhance certain abilities. Six of the ten were either human-werewolf crosses or human-shifter. All became able to take on *any* shape."

Relief slithered through me. Taking on any shape was pretty cool when compared to some of the scenarios I'd been imagining. "That doesn't sound too bad a skill to have."

Jack snorted softly. "Yeah, only if they changed too often, they discovered they couldn't change back to human form. Their body chemistry had altered so much the cells no longer remembered true form, and they got stuck in animal form."

Which wasn't a good thing. Death would surely be better than never being able to regain humanity. "And the remaining four?"

"Were shifter and werewolf crosses, and all four had psychic skills. Three of the four were unaware of the fact. These skills were all enhanced to the point where they became dangerous. I believe all four have

now been transferred to one of the military pro-
grams."

I glared at him. "Don't try putting me in any military program."

He gave me a toothy smile I didn't trust one bit.
"Darlin', you're mine. If you go anywhere, it'll be into
the guardian program."

"That ain't going to happen, either."

"You may not have a choice. If that drug does affect
you, it's either us or the military until we discover the
full breadth of the changes."

Then it was the Directorate. But that didn't mean I
was entering the system without a fight. If Jack
wanted me as a guardian, he was going to have to drag
me there kicking and screaming.

"So what happens now?"

"The drug doesn't appear to have had any ill effects
yet, but even so, we'll begin regular blood tests and cell
scans. We'll also begin regular psi tests, in case alter-
ations start showing there."

"I'm telepathic—you know that."

He nodded. "Entry tests also indicated latent skills
in clairvoyance."

"Which is not exactly a skill the military can give a
damn about."

"On the contrary, clairvoyance provides an excellent means of information gathering."

"Yeah, but as you said, it's latent. As in, not active
and not used."

"Granted. But your telepathy skill isn't. Given it
can be used for both information gathering and as a
weapon, it definitely *is* a desirable skill as far as they
are concerned. You already rate high—this drug could
very well put you off the scale."

I didn't want to be off the scale. Didn't want to use my skills for anything more than defense. But I had a vague feeling Talon had taken all choice away from me. I kicked another stone into the dam and imagined it was the head of a certain golden wolf sinking under the murky brown water.

Jack squeezed my shoulder gently. "You could be one of the lucky ones. It might have no effect at all."

My smile was grim. "You don't believe that any more than I do."

He hesitated. "No. But right now, there's nothing we can do about it. Time will provide our answers. Meanwhile, we have a clone factory to hunt down."

I turned and followed him down the path. "Did you know a company named Konane apparently owns Moneisha?"

He glanced over his shoulder. "No. How do you?"

"Misha told me."

"Interesting. Wonder how he knows—and why he told you."

"Because I asked him."

"Maybe you should ask him a few other things—like whether he knows anything about the clones or the crossbreeds."

"I can if you want."

"Might be worth a try. In the meantime, I'll get a search done on Konane."

"You don't think the crossbreeds are coming out of the same factory as the clones?"

"No, and the evidence that Quinn has collected confirms it."

Rhoan was no longer sitting out in front of the cabin when we arrived. But given the delicious smell of roasting meat that hung on the air, he was probably inside harassing Liander to hurry up and serve the meal.

"I'll never get tired of that smell," Jack said, taking a deep breath. "Which is why I live above a restaurant."

I opened the door for him and waved him on through. "I always thought the smell of food turned a vampire's stomach."

Jack shook his head. "Hollywood myth. You of all people should know better than to believe something like that."

"Hey, some myths sound very reasonable."

"Sounding reasonable doesn't make them so."

He moved over to the table and I looked around for Quinn. He wasn't in the living area, but a second later he came rattling down the stairs. His gaze met mine, dark eyes warm and filled with hunger. The fever surged through my veins, its intensity soaking me in an instant. And the full moon was still two days away. If the mission went on much longer, I'd be in trouble. The fever was still leashed, but the sheer force of it suggested it wouldn't remain that way too long.

"Hey, pretty lady," he said, wrapping an arm around my waist and pulling me close. "Guess what?"

"What?" I said, my voice little more than a husky whisper. God, he felt so good pressed up against me that my hormones were begging me to drop him to the ground and shag him senseless.

"Rhoan and I drew straws. We won the bed tonight."

I linked my hands behind his neck and kissed his chin. "Meaning we're under the stars tomorrow?"

"Afraid so. But the weathermen say it'll be fine."

"It doesn't matter anyway, because I've had scout training. I'll make us a shelter."

His grin was decidedly wicked. "Shame you didn't bring the uniform along. Wouldn't mind seeing you in that."

I raised an eyebrow. "Got a fetish for women in uniform, have you?"

"Especially when they're leggy redheads." His breath caressed my mouth, then his lips found mine and our kiss became a long, slow seduction that had my knees wanting to buckle.

"Enough, you two," came Rhoan's comment from behind Quinn. "Some of us have to stomach food."

I came up for air and accepted the plate my brother shoved at me. "What's this?"

Rhoan gave me a flat look. "What does it look like?"

"I don't know. I think it resembles steak and fries, but it can't be. I mean, it's not black."

He picked a bean off my plate and flicked it at me. His steak, I noted, was very, very rare. "When we get home, you're on cooking duty."

I caught the bean midair and shoved it in my mouth. "That means you do the laundry, bro." Which was a good threat, because Rhoan hated washing as much as I hated cooking. We both hated ironing, which was why our living room was overflowing with clean, unironed clothes. "Maybe you should take some cooking lessons from your lover."

"I can think of better things to do with my lover."

"So can I," Quinn whispered into my ear.

I blew a breath across my forehead, but it did little to ease the fever assailing my skin. Why did I have to meet this man right in the middle of a disaster?

"When you're ready, people," Jack said from the table.

I glanced past my brother and saw Jack had laid the maps we'd found out on the table. At one end was his computer unit, currently lit up with diagrams. I followed Rhoan over and sat down. Quinn sat next to me, his knee brushing mine and sending little tremors of electricity up my leg.

"I scanned in the diagrams you found and did a cross-check of all known military installations," Jack said. "We found three possibles—all of them sold off fifty years ago by the government."

"Any idea who owns them or what they're now used for?" Quinn said, his gaze on the computer screen.

"One was bought by a residential development company and now has several thousand homes on it. Another is currently owned by Hoyle-Brantin, who make household products. The last one is owned by a company called Nashoba, which lists itself as being a cosmetics research and marketing organization."

I raised an eyebrow. "Nashoba is not a brand of makeup I've ever heard of."

"Nor I," Liander said, and flashed me a bright smile. "And I probably use more makeup in a day than you use in a year."

"When you're naturally beautiful like me, you don't need makeup," I said, and ducked the fries thrown at me.

"Considering Nashoba itself doesn't seem to exist," Jack commented, "I'm not surprised you haven't heard of it."

"It's a front for another company?" Quinn asked.

Jack nodded. "The paper trail is a mile long. The computer system is working on it as we speak."

"We seem to be hitting more than our fair share of paper trails lately," Rhoan said.

"And while the computer system searches, what are we going to do?" Quinn said.

"Undertake our own search of both premises."

"How well guarded are they?" I shoved some steak in my mouth and groaned when it all but melted in my mouth. Damn, I'd forgotten how good a properly cooked steak was. I gave a thumbs-up to Liander.

"Nashoba is extremely well guarded. Rhoan and I will be tackling that. Hoyle-Brantin has foot patrols and wire fences. Nothing you can't get around."

I nodded. "You got floor plans?"

He pushed over some paperwork. "It's pretty similar to what you saw in the plans you retrieved from Brown's office though there's a new wing added to the main building."

I took a quick look at them, then kept eating.

"What about the White Phantom Project—did you discover anything about that?" Quinn asked.

Jack shook his head. "There's nothing on the records, and Alex can't recall the project. White Phantom might have been a code name for something else. I've scanned the contents through to her so she can cross-check."

"And the disks?"

He looked at me. "I posted those. She doesn't mind a bit of voyeurism."

Normally, I didn't either, but the thought of watching Brown doing the nasty over and over was enough to turn me off.

"So when do we hit these places?" Rhoan asked.

Jack gave him a wry smile. "Given the approaching

full moon and the fact that three of my current staff are werewolves, as soon as possible."

Rhoan pushed his empty plate away. "How are we stocked in the way of equipment?"

"You and I will have to stop by the Directorate."

"That safe?"

"We'll take the emergency tunnel. Only the directors can get into it, so if someone does attack us, it'll narrow the field of suspects." Jack glanced at me. "I'll take that blood sample with me, too."

I could feel Rhoan's curious gaze but didn't bother meeting it. If he ever found out what Talon had done, he'd kill him. And I wanted to throw the first punch. "Fine."

Jack glanced at his watch. "We'll leave in half an hour. Liander, you right for holding down the fort again?"

"Do I have any other choice?" His voice was dry, yet something in his pale eyes suggested he wanted action almost as badly as he wanted sex. Perhaps I'd been wrong in my estimation that he'd be as unwilling as I to get involved in Jack's schemes.

"Not on this you don't." Jack hesitated and glanced at Quinn. "You'll have to stay here, too. Riley's Directorate, and I can protect her if she gets into trouble. I can't offer you that."

"I'm not expecting you to. Nor will I be left behind on this."

"I can't let you go."

"You can't stop me, and we both know it." The two men stared at each other for several seconds, then Quinn added, "You know my reasons for doing this."

"Yes." Jack hesitated. "Just don't expect my help if things go wrong."

Quinn's smile was wry. "Forgive me for saying it, but I have more than enough politicians, judges, and lawyers ready and able to help me out of any situation. Being a multibillionaire has its advantages."

Jack nodded and rose. "Let's get this show on the road."

Ten minutes later, Quinn and I were in the car and heading back to Melbourne, him driving and me studying the plans for the old army base in Broadmeadows. "There's an industrial estate on one side and an old graveyard on the other."

Humor crinkled the corners of his eyes as he looked at me. "You're voting the graveyard, aren't you?"

I raised an eyebrow. "Can you think of a more appropriate entry point for the dead and half-dead?"

His soft laugh sent tremors of desire skimming my skin. "No one in his right mind would ever call you half-dead."

I grinned. "You were pretty lively yourself, too."

"And will be again, once we get this little jaunt over and done with."

I couldn't wait. I folded the plans and threw them on the backseat. "So, tell me, why can't Jack stop you? Is it simply an age thing?"

"And the hierarchy system."

"Vampires have a hierarchy?"

He glanced at me. "Of course. The older the vampire, the more powerful he is. Having a power system in place prevents an all-out war—which wouldn't be good for *any* race."

That was an understatement if ever I'd heard one. "Meaning the pecking order is merely a matter of waiting for those above to keel over?"

"Crudely put, but yes."

"So what's to stop an underling aiding that event?"

"The wrath of the others that would fall on him or her if it happened."

I couldn't see how that was going to prevent unexplained deaths, especially if the one bumping off the hierarchy was more powerful than everyone else. But then, vampires generally didn't think like the rest of us. "Where do you stand in the pecking order?"

"There are three above me."

"And I'm guessing Director Hunter is one of them? That's why you phoned her—a vampire professional courtesy."

He nodded. I frowned. "Jack said he was her brother—but if she's older than you, and he's younger, how can that be the case?"

He shrugged. "Madrilene and Jack come from shifter stock, and shifters, like werewolves, are extremely long-lived. Perhaps Jack didn't turn until near the end of his life."

My frown deepened. "Madrilene? Do you mean Alex?"

"Yes." He hesitated. "Madrilene is the name she used when we first met."

"Meaning vamps change names over the years?"

"Yes. And yes, I have also."

"So Quinn is not your birth name?"

"First name, no. But Quinn is the anglicized form of my Irish surname, O'Cuinn."

"Interesting." But it wasn't doing anything to explain how Jack could be just over eight hundred years old and Director Hunter more than Quinn's twelve hundred. By my reckoning, there was at *least* a century unaccounted for, shifter stock or not. But obviously, Quinn wasn't going to explain it. If I wanted answers,

I'd have to ask the source. And whether he'd explain or not was another matter.

"Given what you said about the vampire hierarchy, and the fact that you're older and stronger than Jack is, what's stopping you from putting commands into his mind?"

"He's strong enough to keep me from controlling him. I could overwhelm him and kill him, mentally and physically, but I don't have the strength to keep him under my control."

"Of course, I only have your word on that."

"My word not good enough?"

"A question I can't answer as I don't really know you." I crossed my arms, for a moment regarding the rain-washed road ahead. "Why are you going so determinedly after the people behind the cloning?"

"Jack's already told you—the source material was a friend of mine."

"How good a friend?"

He glanced at me. "Not sexual, if that's what you're implying. He was born Hieremias, son of Glaucus, though he changed it to Henri Glaucus for ease of use in later years. We'd been friends for over a thousand years."

It was hard to imagine knowing *anyone* for that length of time. "How did he die?"

His swift look was cold, hard, and sent shivers down my spine. And yet there was something else in his dark eyes. Something akin to pain.

"Broken heart. He walked into the sunshine and stayed there." He hesitated. "Or so I thought."

What was the betting that it was another bloody werewolf behind the hurt? Geez, I wanted to explore possibilities with him, but did I really have the energy to fight the pain inflicted by the ex as well as what had happened to his friend? Then I remembered the magic we'd created while making love, and thought, *Hell, yeah.*

"Obviously he was captured before he cindered if there are clones of him walking around."

"Yes." He paused again. "When I first saw the clone in Sydney, I was overjoyed, thinking I'd been wrong, that Henri hadn't committed suicide. But a mind search quickly revealed the truth. The clone's memory of life had only started seven and a half years ago."

"So is that why you were attacked here in Melbourne? Because you killed the clone?"

"Possibly—especially if they were aware of my history with Henri. They would have had to realize I'd start searching for him."

"Because of your friendship?"

"Because I owe Henri my life more times than I care to remember."

A loyal vampire. Interesting. "So why would they be cloning Henri? What has he got that a million or so other vamps haven't?"

He gave me a thoughtful look. "You don't read newspapers much, do you?"

I frowned. "What's that got to do with it?"

"Henri was a supreme athlete, and ten years ago was the only man alive who could say he raced in the original Olympics for real, not just in hologram."

"Whoa . . . that makes him—"

"Ancient," Quinn cut in. "When the modern Olympics began, he was a semiregular competitor. When they restarted after World War II, he competed again."

"How? He's vamp, and most events are run in the day."

"He's a very old vampire. Only the midday sun will kill him."

"So how did he race? Nonhumans weren't allowed to compete back then."

His smile was wry. "Back then, they didn't have the technology to separate human from nonhuman. He won quite a number of medals over the years."

"And when the alternative Olympics started?"

"He was a star. He won nearly all track events in the three alternative Olympics before his death. This year, the Australian Olympic Council commemorated his achievements by nominating him for the Sporting Hall of Fame. He was the first vampire ever to be selected, and his story was splashed all over the media."

I was going to have to start taking more interest in the local news. "Whoever is behind this cloning couldn't have known Henri's love affair was going to go wrong and that he'd kill himself."

"Couldn't they?"

The Irish lilt was gone, replaced by harshness. For several seconds I just stared at him. "No way. Why go to that sort of trouble when it would have been simpler to kidnap him?"

"Because this way no one went looking for him."

And in that moment, I understood the pain I'd glimpsed in his dark eyes. *He* hadn't gone looking for his friend. I reached across, placing my hand on his arm. His muscles jumped under my fingers, as if he was resisting the comfort offered. "You couldn't have known."

"But I could have *checked*."

"You would have killed yourself."

His smile was grim. "Maybe. Maybe not."

I had a feeling he wouldn't have really cared either

way as long as he'd discovered the truth. "Did he tell you he was going to commit suicide?"

"No, but I've known him forever. I should have guessed what would happen."

"How could you guess that a man who had lived so many years would kill himself over a worthless were-wolf?"

"Exactly," he growled, then glanced at me, his expression no softer. "Present company excluded."

Present company *not* excluded, and we both knew it. He might allow himself to want me physically, but he would never allow himself to want anything more. Because of his ex. Because of his friend's ex. Which meant no matter how hard I fought to keep exploring, in the end we would part. And that was a damn shame, because we could have been good together. More than good.

"What happened to her?"

"She's dead."

No surprise there. "She didn't tell you anything before you killed her?"

"I didn't kill her. She was dead when I found her."

"And you didn't think that a tiny bit suspicious?"

"Marnie loved fast cars and high speeds. She lost control on a wet road and slammed into a tree. There were witnesses. I thought it justice and let it go."

"Did you question the witnesses?"

His glance was dark. "No. At the time, I had no reason to believe it was anything more than an accident."

"And now that you do?"

"I cannot find the witnesses."

Surprise, surprise. "But why would they snatch someone so famous for the clones? Even if he was the best of the best, surely they must have known the emergence of the clones would eventually raise eyebrows?"

"Not really. Henri's death was widely reported and ten years is enough time to wash away the public's memory of him. Besides, the clones do not resemble him *exactly,* even if they are genetically identical."

"But if you are old friends with Director Hunter, then she would have been aware of your friendship with Henri. Why didn't she mention Gautier's resemblance to him?"

His expression darkened. "Because she was hoping Gautier would lead her to his source."

I studied him for a moment, then said, "And because she knew you'd want immediate action, therefore possibly fouling her own investigation."

"Yes. Not that her investigation has given any results so far."

That was because Gautier was a sneaky bastard. "And in the year you've been hunting these clones, you've made no inroads on where they might be coming from?"

"No. But I'm fairly certain they're not military."

"Why?"

"Because while I have no doubt the military are striving to create the ultimate soldier, I very much doubt that they would allow their creations to walk the streets and raise suspicions."

"So you think it's a private company with visions of taking over the world?"

He smiled. "Maybe just a country or two. Conglomerates these days are into power as much as money. Control the government, and you have the power."

"So bribing or blackmailing politicians has fallen out of favor?"

"Bribing and blackmailing can be traced. Clones would raise far fewer suspicions."

"Clones can be traced as easily as blackmail. The Directorate, and many other government departments, are beginning to install cell scanners and now have regular blood tests in place."

"The cell scans wouldn't pick up irregularities because there would be none. For all intents and purposes, the clone would be identical to the original. And I doubt the blood scans would pick up anything—they haven't in Gautier, have they?"

"Well, no." I frowned. "Why is that, if he is a clone?"

"I have no idea. Perhaps they wean the accelerant off and wait until the blood tests are clear before they slot in their replacements."

"But if they're cloning to grab power, why not start cloning politicians? Why a guardian?"

"Because the process is not yet perfected. While Gautier appears to be without problems, most of the other clones I have come across seem to have the sort of problems usually associated with extreme age."

"Which would surely be connected to the amount of accelerant they're using to develop these things quickly."

"Not necessarily. When cloning was first being explored back in the twentieth century—well before the growth accelerant was discovered—it was noted that cloned species seemed to have age-related problems."

"That didn't stop them."

He smiled. "It's still not stopping anyone. Science and morality are not often bedfellows."

The car crested a hill, and Melbourne lay before us, a sea of bright lights that was quickly lost to the trees again. The shrill ring of my cell phone cut through the brief silence. As I took it out of my pocket to answer it, he gave me a hard glance, and said, "I hope you were intending to turn that off before we broke into the grounds of Hoyle-Brantin."

"Nah," I bit back. "I was intending to leave it on, just so we could have the thrill of being discovered when it rang."

Though the truth was, I'd actually forgotten it was on. I pressed the receive button, expecting it to be Talon demanding to know where I was and why I wasn't panting for him.

Only it was Misha.

And he sounded no happier than Talon would have been.

Chapter 12

hat in hell have you done to Talon?" he said, his fury evident even down the line.

"What in hell does it matter to you?"

"He's harassing me."

That raised my eyebrows. "How can he harass you when you've gone back to your pack and neither he or I know which of the silver packs you come from?"

"I'm back because it turns out my mother was embellishing the truth. My sister had an accident but it wasn't anything major. Mother just wanted me to meet someone she considers a perfect mate."

I had a feeling he wasn't telling me the truth, though the bit about meeting a mate was typical mother behavior. I'd witnessed similar contrivances throughout my teenage years, before we'd been kicked out of our pack. At least neither Rhoan nor I had to worry about that—though part of me wished that we did.

"So what do you want me to do? You're a big boy—deal with it yourself."

"I've tried reason, but he's off the rails." Misha hesitated. "He told me you two were exclusive."

I snorted. "As you said, he's off the rails."

"So if I get rough, you have no objections?"

"Not as long as you leave me enough to kick."

Misha chuckled, and the tension I'd been hearing in his voice eased. "Sorry to get hostile on you, but the last few days have been a bitch, and Talon was the last straw."

So he had rung me to complain? Somehow, I doubted it. Misha was a nice man, yet he was also a very successful businessman, and had always handled problems quickly, often ruthlessly. If he was seriously pissed off with Talon, he'd have done something about it. That he'd called me instead suggested there was an ulterior motive behind his call.

Or was Jack's warning about Misha making me see things that weren't there? "Is that all you rang for?"

"Hell, no. I wanted to know if my car was still in one piece."

I smiled despite my reservations. "It's parked safely at the Crown Casino."

"Why is it parked there?"

"Long story. But it's in one piece."

"A miracle." He hesitated, then added, "Don't suppose you're intending to drive it home anytime soon?"

His voice had dropped several octaves, sliding across my senses like warmed chocolate. Jack might have implanted doubts about him, but that didn't stop me from wanting him.

Though given the moon heat, I'd want the devil himself if he had a nice enough bod.

"I'm on assignment at the moment, but if you can wait, I'll be there."

"I thought you said you were nothing more than a gofer?"

There was an underlying hint of steel in the warmth of his voice that made me frown. "Even gofers at the Directorate get drafted when the need arises."

"So that's what has made Talon crazy," he commented. "You're not at his beck and call."

If Talon was acting crazy, it was because I'd said no—something he was not used to hearing. I doubted he was going crazy over missing me sexually. As good as we were together, he had seven other mates to keep him satisfied.

A hand touched my thigh and warmth scooted across my flesh. My gaze jumped to Quinn's. His face was expressionless as he said, "We're here."

I glanced across the road and saw the old graveyard. "You can't park along this section of Camp Road."

"I realize that, but I don't know the area." His voice was patience itself, but something in his dark gaze hinted at annoyance. Or anger. At what, I had no idea. "You're the one that read the street directory," he added.

"There's a playground ahead on the left. You can park there."

"Who's that?" Misha said into my ear.

"No one important," I replied, and could have sworn Quinn's expression tightened a little. Which was stupid. He was getting what he wanted, and he wanted nothing more. "Look, I have to go. I'll call back."

"Riley, wait—"

I didn't wait, just hung up on him. I'd apologize later, but at present, I had work to do.

I turned off the phone, climbed out of the car, and sniffed the air. The breeze was cold and filled with the scent of rain. Overhead, dark clouds shuttered the light of the stars, and the moon was nowhere to be seen. Yet the power of it crawled under my skin, igniting the fire deep inside. The metal in the car had, to some extent, protected me, but there, out in the open, there was no escape. The fever burned and would need release soon.

But the full moon was still two nights away, and the vampire half of me was keeping the fever within control—for the time being. But while it might be contained, the wolf part still raged, and it hated the restrictions of so many clothes. If I was to remain in control, I needed to appease at least one need. I shucked off my coat and threw it back in the car. My stilettos quickly followed.

"What are you doing?" There was an edge in Quinn's voice as he walked around the back of the car.

"The moon is high and the fever burns. I need to feel the ground under my toes. The wind on my skin." Plus, I couldn't exactly creep around wearing spiked heels, which was all I had with me unless I went home.

His gaze was a caress of heat that slid down my body, lingering on the way the black cotton shirt fit across my breasts and the way the skirt clung to my hips and thighs. Not naked, but not leaving much to the imagination, either.

When his gaze rose to meet mine again, the fever that burned through my blood seemed to echo in his dark eyes. "Do you need relief?"

"Relief?" I arched an eyebrow. "That makes it sound like I've got some disease." And *that* rankled.

"You know what I mean."

"Yes, I do, and no, I don't." I hesitated, giving him my best sweet-as-pie expression—a sure sign the inner bitch was coming out. "Besides, one of the guards might be a wolf. We could celebrate the moon together."

His gaze narrowed dangerously. "The idea is to get in and get out, unobserved."

"Which you can do if I play distraction."

"We stick to the plan," he growled, and grabbed my arm, propelling me down the footpath.

He was only an inch or two taller than I, but I was practically running to keep up with his long strides. I could have pulled free of his grasp easily enough, but truth be told, I liked his touch. And right then, with the moon burning through my system, I didn't care if it was rough or gentle.

We climbed the small fence and strode through the cemetery. The wind stirred the dark pines surrounding the small graveyard so that it sounded like the whisperings of the dead. But if the dead had once lived there, they'd long ago moved out. The tombstones were worn with age and barely readable, the graves overrun by weeds and neglect. Even the dead had pride, and the place would not look so desolate if any of them still remained.

The fence surrounding the old army camp was just as neglected. It wasn't electrified. It wasn't even taut. "I doubt if anything more serious than cleaning products is in development behind that wire."

"No, but we still have to check."

I scanned the nearby darkness but could see nothing except shadows. I switched to infrared. The only thing to find were the small blurs of heat going through the rubbish bins that lined the back of the building ahead.

"Rats," I muttered, my stomach turning as I remembered a drunken teenage eating dare and the resulting days of sickness.

"If rats are all we find, I'll be happy."

He held up the wire and I ducked through. "I thought you wanted to find your friend?"

"I do, but I doubt he'd be here. Whoever is behind this cloning is very clever and very cautious. Lax security would not be part of it. It's too much of a risk."

"But maybe that's why he's been so hard to find. We're looking for one thing, while he's hiding under our very noses."

"I have no doubt he's hiding under our noses, but I don't think this place is it."

"Why?"

"You said it yourself. Smell the air."

I already had. "Ammonia." But it was overwhelmed by the richness of sandalwood and man.

He nodded. "This place *does* make cleaning products."

"That doesn't mean it can't also be making clones. The base is huge, and from a look at the plans, they're only using a small section of it."

He studied me for a minute. "You're looking for an argument, aren't you?"

Right then, arguing was the *last* thing on my mind. I raised an eyebrow. "What makes you think that?"

"Because two seconds ago you were saying you didn't think anything more than cleaning products was being made here, and now you're arguing it could be a front."

"I'm just playing devil's advocate."

"You're definitely playing. I'm just not sure what the game is yet."

I gave him my most innocent smile, but it didn't seem to offer him any comfort.

"This way," he said, after a pause.

He turned and led the way to the right. The wind stirred the gums and pines scattered around us, and rattled the loose tin on the roof of the buildings just ahead. From behind us came the steady growl of traffic along Camp Road, and from up ahead, the solo roar of an engine.

"There's a car headed our way."

"More than likely a guard doing his rounds."

I glanced at my watch. "It's right on nine, so maybe they do either half hourly or hourly checks."

"How close is it?"

"A distance off yet."

"So we've got time to get to the main building if we run?"

"I think so."

He grabbed my hand, fingers hot as they encased mine. "Blur," he ordered, and tugged me forward.

We made it to the main building a heartbeat before the car came into view. The sweep of lights as it turned the corner turned night into day, almost pinning the two of us in brightness.

I crouched in the corner shadows beside Quinn, watching the car and feeling nothing along the sensory lines. Which meant the guard was human. Anything else I would have felt.

"He's bored," Quinn said, his breath brushing warmth past my ear. "And hates his job."

My thigh rested against his, and electricity seemed to spark the air between us. The fever began to burn so bad, sweat trickled down my back, despite the ice in the wind. I was still in control, but it wouldn't take much to push me over the edge. I had a feeling Quinn knew exactly what my state was and that he wasn't about to make a second offer of relief. Next time, I'd have to ask. If he thought I wouldn't, he was sorely wrong.

"He's obviously neither psychic nor shielded if you can read him so easily."

He didn't answer immediately, his expression distant. After a minute, he blinked and glanced at me. "I've searched his mind. There's nothing here to find."

"We should still check."

He nodded and rose. We checked, and found exactly what we expected. Nothing.

"Hope Jack and Rhoan have more luck than we had," I said, as we made our way back to the car.

"I suspect they won't. This is all too well planned to be uncovered so easily."

"I would hardly call going through a mountain of files easy."

"But what did we really find? Plans that may very well be nothing more than a dead end."

He lifted the wire for me. I ducked through, then stopped.

The dead had returned to the graveyard.

There were eight of them, and they formed a rough semicircle around us. They were all males, all naked, and all rather lacking in the manhood department. Their bodies were muscular, almost too perfect, and their skin shone with a luminosity that reminded me of the moon. But any vague resemblance to humanity ended right there. The flesh of their arms gave way at the elbow to the soft golden fur of a cat, and they had claws rather than hands. Instead of faces, they had the heads and beaks of an eagle. On their backs, fanning lightly in the wind, brown-and-gold wings that arched high above them.

"Gryphons," I said. "Sort of."

"Humans bred with gryphons, I would suggest." Quinn stopped beside me, his shoulder brushing mine. The moon fever sang in response, and my whole body began to tremble, a sharp warning I was roaring toward the point of no return.

I clenched my fists, fighting the need in me. "Why then do I sense them as the dead rather than gryphons?"

"I don't know." He flexed his hands, then glanced at me. "I hope you have more of those punches in you."

"I most certainly do." I watched them watching us and wondered why they hadn't yet moved. "I gather you can't touch their minds?"

"No, they're shielded, though I can't see any wires on them." His fingers captured mine, raising my hand to his lips. His kiss was feather-soft, erotic. "Good luck."

He released my hand and faded into the night, moving swiftly to the right. That was obviously what the creatures had been waiting for. With a blur of wings, they rose, five swooping toward Quinn, three to me.

The insane part of me was quite offended by the fact that Quinn was considered the greater threat.

The sweep of their powerful wings filled the night

with a maelstrom of air. Dirt and leaves swirled around me, making it difficult even to see.

As the three of them arrowed in, I turned and ran, heading for the protection of trees. I might be offended but I wasn't a fool, and I didn't have eyes in the back of my head. At least the thick pines gave me some protection against an attack from above or behind.

A clawed paw the size of a spade swept through the air. I ducked and swung, kicking the creature in the gut. The blow bounced off the gryphon's rippled abs and jarred the whole of my leg. I briefly wished I hadn't taken off my shoes. Spikes were a far better weapon than bare feet.

The air screamed a warning, and I ducked blows from the other two creatures. They were so close that the wind from their wings was a vortex that tore at my hair and clothes, filling the air with pine needles and my lungs with dirt. I coughed, squinting to see through the muck surging around me.

The first creature banked toward me, arrowing in from a sharp angle. He flew low under the trees, beaked mouth open as if screaming, though no sound came out.

I danced away from more blows from the other two, then rocked backward as the first creature swooped close. Claws lashed out, scouring my arm and leaving three bloody rents. I swore and leapt forward, onto its back. It screamed then—a high sound that was neither bird of prey nor cat nor human. I hung on for grim life as it bucked and twisted, then we were out of the trees and surging skyward.

His smell hit me, and despite what I'd sensed before, it was not the mustiness of animal and death. It was honey and rain, a sweet, refreshing aroma that had the already rampant moon heat surging anew. But these things weren't trying to fuck me, they were trying to kill me, and the moon heat wasn't yet strong enough to overcome the instinct of survival.

I drew my legs up underneath me, knees bent, feet pressed into the middle of its back, then released one wing and grabbed the other with both hands. It was a precarious stance and had he twisted then, I would have been gone. But he didn't, seemingly content to surge for the stars. His wings pumped the night, gleaming a rich, burnished gold, beautiful and powerful.

And I was about to destroy them.

Pushing away a touch of regret, I glanced down at the rapidly disappearing ground. It had to be done right then, or the fall could kill me. Taking a deep breath, I pushed up and twisted backward with as much force as I could muster.

I had the inhuman strength of a vampire at my call. The wing stood no chance.

With an odd sort of popping sound, the wing tore free of flesh, then it and I were tumbling earthward. The creature's screams filled the air, along with its blood. It spiraled out of control, the one remaining wing pumping frantically but doing little. More screams filled the night as the other two creatures swooped to the aid of the first, each catching an arm, wings a blur as they tried to ease the rate of its fall.

Unfortunately, there was no one to ease my fall. I twisted, hitting the ground feetfirst, then collapsed forward into a roll to ease the pressure on my spine. It didn't seem to make much difference. My breath left in a whoosh of air, and, for a moment, stars danced so close it felt like I could reach out and grasp them. The pain filling every fiber became a darkness that threatened to consume me.

I fought it, breathing deep. Heard the screams that weren't human and knew those things were coming after me again. I had to get up. Had to move.

With a groan, I rolled to my feet, but immediately dropped as a creature swooped. I surged upward as it skimmed past, avoiding its claws to sink my fist into its groin. It made an odd sort of coughing noise and came to a hovering stop. It hunched up, but the claw at the end of its closest foot caught my shoulder, slashing deep even as the blow knocked me sideways.

Pain burned white-hot through my body, and sweat beaded my brow. Gritting my teeth, I scrambled upright, grabbed the leg of the creature, and swung it around as hard as I could before releasing it. It flew awkwardly through the air and hit a nearby pine with enough force to shake needles loose. But it obviously wasn't hurt, as it pushed upright almost immediately.

The third of the creatures arrowed in. I ran, and had to resist the sudden urge to shift into my other form. A wolf wouldn't have a hope against flighted creatures, and the only weapon I'd have would be teeth. Nor could I use telepathy—if Quinn couldn't touch their minds, there was little chance I could.

Wrapping the night around myself, I grabbed several stones and tossed them into the pines. They clattered against the trunks and plopped into the soft carpet of needles. My attacker swung toward the sound, giving me time to catch my breath.

But the gryphon I'd torn the wing off was on the move, beak in the air and making a strange snuffling sound—much like a dog did when tracking. I swore under my breath. Obviously, gryphon and human wasn't the only thing in the mix. Its head swung my way and, with a scream, it ran toward me.

I backpedaled fast, not daring to take my eyes off the thing. It was faster than I'd expected. Talons raked my stomach, drawing blood. I dropped my cloak of shadows and bit my tongue to hold back the scream. Grabbing the creature's wrist, I twisted around and pulled hard, yanking it up and over my shoulder. It sailed past me and landed with a crash on its back. As feathers flew upward, I stiffened my fingers and knifed them toward the creature's eyes. It moved, and I hit cheek instead. Felt flesh and bone give as its cheek caved in.

Bile rose in my stomach. Shuddering, I dropped, sweeping my leg and knocking the creature off its feet again as it struggled to rise. It roared in frustration and lashed out. The blow caught the side of my face and sent me staggering.

The creature was up and at me almost instantly. Air became a torrent of dirt, telling me the others were also close. I faked a blow to the creature's head, then spun and lashed out at its groin instead. The force of the blow shuddered up my leg, but the creature dropped, clutching itself and making an odd sort of keening sound.

The others hit me. I ducked and weaved, but there was no way on this earth to avoid every blow. I was vampire-fast, but even the wind itself would have had trouble in this situation. Red heat flashed through me, and the smell of blood and fear sat heavily on the whirlpool of air surrounding us.

I hoped like hell Quinn was faring better, because I was in deep trouble and in need of help.

Fast.

From the side of us came an odd popping sound, then the head of the lead creature exploded. Blood, tissue, and gray matter went everywhere. As it dropped lifeless at my feet, the second creature met with the same end.

The wind chose that moment to die, and I smelled the familiar aroma of musk and man. Anger surged, replacing the relief.

But before I could say anything, before I could do anything, something hit the back of my head and unconsciousness claimed me.

*P*ain woke me. It wasn't sharp, just a constant, maddening ache, the sort that set teeth on end. Even breathing hurt.

But it was a distant cry compared to the burning at my wrists and ankles, and the desperate, hungry blaze seething through my veins. My whole body trembled with its force, and it was an intensity that could so easily drive me mad.

One that *would* drive me mad if I didn't get some loving soon.

I twisted, trying to at least ease that ache myself, even though it would provide temporary relief, at best. But I barely could move my hand more than a few inches, and the clink of metal told me why. I'd been chained. By silver, if the burning at my wrists was anything to go by.

A soft chuckle filled the silence. Talon was there, watching.

I opened my eyes. The room was large, the color a warm gold that was soothing despite the situation. To the right were large windows through which dawn's light filtered, adding to the airy feel. It was an effect that was somewhat spoiled by the thick bars on each window—not that they would stop an escape if I managed to get out of my chains. The closest window was open, and the caressing breeze cool, filled with the salty tang of the ocean.

Directly opposite was an open doorway through which a bath and several towels were visible. To the left, another door, that one closed. There was nothing else in the main room but a satin-covered bed, and it was there that Talon sat. He was fully dressed, which in itself was surprising.

"You stupid bastard." My voice was little more than a cracked whisper, but he was a wolf and would have no trouble hearing it. "You have no idea of the trouble you've landed yourself in."

"I think not." His smile was all arrogance, his eyes chips of golden ice. "Government departments tend to turn a blind eye to the sexual practices of werewolves."

"This is kidnapping, and that's a crime."

"But that's not what anyone believes, because I rang up stating you are ill. You're on sick leave, as of an hour ago."

I shook my head, unable to believe he'd go to such lengths. "I was on special assignment. With my boss. I have no idea who you spoke to, but it won't matter. They'll know the lie."

He shrugged. "I wasn't fool enough to ring from my phone, rather a pay phone. And I used a voice modulator. They won't find you."

"Rhoan knows who my mates are. He'll find me."

Talon crossed his arms and laughed. It was a cold, dismissive sound that made the anger boil that much faster.

"That pansy couldn't find his way out of a flower shop," he said. "Besides, we're not at any of my known addresses, but a holiday house recently purchased by a subsidiary of one of my companies. It'll take them weeks to nail down the paper trail. By then, we'll have shifted."

"Never underestimate Rhoan. He's very, very good at what he does—and in case you've forgotten, what he does is track down and kill people." And Talon was dead meat if Rhoan found us like this.

He rose and walked toward me, all grace and powerful elegance. The smell of his lust fanned the already out-of-control fire.

I swallowed, but it did little to ease the aching dryness in my throat. "How did you find me?"

His smile was all arrogance. "The chip in your arm is not for birth control—we took that out over a year ago. It's a tracking device."

So that's how he'd found Quinn and me at the Directorate. He hadn't raided my apartment, as I'd presumed. He'd simply followed the signal. It had to have a limited range; otherwise, he would probably have made an appearance at the old farmhouse.

The sweat running down my face dripped into my eyes and stung like crazy. I blinked, but it didn't seem to help my vision any. Everything was blurry, tinged with red. I hoped it was blood, but had a bad feeling it was something far worse. Despite what Hollywood seemed to think, the moon fever didn't often turn werewolves into desperate killing machines. But on the few occasions it *did* happen, it was because the wolf had ignored the call of the moon for too long. The desire for sex mutated into something far more deadly— bloodlust.

Why would Talon want that? What good would it do him?

He stopped. I lashed out with a fist, but the blow was brought up short as the manacles bit into my wrist. I hissed in pain and frustration, and he smiled.

"Do you wonder why you're here, and chained?" He reached out, idly fondling a breast.

Part of me hated it. Part of me wanted anything he was willing to give. I knew which part would win. Had to win, or there would be trouble.

"You want a kid, and I won't give it to you willingly."

"Very good." His tone was distant, his gaze intent, as his caress moved from one breast to the other.

I couldn't help pressing into his touch. I needed it as badly as an addict needed her next fix.

"The scans I took the other day indicated you were close to ovulation. I cannot risk another wolf impregnating you after all the trouble I have gone to."

An insane thought when all wolves were chipped to prevent pregnancy happening. But then, I guess Talon wasn't exactly chummy with sanity at that particular point in time. "There's no guarantee I'll even carry to term."

"Which is why I have arranged for you to be moved to one of my laboratories. Our perfect child will be given every medical chance there is."

"There is no such thing as a perfect child." We all had faults, though right then I doubted whether Talon would agree—at least when it came to *him*.

He didn't seem to hear me, and his voice, when he spoke, was distant. "Perfection is something I have chased for a very long time."

His caress moved down my stomach. I was burning, eager, hungry. My heart raced, and the smell of sweat and lust filled every breath. But the need to become a wolf, to rend and tear and taste blood, was almost as strong as the call of the moon. My teeth and nails were elongating in anticipation of the change, becoming more wolf than human. The only thing stopping me from fully completing the shift was the silver on my wrists and ankles.

"Why do this?" The words were slurred through my teeth. I rattled the chains to indicate what I meant.

"Do you not remember your folklore?"

I shook my head. Right then, I was having trouble remembering my own name.

"Wolves who mate when the moon fever turns to bloodlust will always conceive."

My smile was bitter. "That's no folklore—that's a truth I owe my existence to."

He raised an eyebrow. "What do you mean?"

"Just what I said. I was conceived when my mother was in bloodlust." She'd been trying to make it home to our pack, but her car had broken down on the outskirts of a small country town. In some ways, it was lucky the graveyard and that newly risen vampire had stood between her and the people in that town, because it had allowed her to slake both desires without killing any humans.

"Then let us hope it is a case of like mother, like daughter." His fingers slipped though my slickness, and I shuddered, arching into his caress, relishing it, as hard and as rough as it was. He chuckled. "You are close, aren't you?"

Closer than he knew. The need to mate warred with the need to sink teeth into his flesh and howl my victory to the moon. I took a deep, shuddery breath, suddenly thankful for the silver chaining me. It was the only reason I was still in human form, still lucid.

"ARC1-23 was the wrong drug to use."

He raised an eyebrow. "When did you find out?"

"A couple of days ago." My words were little more than a pant of air, my body twisting, thrusting, desperate for the relief his fingers were offering.

His lust swam around me, as thick and as heavy as the erection pressing against the restraint of his pants. God help me, I wanted to feel him inside, wanted it so bad I was whimpering.

"That drug has an extremely high success rate. You will conceive when I finally fuck you, little wolf, and you will remain in my care until you give birth."

"Like hell." But my words held little force. The pressure was building, ripping through my nerve endings with the force of lightning. A few more sweeps of his hand, that was all it would take . . .

With a soft chuckle, he stepped away. I lurched forward, trying to grab him, trying to make him finish what he'd started. But the chains brought me up short again. I cursed him, long and hard.

"And that," he said, his voice rich with amusement, "is why I shall be raising our child, not you."

Though his features were half-lost to the growing haze of red, the icy determination in his expression was still very evident. Odd. I'd half expected to see a madness equal to what burned through my veins. He *had* to be mad if he thought he could get away with something like this. Even if he *did* make me pregnant, there was no way I was ever going to sit back and let him have our child.

"Ten of the fifty on that first trial failed to conceive. I might be one of those."

"Our tests over the past few months show that your body has been reacting favorably to the drug."

But maybe it was reacting in ways he wasn't expecting—or testing for. "What about the other ten? The ones that transmuted?"

He raised his eyebrows. "What about them?"

"They were half-breeds, just like me."

His amusement fled, and his face became stony. "What do you mean?"

My laugh was bitter. "Have you never wondered why I am so fast, so strong? I'm not just a werewolf, I'm a vampire."

He crossed his arms, eyes and voice flat as he said, "Impossible. Vampires aren't fertile."

"Except in the few instances when the change takes place within twenty-four hours of death. My mother was raped by such a vampire."

"No."

"Why do you think I was exiled from our pack? They allowed me to be raised out of loyalty to my mother, but once I hit puberty I was ousted."

"No."

He said it more forcefully this time, and I snorted. "What's wrong? Don't you like the fact you've been fucking a half-breed all this time?"

He didn't answer. I stared at him, saw the sudden loathing in his eyes, and realized the words said in jest were true. Talon was a man who believed in the superiority of the werewolf race, but I'd never realized that opinion also meant he'd have little tolerance for half-breeds.

"Our scans never indicated you were anything other than wolf." His voice was flat, yet held a note of anger that caressed my skin as hotly as his lust had moments before.

"They wouldn't, because for all intents and purposes I *am* wolf. It's not until you do a complete DNA check that you see the differences."

For several more seconds, he just stared. Yet the force of his anger rose and rose, until it was a wave that burned through every fiber of my being. His fists clenched, warning enough that a blow was coming. I dropped my shields and reached desperately for his mind—only to hit a psychic shield. For the first time in two years I noticed the thin wire entwined through the white gold chain at his neck. He was shielded against mind intrusion, had been for as long as I'd known him.

A laugh bubbled through me. So much for all my cautious restraint over the years.

His fist hit my stomach, and the laughter gave way to a desperate battle to breathe.

He continued to hit me, again, and again. I shuddered, twisting and fighting to be free, the need to tear him limb from limb as fierce as the need to survive.

"Coward," I spat between blows. "Step closer and try that."

I was trembling, aching, bloody. Everything had gone red, only it wasn't blood. Rage and the wolf had control and the consuming pain meant nothing.

I wanted, needed blood.

If he took one step closer, I could grab him and rip him to pieces. My fingers curled in anticipation. I wanted to taste him. Wanted to tear my teeth through his sweet flesh, and watch his blood pour from his body. Wanted to see it mingle with mine on the fine gold carpet.

He either didn't hear or didn't want to hear. As he drew his fist back for another blow, the door to the left of us crashed open and Talon was ripped away from me. I closed my eyes and howled in anger and frustration.

Hands were on me, shaking hard.

"Riley? It's Quinn. You're safe. It's okay."

His voice was muted, lost in the roar of need. I lashed out, raking his cheek with hooked fingers. The smell of blood filled the air, stirring the lust to greater heights. I twisted, thrusting my fingers into my mouth, sucking the blood and skin from under my fingernails. It was a sweetness that made me salivate, yet there was nowhere near enough of it to satisfy the hunger in me.

"Riley—"

"Don't take off those chains," a second voice warned flatly. "She's in bloodlust, and could kill us both if you set her free."

"So what in hell do we do?"

"Not we, you." The second voice was vaguely familiar, though his name failed to traverse the haze of heat and lust filling my mind. "You'll have to fuck her while she's chained."

"For Christ's sake, look at the mess—"

"You have no other choice. Four of us barely controlled her when we were trying to treat her wounds. The bloodlust triples her strength."

Quinn didn't answer. I couldn't see him, couldn't sense him. Didn't know if he was still close or not. I threw my weight against the chains, testing them, trying to break free. White heat burned into my wrists and ankles, and my skin became slick with moisture. Moisture that smelled sweeter than sex. But I couldn't get to it, couldn't taste it. The chains weren't long enough.

He forced a breath out, a sigh that was somehow filled with anger. "Take care of that bastard, then, and make sure he can't escape."

Fingers caressed my face. I turned, snapping at them, catching nothing but air.

"I will," the second voice said softly. "But I'm afraid that's not all you'll have to do."

"What?" There was an edge in the rich tones that suggested anger.

"She needs the taste of blood."

"I'm a vampire. She shares my blood willingly, and she treads the path to becoming a vampire."

"I know, but she is part vampire anyway, so maybe she's immune to the curse."

"Gift, not curse."

It was tightly said, the anger more evident this time.

"Either way, it is a chance we have to take. You could survive what I cannot. Look at her teeth."

There was a pause, then, "Wolf-sharp."

"And she won't just bite, she'll savage. I may be wolf, but I dare not risk such a bite, especially given it'll take more than a few minutes to cure her thirst. She'd more than likely suck the life from me. Nor can we call in a medical unit, simply because few doctors have seen a werewolf in bloodlust, let alone know how to treat it."

Quinn took another deep breath, then released it slowly. It hit like a blow. I lunged toward him, snarling and snapping.

"Keep an eye on everything while I do this."

"Be careful."

"I'm not a fool."

The door slammed, and silence fell. The scent of sandalwood caressed the air, suggesting Quinn was still close. I waited, muscles quivering, ready to lunge should he step within reach.

Material rustled. A zipper slid down. Shoes were kicked off. Anticipation quivered through me, bloodlust and moon lust at war through my system.

His fingers pressed into me, and the moon heat surged, momentarily overwhelming the red tide. His touch slid back and forth through my slickness, and pleasure stormed through every nerve ending. Then he slipped two fingers inside, stroking hard. I shuddered, writhed, until it felt as if every fiber of my being was about to tear apart from the sheer force of the pleasure. Then everything did shatter and I howled the glory of it to the moon I couldn't see.

But it was nowhere near enough to satisfy the hunger.

He stepped closer. I snapped at him. He raised an arm and pressed it against my mouth. I reared back enough to rip into his flesh, tearing deep. He made no sound, but as his blood filled my mouth, he thrust himself into me, stroking hard and deep. It was a sensation unlike anything I'd ever experienced. Ecstasy itself.

He made love to me hard and long, until the quivering in my body eased and the lust faded under the taste of his blood and sweat. Eventually, there was nothing left but sweet relief and the need to sleep. It was a need I was finally able to give in to.

When sanity finally resurfaced, it was to the awareness of satin rather than wall pressing against my spine. The room was filled with a dusky light that spoke of sunset, and my body was sated, the aches distant. But all I could taste was blood. All I could remember was the rich flavor of his flesh as my teeth tore and slashed . . .

My stomach roiled and I clambered off the bed, running for the bathroom. I barely made it.

When there was nothing left to bring up, I flushed the toilet and leaned back, closing my eyes. Beneath the taste of bile, blood still lingered. I had to get up and find something sweet to rinse my mouth out with; otherwise, I'd be sick again. But right then, I didn't have the strength to move.

Footsteps approached. The softness of the tread and the scent in the air said it was Quinn. I didn't open my eyes. Didn't want to see the damage I'd done.

"How did you find me?"

"I saw Talon snatch you, but the creatures stopped me from coming to your aid." He stopped in front of me, a warmth I could feel rather than see. "When I could, I called Liander, and he did a search for all of Talon's known addresses."

So Liander was the other voice I'd heard. "This place was only recently purchased by a subsidiary company, so how did you find it?"

"The subsidiary is one of the ones Jack had uncovered. Given this was a recent purchase, we took a chance."

And Talon had thought he was being so clever. But any amusement I might have felt was smothered under the apprehension of what had happened there. What I'd done.

What he'd done.

"I don't want to become a vampire on my death." It came out little more than a cracked whisper, and I swallowed to ease the dryness. But that only succeeded in pushing the bitter taste down my throat again, and my stomach stirred in warning. "I hate the taste of blood." Not that I'd ever tasted human blood before the moon madness, but I'd hunted enough rabbit over the years, and every time I'd sunk teeth into flesh, the rush of warm blood into my mouth had made me want to vomit. Rhoan reckoned I was a vegetarian who just wasn't willing to admit it yet.

"Many vampires hate the taste in the beginning." He pressed a cup into my hand. "But you and I would have to share blood thrice, and perform a ceremony on the third occasion, before you'd turn into a vampire on your death."

I looked up, surprised. "I never knew that."

He raised an eyebrow. "If it were not so, don't you think the world would be overrun with vampires by now?"

"I never really thought about it."

He moved my hand, pressing the cup to my lips. "Rinse your mouth out. You'll feel a little better, believe me."

It wasn't water in the cup, but something that was both sweet and spicy. Whatever it was, it worked, and I did feel better once the bitter, metallic taste had fled my mouth. He took the cup, rinsing it quickly under the tap.

His arm was bandaged from wrist to elbow, and the fact that it wasn't in a sling at least meant I hadn't bitten through bone. But he used his left hand rather than his right to wash the cup and turn off the tap.

"How much damage did I do?"

He shrugged. "It's nothing my body can't heal."

"That doesn't answer the question."

"No." He held out his left hand, and I placed my

fingers in his. He pulled me up and placed a gentle kiss on my forehead, his lips lingering, breath warm against my skin. Then he stepped back. "I shall have scars from wrist to elbow."

If he was going to end up with scars, I'd done everything *but* break bone. I briefly closed my eyes. "I'm sorry."

"You were only obeying the needs of your body. The fault lies with another."

Though it was evenly said, something in his expression made me realize our time together was coming to an end. He might still want me, but he was ready to move on.

I took a deep breath, but it did little to ease the sudden rush of anger. The wolf might be sated, but, by Christ, I still wanted to smash Talon's face in. Not only for what he'd done to me, but for his utter destruction of whatever chance there'd been for me and Quinn to continue on a little longer.

"Is he dead?"

Cold fury flashed in his eyes. "No."

"Good, because I owe him a punch or three."

"When we find him again, I'll make sure you get your chance."

Disbelief ran through me, and my gaze searched his. "You let him escape?"

"Not intentionally. Some of his men arrived while I was tending to you. By the time I realized what was happening and went to Liander's aid, Talon had fled."

"Fuck."

"*That* has already led to more than a few problems."

Again anger surged. "Don't be blaming me. The bloodlust was not something I could have controlled."

"Wasn't it? If you'd taken my offer of relief in the

parking lot rather than playing games, none of this would have happened."

"Maybe the bloodlust wouldn't have happened so quickly, but he still would have snatched and chained me. From there, it was only a matter of time."

"We would have found you before that time was up."

Maybe. And maybe not. Talon would have smelled the thickness of my need and known how close to the edge I was. Maybe the only reason he'd come to this house was because he knew he didn't have much time to restrain me.

Which pointed me to another point. "Why didn't you make sure he couldn't escape? Touch his mind and force him to do what you want?"

"He had a shield on."

"So? You could have removed it."

"Could have, only I had more pressing problems."

Meaning me. "I was chained. You could have done whatever you wanted."

"Not when I could feel your agony."

My anger partially evaporated at his soft words. He cupped my cheek, his thumb brushing my lips. My gaze rose to the heat of his, and my pulse accelerated. The moon might be lost to the brightness of the day, but simply being close to Quinn had me wanting him.

It was just a damn shame he lived in Sydney. That after this case was solved and forgotten, he'd walk away without a second's thought, because I was a wolf and we were okay to fuck but not get involved with.

Not that I actually wanted involvement—but I definitely wanted to explore the breadth of the attraction between us.

"Do you think Talon was behind those things that attacked us?" I asked.

"No."

"Why not?"

"Because I doubt he'd set his creatures on us, then kill them to save you. And because there was someone else there, someone who came to watch."

There was an edge in his voice, and I raised an eyebrow. "You caught them?"

"No. But I saw the van and I was able to catch a glimpse of the number plate as they drove off. Jack's running it, and the company name, through the computer." He hesitated, and his half smile made my pulse do several flips. "It appears we were off track when we were doing our search for Genoveve."

No real surprise there, as we were only going on what we'd found—and we'd found very little. "The truck was from them?"

"Yes. Only it's not a military or research concern, but rather a confectionary company."

I blinked. Confectionary? "How does that connect with cloning or crossbreeds?"

"God only knows. Maybe they nicked the van and were using it simply because it wouldn't normally come under suspicion."

"Too much of a coincidence that my kidnappers were also taking me to a place named Genoveve." I frowned, absently chewing my lip. "You know, I have a bad feeling I've seen that name before."

"Most likely on the supermarket shelf."

"No, somewhere else."

He frowned. "Like where?"

I opened my mouth to say I'd tell him if I knew when the memory finally hit me.

It had been almost a year ago that I'd seen the name, and, given the circumstances, it was a wonder I'd remembered it at all.

I'd been on a date with a new mate, and we'd gone back to his office for reasons that now escaped me. Genoveve had been one of the files we'd swept off the desk in our haste to clear enough space to make love.

I closed my eyes, part of me unwilling to believe that I might have been betrayed yet again.

Because my date that night had been the director and owner of Rollins Enterprises.

Misha.

Chapter 13

Quinn's grip on my arms tightened. "What?"

"It might be nothing." At least, I hoped it was nothing. Surely fate would not be so unkind as to betray me twice.

"Tell me."

I took a deep breath and released it slowly. "I'd always thought the name was familiar, and I've just remembered why. The second of my two mates had a file on his desk that bore the name Genoveve Confectionary."

"Did you get the chance to look at it?"

"Why would I bother? It was over a year ago that I saw it, and we were in a mating rush at the time. You're lucky I even remembered it."

He released my arms and stepped back. "What is his name?"

"Misha Rollins."

"The same Misha who was on the phone to you when we pulled up at the cemetery?"

I stared at him for a second, taking in the implications of his words, a cold sensation forming in the pit of my stomach.

"There are more than a dozen Camp Roads in Melbourne, and even if he *was* behind the attack, there is no way they could have pinpointed us so quickly."

Yet I remembered Talon's words. Remembered the tracking device in my arm. And he'd said *we*. Did that mean he and Misha were partners in this madness? But if that were so, why would they set their creatures on us, then shoot them?

It didn't make any sense. None of this was making any sense.

"He had your phone number, and you left your phone on."

"But they didn't need satellite tracking—I've apparently got a tracker in my arm."

"Then we had better get it out."

"Misha's *not* behind the attack." I had to believe that. Had to. Otherwise, I might never trust my instincts again.

Quinn's expression was cold. "Why don't we go question him, then?"

"Why don't we wait for Jack and see what he has to say?"

Though his expression didn't alter, his anger whipped around me. "Fine."

He spun on his heel and walked out. I watched him go, though right then all I wanted to do was grab him and make love to him. It wasn't the moon heat. Rather a desire to hold on tight to something that was good. Something that was slipping through my fingers.

With a sigh, I flicked on the water in the shower and stepped under it when it was hot enough. After washing the blood and sweat from my skin, I studied my various wounds. My stomach was tender to the touch, and the rainbow display of colors was broken by three pale pink scars. My arms bore several more healing slashes, as did my shoulders and thigh. Though I couldn't remember changing shape during the night, I must have, because there was no other way such cuts would have healed so fast.

Once I'd dried myself, I went out to check for clothes and discovered my bag sitting at the end of the bed. Liander must have brought it down from the farm. I shoved on my skirt and a shirt, mighty thankful for the extra undies I'd thrown into my bag when I'd packed for the club days ago. Once dressed, I wandered down a wide hallway, through a shadow-filled living room, and found myself in a kitchen bigger than my entire apartment. Through the windows, lights sparkled, testimony to the fact that many houses lay on the slope below us. In the distance, glistening white-caps pounded toward a shore I couldn't see.

Liander sat at an ornate glass table reading a newspaper, but he glanced up as I walked in. His left eye was black, and bruises littered his pale arms.

His gaze raked me, lingering on the healing wound on my thigh. It wasn't a sexual look, just a concerned one. "Feeling better?"

"Much. How about you?"

He shrugged. "I think my ego is bruised more than my body. There were only four of them, yet they got the better of me."

"Only four? Gee, you're slipping."

My voice was dry, and a smile tugged his lips. "Once I could have taken double that number."

"It's a long time since you were in the military."

"It shouldn't matter. I do keep in shape, after all."

"But not fighting fit—you've had no reason to, after all."

"True."

I walked over to the fridge to grab something to eat, but there wasn't much more than old-looking fruit. Obviously, despite what Talon had said, he really hadn't intended to stay there long. I picked out one of the better-looking peaches and slammed the door shut. "Where's Quinn?"

Liander nodded toward the French doors to my right. "Out on the patio, calling someone to get some information on Misha." He hesitated, his expression tightening. "He's using us all, you know."

"Yeah. All he's interested in is finding out what happened to his friend."

"His friend being the DNA provider for these clones?"

I nodded and bit into the peach. "I gather Rhoan filled you in on what's been happening?"

Liander's gaze met mine. "There are no secrets between us, Riley."

I remembered what he'd said to Quinn when I was in the bloodlust, and realized then he knew what we were—knew, because Rhoan had told him. It was extraordinarily pleasing to know that my brother had found someone who loved him just as he was.

Though I doubted Rhoan himself was fully appreciative of the fact.

Liander folded the newspaper and leaned back in his chair. "Rhoan also told me about Quinn's history with werewolves. Be careful with him."

I swiped a hand at the peach juice running down my chin. "First my brother, now my brother's lover."

Exasperation edged my voice. "Will you both give me credit for having a little common sense?"

He smiled, but the concern in his silver eyes remained. "You're generally one of the most sensible people I know, but emotions rarely have anything to do with common sense."

"I haven't known Quinn long enough to get emotional. Right now, he's just another lover." A lover I *could* get attached to, if he ever gave me the time. But he wouldn't, so why was everyone worrying? "Were the men who came to rescue Talon human?"

He shook his head, his smile telling me he wasn't fooled by the change of topics. "Wolves."

"And their smell?"

He shrugged. "Like wolves. Men."

Not clones or lab-created creatures then. Which I supposed was a good thing—at least it suggested Talon's madness was just the common, everyday type, not the "I-will-dominate-the-world" variety.

"And Jack's been informed of events?"

"Yes." He glanced at his watch. "They should almost be here."

I raised an eyebrow. "That wise? I mean, these people keep on finding us, so it might be better if we remained in a couple of different groups." Though, if I had a tracker in my arm, maybe I was the reason they kept finding us. Talon might have inserted it, but there was no telling if anyone else had discovered the signal.

"Probably, but I'm not calling the shots. Jack is."

And Jack would do what Jack wanted. Maybe he *wanted* to bring them to us. It would certainly be one shortcut to finding out who was behind all this.

I finished the peach and tossed the pit in the nearby rubbish bin. From outside the house came the sound of an approaching car. Liander rose, then moved with deceptive casualness to the window and looked out.

"Jack and Rhoan," he said after a moment.

He went to the front door, and I looked around as Quinn came in off the patio. "Your sources able to tell you anything about Misha?"

"Not yet," he said. "They'll get back to me in an hour or so."

I crossed my arms. "Are you going to share what they find with Jack?"

"Yes," he said.

No, he meant.

I smiled grimly. "And do you intend to kill whoever has held Henri captive all these years?"

"Killing is not my style."

"Tell that to the clone in the toilet."

"He was a clone. That's different."

I wanted to ask how, but my brother chose that moment to walk in. His glance took in the two of us, and his gaze narrowed slightly.

"You okay?" he asked, pulling me into a fierce and protective hug.

"I'm fine," I replied. "Just make sure you leave enough for me to kick if you find Talon before I do."

"I'll try to remember," he said, then pulled back a little. "Did he tell you anything?"

"Not anything new. Just the same old obsession."

"The bastard definitely needs to be taught a lesson or two." He shifted to one side and wrapped an arm around my shoulder.

Jack tapped the table, bringing our attention back to him. "Our search at the second former army base revealed nothing more than cosmetic manufacturing. And our computer search for Genoveve Confectionary has yielded little for the moment. It would seem the owners are hidden behind yet another paper trail."

"We may have hit a shortcut," I said, before Quinn had the chance. "A year ago Misha had a file bearing the name Genoveve Confectionary on his desk. I think it's worth asking straight out what his involvement with them is."

Jack contemplated me for a second, green eyes narrowed but glinting with familiar amusement. He was still playing his games, still trying to reel me in, but in this case, I had no intention of sidestepping such attempts. Whoever was behind these creatures had to be stopped, and if I could play some small part in that, then I would. If only to ensure these bastards stopped coming after *me*.

"You know, that could be a very good idea," he said casually. "Especially if you arrange to meet him somewhere other than his office."

"Play bunny bait, you mean, while you search his office."

He gave me a toothy grin. "Darlin', I'm glad you're on my side."

"The only side I'm on is Rhoan's and mine."

"For now."

"For ever."

He shook his head. He wasn't going to give up his little dream, no matter what I said. And I guess he was right to persevere. After all, depending on what the drug did to my system, I might be forced to step into the guardian system whether I wanted to or not.

"That could be dangerous for Riley," Quinn said. "Especially if Misha *is* behind either the clones or the crossbreeds."

"She's not guardian," Rhoan added. "You can't ask her to do something like that because she hasn't had the training."

"All she has to do is what comes naturally to a wolf when the moon rides high."

"They've shot at her and tried to snatch her," Rhoan said. "I don't think it's wise to send her out alone."

"I won't be." Jack glanced at me. "Do you have a problem doing this?"

"No." Hell, truth be told, when darkness hit tonight and the fever burned through my blood, I wouldn't really give a damn who I danced with as long as I danced. "But there is another problem."

His gaze sharpened. "What?"

"Talon put a tracer in my arm."

"We have some trackers in the car. We'll tune them to the tracer's frequency. If something does happen, at least we can find you."

Talon could, too, but that was a good thing. My fists wanted a serious word or two with his face.

"I hope you're not going to try to make Quinn and me sit this one out," Liander said, voice steely.

"No. Your field of expertise with the military was electronics, which could come in handy when we're breaking in to the office. Quinn will be playing bodyguard to Riley, just in case Talon attempts another snatch."

Quinn didn't say anything, but it was more than obvious he wasn't happy about being left out of the business end of things. And I had to wonder if he'd actually be there when I came back out of the club.

Jack tossed me his phone. "Let's swing into action, people."

It was close to nine by the time we reached the Blue Moon. The night sky was filled with stars, the moon a silver luminance that sang through my veins, and every nerve ending felt as if it were being stretched taut.

Quinn stopped the car in the shadow-filled lane across the street, contemplating the blue-lit building for several seconds before looking at me. "Looks like they've got a good crowd."

His expression hadn't changed any in the last few hours, and his eyes were still obsidian stone. If we'd had some sort of relationship, I might have been tempted to think he was annoyed—even jealous—about my dancing with Misha. But given his take on werewolves and the fact he didn't want anything more from me other than a good time, that was ridiculous.

"I've got a permanent table booking the last two days before the full moon, so I'll get in okay." I swept my gaze from the small line of wolves waiting to get in to the man standing in front of the door. Jimmy. A little bit of tension slid away. At least there was someone else close by who I could trust if Quinn disappeared and I got into trouble.

Quinn twisted around and grabbed the tracker from the backseat. A soft, clear beeping filled the silence. "Have you any idea of the range of this thing?"

"No, but it would have to be two or three kilometers, at least. Talon used the tracer to find us at the Directorate, and neither his office nor his house is close by."

Quinn nodded. "Be careful in there. If you need help, just drop your shields and yell psychically."

I raised an eyebrow. "Is it safe for you to drop your shields? I mean, you're stopped right outside an overflowing wolf nightclub—won't the combination of auras be overwhelming?"

"No."

"Why not?"

He hesitated. "Because I won't be dropping my shields. I'll hear you through them."

"How?"

"We've shared blood. Psychically, I'm now more attuned to you."

"Meaning you can read my thoughts anytime?"

"No, because your shields are too strong. But drop them, and call, and I'll be there."

If I called now, would he come? Not to me, but with me? In me? Somehow, I doubted it. And besides, if Misha *was* behind any of this, I needed to be at fever pitch. Needed my aura to hit him hard and fast, so that he had no time to think, just react. And during our mating, I'd get my answers—either verbally, or by reading his mind.

"I have no idea how long this will take."

He shrugged. "I'm not going anywhere."

So he said. I put my hand on the door handle, then hesitated. "Quinn—"

"There's nothing between us," he said softly. "Nothing other than great sex, anyway."

He wasn't wrong—as yet, there *was* nothing more than great sex. But we'd only known each other a few days, and the indications were, even then, that there *could* be something else there. Whether it was a deeper relationship or simply friendship and good sex was something only time would tell. And no matter what warnings Rhoan and Liander might give, I was more than willing to chance fate and explore options. "Great sex is somewhere to start."

His gentle smile made my heart do a familiar flip-flop. "I am not the sharing type, Riley, and I do not want to be dragged into the whole werewolf culture. It's just not me."

I raised my eyebrows. "Even at the cost of losing great sex?"

"Even at." His gaze left mine. "You'd better get going. He's probably already inside."

"Probably." I studied his profile a moment longer, then leaned across the car to place a kiss on his cheek.

Only he shifted, and my kiss found his mouth instead. It was a long, glorious possession that left me gasping for breath and wanting him more than I'd ever wanted anyone in my life.

"Go," was all he said, the lilt of Ireland so rich in his voice his word was almost lost.

I went. Right then, I had no other choice.

Jimmy gave me a cheery hello and opened the door, ushering me in past a chorus of complaints and groans from those still waiting. A second guard waited near the inner door—Jimmy's brother, Stan. He was slighter smaller, slightly thinner, but other than that, almost an exact replica of Jimmy. Only he had all his own teeth.

"Hey, Riley," he rumbled. "Misha was asking for you as he came in, about ten minutes ago."

My smile felt tight. "Thanks, Stan."

He nodded. "We're packed tonight. Just as well you booked a table."

"Yeah." I grabbed a locker key as usual, then headed inside.

The hologram stars burned across the ceiling, their light not yet dimmed by the glow of the blue moon, which was only just beginning to rise in the distant corner.

The dance floor was a sea of naked, gyrating flesh, and most of the tables were occupied. The air was as hot as the music and rich with the scent of lust and sex.

I breathed deep, allowing the atmosphere to soak through every pore, right into my bones.

If I wanted to be involved with Quinn on a deeper level than I was, I'd probably have to give up this sort of dance. But it was what I was. The freedom and excitement of these moon dances were part of my nature, and I'd be damned if I'd drop them just because it offended his human sensibilities. I wasn't human, and he shouldn't judge me by those standards. And asking me to give up the moon dance would be like asking him to stop drinking blood. It wasn't fair, and it wasn't right.

I made my way down the stairs and into the change room. Misha might be watching, so everything had to follow the pattern I'd set over the past year, right down to taking a shower and stowing my clothes.

When I walked back out I was as naked as everyone else. I scanned the tables until I found mine, but he wasn't there. Which meant he was either somewhere on the dance floor or in one of the back privacy booths or rooms with someone else.

I moved onto the dance floor. The rich aroma of sweat and wantonness swam around me, and my breath caught, then quickened. The press of flesh made my skin burn and my already erratic heart race that much harder.

Hands caught me, whirling me around before pulling me into a body that was strong and lean and brown. Teeth flashed brightly as he wrapped his arms around my waist and led me into a dance that was both sensual and playful.

The moon and the atmosphere and my own raging hormones had me ready to take or be taken. Had it been another time, another day, I might have done both, right there, right then.

The stranger brushed a kiss across my lips, a caress that was teasing yet filled with the promise of heat. "I want you," he said softly. "Are you free to take this dance a little further?"

His voice was as playful as his dance, and I liked the fact he asked first rather than trying to take, as many on the dance floor would have. The crush of his body against mine felt so good, so tempting. I took a deep breath and tried to remember that I was there for a reason.

"Unfortunately, no, not at the moment," I murmured, pressing just a little bit closer. He wasn't much taller than I, so the heat of him caressed all the right places.

His green eyes gleamed with amusement and desire. "I'm Kellen."

"Riley."

"You a regular here?"

"Yes. You?"

"First time. But I believe I've found reason enough to come back again."

I grinned, liking the mischievous yet determined glint in his eyes. The way his body fitted mine so neatly. "I shall keep an eye out for you."

He raised my hand and kissed my fingers. "Do that," he said, and whirled me back into the madness.

I found Misha a few seconds later. He was just off the center of the wildly gyrating crowd, dancing with several silver wolves. His gaze was molten when it met mine, his hunger a live thing that stole my breath and ate at my skin. That surprised me. Misha had never been one to wait for pleasure, and the three he danced with looked more than eager.

He caught my hand, pulling me close as he spun us

away from the silvers. The flash of their anger burned after us, but was quickly lost in the sea of hunger washing past.

He didn't say anything, just pulled me into the thick of the dance, right into the very heart where the press of bodies was at its strongest and the smell of sex so powerful it was almost liquid. I could barely breathe, desire was so fierce, yet I was not so far gone that I couldn't sense the anger in him.

He wrapped a hand around my neck and pulled me close. His kiss was fierce and hard and long.

"You should have asked, Riley," he said eventually. "I would have answered your questions."

I wrapped my arms around his neck, still playing the game though I knew the game was over. "I came here to ask you questions."

"Maybe. And maybe you were meant as a distraction."

I couldn't move, couldn't retreat. Truth be known, didn't want to do either. He was too close, felt too good. "What makes you think that?"

"The fact that three minutes before you walked in I was notified that someone had broken into my Collins Street office." His smile was tight. "They can look all they like. They won't find anything."

"And you're so sure that you'll let them look?"

"Oh yes."

Heat pressed through me, against me. Heat that was Misha as well as the other wolves crushed against us. Every breath was an intake of hunger, and in the blue wash of the lights sweat glistened like diamonds against my skin. I could barely even think, the fever was so bad, and yet I knew I had to keep my wits about me. I could not afford to forget that Misha might well be the enemy.

"How did you know?" My breath was little more than a pant of air.

"I have always preferred to rely on more than the latest in technological wizardry."

He didn't explain it and I didn't have enough air left to ask. His hands tightened against my waist, his fingers hot and bruising as he lifted me onto him. I wrapped my legs around his waist and began to move.

"The bait will earn her answers tonight, believe me," he growled.

I didn't answer. Couldn't answer. My blood burned, my heart hammered like a steam train, and all I wanted was to ride this lean and angry man until the slow waves of pleasure lapping my skin became a molten force that would not be denied.

And that's exactly what I did.

We climaxed as one, the strength of it tearing a strangled sound from my throat as his body slammed me into the backs of others, his movements fast and furious.

The shudders eased. He was still hard inside, but that wasn't surprising, simply because the power of the moon was at full force. The moon heat granted all wolves the potency to celebrate again and again during the weeklong phase, but tonight and tomorrow were peaks, with recovery time down to zero. Perhaps it was nature's way of making up for the change she forced us through at the full moon. The night of the full moon was the one night we had no control over which form we took. That night, we ran solely as wolves.

He began to move inside me again. His expression

was tight, intent, and I knew he intended to exact payment in full before he said anything more.

The fact that he was there, fucking me, when he was well aware that his offices were being broken into and examined assured me there would be nothing incriminating found. Whether that evidence was somewhere else or whether there was simply nothing to be found was anyone's guess.

We stayed in that sweating, gyrating mass for an hour before moving out. We continued at the table, in the shower, against the wall, on the stairs. Each time was hard and furious, and most of the time he took without giving. The wolf in me was having a damn fine time, but the woman was getting a little pissed.

He finally led me back to the table, and I heaved a silent sigh of relief. I was bruised and aching and only partially satisfied, and knew it was intentional. He was making me pay for what he saw as a betrayal.

I slid onto one of the benches and grabbed a beer off a passing waiter. I didn't drink it immediately, instead pressing the icy bottle against my fevered forehead.

Misha sat down on the opposite side. "Ask your questions."

His silver eyes gave nothing away.

"Tell me why you had a file bearing the name Genoveve Confectionary on your desk a year ago."

"It was a company I was considering buying." He raised a pale eyebrow. "You have a very good memory."

"Exceptional, considering the circumstances."

The smile that played across his lips was at odds with the ice of his gaze.

"And did you?" I prompted, when he didn't say anything.

"No."

"Who did?"

"Konane."

"The same company who owns Moneisha?"

"Yes."

I flipped the cap off the beer and took a long drink before asking, "So who is the owner of Konane?"

He smiled. "Try another question."

His expression said he'd tell me. Eventually. I wondered how many hours' "payment" he would exact before he did. "So what has chocolate and research got in common?"

"Maybe the owner was simply diversifying his portfolio."

Something in the way he said that itched at my instincts. "You don't believe that."

"No."

"Why not?"

He leaned back in his seat and studied me for a second, his expression both arrogant and amused. "Because the owner of Konane and I share similar interests, and have, in the past, been business partners."

I forced a smile. "You never told me you were interested in chocolate."

There was something cold and hard about his expression. I had the strangest feeling that *this* man, the man who had taken me so ruthlessly that night, was the real Misha. That the Misha I'd been allowed to see the previous twelve months was merely a means to an end. What that end was I had no idea, but had a bad feeling I'd better find out.

I lowered my shields and reached out with my mind. I wasn't surprised to hit a wall around his thoughts—but it wasn't electronic. His shield was as natural as mine and just as strong.

I took another drink of beer and tried to ignore the urge to leave. I had a job to do, and besides, the moon still burned through my blood.

"It wasn't the chocolate that caught our interest," he said softly, "but the fact that Genoveve was supposedly built over the top of a military installation."

Would the plans in Alan Brown's office match the installation Genoveve was supposedly sitting on? Probably. "I've read about the World War II tunnels and arms caches they've uncovered in and around Melbourne, but never have I heard a whisper about anything bigger."

"No one knew about those tunnels until they were excavated. All the plans were supposedly destroyed after the war and most of the tunnels concreted up."

If the plans had been destroyed, how had Alan Brown gotten hold of them? And why hadn't he destroyed them? I finished my beer and pushed the bottle away. "So why would you think there's any truth to the rumor about what's under Genoveve?"

"Because I talked to the man who found an entrance. As did the man who owned Konane."

"So why does an old military installation hold such fascination to you and the owner of Konane?"

"Because the search for perfection sometimes takes roads the government does not approve of, and in such cases, it is best if the search is conducted in secret."

Oh God . . . Was he saying what I thought he was saying?

He smiled. "I am not involved in Genoveve or the research being done on nonhuman cloning."

"I only have your word on that, and right now, I'm not inclined to trust it."

"I swear on the life of my mother, I have told no lies here tonight."

No lies, but had he told the absolute truth? I had a feeling the answer was no. "So, you have absolutely nothing to do with cloning?"

Amusement momentarily danced in his eyes. "I am not involved, in any way, with the current cloning endeavors. If you want an honest opinion, I cannot see the sense in it. Until we fully understand all the intricacies of creation, cloning will always be an avenue of imperfect research."

"You cannot understand something if you do not research it."

"True. But right now, it is research that is simply throwing good money after bad. How many years has man being trying to clone himself? Where has it led? He can now create imperfect or sickly images of himself every fifty or so attempts."

"The body-part farming came out of the cloning research, and that in itself is very profitable."

He shrugged. "Only marginally. The government has a tight fist on marketing and research."

But the black market was booming, and the government was having little luck stopping it. "So what research were you planning to conduct under Genoveve, and why didn't you end up buying it?"

He smiled. "My companies, like many others, are seeking to unravel the secrets of a vampire's long life. There is a fortune to be made with such knowledge."

That was an understatement, given the human fixation with youth. "So, when you said Moneisha had been successful in pinpointing the cluster of genes that make a vampire a vampire, you were actually talking about your own research?"

"In part. I was trying to discover how much you suspected."

"Why?"

He studied me for a moment, then said, "Because I was told to."

I raised my eyebrows. I really couldn't see Misha bowing to the rule of another, but then, what did I really know about him? "Who by?"

He merely smiled. I changed direction again.

"Have you succeeded in pinpointing the vampire genes?"

"In part."

I studied him for a moment. "Research like that doesn't need to be conducted in a secret installation."

"It does when your test subjects are unwilling participants."

"You're snatching vamps off the street?"

"No. I intended to, simply because the government's recent regulations have made it tough to get enough skin and blood to conduct research. But I never bought Genoveve, simply because I was outbid. All my companies conform to regulations."

Currently conform, he meant. But I had a suspicion they wouldn't in the future. "You know Jack will check."

He shrugged. "He will find nothing out of order."

"And is the vampire research all that your companies do?"

He smiled. "No."

"Then what?"

"My companies partner several others in drug research."

What was the betting he had a finger in the pie that had made ARC1-23? "Does that mean you knew all about Talon trying to impregnate me?"

Again amusement glittered in his eyes. "Yes."

Anger whipped through me, and my fingers clenched. "And you approve?"

"No."

"Then why the hell didn't you warn me?"

"Because again, I was warned not to."

I snorted softly. "And you never go against orders? Bullshit, Misha."

"There are lots of things happening you don't understand. Lots of restrictions on me that I cannot countermand, no matter how I might wish to."

That raised my eyebrows. "Care to explain that sweeping statement?"

"Not yet."

I blew out a breath and thought about the bits and pieces he'd told me over the last few days. "You told me to imagine the supersoldier you could build if you could have all of a vamp's abilities and none of the restrictions. Is that what you're doing? Trying to build a supersoldier by crossing human and vampire genes?"

"Perhaps." He smiled idly.

"Then what about hybrid nonhumans?"

"What about them?"

"Are you involved in creating them?"

"I've already said no."

There wasn't a flicker in his face or his eyes, and yet I sensed that he'd just told his first outright lie. "Then you know nothing about an attack that occurred shortly after I'd been speaking to you on the phone."

He raised an eyebrow. "I want to fuck you, not kill you."

I leaned back, partially wanting to trust him but mostly not. "That didn't answer my question."

"Yes, it did." He hesitated. "I actually tried to warn you, but you hung up."

"So you knew about the attack in the graveyard?"

"Yes."

"How did they know where I was going to be?"

He glanced down at the arm that held the tracker, giving me the answer in an instant. I swore softly. "Then how did you know about the attack?"

He gave me that smile again and didn't answer.

I tapped my fingers against the table. "So are you going to tell me who owns Konane?"

His gaze swept down my body, and the fever that had lain in wait ignited. His silver eyes met mine, echoing the hunger that burned through me. I didn't want to want him, but at that moment, I had no choice. And I needed the answer he'd yet to give.

"I want another two hours out there," he said, nodding toward the heaving crowd on the dance floor.

"Why?"

His smile was sweet, and yet there was something cold about it. Something very calculating. And in that moment, I saw the similarity between him and Talon. "It doesn't matter why."

I guess in the end it didn't. He got his two hours. Then I got the name.

Talon.

Chapter 14

I headed for the toilets and had a long, hot shower. It didn't do much to ease the aches of my body, but at least I felt cleaner. And the moon's heat no longer flicked through my veins. Misha had finally seen to that, if nothing else. Maybe he thought it would ensure I'd see him again.

But if that had been his thinking, then he didn't know me very well at all. Though what did I really know of him? Or Talon?

At least my questions had been answered—whether truthfully or not still remained to be seen.

But the night *had* achieved something else—it had solidified my determination never to become a guardian. Because guardians, whether male or female, often used sex to gather information, and being with Misha had given me a small taste of what that was like. I had no problems with having sex with someone I didn't know. I'd done that most of my life, in many different werewolf clubs, and enjoyed myself immensely. But having sex with a stranger for the sole purpose of gathering information almost smacked of prostitution, and that sat uncomfortably.

Yet wasn't that exactly what I'd just done? Sure, I knew Misha, but did that really make a difference? The fact that I'd gone into the situation ready and willing to do what was necessary proved I was more like my brother—and more capable of undercover work—than I'd thought.

And that was the most uncomfortable thought of all.

I rubbed a hand across gritty-feeling eyes then glanced at the clock on the wall. It was just past two, and I really had to get moving. I stood under the hot water for a few more minutes, then toweled myself dry and got dressed. Stan and Jimmy gave me cheerful good-byes as I made my way back to the shadows of the lane.

Quinn leaned against the car hood, his arms crossed, face impassive. "Are you okay?"

I shrugged. "I got the answers to everyone's questions."

"The answers can wait. You look like hell."

"Strange. That's exactly what I feel like." I stopped several feet away, wishing he'd take me in his arms and hold me. Just hold me. Nothing more—not right away, anyway. I simply needed the comfort of a touch that wasn't hard or rough or calculating.

But he didn't move, and I didn't ask.

"Misha knew Jack and Rhoan were breaking in to his office."

"That explains the unhappy vibes I've been getting from you."

Was it any wonder he was getting unhappy vibes? Both of my mates were apparently using me for their own ends and never once had I suspected them. So much for trusting my damn instincts.

"Talon made an appearance at the club tonight," he continued.

Alarm shot through me. "What?"

He nodded. "Went in about forty-five minutes ago and left about ten minutes later."

"Wonder why?" It made no sense, especially considering he'd seemed determined to kill me after he'd learned of my mixed heritage.

"Maybe he's reconsidered."

"No." Talon rarely changed his mind about anything. If he'd come to the club, it would be for some reason other than wanting to conceive a child with me. "Did you try and stop him?"

"No, but I followed him in."

I hadn't sensed either of them. "What did he do?"

"Watched you and Misha."

"Misha implied that he and Talon had been partners in the past. Maybe they still are. Maybe Talon came into the club for that reason."

"And maybe realized that while he might not personally like your mixed heritage, you're still too good a morsel to pass up for research."

A chill ran through me. I had a feeling he'd hit the nail right on the head.

Quinn studied me for a second, then wrapped his fingers around my arm and pulled me into his embrace. He didn't say anything, just held me, and it felt so good and warm, and so damn *right,* that I wanted to cry.

"We'd better keep an eye on Talon. I fear he may be more involved than we currently think."

"He is. He owns Konane, and he owns Genoveve."

He kissed the top of my head, his lips a feather-light brush of heat. Then he held me away from him, and the night seemed suddenly colder.

"If that's the case, we'd better get moving."

I nodded, though I really didn't want to go anywhere but back into his arms.

"Here, put this on, then get into the car." His voice was even, yet I had a sense of controlled excitement. Perhaps he, like me, sensed that the resolution of this whole mess was drawing close.

I took the thin strap of metal he held out. "What is it?"

"It'll disrupt the chip's tracking signal and ensure we're not followed."

I strapped it onto my forearm as I climbed into the car. "Any word from Rhoan or Jack?"

"They're finished and waiting at Liander's."

We drove in silence to the workshop. Rhoan, Jack, and Liander were seated in the small dining-cum-living room behind the main workshop. Rhoan rose from the sofa he and Liander were sharing and pulled me into a hug. I hugged him back, glad to have someone in my life who was stable. Constant. Someone who loved me for what I was, not what I could do for him or produce for him. Someone who would always accept me as I was, vampire bloodline, wolf heritage, and all.

"You okay?" he whispered.

I nodded, not daring to answer in fear that the tears stinging my eyes would choose that moment to break free.

"Sex for information is never pleasant the first time."

"That's the trouble—in the end, the sex was *more* than pleasant." I shivered. "I don't want to become a guardian."

But it could happen, and I very much suspected that Jack was right. That I'd not only be good at it, but I'd enjoy it. Even the information-gathering, sex-with-strangers bit.

"Then fight it for as long as is practical." He stepped back, his face stern but eyes smoky with understanding. "You need a hot drink?"

"Coffee, with a chaser of bourbon."

He squeezed my hand, then walked across to the minibar. I sat down on a hard wooden chair next to Quinn.

"So," I said, voice edgy, "what happened to cutting all the alarm systems?"

Liander looked more than a little affronted. "I may be rusty, but I'm not *that* rusty."

"Then how come Misha knew you were in his office going through his files when I walked into the Blue Moon tonight?"

"He couldn't have," Jack said. "Believe me, we were very careful."

"Electronically, perhaps, but Misha implied he had more than electronic security systems present."

"He did, and they never saw us."

"Someone—or something—did."

Rhoan handed me the alcohol and I drank it in one gulp. It burned all the way down, but at least it took the edge off the cold knot sitting deep in the pit of my stomach.

"Then he didn't answer any questions?"

"No, he was quite happy to talk. He reckons he has nothing to hide."

"And you believe him?" Quinn asked softly.

I met his gaze, momentarily getting lost in the depths of his dark eyes. "No, I don't."

"So, why Genoveve?" Jack asked.

"Apparently, it's built over the top of a World War II military bunker. He was planning to use it for non-government-approved research."

"Was?" Jack asked.

Rhoan held out a steaming mug and I accepted it with a small smile. "Yeah. He was outbid by the same company who owns Moneisha."

"Konane?"

"Yep. And Konane is owned by Talon."

Liander groaned. "We had him, and we let him escape."

"And he's probably out of the damn country by now." Rhoan sat on the arm of the sofa and threw an arm around my shoulders. "We'll never find him."

"We will," Quinn said softly. "He was in the Blue Moon tonight, watching Misha and Riley. And he was furious."

"Interesting," Jack murmured. "It suggests that he still has some interest in Riley. Maybe we can put that to use."

"No," Rhoan and Quinn said together.

Jack ignored them, staring at me. "This all goes far deeper than one werewolf and one company, but right now, he's the only lead we have. He has to be caught, and he has to be questioned."

"Agreed," Rhoan all but spat, "but why use Riley as bait again? She's done more than her fair share for kin and country."

"I know she has." Jack's voice was filled with a contriteness that didn't show in the green of his eyes. "But Talon is not interested in you or me. And, because of Gautier's influence, we dare not trust any of the other guardians at this moment."

"We know where Genoveve Confectionary is. Why don't we just raid the damn place?"

"Because we don't know where the entrances to the underground sections are, and by the time we find them, the evidence we need might well be destroyed."

I sipped my coffee and met Jack's gaze evenly. While I was aware that he was reeling me in a little bit more, the reasons why I'd walked into the Blue Moon earlier tonight still held true. Whoever was behind this had to be stopped, and if I could play a part in that, did I really have the right to walk away?

And would walking away be any safer? They'd first come after me at the train station, and that was way before I'd really gotten involved in this investigation. Maybe walking would only make things worse.

Besides, the wolf within had had enough and wanted revenge in a *bad* way.

"Do not forget that ten guardians have already died, or that Kelly may have made it eleven," Jack added, talking to Rhoan but his gaze not wavering on mine.

I closed my eyes, not wanting to think about the other guardians. Not wanting to think that Kelly might have joined their ranks.

Dammit, she *couldn't* have. I didn't make friends all that easily—surely fate wouldn't be cruel enough to snatch her away.

"We *have* to stop this now," Jack added softly.

"Riley's not even a guardian!" Rhoan was off the chair,

fist clenched and expression livid. "How in hell can you expect her to survive what those others could not?"

"Because she *is* a survivor," Jack bit back. "And because she's a dhampire, just like her brother. That is more of an advantage than either of you realize."

"She's also sitting in this damn room, not in another building," I interrupted. "Rhoan, calm down and sit. Jack, just give me a goddamn chance to drink my coffee and catch my breath, will you?"

With the coffee in hand, I rose and walked out onto the balcony. The night air was as sharp as ice, and I breathed deep. It didn't clear the fear stirring through me. Fear not of what I had to do, but what I might become.

I leaned against the wrought-iron balustrade and sipped the aromatic hazelnut coffee. The wind whispered through the nearby trees and stirred the hair from the nape of my neck. It felt like the fingers of ghosts.

I closed my eyes and tried to gather calm from the cool of the night and the brightness of the stars.

Though I heard no sound, the teasing caress of sandalwood momentarily overwhelmed the scent of hazelnut and told me I was no longer alone. He leaned on the balustrade, his body separated from mine by several inches, yet close enough that the heat of him burned across my skin.

"Is it the moon?" he said softly.

"Partly. Jack seems to have forgotten that Rhoan, Liander, and I all turn into wolves tomorrow night."

"It'll surely be over by then."

I opened my eyes. The stars seemed to reflect in his night-colored gaze. "You didn't come out here to try to stop me?"

His smile was bittersweet. "What right have I to do that?"

"Whatever right you do or don't have didn't seem to matter a few minutes ago."

He shrugged. "Jack's suggestion caught me by surprise."

"But now that you've had time to think, you realize it might be the quickest way of finding your friend."

He held my gaze steadily. "Yes."

I looked away and took a sip of my coffee. "There are a great many risks in doing this, and Talon is no fool."

"Neither is Jack. Trust him."

"It's Talon I don't trust." I glanced skyward. "And he's the one who put the chip in my arm. If he snatches me, the first thing he'll do is take it out."

"But he won't suspect that I, too, carry one."

I glanced at him sharply. The smile that touched his lips never reached his eyes. "You're not going in there alone."

"If anyone should go with me, it's Rhoan. He's trained for this sort of stuff."

"And I have centuries behind me. Life and time provide far better training than your Directorate ever could."

"Jack won't allow it."

"Jack can't stop me."

"But Talon might not be tempted to snatch me if you're with me."

"Oh, I think he will. For a start, I gave him a broken nose when I rescued you, and I'm sure he's itching to return the favor. And second, I've killed a lot of his precious clones."

I had to admit, I felt far better about being bait with

Quinn alongside me. I probably wouldn't be any safer, but at least I wouldn't be alone.

"Thank you," I said softly.

He grimaced. "My reasons are purely selfish, so don't read too much into it."

"Meaning if it's a choice between me and your friend, you'll save your friend?"

The warmth fled from his face, leaving it emotionless. "Yes."

Fair enough. He'd known his friend for many centuries. He'd only made love to me a couple of times. Had our positions been reversed, I probably would have made the same decision.

I think.

"There is one thing we should do before we get in there," he continued. "Just in case we're separated."

"What's that?"

"Develop a psi link between us."

"Psi links can be nullified by psychic deadeners, and I'm betting Talon will have the latest installed." Though the latest deadeners hadn't worked with Quinn in the Directorate, they'd certainly stop me. "He couldn't take the risk of not doing so if he's developing vampire clones."

"But we've shared blood."

"So? A deadener is a deadener."

"And it works on one specific section of the brain. Because we've shared blood, our psychic connection will work in a whole different area."

"You're shitting me?"

The smile that tugged his lips made my pulse skip. "No, I am not."

I tilted my head slightly and studied him for a moment. "Why?"

He shrugged. "Because unless it comes down to that choice, I intend to get us both out of there alive."

"And once the link is formed, can it be broken?"

He hesitated. "No, but I'm in Sydney most of the time, so it won't matter."

"And on the odd occasion you're not?"

"It still won't really matter. The link is basically a locked door between two rooms—your mind and mine. And like any locked door, you have to knock to gain entry."

"No master keys?"

Starlight twinkled briefly in his eyes. "No keys."

"Then what do we do?"

"Put your coffee down."

I did so.

"Now, raise your left hand and touch your fingertips to my temple, then close your eyes."

He echoed my movements, his fingertips so warm against my head.

"Now, imagine yourself standing on a vast dark plain. In the middle of this plain there is a wall you cannot see past. Imagine that wall as your psi shields."

It was harder than I thought it would be. I'd always taken my psi shields for granted—they were a gift of my heritage, something I'd had since birth, and they'd strengthened greatly over the years. Rhoan had taught me how to lower them once he'd become a guardian, but that was about it for training. No one had ever told me I could create "doors." Maybe it was something not everyone could do.

Sweat trickled down my face and I resisted the urge to swipe it away. The dark plain was forming, and so too was a wall. It was red, endless, and seemed to shimmer slightly.

"Now," Quinn intoned softly, "imagine there is a door on the left edge of that wall."

"The wall is endless."

"Then either you have not envisaged an end, or you have psi talents you have not yet tapped. Imagine the door as far left as you can see without moving."

Again I did as he bid, but the effort left me trembling.

"Now, push that door open and see me there."

I took a deep breath and envisaged that door slowly opening. It felt like I was trying to move a damn mountain. I pushed and pushed, and finally, with a snap, it opened, and I fell flat on my psychic face. I looked up, imagining Quinn standing there, imagining him laughing.

And suddenly he was laughing, not out loud but deep inside. It was a caress of warmth that stirred the fibers of my soul, intimate in a way that went beyond touch, beyond sex.

No one has ever fallen through a door before.

His mind voice was as rich and as sexy as his regular voice, though why I found that surprising I don't really know.

Well, I've never liked doing the obvious. I picked my psychic self off the floor, and added, *So this door will remain open now unless one of us closes it?*

Yes, but I think it best to close it now, simply because you are a wolf and your aura is reaching a peak. The minute we're inside Genoveve, open it.

Meaning he wasn't as immune to my aura as he was pretending? I couldn't be sad about that. *So how do I close it?*

Simply imagine the door closing, and it will be done.

There was no "simply" about it. Closing that psychic

door proved every bit as hard as opening it. But maybe that was because part of me simply didn't want to lose the intimacy of it.

It slammed shut the last few inches, as if given a push from the other side. A gasp escaped my lips, and I opened my eyes. His gaze met mine, warm and sexy.

I dropped my hand from his temple. "It must be amazing to have sex like that."

He raised an eyebrow, his fingers sliding from my temple to my cheek. "You've never made love to another psychic?"

"Well, obviously I have, because you're psychic and I discovered this evening that Misha is as well. But never once has anyone suggested dropping shields and entwining our minds as intimately as our bodies."

"It's an amazing experience."

His fingers were warm against my cheek, drowning me in sunshine and desire. My heart was hammering so loud I was sure they'd be able to hear it in the living room. I cleared my throat and somehow managed to stutter, "I'll have to take your word for it."

"Maybe one day—"

He didn't finish the sentence simply because his lips met mine. On the kissing scale, it blew the top off anything I'd experienced so far—even with him. It was a wild and erotic possession that was both passionate and intimate. And it totally and irreparably smashed the lie that he didn't want anything more than sex. *No one* could kiss like that and say it was just about sex.

Yet he wouldn't admit it, not in words, and I had no doubt that at the end of this mission he would still walk away.

Which was damned annoying.

I pulled back. We were both breathing heavily, and

his desire was as evident as mine. "Too much more of that and you might just find yourself being ridden right here on the balcony."

"And you think I would have minded?"

"Well, no. I just didn't think you were an exhibitionist."

"With you, I could be."

I grinned. "Remind me to take you up on the offer sometime."

Amusement lingered on his lips, but there was a sadness in his eyes that stirred my heart.

"It won't happen, Riley."

Like hell it wouldn't. My wolf soul had his scent in her nose, and she wasn't about to let him go easily. He picked up the coffee cup and offered it to me. "Have I stirred things up too much?"

"The fever is controllable enough." Which was surprising. Even though I'd been with Misha for five hours, the moon heat should still be raging through my system. The full moon was less than a day away, and given the intensity of need earlier in the week, I should have been at fever pitch by now.

Maybe it was the situation. Maybe fear of playing bait a second time was overwhelming the power of the moon. Whatever the cause, I had no doubt that later on in the day my need would burn. I was a werewolf, and there was no escaping such a basic part of what I was.

"We should get moving." He glanced at the sky. "Dawn will be soon."

My stomach curled. I threw the rest of my coffee over the balcony, then walked back inside. "What's the plan then?"

Rhoan groaned. "Riley—"

"There's no other way, and we both know it."

"I'm going with her," Quinn said, his gaze challenging Jack.

Jack didn't look all that surprised. "I don't think you should. As I said before, I can protect Riley but not you."

"If things go down the tube, your protection won't matter to her or to me."

"True." Jack glanced at me. "I won't bother telling you it'll be rough in there, simply because you know what Talon is capable of better than any of us. I will tell you that no matter what, you do what you have to do to survive. Even if that means killing."

I stared at him for a moment, throat dry, then nodded.

"We'll insert microchips under both your armpits so we can track either of you," he continued, "and set you up with weapons. Then I think it's time for you to return home, Riley."

And wait for the net to fall, obviously. "They'll do weapons search, surely."

Jack's sudden grin was devious. "But they'll be looking for weapons that look like weapons."

I raised an eyebrow but didn't bother asking him to explain. I'd see them soon enough anyway.

Jack thrust up from the seat and repeated what had to be one of his favorite expressions: "Let's get this show on the road, people."

*W*alking through the front door of my apartment had never proven so nerve-racking. While I'd sensed no intruders, that didn't mean there couldn't be. After all, I couldn't sense humans, and the things that had attacked Quinn in his apartment had smelled like humans to him.

Quinn had stopped at the door, and it wasn't until I'd checked all the rooms that I realized why. He couldn't enter without an invitation.

I grinned at him. "You wanna come in?"

"It would be easier to play bait from inside rather than the hall," he said, voice dry. "But remember, there are consequences."

I nodded. "Once invited, never refused."

"Meaning I can come and go as I please, whenever I please."

"Meaning you could come in for a little midnight fun when you're down in Melbourne?"

He gave me a smoky sort of look that could have meant anything. "Maybe."

Couldn't be sad about that, either. "Quinn O'Conor, you are welcome to step over the threshold of my home anytime you please."

He stepped through the door, then took my hand and brushed a kiss across my fingertips. Warmth spread like quicksilver through my body, and deep inside, my soul trembled.

"Thank you."

"You're most welcome."

I took my hand from his, then walked into the kitchen and grabbed a soda and a synth blood pack from the fridge. Quinn was standing near the window when I came back out, the early-morning sunlight streaming in through the glass surrounding him in a halo of gold.

He accepted the blood pack with a smile, and said, "I can't see any of them."

"You're not supposed to." I dropped my bag and

popped the soda. "Rhoan and Jack are guardians, and good at what they do."

I gulped down the soda, then walked back into the kitchen to dump the can into the rubbish bin. Quinn was watching me as I walked back out. "You're favoring your right leg a little. You'd better shift the position of the knife."

"Easier said than done."

I bent and tried to adjust the weapon. Just getting my hand down the side of the boots was hard enough, and I fleetingly wished I'd gone for something more flexible in footwear. But Talon had liked them and might be inclined to leave them on. They were practically a second skin, and under normal situations would have shown any weapons shoved down them.

But the Directorate's knives were far from normal—three of them were thin, clear sheets of plastic that were as rigid as steel and could slice through just about anything—or so I'd been assured. The other was almost identical, only it was made of a special compound that reacted with blood and disintegrated—revealing the silver strip that ran down the heart of it. Ideal, Rhoan assured me, for pinning werewolves and other shapeshifters to human form. Personally, I preferred the microscopic hand laser secured in the topknot of my hair.

Quinn had those and more, but I had a suspicion that he wouldn't use them unless he absolutely had to.

When I finally got the knife in a comfortable position, he wrapped his fingers around my arm and pulled me close. I rested my cheek against his chest, listening to the slow beat of his heart, feeling safer than I ever had in my life.

An illusion, but one I could have easily surrendered to.

"It's close to nine," I said, after a long while. "Hope they get here soon." Before whatever courage I'd started with got up and walked away.

"There's a van moving up the street," he said, his voice a rumble that vibrated through my ear. "There are eight people inside."

"I think I should be offended that Talon's only sent an extra two to deal with me."

He laughed softly and brushed his lips across the top of my hair. "They're expecting the element of surprise."

"They should also be expecting a fight."

"Talon's never seen you in action, has he? And six were quite enough to overpower me."

I looked up at him. "You never satisfactorily explained that."

He grimaced. "It was simply the fact that they were all the spitting image of Henri. I wasn't expecting it and it shocked me. In a life-or-death situation, a second's hesitation is all it takes to change the odds."

And it was almost his death. "So why the garden center?"

"As I said, I suspect they wanted it to look like a random vampire killing."

It made sense. Given the amount of vamp murders that had happened over the past few weeks, no one would have raised an eyebrow. And while the Directorate would have investigated, if it had looked like a singular event rather than gang-related, it probably would have been given lower priority.

"They're getting out of the van," he said softly.

Tension wound through my limbs, and my stomach began doing tight circles. "Clones?"

"Mix of clones and werewolves."

I took a deep breath, then raised on my toes and gave him a kiss. "Good luck."

His lips lingered on mine, his breath warm against my skin. "You too."

The doorbell rang. I took another breath, then broke away from his grasp and shook nerveless fingers. "Yes?"

"Special delivery," a gruff voice answered. "Needs to be signed for."

I glanced at Quinn a final time, saw his tension in the set of his shoulders, then walked to the door. My fingers shook as I clasped the handle and undid the deadlock, but I never got the chance to open the door. Instead, it was thrust open by those on the other side, striking me in the nose and flinging me backward.

I hit the ground with a grunt, but rolled immediately to my feet. There was blood gushing from my nose and people flowing through the doorway. They smelled of rubbish left too long in the sun. Whatever method Talon was using to create the things was also killing them.

Then there was no more time to think as two of them rushed at me. I ducked the blow of the first creature, but missed the second. His fist smashed into my chin and the force of it had me sprawling backward. I hit the floor a second time, my breath leaving in a whoosh of air. For a moment, stars danced, the world went dark, and the bitter taste of blood filled my throat.

Someone who smelled of sex and death fell on top of me. Though gasping for breath and fighting the blackness threatening to invade my mind, I still heard the creature snarl. He smelled and looked like a wolf, but his teeth were extending, saliva dripping from the ends in expectation of a feed.

The bastard wasn't going to feed off me, not if I could help it.

With as much force as I could muster, I slammed the heel of my hand into his face. Bone and cartilage shattered under the blow, and he screamed. I thrust him off, scrambled to my feet, and swiped a hand at the blood running from my nose.

Air rushed from the left. I pivoted on one foot, kicking hard. The blow landed in the gut of the clone rushing at me, but didn't seem to have the slightest effect. He grabbed my foot, twisting it hard, making me yelp. His smile was greasy and overconfident and I saw why a second later when he raised the gun. I jerked my foot from his grasp, heard the slight "pop," felt a brief sting of pain in my arm. Looked down, and saw the dart.

Being drugged was better than being battered unconscious.

Even so, I went down fighting.

Talon would expect nothing less.

Chapter 15

Awareness snuck in slowly, and with it came a sense of déjà vu. Voices surrounded me, some that were tinny and some guttural. Lights as bright as the sun burned into my closed eyes. The air was a cool caress and yet my skin burned.

As awareness sharpened, it formed a picture of rising pleasure and lingering pain. My arms were raised above my head, the pins and needles in my fingers suggesting they'd been that way for some time.

Sweat stung the air, mingling with the heady aroma of sex and lust. The moon fever seared through my system, the sheer strength of it a warning that the time of changing was near.

My back was pressed against something cold and hard, my stomach against flesh as hot as the sun. My skin was on fire and every muscle quivered.

Hands were on me, bruising and familiar. Heat

filled me, thrusting deep, pushing me toward the crescendo I both wanted and hated.

As before, it wasn't a dream. Talon was in me, and I was responding as strongly as I ever had.

Pleasure spiraled, until it became a force that would not be denied. I came at the same time he did, but bit my lip against the strangled gasp rising up my throat. My body might be conditioned to respond to his touch and his smell, but I wasn't a willing participant in this mating, and I'd be damned if I'd give him the satisfaction of knowing he could still make me come.

He gave one last thrust, then withdrew and stepped back. The room behind him was narrow and long, the wall opposite all glass. Comfy chairs followed the curve of the glass, and behind these, several sofas. It reminded me of the private boxes often seen in sporting venues. The only thing that differed was the long control panel and desk to my left.

My gaze finally met Talon's. Amusement shone in his golden eyes and his expression was all arrogance. My fingers clenched, but with my hands chained above my head there was little leeway to swing a punch.

"I guess this means you've decided it's still okay to fuck a half-breed, huh?" I said dryly.

He sauntered over to the sofa and sat on the back of it, one leg swinging idly. "Fuck, yes. Have a child with, no. I am the pinnacle of the werewolf race. I can breed with nothing less than similar perfection."

I raised an eyebrow at that. He *was* perfection, but only in body. The heart and soul left a lot to be desired. "Then you're going to die childless."

A smile played about his lips. "Perhaps."

I didn't trust that smile or the glint in his eyes. They

bode me no good. I shifted slightly, testing the chains around my legs. They were as tight as those on my hands, but the brush of leather against my thigh said I still had my boots on. Though the knives were a fat lot of good if I couldn't get to them. Still, there *was* one good thing. The chains weren't silver.

"So why bring me here at all?"

"Because you are a dhampire, and one with few problems, which is extremely rare. Examining your genes will greatly enhance my research."

"I thought you were breeding clones?"

"I am. But I'm also exploring the DNA of different races in the hope it'll explain why my clones are dying."

"Here's a news flash. You want to create dhampires, all you have to do is wait by the grave of an undead. Grab him when he rises and milk away. His seed is viable for up to twenty-four hours."

"The newly risen are extremely violent, and I have not the resources to waste just yet."

"Yet you can keep throwing them at Quinn." And me.

He shrugged. "He was getting dangerous."

"Because he was getting close?"

"Yes."

"And where is he now?"

His eyes glinted at me. "Do you care?"

I rolled my eyes. "He's a vampire, for God's sake."

Talon snorted. "At least you have some taste left. He's downstairs, in a cell. He'll prove a good test for my latest batch."

"He's not a guardian." It was a guess, but a fairly certain one.

His smile flashed. "No. He is something better—an extremely old vampire."

Part of me ached to ask about Kelly, but I didn't. Mostly because I needed to be strong at that moment, and if I knew for sure she was dead, strong was the one thing I *wouldn't* be. "And is that what you plan for me as well?"

"Oh no, little wolf. You will spend your days in my labs here in Genoveve and your nights in my bed."

His voice was a low and familiar caress I felt deep inside. Given the fast-approaching full moon, desire was almost automatic, but it was accompanied by a churning in my gut. I really didn't want him to touch me, but if push came to shove, there might be little choice.

"Tell me, did you send those sickos in the van after me?"

Anger flickered in his eyes. "No."

"Then who did?"

"Someone who is of no consequence to you now."

Meaning he expected me to stay here like some good little puppy? The man was an idiot. An insane idiot. "Then why were they bringing me here first?"

"Because those guards were mine, and obey my orders first."

I raised an eyebrow. Dissension in the ranks had to be good for us. "And your orders were?"

"To bring you here so I could claim what I wanted first." He paused. "It was before I realized you had tainted blood, remember."

Tainted blood? That was almost as bad as Quinn asking me if I needed "relief." "So was the man giving orders Misha?"

Talon snorted. "Misha is a fool who plays a dangerous game."

"Then who is in charge?"

His golden eyes twinkled with amusement. "Someone you know, little wolf. Someone you've had dealings with for some time now."

Well, gee, that narrowed down the field. It could be a past lover, or a friend, or the guy I bought coffee off most lunchtimes. "I don't suppose you can be a little more specific?"

"I don't suppose I can."

My fists clenched, but it was pretty much a useless gesture of irritation. "Do you really think the Directorate is going to let you grab one of their people and not do anything about it?"

"You're a secretary, not a guardian. I hardly think they'll miss you."

"Rhoan will."

His smile reminded me of a shark. A conceited one at that. "Neither Rhoan nor the Directorate knows anything about Genoveve or this facility. They concentrate their efforts on Moneisha and I'm quite happy for them to continue to do so."

His arrogance would be his downfall—and I hoped like hell I would be there at the end to witness it.

He rose and sauntered over to the window, staring out. I closed my eyes, imagining that dark plain and the door I'd created.

Talon's voice made me start.

"My father started this research a long time ago, and I have every intention of finishing it."

"So your father was as mad as you?" My comment was absent, my concentration on opening that door. Sweat trickled down my forehead.

"My father was a genius. He saw the potential in the werewolf race, a potential that was not being realized simply because breeding was not being selective enough."

The dark plain rolled before me, the red wall shimmering brightly. I grasped the door handle and thrust my weight against the door. It still felt like I was trying to move a mountain, and I wondered if it would get better with time—and usage—or whether this sort of mental stiffness was natural.

Talon droned on. "He spent his life studying the DNA sequences of the genes within an adult werewolf, how the proteins are made, and how they are used to construct the adult body. I am the result of his research."

My eyes flew open. "You're a *clone*?"

He glanced over his shoulder. "I prefer to call myself a natural creation of the lab. I am everything my father and the werewolf race is not."

I stared at him, dumbfounded. And yet it explained his size. And the overwhelming power of his aura. It *wasn't* natural. "But . . . why then do all your clones reek of death if your father perfected the research?"

"Because much of the research was lost in a fire that took my father's life. And because I use an accelerant so I have fully functioning adults to test. Vampire genes are more elusive than werewolf."

"So why are you working on vampire clones if your father saw the potential of werewolves?"

"Because the vampire is faster than the wolf and has the gift of shadowing. Pinpoint the sequences that give birth to this difference, add them to the werewolf, and you have a creature of unstoppable power."

"And yet you're rejecting me because I'm not full

were. That really doesn't make sense, even for a madman."

His smile was condescending. "My creations will be all wolf—they will just have a few extra sequences that will give them greater skills."

"Then they are not wolf."

He snorted. "Like I am not a wolf, just because my DNA has been enhanced? No, my creations will be weres, and they will be all-powerful."

And he planned to be the force behind that power. God only knew what he intended to do with it. "Is Misha working with you in this? His company is certainly working to pinpoint the vampire genes."

Mirth played about his mouth. "Misha refuses to see the benefits in cloning."

So Misha had been telling the truth in that respect, but could I trust the truth of everything else he'd said? Somehow, I suspected not. "So he's your partner?"

"Not in Genoveve."

So, again, Misha had been telling the truth. Question was, why, when he was obviously involved not only with Talon in other ventures, but also with the man who controlled them both?

A light flashed on the panel to my left. Talon sauntered over and picked up the phone. The voice on the other end of the phone was guttural and edged with some sort of accent, making it difficult to pick up any words from where I stood.

Talon hung up, then walked over to me and grabbed my face with one hand, his fingers digging into my cheeks. This close his aura was smothering, all heat and longing and need. "Business to attend to," he said, then kissed me hard.

God help me, the fever rose, and it was all I could

do not to arch into his body. But when he stepped back, I spat in his face. He laughed and wiped the spittle away with an arm. "We shall see how feisty you are once that fever has had time to burn."

He walked out. I closed my eyes and conjured the psi door again, pushing with all my might. This time it opened, and I didn't fall on my face.

Are you all right?

Quinn's mind voice was flat and soft, yet his anger and concern seemed to resound through every fiber, providing both warmth and strength.

Yes. You?

Nothing worse than bruised ribs. I'm currently locked in a cell, but I have all the hidden weapons.

As have I. I'm chained in what looks like a control room over what I'm presuming is an arena.

Is Talon with you?

Just left.

And the fever?

Burns. Right then the force of fear made me able to ignore it, but I had a suspicion Talon only needed to walk into the room and that would be the end of any pretense of control.

Can you escape?

I tugged experimentally on the chains. Concrete dust sprinkled downward, making me sneeze. *Probably take me a while, but yes.*

Then start trying. This cell has laser bars, and I can't get out until they're down.

So you're not holding out hope that Rhoan and Jack are going to come rushing to the rescue any minute now?

It's five in the afternoon. If they're rushing, they've got a strange way of showing it.

Something has gone wrong.

Obviously. He hesitated, then added. *They'll be here, of that I have no doubt. I just don't think we can afford to sit around and wait for them.*

Not when Talon plans to use you as a punching bag for his latest batch of clones.

Shifting my right foot, I began turning and twisting and tugging at the chain, until the skin around my ankle was raw and pain burned up my leg. The ring in the wall began to move, the small puffs of dust providing hope.

It came away suddenly, the chain lashing out across the carpet, then snapping back like a pissed-off snake.

I started on the ring holding my other leg captive and was slick with sweat and trembling by the time it came loose. I edged the chains behind my legs just in case Talon came back in, then started work on the chains pinning my arms together.

Maybe it was the fact that the ring was higher and I was able to hang more weight off it, but that one came out quicker. Even so, my wrists were red and raw.

I'm free. Still wearing chains, but free. I rattled past the long control panel and began going through the drawers of the desk.

Great. Now comes the more difficult part—finding me.

Unfortunately, Talon has not been considerate enough to leave floor plans lying about.

Quinn's amusement shimmered through my mind, momentarily dulling the ache in my wrists and ankles. *I'll have a word with him when I meet him.*

The third drawer down was locked. I forced it open, and found several keys. The fourth key opened the locks around my wrists, the seventh the ones around my ankles. I had no idea what the rest opened, but I wasn't about to leave them behind.

I puddled the chains under the desk and walked back to the control panel. *Any idea where you are?*

No. There are no signs and no movement whatsoever.

I scanned the many screens and eventually found what looked like pictures from security cams. I pressed a button, and the picture jumped to a different setting. I kept pressing. The first person I found was Talon. He was in a lab, peering into a microscope, and just the way he stood suggested he was far from happy. And that made *me* extremely happy.

I moved on, eventually finding what looked to be a series of crisscrossed red lights. *Those lasers bars . . . are they red and on all four sides?*

Yes.

Then I think I've found where you are. I glanced at the top of the screen. Sublevel three. *All I have to do now is find how to get there.*

Be careful.

No . . . really? And here I was all set to go running down the halls.

His laughter reminded me of a summer breeze—so warm and rich. *Anyone would think you did this for a living.*

My clothes were nowhere to be found, so I walked over to what looked like a cupboard. Inside, there were several leather jackets and Talon-sized pants, as well as a white lab coat. I put on the coat, rolled up the sleeves, then undid my hair to retrieve the finger laser. The knives I left where they were.

On my way. Hopefully.

I opened the door and peered out. The corridor was long and curved around to the right. I glanced up. Two security cams, one just above me, another right on the curve.

Shoot them out.

I do that and it'll raise the alarm.

The mere act of walking out could do that. You have no idea who's watching.

I slipped the laser onto my fingers, adjusted the trigger, then raised my hand and fired. Black glass shattered, falling to the floor as softly as snow. I did the same to the second camera, then listened for any sound that might indicate the alarm had been raised.

Nothing.

I edged out. The silence was eerie, the air cold. Shivering, wishing I had more than a thin coat on, I edged down the corridor.

As I moved around the corner, a slight hum filled the silence. I froze. Sweat trickled down my back, and my finger trembled against the laser's trigger. The humming stopped. I let loose the breath I'd been holding, but in that instant, footsteps echoed, coming down the hall toward me.

I swore under my breath and looked around quickly. No doors and nowhere to go but back to that room. I might not have gotten far, but I wasn't about to retreat. I sniffed the air. Pine and coffee. Not Talon, then.

Taking a deep breath, I pushed away from the wall and walked down the hall, the rap of my bootheels as loud as the beat of my heart. His scent got sharper, and a second later I saw him—a small brown man clutching a clipboard and wearing a furtive expression.

He stopped when he saw me. "Who the hell are you?"

"Research." I continued walking toward him.

His frown increased. "What division?"

"This one." I popped the buttons on my lab coat and flashed him.

The clipboard dropped to the floor and his jaw just about did the same. That's when I hit him. His head snapped back and he hit the floor with a crack that made me wince. I dragged him to the side and checked that he still had a pulse.

He did. I grabbed the pass from around his neck, wrapped the coat around me as best I could, picked up the clipboard, and continued on. Elevator doors came into view. So too did another camera.

I kept my head down and kept on walking. The doors slid open. I walked in, pressed sublevel three, then stepped back and waited.

And waited.

Heart thumping, fingers trembling, I pressed the button a second time.

Still nothing.

Then I saw the keycard slot beside the panel. Cursing under my breath, I swiped the stolen pass through the slot and the elevator doors slid closed.

I flopped back against the wall and took several deep breaths. Until I saw the camera. The whole place was worse than the damn Directorate for spying on people. But I didn't move, hoping my disheveled and sweaty state would have any watchers thinking I was nothing more than another of Talon's floozies. Which I guess I was.

The elevator stopped at sublevel three and the doors opened. I peered out. Darkness crisscrossed by red lines greeted me. I switched to infrared and scanned the room. Heat fluttered down the far end of the room. There was nothing—or no one—else near.

Hurry, Quinn said.

"Like I'm not," I muttered, and heard the distant

ring of amusement, felt it wash through my mind as sweetly as a kiss.

It seemed to take forever to weave through the web of lasers. Hurrying wasn't a priority when the slightest wrong move could result in body parts being sliced off.

Eventually, I reached his cell, and the sheer relief of seeing him again had me shaking. I retrieved the keys from the pocket of the coat, found one that looked right, and slid it into the lock. The lasers withdrew, and Quinn was free.

He didn't move, just studied me in a detached sort of way. Though I wanted nothing more than to lose myself in the safety and warmth of his arms, it was a risk I couldn't take. The fever was knife-edged.

"And if we meet Talon?"

He was reading my thoughts better than I was his. But then, he'd had more practice. I shrugged. "I'll deal with it."

He nodded, accepting my answer though we both knew there was only one way to deal with the heat that burned through my bloodstream.

"Let's go."

He led the way back through the maze of lights. A soft humming filled the silence. The elevator was on the move again.

"You hide left, I'll hide right. If it stops here, we'll attack," Quinn said.

Mouth dry, I wrapped the shadows around my body and pressed back against the wall. The movements of the elevator vibrated into my spine, and I closed my eyes, hoping against hope it didn't stop.

It did.

Eight people walked out and began moving toward the laser cells. They smelled of death, and a sliver of relief ran through me. A single werewolf in the mix could have spelled trouble.

The elevator door closed and cut off any immediate retreat.

Go, Quinn said, and I did.

I might be vampire-fast but my heels still rapped against the floor and gave the game away. There was a shout and the last vampire in line spun, his fist flying in a blur. I ducked, then punched, my blow smashing into his ribs with enough force to elicit a groan.

Out of the corner of my eye I saw the flash of movement. I swung, kicked the first vampire in the head, then twisted away from the hands grabbing at me. Only to fall into the grasp of another. His arm snaked around my neck and I cursed, mule-kicking. I hit nothing but air and he laughed, his breath foul as it brushed past my cheek. I twisted and grabbed his balls, squeezing hard. He made a strangled sound, his grip around my neck loosening. I tore free and thrust him into the path of another. They went down in a tangle of arms and legs.

Another vampire lunged for me. I backpedaled fast, barely avoiding his fist. I ducked a second blow, then pivoted and kicked him in the gut. The blow bounced off the vampire's flesh and jarred my whole leg. The bastard obviously had bricks in place of stomach muscles.

I danced away from another blow, then lashed out at the vampire's jaw. Though his head snapped back, he snarled—or smiled. It was hard to tell when all I saw was the flash of teeth. I hit him again, but he caught the blow in his fist and twisted hard. Pain burned white-hot up my arm, and a scream tore up my throat—a scream that became more intense as his teeth slashed into my arm. The sound of his greedy sucking churned my gut.

Shuddering, I twisted, sweeping the creature off its feet again. Pain twisted up my arm as his teeth were ripped from my flesh, and he roared in frustration. I lashed out, the blow catching the side of his face and sending him staggering.

He didn't get far. There was a blur of red heat, then Quinn was in front of me, his fury so great it scorched both skin and mind.

He wrapped his fingers around the vampire's neck and pulled him close. "Where is the man who is being used to produce the clones?"

The vampire cursed him, but the words abruptly cut off. Silence fell. No conversation, no movement from either vampire. But I knew what was happening. Quinn was raiding the other's mind.

I thrust up the coat's sleeve and checked the wound. It was as bad as it felt but before I could shift shape, there was a crack of bone and Quinn's hand was on mine. The vampire lay limp behind him.

"Let me," he said softly.

He raised my wrist to his mouth and flicked his tongue across the wound. The sweet bliss of the caress made me jump, a whimper escaping my lips. His dark gaze burned into mine, his breath fiery against my skin. He licked at the wound as a cat might, washing away the blood, cleaning and healing the wound. It was erotic and sensual and undeniably exquisite.

My breath caught somewhere in my throat and the fever battered the walls of control. "Quinn, don't."

It was a soft and breathy plea, but one he ignored. Sensations tumbled through me. I quivered under the gentle eroticism of his touch, clenching my thighs as the pressure built and built, until I felt so tightly strung everything would surely snap. Then it did, and I was unraveling, groaning, with the intensity of the orgasm flowing through me.

It had only taken a few minutes, and as I opened my eyes and met his dark gaze, I knew it had been deliberate. He'd lifted the lid off the pressure cooker inside me, giving me more of a chance to control it a little longer.

"Thank you."

"Blood as sweet as yours should never be wasted." He kissed my fingers, his lips warm against my skin, then released my hand and stepped away. "We have to get going."

At that moment, I would have I followed him anywhere, but I settled for the elevator. "Did you get anything from the vampire before you killed him?"

"The location of Henri and the nearest exit."

"So we get Henri first, then retreat?"

"No. I get Henri and you get the hell out of here."

"Quinn—"

The doors opened. He pressed a hand into my back, guiding me inside. "It's for the best. There's an exit not far from the elevator. The alarm doesn't appear to have gone out yet, but it soon will. That's when it'll get dangerous."

"You can't fight all these creatures alone."

He took the pass from me, swiping it through the slot before hitting the first-floor button. "I can fight a whole lot better knowing you are safe. Please, do what is sensible."

I took a deep, shuddering breath. Part of me wanted to stay and fight by his side, but the rest knew he was right. I wasn't trained for this sort of work. I could fight, but I didn't want to kill, and that could get dangerous for not only me but Quinn as well.

"Okay."

A smile tugged his lush lips. "You are the most surprising woman I have ever met."

I raised an eyebrow. "Because I do what is sensible?"

"Because you do so without arguing first."

"I do not have a death wish, and this is not a situation I'm enjoying." Besides, though there were no windows and clocks to be seen in this place, I knew night was falling. The full moon was close to rising, and the force of it had my whole body tingling. Soon I would be wolf, and while teeth were a good weapon against one, against many they would be useless.

I lightly touched his cheek. "Please be careful."

He caught my hand and kissed my palm. "I'm a very old vampire, and I didn't get this way by being careless. And one crazy young werewolf with Hitler delusions will not take me out."

Maybe. But that crazy young werewolf had an army of dysfunctional clones at his back, and *they* very well might.

The elevator stopped, and the doors opened. Quinn released me and peered out. I retrieved a couple of knives from my boots and put them in the coat's pockets.

"Clear." He tugged me out. "Go left and take the first corridor on the right. The exit is at the very end."

I didn't move, etching his face in my mind, just in case something happened and I never saw him again.

"Go," he said softly and released my hand.

I stepped forward, brushed a quick kiss across his lips, then turned and walked away. But I'd barely gone ten steps when a strident ringing cut through the silence. I froze, my heart sitting somewhere in my throat and beating ten to the dozen.

Run, Quinn said.

I ran. The ringing was deafening, echoing through my ears, but hopefully overwhelming the loud tattoo of my footsteps. The corridor was long, curving around to the left, affording no vision of what was coming the other way. I hadn't seen many people walking the halls, and hoped like hell it stayed that way until I got out.

Should have known my luck was never likely to hold.

Somewhere behind me a door opened, and the sound of heavy footsteps seemed to boom in time with the alarm. They were running toward me, not away.

From ahead, there were more footsteps. I swore softly and checked the laser. Half-charged. I could mow down a few more people before I was reduced to fighting with knife and fist.

The curve of the corridor came to an end, and so, too, did freedom. Talon stood under the exit sign, as naked as when he'd left me earlier, his brawny arms crossed and an arrogant expression on his face. Six clones were at his back.

I slid to a stop and clenched my right hand, my finger against the laser's trigger, ready to fire it should any of them make the slightest move.

"Planning to go somewhere?" he drawled.

My other hand was around a knife. "I've decided I'm not keen on this resort. Don't suppose you'd be kind enough to move so I can get to the exit?"

He raised an eyebrow. "I don't suppose you'd be kind enough to tell me where your vampire lover is?"

"What makes you think I'd know or care?"

"The fact you helped him escape."

"If I helped him escape, he'd be with me, wouldn't he?"

His smile made my skin crawl. "He will never find his friend, you know. This place is a maze, and the corridors bright. No shadows for a vampire to hide in, I'm afraid."

Quinn didn't need shadows and he didn't need to hide. All he had to do was touch the minds of all those he passed and make them see nothing. Far better than shadows.

"So all this racket is because a wolf and a vampire escaped your net? A bit over the top, don't you think?"

He shrugged. "The alarm is automatic when a door is breached."

My heart began to race a little faster. Neither Quinn nor I had breached a door. Did that mean Rhoan and Jack were on the way?

Though surely Talon wouldn't just presume it was us. Surely he would check with security first.

His next words answered my question. "Mark, grab her, will you? Security is paging me."

Footsteps echoed behind me. I swung and dropped, sweeping the laser's light across the legs of three men who approached, cutting through flesh and bone as sweetly as a knife through butter. The smell of burned flesh stung the air, and the three of them hit the floor, screaming and grabbing at legs that were no longer a part of their bodies.

Nausea rose. I swallowed heavily, allowing myself no time to dwell on what I'd done.

Though what I'd done was, in many ways, worse than killing them.

Talon's curse was lost to the sound of more footsteps. I swung back round, cutting down three more clones before the laser petered out. I grabbed the second knife out of my pocket, then lunged forward, the paper-thin weapons glinting like diamonds under the harsh lighting. Two more clones went down, the blades lodged deep in their chests.

Then the last one was on me. I ducked the first few blows, then dropped and swept with my leg, knocking him over. He grabbed at me as he went down, but I broke his hold and punched as hard as I could. My fist mashed flesh, and the ripe warmth of blood spilled into the air. I swung around, grabbed his leg, and twisted it. Bone cracked, and the clone screamed.

My chest heaved as I battled to catch my breath, and sweat trickled down my back. I stepped back from the clone, ignored the bile that rose in my throat, and met Talon's gaze.

My actions might have angered him, but they'd also aroused him.

"Now it's just you and me," I said softly.

"Not really. I have a hundred such creations at my beck and call."

"Then I guess you're not such a perfect specimen of wolfhood after all, are you?"

He raised an eyebrow, a confident smile touching his lips. "You want a fight, little wolf?"

I flexed my fingers. "You think I'm afraid to?"

"I think you're very afraid."

And he'd be right. But it wasn't so much his physical strength but rather his aura. Even from where I stood I could feel it. It was a blanket that was almost smothering, a heat that crawled across my skin like some insidious, insistent demon. Close up, it might be too strong to ignore for any length of time.

He uncrossed his arms, then pressed the band on his

wrist. "Security, I have a problem here that needs to be attended to. Use whatever force you deem necessary to deal with the breach."

Security obviously weren't happy about this, because I heard their squawk from where I stood. Talon cut them off with a curt "Do it," then looked back at me.

"And that," he said, shaking his arms and flexing his fingers, "should be the end of your lover."

"Don't underestimate him." I balanced lightly on my toes, ready to jump out of the way the minute he sprang.

"Oh, I'm not, but even the greatest fighter in the world can be blown to smithereens by the force of a laser—as you've so aptly shown."

"Damn shame the thing ran out of power when it did. I would have enjoyed blasting that smug smile off your face." Taunting him probably wasn't the brightest move, but I just couldn't help it.

His gaze slid down me, a warmth that made me cold inside. "Darkness has fallen outside, little wolf. The moon is only minutes from rising. I shall enjoy beating you into submission, and then I shall enjoy fucking you in wolf form."

Bile rose in my throat. Forcing yourself on someone while both were in wolf form was not only the act of a bastard, it was the ultimate form of degradation and humiliation for a werewolf. It had nothing to do with the power of the moon or the needs of a wolf, because the moon heat ended when the change swept over us. It was an act of rape, of domination, of power. It said you cared nothing for the person you were with, that in your eyes, he or she was no better than the animal whose shape you both wore.

I knew of no wolves who made love on this night.

Most took to the hills, enjoying the freedom of the forests, rejoicing in the rise of the moon.

"You can try," was all I said.

But I knew, like he knew, that I would have to beat him before the change came on. Because in wolf form, he would be stronger. That was the way of nature and something even my vampire genes couldn't get around.

His smile stretched his lips even farther, then he came at me. I waited until he was close, then pivoted, smacking him in the face with a fist before ducking out of his way. His fingers glided down the coat, catching the end and jerking me to an abrupt halt. I cursed him and jerked out of it, spinning away.

He chuckled. "I can smell your arousal, little wolf. And I can see it."

This close his aura *was* smothering. Yet I was resisting and for the moment, that was all that mattered.

And maybe, just maybe, I could use his desire against him.

I slid my hands up my body and cupped my breasts, brushing my thumbs across my nipples. "But do you see anything you like?"

Lust shone brighter in his eyes. He threw the coat to one side, then charged. I sidestepped. The tingling in my body was fiercer. I had to get this over with soon.

He slid to a stop, cursing as he swung around. "You can't have what you can't catch," I taunted.

He charged again. Not thinking, just reacting. His aura snatched my breath and made me dizzy, but somehow, lust remained fenced. Though barely.

I caught his wrist and swung him around, thrusting him back against the wall. Wrapping a hand around his neck, I pinned him in place, then slid my free hand down his body and caressed his thick erection. He thrust into my touch, his body quivering, skin sheened with sweat.

"You want something from me, you ask. Taking is never appreciated."

"You've appreciated it in the past." His words were a pant of air, his quivering growing.

"That was then, this is now."

I kept caressing him, watching the desire grow in his eyes, fighting that part of me that wanted to take him inside and ride him to the end. As he drew closer and closer to the edge, I slid my hand away from his neck and retrieved the last knife from my boot. His orgasm hit, his body jerking and thrusting as his seed spilled out across my hand. I raised the silver-threaded knife and punched it hard into his shoulder.

His eyes flew open, shock registering. Then the blood hit the knife and smoke began to rise from the wound. He screamed and punched me. The force of the blow flung me across the corridor. I hit the wall with a grunt and slid down to the floor, seeing stars and tasting blood for the second time that day.

Then there was no time to do anything more than try to protect myself, because Talon was on me, a whirlwind of fists and anger from which there was no escape.

But it barely lasted more than a few minutes, because the tingling in my body became a power that would not be denied. It swept around me, through me, blurring my vision, blurring my pain. Screaming filling my ears, screaming unlike anything I'd ever heard before. Then, suddenly, there was a blur of red fur, and Talon's weight was gone.

"Rhoan, no!"

Jack's voice, sharp with command.

I scrambled upright, my claws scrabbling against the steel floor. Rhoan, in wolf form, stood above Talon, his deep-throated growl making his whole body quiver, his bared teeth a hairsbreadth away from Talon's neck.

Talon was beyond caring. His eyes were wide and glassy, and he still screamed. His body was aflame with the flicker of golden energy, which usually signaled the change from one shape to the other, but the sliver of silver I'd forced into his shoulder had him trapped in human form.

I'd always wondered just how bad that would be.

Now I knew.

Jack strode forward and grabbed Rhoan by the scruff of the neck, hauling him off. "He's no use to us dead," he snapped, then glanced at me. "You all right?"

I nodded. There was little else I could do. Rhoan walked over and nuzzled me. I licked his nose and wished I was in human form so he could just hug me.

"Then I suggest," Jack continued tartly, "you two go find our missing vampire."

We went.

But Quinn had disappeared.

And so, too, had the body of his friend.

Chapter 16

I plopped down on the dewy grass and drew together the edges of my borrowed coat. The sun had risen just over an hour ago, but the flags of dawn still colored the sky with clouds of orange and gold.

At the foot of the hill on which I sat there was a hive of activity. Trucks lined the rough dirt track that led to the entrance of the underground lab, and people were bustling back and forth, some carrying equipment, others leading prisoners.

To my right, thick black smoke trailed skyward, and the smell of burning flesh rent the air. The clones had been killed and the cleanup had begun.

I rubbed my forehead wearily. I just wanted to go home, take a long bath, and forget this whole episode. Everything except Quinn, that was.

But Jack had ordered me to remain until he had a chance to talk to me, so I remained, watching and waiting and wondering how I was going to sidestep the rest of the mess.

Because it wasn't over yet.

I closed my eyes and lay back, enjoying the caress of the breeze and partially drifting off to sleep. After a while, footsteps approached, and I cracked open an eye.

Jack, not Rhoan.

He sat down on the grass a few feet away, staring up at the sun, his face drawn and tired-looking.

"So why were you late?" I said, when he didn't immediately say anything.

He snorted softly. "Would you believe traffic?"

"No."

"Ah. Well. I guess I'll have to admit we lost the signal."

"Bugger."

"Could have been." He glanced at me. "It was Rhoan who found you. He just started walking, and before we knew it, there you were."

Thank God for the connection of twins. "I'll have to tell him to walk a little faster next time."

A smile touched his lips, but his eyes were all seriousness. "You know what I'm here to say, don't you?"

I took a deep breath and released it slowly. "The job is only half-done."

We'd found the source of the clones, but while Talon had been flirting with crossbreeding, his labs were not the main source of the crossbreeds. And definitely not the source of that weird-looking blue thing that had attacked me in the parking garage.

Jack nodded. "Everything I've found in that lab suggests Talon was not working alone."

"He said he'd worked with Misha in the past." Talon had been so sure of his success that he'd blabbed far more than he should have. "He also said that he wasn't responsible for those two men kidnapping me and that the person behind it all was someone I apparently know quite well."

"Yes. He's been quite talkative in the past hour or so, as well."

Not willingly, I'd bet. "So what has he said?"

He hesitated. "His idea to get you pregnant was all his own."

"No surprise there."

Jack nodded. "No, but apparently, it's been happening for well over a year. ARC1-23 was not the first fertility drug he'd tried, though all the others were legal."

Meaning lack of success had forced him to try other drugs. Meaning I might be as infertile as the doctors had feared. I closed my eyes, not really sure how I felt about that despite the lump that rose in my throat.

"So why wasn't this picked up in my six-month checks?"

He grimaced. "I checked, and it was. But fertility drugs are not on the reportable list, so it never made the overall summary."

"I'm gathering it will in the future?"

My voice was dry, and he grimaced. "*Anything* out of the ordinary will be reported from now on."

Even though it might be a case of shutting the barn door after the stock had bolted.

"Of course," Jack continued lightly, "Talon's desire to create the ultimate werewolf is quite amusing considering he himself is not entirely wolf."

I stared at him. "What?"

"He's a dhampire, just like you."

"He said he was a werewolf."

"And still insists he is. Our tests reveal otherwise."

So much for Talon thinking he was the pinnacle of wolf breeding. "So if Talon is an example of what was achievable, how come everything is going balls up now?"

"Because his father was a very powerful, very wealthy maverick working on his own, and much of his research was lost in a fire that destroyed his lab and took his life."

"That suggests that maybe Talon's not the only successful creation."

"Exactly."

"And maybe one or more of those creations are running the other lab." Which might or might not be called Libraska.

Jack gave me another of his pleased smiles, but I was too tired to get annoyed by it.

"Did all this come from reading his mind?" I asked.

"And the files in his office. Many of them are his father's."

"So you know who Talon's working for?"

He grimaced. "No. That section of his memories has been burned away. Someone with very powerful psychic gifts has been at him in the last forty-eight hours. He's only reciting what they've told him to recite."

"So why has he been so chatty?"

"Their erasing was not as good as it could have been."

"It also means they were willing to sacrifice Talon and this section of their work."

"Quinn was getting close, as were we. This project was probably becoming too hot to hold on to."

That made sense. "What about Misha? Where does he fit in, do you think?"

"I think he's definitely involved, but the force

behind it? I don't think so, especially given his apparent willingness to let us investigate him." He looked at me. "If Talon is right, and the person is someone who knows you, then they may also know what you are."

"No one else knows what we are."

"I knew. Quinn knew. Liander knows."

"You want me as a guardian, Liander loves Rhoan and wouldn't harm a hair on my head because of it, and Quinn wouldn't have used the man he's known forever to be the source of those clones."

A smile tugged Jack's lips. "All true. But if Talon was telling the truth, and the person behind all this *is* someone you know well, then guessing the truth might not be as hard as you think."

I frowned. "But that doesn't make sense. I mean, if they've known all along what I was, why wait until the last week to send a shooter to test me or two things to kidnap me? And why suspect what I am, and yet apparently not Rhoan?"

He shrugged. "I really don't know."

"And here I was thinking the Directorate knew it all."

"We will. Eventually."

Great. In the meantime, I was stuck in the middle of it all, with no option but to remain involved no matter how much I might wish otherwise. I closed my eyes again, and asked the one question I didn't really want an answer to. "So where do we go from here?"

"Misha is the only lead we currently have."

"You can't say that until you've had time to go through all the files in the lab."

"True."

"I don't want anything more to do with Misha."

"I know."

"Then don't ask."

"I won't. But you have to ask yourself how are you ever going to know which mate you can trust and which mate might be another plant."

I knew all that. Knew I was really doing nothing more than blowing smoke, because truth was, I was going to see this through. I just didn't want Jack to think I was going to let it go further. Didn't want him to think he was getting me easily. "I will not become a guardian."

But it might already be too late, and both he and I knew it.

"Riley, if I had any other choice, I would not be asking this of you."

I snorted softly. "Don't try conning me, Jack. Not this time."

He gave me a lopsided smile. "This time, it's the truth. Whoever's behind this has obviously infiltrated the Directorate. I have no idea who else there might be besides Alan Brown and Gautier. All the people on that list you found in Brown's office are dead, and while we are following up everything they worked on, it's going to take time. Which means that Misha is currently our only viable source of information. If we try to put anyone else on his trail or in his bed right now, they'll know we're on to him."

"Misha knows we're on to him. Raiding his office gave that away."

"But I suspect Misha is playing both sides of the fence, and that could certainly work to our advantage."

"Meaning I should just do my duty and spread my legs like the good little doggy that I am?"

Annoyance flickered in his eyes. "We found Kelly's

remains in that place, Riley. She'd been beaten to a pulp in that goddamn arena."

Tears squeezed past my closed eyelids. I'd hoped against hope that her fate would be different from that of the other missing guardians. Had hoped that she was still undercover and merely overdue. But fate seemed set on turning my world upside down just then, and I really should have known that hope wasn't on the agenda.

"That's playing dirty, Jack."

"*They're* playing dirty. I have no choice but to do the same."

I didn't say anything. Just grieved for the loss of a rare friend.

"It's not over, and deep down you know it."

I swiped the tears from my cheeks and gave him what he wanted. "You're wasting breath on the already converted."

He chuckled softly and patted my arm. "You are going to be one of my best."

"No, I'm not. Nor will I approach Misha. I think it best if we just sit back and let him make the first move."

"With that, I can agree." He rose, and stretched, his bones cracking lightly. "Why don't you go find your brother and both of you go home?"

I looked at him. "I think we both deserve a week off for R and R."

His gaze narrowed slightly, but the glimmer was back in his eyes. "Two days."

"Five."

"Three."

"Let's split the difference, then."

He grinned. "Done deal. But if Misha approaches you in that time, I expect to be told."

"Okay." But he wouldn't. I was sure of that, if nothing else.

Jack walked down the hill and disappeared inside the building. I lay in the sunshine a bit longer, then decided I'd better move before the weeds started to claim me.

I pushed upright and headed back down to Genoveve. Rhoan appeared out of the main doors as I neared the road, looking as weary and disheveled as I felt.

He didn't say anything, just pulled me into the hug I'd been wanting all night. The dam broke, and the tears started falling—grief for Kelly, grief for myself, and grief for a relationship that had never been given a chance.

"Don't let him pressure you into anything you don't want to do," Rhoan said, after a while.

I pulled back, hiccuping and wiping borrowed sleeves across my face. "I won't."

"And don't give up on Quinn."

My gaze searched his. "You're the one who told me not to expect anything from him."

He grimaced. "That was before I read his note."

My heart leapt. "He left a note?"

"Yeah, in the cryogenic chamber they must have been keeping Henri in. Here."

He dug a white piece of paper out of his pocket and handed it to me. My fingers shook as I unfolded it.

Thank you for helping me find my friend. Sorry I cannot offer what you are searching for. If we had but met centuries ago . . . Take care. Quinn.

My heart sunk, and I met my brother's gaze. "It's hardly a declaration of intent."

He grinned. "To have written that much means the man at least feels something more than a sexual attraction, especially since he added 'if we had met sooner'."

I glanced down at the note again. "If I do what Jack wants me to do, I can take this"—I raised the note, scrunched it into a ball, and tossed it away—"and do that."

"Give him time, Riley. You haven't known each other very long, and he's had a rough time with wolves."

"I know." I forced a smile. "But I *am* a wolf, and he's a vampire with some very human hangups. I don't think there's a whole lot of common ground between us."

"But a wolf never gives up once the scent of a chase is on."

I gave him a wry smile. "Especially when the scent leads to great sex."

"Precisely. Great sex is something one can never give up on."

"Is that why you're still with Davern?"

"Hell, yeah." He gave me a cheeky grin, then twined his fingers through mine and squeezed them lightly. "Why don't we go home, get cleaned up, then go out and get blindly, stinkingly, drunk?"

I smiled. "That's seems like the perfect ending to a perfectly wretched week."

And it was.

The world has seven wonders. . . .
Riley Jenson will do you two better.
That's nine times the action.
Nine times the passion.
Nine times the kick-ass.

THE RILEY JENSON GUARDIAN NOVELS

by

KERI ARTHUR

A complete nine-book series from Dell Books.
Be sure not to miss any of these exciting novels—
or this series of special previews, to give you a
taste of what you'll get in . . .

Kissing Sin
Tempting Evil
Dangerous Games

And be sure not to miss the rest of the series:

Embraced by Darkness
The Darkest Kiss
Deadly Desire
Bound to Shadows
Moon Sworn

BETWEEN DESIRE AND BLOODLUST
IS THE SWEETEST SIN OF ALL....

KISSING SIN

KERI ARTHUR

AUTHOR OF *FULL MOON RISING*

KISSING SIN

On sale now

All I could smell was blood.

Blood that was thick and ripe.

Blood that plastered my body, itching at my skin.

I stirred, groaning softly as I rolled onto my back. Other sensations began to creep through the fog encasing my mind. The chill of the stones that pressed against my spine. The gentle patter of moisture against bare skin. The stench of rubbish left sitting too long in the sun. And underneath it all, the aroma of raw meat.

It was a scent that filled me with foreboding, though why I had no idea.

I forced my eyes open. A concrete wall loomed ominously above me, seeming to lean inward, as if ready to fall. There were no windows in that wall, and no lights anywhere near it. For a moment I thought I was in a prison of some kind, until I remembered the rain and saw that the concrete bled into the cloud-covered night sky.

Though there was no moon visible, I didn't need to see it to know where we were in the lunar cycle. While it might be true that just as many vampire genes flowed through my bloodstream as werewolf, I was still very sensitive to the moon's presence. The full moon had passed three days ago.

Last I remembered, the full moon phase had only just begun. Somewhere along the line, I'd lost eight days.

I frowned, staring up at the wall, trying to get my bearings, trying to remember how I'd gotten here. How I'd managed to become naked and unconscious in the cold night.

No memories rose from the fog. The only thing I was certain of was the fact that something bad had happened. Something that had stolen my memory and covered me in blood.

I wiped the rain from my face with a hand that was trembling, and looked left. The wall formed one side of a lane filled with shadows and overflowing rubbish bins. Down at the far end, a streetlight twinkled, a forlorn star in the surrounding darkness. There were no sounds to be heard beyond the rasp of my own breathing. No cars. No music. Not even a dog barking at an imaginary foe. Nothing that suggested life of any kind nearby.

Swallowing heavily, trying to ignore the bitter taste of confusion and fear, I looked to the right.

And saw the body.

A body covered in blood.

Oh God . . .

I couldn't have. Surely to God, I couldn't have.

Mouth dry, stomach heaving, I climbed unsteadily to my feet and staggered over.

Saw what remained of his throat and face.

Bile rose thick and fast. I spun away, not wanting to

lose my dinner over the man I'd just killed. Not that he'd care any more . . .

When there was nothing but dry heaves left, I wiped a hand across my mouth, then took a deep breath and turned to face what I'd done.

He was a big man, at least six four, with dark skin and darker hair. His eyes were brown, and if the expression frozen on what was left of his face was anything to go by, I'd caught him by surprise. He was also fully clothed, which meant I hadn't been in a blood lust when I'd ripped out his throat. That in itself provided no comfort, especially considering I was naked, and obviously had made love to someone sometime in the last hour.

My gaze went back to his face and my stomach rose threateningly again. Swallowing heavily, I forced my eyes away from that mangled mess and studied the rest of him. He wore what looked like brown coveralls, with shiny gold buttons and the letters D.S.E. printed on the left breast pocket. There was a taser clipped to the belt at his waist and a two-way attached to his lapel. What looked like a dart gun lay inches from his reaching right hand. His fingers had suckers, more gecko-like than human.

A chill ran across my skin. I'd seen hands like that before—just over two months ago, in a Melbourne casino car park, when I'd been attacked by a vampire and a tall, blue thing that had smelled like death.

The need to get out of this road hit like a punch to the stomach, leaving me winded and trembling. But I couldn't run, not yet. Not until I knew everything this man might be able to tell me. There were too many gaps in my memory that needed to be filled.

Not the least of which was why I'd ripped out his throat.

After taking another deep breath that did little to calm my churning stomach, I knelt next to my victim. The cobblestones were cold and hard against my shins, but the chill that crept across my flesh had nothing to do with the icy night. The urge to run was increasing, but if my senses had any idea what I should be running from, they weren't telling me. One thing was certain—this dead man was no longer a threat. Not unless he'd performed the ritual to become a vampire, anyway, and even then, it could be days before he actually turned.

I bit my lip and cautiously patted him down. There was nothing else on him. No wallet, no ID, not even the usual assortment of fluff that seemed to accumulate and thrive in pockets. His boots were leather—nondescript brown things that had no name brand. His socks provided the only surprise—they were pink. Fluorescent pink.

I blinked. My twin brother would love them, but I couldn't imagine anyone else doing so. And they seemed an odd choice for a man who was so colorless in every other way.

Something scraped the cobblestones behind me. I froze, listening. Sweat skittered across my skin and my heart raced nine to the dozen—a beat that seemed to echo through the stillness. After a few minutes, it came again—a soft click I'd never have noticed if the night wasn't so quiet.

I reached for the dart gun, then turned and studied the night-encased alley. The surrounding buildings seemed to disappear into that black well, and I could sense nothing or no one approaching.

Yet something was there, I was sure of it.

I blinked, switching to the infrared of my vampire vision. The entire lane leapt into focus—tall walls, wooden fences, and overflowing bins. Right down the far end, a hunched shape that wasn't quite human, not quite dog.

My mouth went dry.

They were hunting me.

Why I was so certain of this I couldn't say, but I wasn't about to waste time examining it. I rose, and slowly backed away from the body.

The creature raised its nose, sniffing the night air. Then it howled—a high, almost keening sound that was as grating as nails down a blackboard.

The thing down the far end was joined by another, and together they began to walk toward me.

I risked a quick glance over my shoulder. The street and the light weren't that far away, but I had a feeling the two creatures weren't going to be scared away by the presence of either.

The click of their nails against the cobblestones was sharper, a tattoo of sound that spoke of patience and controlled violence. They were taking one step for every three of mine, and yet they seemed to be going far faster.

I pressed a finger around the trigger of the dart gun, and wished I'd grabbed the taser as well.

The creatures stopped at the body, sniffing briefly before stepping over it and continuing on. This close, their shaggy, powerful forms looked more like misshapen bears than wolves or dogs, and they must have stood at least four feet at the shoulder. Their eyes were red—a luminous, scary red.

They snarled softly, revealing long, yellow teeth.

The urge to run was so strong every muscle trembled. I bit my lip, fighting instinct as I raised the dart gun and pressed the trigger twice. The darts hit the creatures square in the chest, but only seemed to infuriate them. Their soft snarls became a rumble of fury as they launched into the air. I turned and ran, heading left at the end of the alley simply because it was downhill.

The road's surface was slick with moisture, the street lights few and far between. Had it been humans chasing me, I could have used the cloak of night to disappear from sight. But the scenting actions these creatures made when they first appeared suggested the vampire ability to fade into shadow wouldn't help me here.

Nor would shifting into wolf form, because my only real weapon in my alternate shape was teeth. Not a good option when there was more than one foe.

I raced down the middle of the wet street, passing silent shops and terraced houses. No one seemed to be home in any of them, and none of them looked familiar. In fact, all the buildings looked rather strange, almost as if they were one-dimensional.

The air behind me stirred and the sense of evil sharpened. I swore softly and dropped to the ground. A dark shape leapt over me, its sharp howl becoming a sound of frustration. I sighted the dart and fired again, then rolled onto my back, kicking with all my might at the second creature. The blow caught it in the jaw and deflected its leap. It crashed to the left of me, shaking its head, a low rumble coming from deep within its chest.

I scrambled to my feet, and fired the last of the darts

at it. Movement caught my eye. The first creature had climbed to its feet and was scrambling toward me.

I threw the empty gun at its face, then jumped out of its way. It slid past, claws scrabbling against the wet road as it tried to stop. I grabbed a fistful of shaggy brown hair and swung onto its back, wrapping an arm around its throat and squeezing tight. I had the power of wolf and vampire behind me, which meant I was more than capable of crushing the larynx of any normal creature in an instant. Trouble was, this creature wasn't normal.

It roared—a harsh, strangled sound—then began to buck and twist violently. I wrapped my legs around its body, hanging on tight as I continued my attempts to strangle it.

The other creature came out of nowhere and hit me side-on, knocking me off its companion. I hit the road with enough force to see stars, but the scrape of approaching claws got me moving. I rolled upright, and scrambled away on all fours.

Claws raked my side, drawing blood. I twisted, grabbed the creature's paw, and pulled it forward hard. The creature sailed past and landed with a crash on its back, hard up against a shop wall. A wall that shook under the impact.

I frowned, but the second creature gave me no time to wonder why the wall had moved. I spun around, sweeping with my foot, battering the hairy beastie off its feet. It roared in frustration and lashed out. Sharp claws caught my thigh, tearing flesh even as the blow sent me staggering. The creature was up almost instantly, nasty sharp teeth gleaming yellow in the cold, dark night.

I faked a blow to its head, then spun and kicked at

its chest, embedding the darts even farther. The ends of the darts hurt my bare foot, but the blow obviously hurt the creature more, because it howled in fury and leapt. I dropped and spun. Then, as the creature's leap took it high above me, I kicked it as hard as I could in the goolies. It grunted, dropped to the road and didn't move.

For a moment, I simply remained where I was, the wet road, cold against my shins as I battled to get some air into my lungs. When the world finally stopped threatening to go black, I called to the wolf that prowled within.

Power swept around me, through me, blurring my vision, blurring the pain. Limbs shortened, shifted, rearranged, until what was sitting on the road was wolf not woman. I had no desire to stay too long in my alternate form. There might be more of those things prowling the night, and meeting two or more in this shape could be deadly.

But in shifting, I'd helped accelerate the healing process. The cells in a werewolf's body retained data on body makeup, which was why wolves were so long-lived. In changing, damaged cells were repaired. Wounds were healed. And while it generally took more than one shift to heal deep wounds, one would at least stem the bleeding and begin the healing process.

I shifted back to human form and climbed slowly to my feet. The first creature still lay in a heap at the base of the shop front. Obviously, whatever had been in those two darts had finally taken effect. I walked over to the second creature, grabbed it by the scruff of the neck, and dragged it off the road. Then I went to the window and peered inside.

It wasn't a shop, just a front. Beyond the window

there was only framework and rubbish. The next shop was much the same, as was the house next to that. Only there were wooden people inside it was well.

It looked an awful lot like one of those police or military weapons training grounds, only this training ground had warped-looking creatures patrolling its perimeter.

That bad feeling I'd woken with began to get a whole lot worse. I had to get out of here, before anything or anyone else discovered I was free. . . .

A RILEY JENSON GUARDIAN NOVEL

KERI ARTHUR

*In a realm without inhibitions,
there's nothing more seductive
than temptation...*

TEMPTING EVIL

FROM THE AUTHOR OF *KISSING SIN*

TEMPTING EVIL

On sale now

Training sucked.

Especially when the main aim of that training was to make me something I'd once vowed never to become—a guardian for the Directorate of Other Races.

Becoming a guardian might have been inevitable, and I might have accepted it on some levels, but that didn't mean I had to be happy about the whole process.

Guardians were far more than just the specialized cops most humans thought them to be—they were judge, jury, and executioners. None of this legal crap the human cops were forced to put up with. Of course, the people in front of a guardian's metaphoric bullet were generally out-of-control psychos who totally deserved to die, but stalking the night with the aim of ending their undead lives still wasn't something that had reached my to-do list.

Even if my wolf-soul sometimes hungered to hunt more than I might wish to acknowledge.

But if there was one thing worse than going through all the training that was involved in becoming a guardian, then it was training with my brother.

I couldn't con him. Couldn't flirt or flash a bit of flesh to make him forget his train of thought. Couldn't moan that I'd had enough and that I couldn't go on, because he wasn't just my brother, but my twin.

He knew exactly what I could and couldn't do, because he could feel it. We mightn't share the telepathy of twins, but we knew when the other was hurting or in trouble.

And right now Rhoan was fully aware of the fact that I was trying to pike. And he knew why.

I had a hot date with an even hotter werewolf.

In precisely one hour.

If I left now, I could get home and clean up before Kellen—the hot date in question—came by to pick me up. Any later, and he'd see me as the beaten-up scruff I usually was these days.

"Isn't Liander cooking you a roast this evening?" I said, casually waving the wooden baton I'd been given but had yet to use. Mainly because I didn't want to hit my brother.

He, however, didn't have the same problem, and the bruises littering my body proved it.

But then, he didn't really want me to be doing this. Didn't want me on the mission drawing inexorably closer.

"Yes." He continued to circle me, his pace as casual as his expression. I wasn't fooled. Couldn't be, when I could feel the tension in his body almost as well as I could feel it in mine. "But he has no intention of putting it on until I phone and tell him I'm on my way to his place."

"It's his birthday. You should be there to celebrate it with him rather than putting me through the wringer."

He shifted suddenly, stepping forward, the baton a pale blur as he lashed out at me. I ignored the step and the blow, holding still as the breeze of the baton's passing caressed the fingers of my left hand. He was only playing, and we both knew it.

I wouldn't even see his real move.

He grinned. "I'll be there as soon as this is over. And he did invite you along, remember."

"And spoil the private party you have planned?" My voice was dry. "I don't think so. Besides, I'd rather party with Kellen."

"Meaning Quinn is still out of the picture?"

"Not entirely." I shifted a little, keeping him in sight as he continued to circle. The padded green mats that covered the Directorate's sublevel training arena squeaked in protest under my bare feet.

"Your sweat is causing that," he commented. "But there's not nearly enough of it."

"Jesus, Rhoan, have a heart. I haven't seen Kellen for nearly a week. I want to play with him, not you."

He raised an eyebrow, a devilish glint in his silver eyes. "You get me on the mat, and I'll let you go."

"It's not you I want on the mat!"

"If you don't fight me, they'll make you fight Gautier. And I don't think either of us wants that."

"And if I do fight you, and do manage to bring you down, they're going to make me fight him anyway." Which pretty much sucked. I wasn't overly fond of vampires at the best of times, but some of them—like Quinn, who was in Sydney tending to his airline business, and Jack, my boss, and the man in charge of the whole guardian division—were decent people. Gautier was just a murdering freak. He might be a guardian, and he might not have done anything wrong just yet, but he was one of the bad guys. He was also a clone made for one specific purpose—to take over the Directorate. He hadn't made his move yet, but I had an odd premonition that he would, and soon.

Rhoan made another feint. This time the baton skimmed my knuckles, stinging but not breaking skin. I resisted the urge to shake the pain away and shifted my stance a little, readying for the real attack.

"So, what's happening between you and Quinn?"

Nothing had happened, and that was the whole problem. After making such a song and dance about me upholding my end the deal we'd made, he'd basically played absent lover for the last few months. I blew out a frustrated breath, lifting the sweaty strands of hair from my forehead. "Can't we have this discussion after I play with Kellen?"

"No," he said, and blurred so fast that he literally disappeared from normal sight. And while I could have tracked his heat signature with the infrared of my vampire vision, I didn't actually need to, because my hearing and nose were wolf sharp. Not only could I hear his light steps on the vinyl mats as he circled around me, but I could track the breeze of his spicy, leathery scent.

Both were now approaching from behind.

I dove out of the way, twisting around even as I hit the mat, and lashed out with a foot. The blow connected hard and low against the back of his leg, and he grunted, his form reappearing as he stumbled and fought to remain standing.

I scrambled upright, and lunged toward him. I wasn't fast enough by half. He scooted well out of reach and shook his head. "You're not taking this seriously, Riley."

"Yes, I am." Just not as seriously as he'd like me to. Not this evening, anyway.

"Are you that desperate to fight Gautier?"

"No, but I am that desperate to see Kellen." Sexual frustration wasn't a good thing for anyone, but it was particularly bad for a werewolf. Sex was an ingrained part of our culture—we needed it as much as a vampire needed blood. And this goddamn training had been taking up so much of my free time that I hadn't even been able to get down to the Blue Moon for some action.

I blew out another breath, and tried to think calm thoughts. As much as I didn't want to hurt my brother, if that was the only way out of here, then I might have to try.

But if I did succeed in beating him, then Jack might take that as a sign I was ready for the big one. And part of me feared that—feared that no matter what Jack said, my brother was right when he said that I shouldn't be doing this. That I was never going to be ready for it, no matter how much training I got.

That I'd screw it all up, and put everyone's life in danger.

Not that Rhoan had actually said that last one. But as the time drew nearer, it was in my thoughts more and more.

"It's a stupid rule, and you know it," I said eventually. "Fighting Gautier doesn't prove anything."

"He is the best at what he does. Fighting him makes guardians ready for what they may face out there."

"Difference is, I don't want to become a full-time guardian."

"You have no choice now, Riley."

I knew that, but that didn't mean I still couldn't rail

against the prospect, even if my protests were only empty words.

I licked my lips and tried to concentrate on Rhoan. If I had to get him down on the mat to get out of here, then I would. I wanted, needed, to grab a little bit more of a normal life before the crap set in again.

Because it was coming. I could feel it.

A shadow flickered across one of the windows lining the wall to the right of Rhoan. Given it was nearly six, it was probably just a guardian getting himself ready for the evening's hunt. This arena was on sublevel five, right next to the guardian sleeping quarters. Which, amusingly, did contain coffins. Some vamps just loved living up to human expectations, even if they weren't actually necessary.

Not that any humans ever came down here. That would be like leading a lamb into the midst of a den of hungry lions. To say it would get ugly very quickly would be an understatement. Guardians might be paid to protect humans, but they sure as hell weren't above snacking on the occasional one either.

The shadow slipped past another window, and this time, Rhoan's gaze flickered in that direction. Only briefly, but that half second gave me an idea.

I twisted, spinning and lashing out with one bare foot. My heel skimmed his stomach, forcing him backward. His baton arced around, his blow barely avoiding my shin, then he followed the impetus of the movement so that he was spinning and kicking in one smooth motion. His heel whistled mere inches from my nose, and probably would have connected if I hadn't leaned back.

He nodded approvingly. "Now, that's a little more like it."

I grunted, shifting my stance and throwing the baton from one hand to the other. The slap of wood against flesh echoed in the silence surrounding us, and tension ran across his shoulders. I held his gaze, then caught the baton left-handed and started to hit out. Only to pull the blow up short and let my gaze go beyond him.

"Hi, Jack."

Rhoan turned around, and, in that moment, I dropped and kicked his legs out from underneath him. He hit the mat with a loud splat, his surprised expression dissolving quickly into a bark of laughter.

"The oldest trick in the book, and I fell for it."

I grinned. "Old tricks sometimes have their uses."

"And I guess this means you're free to go." He held up a hand. "Help me up."

"I'm not that stupid, brother."

Amusement twinkled in his silvery eyes as he climbed to his feet. "Worth a try, I guess."

"So I can go?"

"That was the deal." He rose and walked across to the side of the arena to grab the towel he'd draped over the railing earlier. "But you're back here tomorrow morning at six sharp."

I groaned. "That's just plain mean."

He ran the towel across his spiky red hair, and even though I couldn't see his expression, I knew he was grinning. Sometimes my brother could be a real pain in the ass.

"Maybe next time you'll reconsider the option of cheating."

"It's not cheating if it worked."

Though his smile still lingered, little of that amusement reached his eyes. He was worried, truly worried, about my part in the mission we'd soon embark on. He didn't want me to do this any more than I'd wanted him to become a guardian. But as he'd said to me all those years ago, some directions in life just had to be accepted.

"You're here to learn defense and offence," he said. "Inane tricks won't save your life."

"If they save it only once, then they're worth trying."

He shook his head. "I can see I'm not going to talk any sense into you until after the sexfest."

"Glad you finally caught the gist of my whole conversation for the last hour." I grinned. "And hey, look on the bright side. Liander's going to be mighty pleased to see you at a normal hour for a change."

He nodded, tossed the towel around his bare shoulders, and headed off whistling. Obviously, I wasn't the only one anticipating a good time tonight.

Grinning slightly, I headed down the other end of the arena, where my towel and water bottle waited. I grabbed the towel and wrapped one end around my ponytail, squeezing the sweat from my hair before wiping the back of my neck and face. I might not have been fighting to full capacity tonight, but we'd still been training for a couple of hours and not only did my skin glimmer with heat but my navy T-shirt was almost black with sweat. It was just as well I could shower here—with the way my luck had been running of late, Kellen would be waiting for me by the time I got home. And as much as most wolves preferred natural scent over synthetic, right now I was just a little too overwhelmingly natural.

I reached out to collect the water bottle, then froze as awareness surged, prickling like fire across my skin. Rhoan had left, but I was no longer alone in the arena.

My earlier intuition had been right—crap had been about to step back into my life.

And it came in the form of Gautier.

Towel still in hand, I casually turned around. He stood at the window end of the arena, a long, mean stick of man and muscle who smelled as bad as he looked.

"Still haven't managed to catch that shower, I see." It probably wasn't the wisest comment I'd ever made, but when it came to Gautier, I couldn't seem to keep my mouth shut.

It was a trait that was going to get me in trouble—if not tonight, then sometime in the future.

He crossed his arms and smiled. There was nothing nice in that smile. Nothing sane in his flat brown eyes. "Still jumping mouth first into situations even the insane would think twice about, I see."

"It's a common failing of mine." I idly began twirling the towel and wondered how long it would take security to react. And if Jack would let them react.

"So I've noticed."

He'd be hard-pressed not to when most of my mouth-first offences of late involved him in some way. "What are you doing here, Gautier? Haven't you got bad guys to kill?"

"I have."

"Then why aren't you outside hunting, like the good little psycho you are?"

His sharklike smile sent a chill running up my spine, and in that moment I realized he was on the hunt.

For me . . .

DANGEROUS GAMES

On sale now

I stood in the shadows and watched the dead man.

The night was bitterly cold, and rain fell in a heavy, constant stream. Water sluiced down the vampire's long causeway of a nose, leaping to the square thrust of his jaw before joining the mad rush down the front of his yellow raincoat. The puddle around his bare feet had reached his ankles and was slowly beginning to creep up his hairy legs.

Like most of the newly risen, he was little more than flesh stretched tautly over bone. But his skin possessed a rosy glow that suggested he'd eaten well and often. Even if his pale eyes were sunken. Haunted.

Which in itself wasn't really surprising. Thanks to the willingness of both Hollywood and literature to romanticize vampirism, far too many humans seemed to think that by becoming a vampire they'd instantly gain all the power, sex, and wealth they could ever want. It wasn't until after the change that they began to realize that being undead wasn't the fun time often depicted. That wealth, sex, and popularity might come, but only if they survived the horrendous first few years, when a vampire was all instinct and blood need. And of course, if they did survive, they then learned that endless loneliness, never feeling the full warmth of the sun again, never being able to savor the taste of food, and being feared or ostracized by a good percentage of the population was also part of the equation.

Yeah, there were laws in place to stop discrimination against vampires and other nonhumans, but the laws were only a recent development. And while there might now be vampire groupies, they were also a recent phenomenon and only a small portion of the population. Hatred and fear of vamps had been around for centuries, and I had no doubt it would take centuries for it to abate. If it ever did.

And the bloody rampages of vamps like the one ahead wasn't helping any.

A total of twelve people had disappeared over the last month, and we were pretty sure this vamp was responsible for nine of them. But there were enough differences in method of killing between this vamp's nine and the remaining three to suggest we had a second psycho on the loose. For a start, nine had met their death as a result of a vamp feeding frenzy. The other three had been meticulously sliced open neck to knee with a knife and their innards carefully removed— not something the newly-turned were generally capable of. When presented with the opportunity for a feed, they fed. There was nothing neat or meticulous about it.

Then there were the multiple, barely-healed scars marring the backs of the three anomalous women, the missing pinky on their left hands, and the odd, almost satisfied smiles that seemed frozen on their dead lips. Women who were the victims of a vamp's frenzy didn't die with *that* sort of smile, as the souls of the dead nine could probably attest if they were still hanging about.

And I seriously hoped that they *weren't*. I'd seen more than enough souls rising in recent times—I certainly didn't want to make a habit of it.

But dealing with two psychos on top of coping with the usual Guardian patrols had the Directorate stretched to the limit, and that meant everyone had been pulling extra shifts. Which explained why Rhoan and I were out hunting rogue suckers on this bitch of a night after working all day trying to find some leads on what Jack—our boss, and the vamp who ran the whole guardian division at the Directorate of Other Races—charmingly called The Cleaver.

I yawned and leaned a shoulder against the concrete wall lining one side of the small alleyway I was hiding in. The wall, which was part of the massive factory complex that dominated a good part of the old West Footscray area, protected me from the worst of the wind, but it didn't do a whole lot against the goddamn rain.

If the vamp felt any discomfort about standing in a pothole in the middle of a storm-drenched night, he certainly wasn't showing it. But then, the dead rarely cared about such things.

I might have vampire blood running through my veins, but I wasn't dead and I hated it.

Winter in Melbourne was never a joy, but this year we'd had so much rain I was beginning to forget what sunshine looked like. Most wolves were immune to the cold, but I was a half breed and obviously lacked that particular gene. My feet were icy and I was beginning to lose feeling in several toes. And this despite the fact I was wearing two pairs of thick woolen socks underneath my rubber-heeled shoes. Which were not waterproof, no matter what the makers claimed.

I should have worn stilettos. My feet would have been no worse off, and I would have felt more at home. And hey, if he happened to spot me, I could have pretended to be nothing more than a bedraggled, desperate hooker. But Jack kept insisting high heels and my job just didn't go together.

Personally, I think he was a little afraid of my shoes. Not so much because of the color—which, admittedly, was often outrageous—but because of the nifty wooden heels. Wood and vamps were never an easy mix.

I flicked up the collar of my leather jacket and tried to ignore the fat drops of water dribbling down my spine. What I really needed—more than decent looking shoes—was a hot bath, a seriously large cup of coffee, and a thick steak sandwich. Preferably with lashings of onions and ketchup, but skip the tomato and green shit, please. God, my mouth was salivating just thinking about it. Of course, given we were in the middle of this ghost town of factories, none of those things were likely to appear in my immediate future.

I thrust wet hair out of my eyes, and wished, for the umpteenth time that night, that he would just get on with it. Whatever it was.

Following him might be part of my job as a guardian, but that didn't mean I had to be happy about it. I'd never had much choice about joining the guardian ranks, thanks to the experimental drugs several lunatics had forced into my system and the psychic talents that were developing as a result. It was either stay with the

Directorate as a guardian so my growing abilities could be monitored and harnessed, or be shipped off to the military with the other unfortunates who had received similar doses of the ARC1-23 drug. I might not have wanted to be a guardian, but I sure as hell didn't want to be sent to the military. Give me the devil I know any day.

I shifted weight from one foot to the other again. What the hell was this piece of dead meat waiting for? He couldn't have sensed me—I was far enough away that he wouldn't hear the beat of my heart or the rush of blood through my veins. He hadn't looked over his shoulder at any time, so he couldn't have spotted me with the infrared of his vampire vision, and blood suckers generally didn't have a very keen olfactory sense.

So why stand in a puddle in the middle of this abandoned factory complex looking like a little lost soul?

Part of me itched to shoot the bastard and just get the whole ordeal over with. But we needed to follow this baby vamp home to discover if he had any nasty surprises hidden in his nest. Like other victims, or perhaps even his maker.

Because it was unusual for one of the newly turned to survive nine rogue kills without getting himself caught or killed. Not without help, anyway.

The vampire suddenly stepped out of the puddle and began walking down the slight incline, his bare feet slapping noisily against the broken road. The shadows and the night hovered all around him, but he didn't bother cloaking his form. Given the whiteness of his hairy legs and the brightness of his yellow raincoat, that was strange. Though we were in the middle of nowhere. Maybe he figured he was safe.

I stepped out of the alleyway. The wind hit full

force, pushing me sideways for several steps before I regained my balance. I padded across the road and stopped in the shadows again. The rain beat a tattoo against my back and the water seeping through my coat became a river, making me feel colder than I'd ever dreamed possible. Forget the coffee and the sandwich. What I wanted more than anything right now was to get warm.

I pressed the small comlink button that had been inserted into my earlobe just over four months ago. It doubled as a two-way communicator and a tracker, and Jack had not only insisted that I keep it but that all Guardians were to have them from now on. He wanted to be able to find his people at all times, even when not on duty.

Which smacked of "big-brother" syndrome to me even if I could understand his reasoning. Guardians didn't grow on trees—finding vamps with just the right mix of killing instinct and moral sensibilities was difficult, which was why guardian numbers at the Directorate still hadn't fully recovered from the eleven we'd lost ten months ago.

One of those eleven had been a friend of mine, and on my worst nights I still dreamed of her death, even though the only thing I'd ever witnessed was the bloody patch of sand that had contained her DNA. Like most of the other Guardians who had gone missing, her remains had never been found.

Of course, the tracking measures had not only come too late for those eleven, but for one other—Gautier. Not that he was dead, however much I might wish otherwise. Four months ago he'd been the Directorate's top Guardian. Now he was rogue and on top of the Directorate's hit list. So far he'd escaped every search, every trap. Meaning he was still out there, waiting and watching and plotting his revenge.

On me.

Goose bumps traveled down my spine and, just for a second, I'd swear his dead scent teased my nostrils. Whether it was real or just imagination and fear I couldn't say, because the gusting wind snatched it away.

Even if it wasn't real, it was a reminder that I had to be extra careful. Gautier had never really functioned on the same sane field as the rest of us. Worse still, he liked playing with his prey. Liked watching the pain and fear grow before he killed.

He might now consider me his mouse but he'd yet to try any of his games on me. But something told me that all that would change tonight.

I grimaced and did my best to ignore the insight. Clairvoyance might have been okay if it had come in a truly usable form—like clear glimpses of future scenes and happenings—but oh no, that was apparently asking too much of fate. Instead, I just got these weird feelings of upcoming doom that were frustratingly vague on any sort of concrete detail. And training something like that was nigh on impossible—not that that stopped Jack from getting his people to at least try.

Whether the illusiveness would change as the talent became more settled was anyone's guess. Personally, I just wished it would go back to being latent. I knew Gautier was out there somewhere. Knew he was coming after me. I didn't need some half-assed talent sending me spooky little half warnings every other day.

Still, even though I knew Gautier probably wasn't out here tonight, I couldn't help looking around and checking all the shadows as I said, "Brother dearest, I hate this fucking job."

Rhoan's soft laughter ran into my ear. Just hearing it made me feel better. Safer. "Nights like this are a bitch, aren't they?"

"Understatement of the year." I quickly peeked around the corner and saw the vampire turning left. I padded after him, keeping to the wall and well away from the puddles. Though given the state of my feet, it really wouldn't have mattered. "And I feel obligated to point out that I didn't sign up for night work."

Rhoan chuckled softly. "And I feel obliged to point out that you weren't actually signed up, but forcibly drafted. Therefore, you can bitch all you want, but it isn't going to make a damned bit of difference."

Wasn't that the truth. "Where are you?"

"West side, near the old biscuit factory."

Which was practically opposite my position. Between the two of us we had him penned. Hopefully, it meant we wouldn't lose him.

I stopped as I neared the corner and carefully peered around. The wind slapped against my face, and the rain on my skin seemed to turn to ice. The vamp had stopped near the far end of the building and was looking around. I ducked back as he looked my way, barely daring to breathe even though common sense suggested there was no way he could have seen me. Not only did I have vampire genes, but I had many of their skills as well. Like the ability to cloak under the shadow of night, the infrared vision, and their faster-than-a-blink speed.

The creak of a door carried past. I risked another look. A metal door stood ajar and the vamp was nowhere in sight.

An invitation or a trap?

I didn't know, but I sure as hell wasn't going to take a chance. Not alone, anyway.

"Rhoan, he's gone inside building number four. Rear entrance, right-hand side."

"Wait for me to get there before you go in."

"I'm foolhardy, but I'm not stupid."

He chuckled again. I slipped around the corner and crept toward the door. The wind caught the edge of it and flung it back against the brick wall, the crash echoing across the night. It was an oddly lonely sound.

I froze and concentrated, using the keenness of my wolf hearing to sort through the noises running with the wind. But the howl of it was just too strong, over-riding everything else.

Nor could I smell anything more than ice, age, and abandonment. If there were such smells and it wasn't just my overactive imagination.

Yet a feeling of wrongness was growing deep in-side. I rubbed my leather-covered arms and hoped like hell my brother got here fast.